BY LAURIE R. KING

MARY RUSSELL

The Beekeeper's Apprentice	Beekeeping for Beginners:
A Monstrous Regiment of Women	A Short Story
A Letter of Mary	Pirate King
The Moor	Garment of Shadows
O Jerusalem	Dreaming Spies
Justice Hall	The Marriage of Mary Russell:
The Game	A Short Story
Locked Rooms	The Murder of Mary Russell
The Language of Bees	Mary Russell's War
The God of the Hive	Island of the Mad

STUYVESANT & GREY

Touchstone	The Bones of Paris

KATE MARTINELLI

A Grave Talent	Night Work
To Play the Fool	The Art of Detection
With Child	

AND

A Darker Place	Califia's Daughters (as Leigh Richards)
Folly	Lockdown
Keeping Watch	

ISLAND OF THE MAD

ISLAND OF THE MAD

A NOVEL OF SUSPENSE FEATURING
MARY RUSSELL AND SHERLOCK HOLMES

Laurie R. King

BANTAM BOOKS
NEW YORK

2019 Bantam Books Trade Paperback Edition

Copyright © 2018 by Laurie R. King

All rights reserved.

Published in the United States by Bantam Books, an imprint of Random House, a division of Penguin Random House LLC, New York.

BANTAM BOOKS and the HOUSE colophon are registered trademarks of Penguin Random House LLC.

Originally published in hardcover in the United States by Bantam Books, an imprint of Random House, a division of Penguin Random House LLC, in 2018.

Map by Jean Lukens and Robert Difley

ISBN 978-0-8041-7798-6
Ebook ISBN 978-0-8041-7797-9

Printed in the United States of America on acid-free paper

randomhousebooks.com

2 4 6 8 9 7 5 3

Book design by Jo Anne Metsch

To Mary Alice Kier,
Fellow devotée of La Serenissima

The world is but a great Bedlam,
where those that are more mad lock up those that are less.

—THOMAS TRYON, 1689

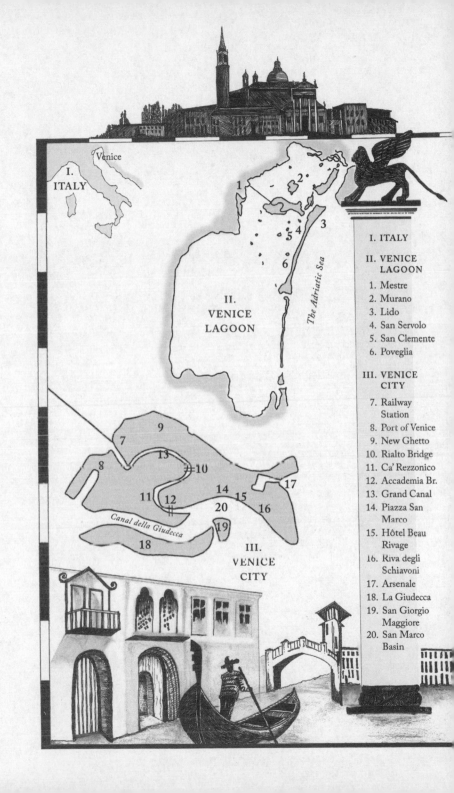

Venice

I.
ITALY

II.
VENICE
LAGOON

The Adriatic Sea

III.
VENICE
CITY

Canal della Giudecca

I. ITALY

II. VENICE
   LAGOON

1. Mestre
2. Murano
3. Lido
4. San Servolo
5. San Clemente
6. Poveglia

III. VENICE
    CITY

7. Railway
   Station
8. Port of Venice
9. New Ghetto
10. Rialto Bridge
11. Ca' Rezzonico
12. Accademia Br.
13. Grand Canal
14. Piazza San
    Marco
15. Hôtel Beau
    Rivage
16. Riva degli
    Schiavoni
17. Arsenale
18. La Giudecca
19. San Giorgio
    Maggiore
20. San Marco
    Basin

ISLAND OF THE MAD

Chapter One

....

SHERLOCK HOLMES AND I STOOD SHOULDER TO SHOULDER, gazing down sadly at the tiny charred corpse.

"She should never have left us alone," I told him.

"She had no great choice in the matter."

"There's always a choice."

"Strictly speaking, perhaps. But it's best that she disappear, at least for a time. Even putting aside the death penalty, I cannot see her thriving in prison."

I had to agree. "She is probably better off in Monte Carlo." And so saying, I snatched up the smouldering pan and tipped my attempt at a chicken dinner into the rubbish bin. Our long-time housekeeper, Mrs Hudson, had recently abandoned us, selfishly choosing freedom over being tried for murder—and thereby risking our lives to my poisonous culinary skills. "Cheese sandwiches, then? Or shall we walk up to the Tiger?"

He glanced at the kitchen clock. "Do you suppose Tillie might have a table, up at the Monk's Tun?"

———

Three hours later, we were making our leisurely way towards the gate in the stone wall encircling our house. I had pocketed a torch as we left, but the midsummer sky held enough lingering brightness that we did not need it as we returned across the Sussex Downs. Tillie had outdone herself, with a perfection of cool dishes on a warm afternoon: subtle lettuces, an iced soup, cold meats, hot rolls, and a strawberry tart the likes of none in the land.

The one drawback was, the Monk's Tun had begun to collect a reputation. Not that I begrudged Tillie her success—although I might wish we had not chosen to stop in the same night as a carload of Young Things on their way up from Dover.

Not that they were drunk, merely festive; nor were they loud, exactly, merely difficult to ignore. They were my age—in fact, two of them I dimly recognised: a young man with dark Byronic curls who had been the year before me at Oxford, and a girl whose face appeared in the illustrated Society pages of the newspapers. My eyes kept going to them, two sleek girls in Paris frocks, two clean, tanned lads in casually worn suits that would have cost Tillie's bar-man a year of his salary.

The second time Holmes had needed to repeat something, he craned around to look at the table of merrymakers on the other side of the old room.

"Friends of yours?"

"Good heavens, no."

"Then why are you watching them so closely?"

"I wasn't. Not really. Just—they seem like an alien race, down here in Sussex. Don't you think?"

His grey eyes fixed on me, but before he could speak, Tillie came up to greet us, and the next course arrived, and the moment was lost.

However, Holmes never forgot anything. When he pushed open the gate an hour later, he said, "Russell, do you regret the choices you made?"

Little point in pretending I didn't understand. "Regret? Never. I might occasionally wonder what life would have been, had things been different, but it's mere speculation. Like . . . like trying on a dress I'd never actually wear, just to see what it feels like."

He closed the gate and worked the latch. We picked our way through the grassy orchard, hearing the faint texture of sound from the hives—drones cooling their homes from the day's heat. Near the house, the sweet odour from the old-fashioned climbing rose drew us forward. Mrs Hudson had planted the flower, long before I knew her. Mrs Hudson, now gone away, to . . . But before yearning could overcome me, the night was broken by the jangle of the telephone bell.

Neither of us hurried to catch it.

And neither of us suggested, when the machine ceased its clamour before we were halfway through the kitchen, that we ask the Exchange to restore the connexion.

Instead, Holmes pulled a corkscrew from the drawer and a bottle of chilled honey wine from the cooler. I fetched a pair of glasses from the cupboard. We left the door open, to chase away the aroma of cremated chicken, and settled into our garden chairs. The night smelled of blossoms and honey. The low pulse of waves against the Sussex cliffs obscured the sound from the hives. The wine was cool, but faintly sad as its summer freshness faded, giving a hint of bitterness to come.

And the telephone rang again. At this time of night, the sound was ominous.

With a sigh, I put my half-empty glass onto the stones and went through the terrace doors.

I spoke our number by way of greeting, to be answered by a voice from the local Exchange. "Evening, Mrs Holmes, sorry to ring so late but the lady said it was an emergency, so I told her I'd keep trying you. And the girl at the Monk's Tun said you'd left there. Do you want me to connect you again?"

Life in a rural area is rich in many things, but privacy is not one of them. "Hold on a moment, I'll get Holmes." The word *emergency* generally summoned Sherlock Holmes.

But to my surprise, she said the woman had asked for me.

"Did she leave a name?"

"She said to tell you it was Veronica Fitzwarren."

Ronnie. Oh dear.

I pulled up the chair we kept near the telephone, and sat. "Yes, you'd better put me through."

Ronnie Fitzwarren—she'd been Lady Veronica Anne Beaconsfield when we met in 1917—was my oldest friend on this side of the Atlantic. My very first morning at Oxford University she stepped into my rooms and took charge of my life, turning what might have been three years of solitary academic pursuit into a time of exploration, community, and occasionally fun.

On the surface, we had little in common: Ronnie was short, round, vivacious, an English aristocrat down to her Norman bones, not greatly interested in her books, and dedicated to a series of Good Works. I, on the other hand, was tall, thin, aloof, of mongrel blood, and far more interested in the academic elements of human beings than the personal.

Ronnie taught me the meaning of friendship: once she'd laid claim to me, we were bound together. After University, however, our lives had drifted apart—until, on the eve of my twenty-first birthday, we happened to meet. At the time, I had just begun to realise how torn I was between a life of independence and a life with Sherlock Holmes. The conundrum was brought into greater focus in the time that followed by Ronnie's interest in a woman religious leader with some dubious connexions—and, by Ronnie's attachment to a troubled young demobbed officer with a weakness for hard drugs.

I'd dragged Holmes into the case, a mutual involvement that brought us together in unforeseen ways, revealing a surprisingly generous side to the man who had been my informal tutor since I met him at the age of fifteen.*

Holmes coaxed, cajoled, and bullied Miles Fitzwarren into sobriety,

---

* The Beaconsfield case is described in *A Monstrous Regiment of Women;* the meeting and apprenticeship of Russell and Holmes are found in *The Beekeeper's Apprentice* and *Mary Russell's War.*

turning him from a man so befuddled he'd mistaken Ronnie's dead father for her sciatic uncle, to a man serving His Majesty's government with honour and distinction.

Ronnie married Miles in 1921. Their son was born the following year. Two years after that, an Irish sniper's bullet left her a young widow with a small child and a complicated financial situation—and yet, far from my stepping up to be a faithful friend in her time of need, the past year had found me mostly absent from England, and from her life.

Letters, quick visits, and presents to the child did not assuage my guilt: she'd rescued me; I'd abandoned her.

The word *emergency* in Ronnie's situation could mean nothing good. But my friend seemed in no hurry to tell me about it. Instead, the familiar voice launched into cheery exclamations over how long it had been and was it as warm in Sussex as in London. Then she asked, rather pointedly, if I thought the Exchange had left the line. Following the giveaway clicks, Ronnie's voice went more sober.

"Mary, I actually phoned you a couple of hours ago—I didn't know the woman would continue to try you. It could wait till morning . . ."

"I'm glad to hear it's not drop-everything urgent, but since you've reached me, why don't you go ahead and tell me about it? Is it Simon?" The child was occasionally sickly, but in summer?

"Simon? No, he's super, why? Oh, I mean, I know why, but no, he's doing marvellously. I'm sorry you missed his birthday party last month. Mother hired a pony ride—she found this funny little man with ponies down in Brighton and Simon climbed right up, never a hesitation, you should have seen it . . ."

I waited through a proud mama's recitation of genius, studying the room, wondering if Holmes might rid it of Mrs Hudson's homely touches, wondering if Ronnie would notice if I gently laid down the earpiece to go fetch my wine glass—which was no doubt serving as a swimming pool for midges. When Ronnie paused for a breath, I hastened to interrupt. "That all sounds perfectly super. So if not Simon, what's the trouble?"

"Do you remember my Aunt Vivian?"

"The one—" I stopped to reach around for a diplomatic word, but Ronnie wasn't bothered.

"In the loony bin, yes."

"I only met her the once, but it was . . ."

"Terrifying?"

"Memorable."

My old friend laughed sadly at the understatement. "I know. Well, she's vanished, into thin air."

A solid twenty minutes later, I removed the telephone receiver from my numb ear. Five more minutes passed before I stood and went back through the terrace doors.

As I approached, Holmes stretched out an arm and removed his clean handkerchief from the top of my wine glass: no drowned midges.

"That was Ronnie Beaconsfield—Fitzwarren, rather," I told him. "Her aunt has disappeared."

"The mad one?"

"Yes."

"Wasn't she in Bedlam? Escape from there is not an easy matter."

I glanced over at him, but his face was in shadow. "Holmes, that sounds oddly like the voice of experience speaking." He did not reply, which meant that here was yet another episode in his life he had neglected to mention—probably because there was something embarrassing about it. "No, in fact, she'd been given a week's home leave, with a nurse in charge, in order to celebrate her brother's—her *half*-brother's—fiftieth birthday. The Marquess of Selwick? Vivian and the nurse were headed back to the asylum on Friday, but they never arrived."

"And your friend wishes you . . . ?"

"To look into it, yes. She has a young child, so her movements are somewhat restricted."

"The child hasn't a governess?"

"Only a few days a week. The widow's pension Ronnie gets doesn't leave her with many luxuries."

"Veronica Beaconsfield is living on an Army pension?"

"Ridiculous, I know. But I suspect that her uncle the Marquess made some bad investments, since he's never moved back to the London house since the War—ironic, considering that Ronnie's father was something of a financial genius—and the other uncle, on the mother's side, married an American who's rather tighter with her dollars than he anticipated. Neither are keen on providing Ronnie an allowance to live in her own place in London. I'm sure it'll be sorted out in the end, but until then . . ."

He grunted. I took another sip from the too-warm wine.

Peace returned. As did the midges. Holmes gathered the near-empty bottle and the glasses and took them into the house, leaving me to listen to the sea and think about beehives, and carefree Young Things, and Ronnie's mad aunt.

As I remembered it, Vivian Beaconsfield had always demonstrated a particular antipathy for her half-brother Edward, Lord Selwick. I was pretty sure that most of her overt violence had been aimed at him. Perhaps her willingness to celebrate the anniversary of the Marquess' birth had been a sign of healing.

Or had it been something else?

Chapter Two

....

1922

THE LADY VIVIAN BEACONSFIELD WAS THE THIRD AND youngest living child of William Reginald George Beaconsfield, Seventh Marquess of Selwick. The Marquess had married twice, with sons Edward and Thomas by his first wife, then Lady Vivian with his second. Edward, the heir, was sixteen when his little sister came along, thus nearly entirely fledged from his native Surrey nest. His brother, Thomas, was only fourteen, and though both had been at boarding school when Vivian was born, Thomas was the one who returned home during the long holidays, the one who was actually interested in running the estate. As I remembered, from various things Ronnie had said over the years, Lord Selwick—her Uncle Edward—had no interest in the countryside until he had been forced to return during the War, preferring the bright lights and the halls of power to bucolic Surrey.

Vivian's mother died of a fever in the winter of 1912, when her daughter was twenty-one. The following year, the aged Seventh Marquess faded away as well, and Edward inherited the title and lands. The new Marquess was happy at Selwick Hall in London and the family château in the south of France, leaving his brother to oversee things in Surrey. Thomas Beaconsfield—now with a lesser title of his own, Earl of Pewsley, a reward for steering some very important men away from some very costly financial mistakes—came to be known by the jocular nickname of "Lord Waterloo" for his idiosyncratic habit of commuting up and down between London and Surrey. He was often joined on these journeys by his wife, who was active on various Arts ventures, and Ronnie, who came to Town for tutoring. But they went home each night to Selwick, and to Vivian, his fragile younger sister.

Then came the War. Despite his title, his age, and his responsibilities, Thomas Beaconsfield enlisted, and volunteered for the Front. There he died, a bare twelve months later. His wife and sixteen-year-old Ronnie were bereft. His twenty-four-year-old sister was devastated.

Vivian had always been eccentric, and vulnerable—even physically so, being delicate of bone, pale of hair and skin. Her coming out in 1910, at the alarmingly late age of nineteen, had been a trial for all concerned, and she fled London even before the Season was at an end, with no sign of a ring or even an agreement. She spent some weeks in Europe before returning to her refuge in the country, there to remain.

Selwick having no master and London being under attack, Edward had little choice but to return home. Ronnie and her mother spent much of their time away, burying their grief in war work and grim preparations for University exams. The Marquess had moved their things into the east wing, that he might take up residence in the main house. His sister, Vivian, was moved to the women's side as well.

That disruption, added to the deaths of both parents and brother and the long absences of sister-in-law and niece, seemed to push Vivian's eccentricities into something darker. The servants' reports of her behaviour grew more and more alarming—her habitual country walks would extend long after sunset; her shyness grew into a pathological avoidance of former friends. There were occasional outbursts of temper that would be followed by unnatural, almost cringing withdrawal. She grew ever thinner, would pick at her finger-nails until they bled, bit at the corner of her mouth, nervously pulled locks of hair. Ronnie and her mother, coming back from London in June to help with harvest chores, found a quivering and nervous woman. One day, the maid discovered a sharp little kitchen knife in Vivian's pocket. The next afternoon Ronnie came upon her, weeping uncontrollably in the morning room. A few days after that, one year to the week after Thomas' death, Vivian tried to murder the Marquess with a fireplace poker.

Her first committal to a private institution was voluntary, lasting three months. Vivian returned home, rested and eating, seeming restored to sanity. In a few weeks, the darkness began to return.

It became a pattern: irritability, silence, the first signs of chewing at the edges of her body, then an outburst—invariably against Edward, which even he agreed was something of a blessing, since he was the one most able to defend himself. Committal would follow, as she acknowledged that she was in need of a "rest." This went on for three and a half years. Then came the fifth such cycle, in 1920. Instead of attacking her half-brother, Vivian went after herself, using another purloined knife. A chambermaid found her. The next committal was not voluntary.

By this time, Vivian Beaconsfield had exhausted the patience of private hospitals. For some ungodly reason—a mix-up? Her brother's pique?—she was taken to Bedlam, London's home for the mad since the fourteenth century. Her sister-in-law was appalled, her brother refused to speak her name—but strangely enough, Bedlam of all places saved her life.

One's first reaction to the name—which in fact was Bethlem Royal Hospital—was a queasy horror: Bedlam as a charnel-pit of cries, filth, brutality, the chaining of inmates, and visitors in Regency silks paying to be amused by the inmates' antics. However, even by Dickens' time, the humane treatment of the insane had made enormous progress. Now, Bedlam housed the educated mad, from schoolmasters to seamstresses, with a handful of talented artists for whom the outside world was too much. Nonetheless, the hospital's image was softened neither by its location in a rough district south of the River, nor by its hulking grey appearance. I admit, despite my intellectual knowledge of improvements, my thoughts of the place tended towards Hogarth's image of writhing and half-naked lunatics.

Still, Ronnie felt that her aunt was happy there—that yes, the blood in Lady Vivian's veins might run a shade bluer than that of the other inmates, but she seemed to have found her peers.

Ronnie took me once to visit her aunt. It was a wintry October afternoon in 1922, and not an ideal time to be crossing London with an infant in arms. Still, my old University friend was determined to introduce her young son to his great-aunt, and asked me to accompany her— why, I was not sure, other than my being one of her few friends who might not be shaken to the core by a trip to Bedlam. But as we motored through the rough streets of the South bank, I noticed how closely Ronnie held the child, and how warily she eyed the windows. Perhaps I was more of a bodyguard—certainly more so than the white-haired driver.

Bedlam was tucked behind high stone walls, the better to keep the wandering mad on one side and any tormenting onlookers on the other. The hinges screeched as the iron gates were pulled open by the guard, an aged fellow who looked barely adequate to corral young Simon, much less several hundred of London's mad.

Inside the walls, the dark and dirty stones of Southwark gave way, unexpectedly, to a garden: trees, lawn, a flower bed neatly mulched over for winter. Over to our left, some well-bundled women walked along a path-way, giving no indication that they were even aware of the gates, much less eager to flee through them.

Had it been a sunny morning, the stone façade might have given off an air of dignity, even welcome, but as we circled around to park, it simply . . . loomed. Four storeys high, with sixty or more windows on each floor, centred around a portico with columns resembling massive bars and a high dome that looked like a stone tea-cosy. The portico, ten steps above the drive, faced north, putting the entranceway in shadows. Even young Simon protested, although that could have been a reaction to the slowing of the motor. Ronnie wrapped the blankets around him as the driver came back to open the door. Bitter air rushed in—along with a high, drawn-out wail from the building itself that raised the hairs on the back of the neck. Ronnie gathered her soft armful and dashed up the steps, with me hastening to follow her through the columns to the hospital doors.

Inside, visitors were greeted by two immense stone carvings of male nudes, one cringing but hopeful, the other stretched in agony and bound by chains (named, I later found, Raving Madness and his brother, Melancholy). But the air was warm, as were the greetings of the staff, and smelled less of the expected despair and cabbage than it did of coffee and furniture polish.

The porter, a nurse, and soon the hospital superintendent himself appeared, greeting Ronnie as an old friend and making much of the tiny creature, yawning and stretching in her arms. Our coats were taken, our hats (and their pins) laid aside, and we were ushered across a hallway to what looked like a Victorian sitting room, with solid furniture, marble statues, potted palms, ancestral portraits, and comfortable chairs dotted with crisp white antimacassars. A radiator ticked on one side and a fire crackled on the other; the curtains were drawn back from high windows that looked out on a neatly tended garden. Despite the cold, three women strolled the paths, one of whom appeared to be carrying on a learned debate with an invisible friend.

The nurse who had brought us in lingered to coo over the lad, clearly tempted to prise him bodily from his mother's grasp. Before open battle could break out, an older woman in a grey dress stepped through the doorway, her authority sending the attendant scurrying back to work.

This woman Ronnie had no hesitation about, freely plunking the armload of blankets into the experienced hands, then turning to introduce me. It was the hospital matron, competent, iron-willed—and with an unexpected trace of humour at the back of her eyes. The sort of person no young mother would hesitate to entrust with her progeny—or her beloved aunt.

"How is she?" Ronnie asked once the initial fuss over the five-month-old was over.

"A bit sad," Matron replied without hesitation. "Her favourite nurse has just left to be married, and a patient she was friends with was moved to a private hospital nearer her family. But she'll be much cheered to see you."

"I'm so sorry, I should have come sooner, but—"

"Child, that's not what I was saying. Indeed, you'd have worried her by coming here in a . . . vulnerable state. Your letters have been quite pleasure enough."

Ronnie looked at the child in Matron's strong arms. "She will be fine with him, won't she? I needn't . . ."

"Worry about the little mite?" Matron gazed at the pink face with affection, then transferred him easily back to Ronnie's care. "She'll be perfectly fine with him. She's in a good phase at present. Even when she's not, the only person she tries to hurt anymore is herself."

With this sorry pronouncement, Matron left us alone with our thoughts and the child.

In a few minutes, the door opened, and in came two women. One was a tall, black-haired Sister in a dark blue uniform with stiff white collar, cuffs, and belt. Her right hand grasped the other woman's arm—which might have brought to mind control, strait-jackets, and shackles except that there was a degree of what almost seemed like affection in the gesture. I did not know if she showed that respect to all her patients—Vivian had to be one of the most high-ranking patients she would ever treat—but to my eye it looked more like helping a myopic friend across an uneven floor than it did controlling a certified lunatic.

Once inside the Sister let go, allowing Vivian Beaconsfield to continue across the room towards her niece.

At first glance, my eyes interpreted the figure as Ronnie's ancient grandmother: tiny with age, white-haired, kept upright by the nurse's assistance.

Certainly she was small—and she did look older than the early thirties I knew her to be, with thin, somewhat greasy pale blonde hair scraped back against her head. She wore normal day clothes, somewhat out of date and with the dullness of coarse laundry soap. It also lacked the belt its side-loops intended. However, the woman herself seemed neither worn nor particularly dull. Vivian greeted Ronnie with warmth, acknowledged my introduction with a hand-clasp, then bent over the infant with all the proper exclamations. She looked less mad than tired, like a woman recovering from a long and dreary fever.

Aunt and niece settled on chairs before the fire to examine young Master Fitzwarren in all his splendour, and were soon oblivious to the world. The nurse remained near the door, which might have been a hospital requirement, although she did not appear impatient or eager to get away. I moved over to her side. She was nearly as tall as I and only a few years older, with short, neat dark hair—short hair perhaps being an advantage to those working with the aggressively insane. She wore no more makeup than I did, not even to lessen the prominent mole along her jaw-line. I nodded towards the Beaconsfields. "I don't imagine your patients get to see many children."

"You'd be right there." Her accent was London, although I'd have said to the north of the River and some miles west. "A sweet world it would be if the mad could be put in charge of the nursery."

I smiled at the image, and held out a hand. "Mary Russell. I've known Ronnie since University."

"Rose Trevisan. I've known Miss Beaconsfield since she arrived." *Miss Beaconsfield,* I noted, rather than *Lady Vivian.* Socialist doctrine, hospital policy—or simple ignorance of titles? Her own name sounded Cornish, but her black hair and olive skin suggested that her people were of a more recent immigration.

"I hope she's doing all right here, Sister?"

"You knew her before?"

"I met her once, five or six years ago. That was before . . ."

"Before her troubles descended," Nurse Trevisan provided.

"Yes."

"She's doing well. Finding peace."

"I'm glad to hear that. Bedlam—sorry, Bethlem—has a rather dubious reputation, but Ronnie says her aunt is happy here."

The nurse smiled. "An evil reputation can be a protective wall. Those who imagine a vicious dog behind a fence don't climb over and discover the spaniel."

It was a startling thought. The wail that had greeted our arrival was far from contented—but before I could say anything stupid, "Miss Beaconsfield" looked up from her great-nephew and called her attendant over to admire him.

We took tea, an oddly normal ritual undermined in part by the pre-buttered scones (rendering knives unnecessary) and institutionally sturdy tea service (which, if broken, would have nothing resembling a sharp edge). The conversation flowed nicely when it ran through the safe territory of books and babies: Ronnie kept her aunt well supplied with reading material, and Vivian's memories of an infant Ronnie were fond. When those streams ran dry, it was up to Ronnie to supply news, there being little point in asking what her aunt had been doing. Politics was too complicated, mutual friends too few—although when Ronnie happened upon the topic of a formal wedding she'd attended a few weeks before, Vivian's face came alive, and she wanted to know every detail of dress and music and the foods served.

Eventually, Ronnie's grasp of the details grew thin, and Vivian sat back with a tiny sigh. The garden outside was fading in the dusk, and Nurse Trevisan—who had remained in the room, reading a book in the corner—took out her watch. As she stood, we heard raised voices from the hallway outside, building in fury to a scream and a scuffle, then silence.

Ronnie bit her lip, not looking at her aunt, but the older woman reached out to take her hand. "Dear child, a disrupted mind is not a pretty thing. I thank you for not coming in recent months. The memory of my dishevelled hair would forever lie between us."

Ronnie gave out a noise that was halfway between a sob and a laugh, and gripped her aunt's hand. "Oh, Auntie Viv, I've missed you so, I wish I . . . I could *do* something for you!"

"Nonsense! Your letters have been life-savers. I treasure the photographs you have sent. Those are the world to me."

"But, isn't there anything you need? Would you come and live with Simon and me? Oh, anything at all, Auntie, just ask."

"Ronnie, dear, I need to stay at Bethlem for a time. I'm safe here. Although if you'd like to send me a present, I'd adore a pot of your mother's damson preserves, when she makes some. If you posted it to Nurse Trevisan, she could dole it out to me." She glanced across the room at the nurse, who smiled back at her. "Oh—and I nearly forgot!" She patted at her garments until she heard a crinkle, and pulled out a folded drawing. "This is for the young man. Not terribly colourful, but all I have is a regular pencil. Ah—perhaps if you send me some pastels, I might do a better one for his nursery wall."

When Ronnie unfolded the paper, her face went soft with delight. She held it up for me to look at: a black-and-white Pierrot with ruffled collar and rounded hat. His expression was bashful yet mischievous, perfect for a child's room; my hand wanted to smooth away the fold lines across his face.

Ronnie let me hold it as she prepared to depart, bundling the boy, embracing her aunt, taking her leave of Nurse Trevisan. It was near-dark outside, the motor a rumbling oasis on the forecourt, and I laid the drawing on the seat to help Ronnie climb in with her arms full of child and blankets.

As we drove through the gates of Bedlam, back into the streets of London as if we were crossing over from a calm island, young Simon began to raise protests that sounded eerily like the voice of madness. I folded the drawing and tucked it away in Ronnie's handbag. When she'd got the boy settled, she remarked, "Aunt Vivian used to do the most beautiful watercolours. We have some at home—that one of the cottage, that I have in my sitting room?"

"Yes, I remember. I wonder if she's started again? I imagine it would do her good."

"I hope so. Mummy says Auntie Viv closed her sketch-books the day Daddy died, and hasn't touched them since. She'll be so happy to know that Auntie Viv's drawing again."

Drawing, yes—although I had to think that Pierrot was a rather mixed image for a child's room: a too-trusting, isolated figure of derision, rejected by his love and mocked by his betters, the most poignant of the commedia dell'arte characters.

And what on earth had the woman meant by *I'm safe here*?

Chapter Three

....

"THE LADY VIVIAN SOUNDS LESS OF A LUNATIC THAN many of those freely walking the streets of London," Holmes remarked. His pipe had gone cold, and he fished around for the ceramic bowl to knock out its burnt remains.

"She came very near to killing herself," I noted. "And she's been known to attack her brother with a steel poker."

"I have been tempted to do the same to mine," he murmured.

"She ended up in Bedlam, Holmes. That says a lot."

"Although you say she's not there now?"

"She's been doing so well the past few months, Ronnie says, that there's been discussion about moving her to Bedlam's other facility down in Witley, which is a sort of halfway-house where patients are sent to test if they are ready to be de-certified. So when Vivian got news of her brother's celebration and asked if she might attend—taking an attendant in case of distress—the doctors agreed to issue her a pass. The party was on Saturday. Vivian and the nurse went the Monday before. All seemed fine until Thursday, when she told Ronnie's mother she was feeling overly tired, and thought she should return to London. She and the nurse left the next morning, and the birthday celebration went on without her. But the following Monday, the hospital sent a wire to say that Miss Beaconsfield—which seems to be what they call her there—would require hospital permission if she wished to prolong her stay."

"She planned her escape."

"Someone did."

He looked up from his half-filled pipe, one eyebrow going up.

"When she arrived, last Monday, Vivian told Ronnie's mother that she wanted to wear her diamonds for the celebration. These aren't the Beaconsfield family jewels—which, since Edward isn't married, Ronnie's mother planned to wear—but a set left to Vivian by her mother. A heavy, old-fashioned necklace, tiara, bracelet, and earrings. So when Lady Dorothy got the Beaconsfield necklace out of the bank vault before the party, she brought Vivian's as well."

"And the mad aunt took those with her."

"Those, and an assortment of other small valuables. The house being in such turmoil with the party, no one noticed—or rather, Lady Dorothy noticed on Friday night that the jewellery was missing, but she wasn't about to bring it to the Marquess' attention, since it would have caused a fury. She planned to go down to Bedlam on Tuesday and quietly retrieve them. Except that Monday night, she learned that her sister-in-law was not there."

"And the attendant?"

"No one has seen her, either."

The words fell into the night, turning the June air cool. After a time, Holmes stirred, and struck a match to hold to his pipe bowl. Our surroundings danced for a moment in the brightness, then darkness fell again as he shook out the flame.

"Three possibilities?" he suggested.

"I agree. One, Vivian planned her escape from Bedlam, and the nurse is in on it. Two, the nurse fell to temptation, and has either abducted Vivian or done away with her. Or three, someone else has set it up to look as if the madwoman has struck."

"Why not: four, that Vivian Beaconsfield planned her escape, and has done away with the nurse?"

"I can't see that," I said. "True, the woman's hold on reality appears slippery. But nothing in her attitude or her background speaks to cold-blooded murder."

"Fireplace pokers?" he murmured.

Well, there was that.

"In any event, I told Ronnie I'd see what I could do. I'll go up to Town tomorrow and talk with her, then probably take the train down to Selwick to have a word with the family."

"And the servants," he added.

"And the estate manager, who will know about insurance and the condition of the Beaconsfield finances."

"Shall I begin enquiries about the principals? The Marquess, Vivian herself, the nurse?"

"Don't bother with Ronnie's mother. Lady Dorothy hasn't the imagination for crime. The others, yes. If you can keep it *very* quiet."

Sherlock Holmes did not dignify my caveat with an answer.

Chapter Four

....

HOLMES CAME UP TO TOWN WITH ME THE NEXT MORN-
ing, both to set his enquiries under way and (of greater concern) to do
some work at the British Library. We went our separate ways at the
Victoria station, he to his books and me to my family in turmoil. As we
parted, I told him not to expect me back in Sussex for a day or two. His
hand came up in a half-wave of acknowledgment.

Ronnie lived along the southern edges of the Maida Vale area. As I
walked over from the Edgware Road stop, I thought my preoccupation
with her Aunt Vivian had begun to invade my hearing as well as my
mind: uncanny wails seemed to echo through the streets as I neared,
eerie ululations that grew ever louder as I approached her door. It took
some pounding to draw her attention, but she eventually came, looking
harried and unkempt and not far from tears herself.

Behind her, young Master Simon broke off his full-throated protests
to eye the cause of this outrageous interruption.

"Mary, sorry! Hope you haven't been here long—come in, I'll put on
the kettle. I don't know if Simon is teething, though it seems unlikely at

his age, or if he's coming down with something. He may simply be constipated—Nurse is determined to introduce him to the pot and he's equally deter—"

Fortunately for my delicate sensibilities, the young man decided we'd had long enough on our own and opened his mouth again.

I'd never realised how difficult it could be to carry on intelligent conversation over an unhappy child. Or even carry out intelligent thought: I could well see why the lad's nurse had taken to her bed with a sick head-ache. After five minutes of trying to speak over the roar, I told Ronnie I wouldn't take tea, thanks, but thought I'd set off for Selwick right away, and see her on my way back through Town.

I could only hope that by the time I returned, the nurse would either be recovered, or replaced.

Standing in the flat's doorway while the three-year-old scion of the Beaconsfield clan expressed his utter fury from around her knees, Ronnie handed me a photograph of her aunt, and managed to convey the information that her mother would be home and expecting me. I made my hasty escape, thanking all the domestic gods that I had not been chosen to reproduce. I took a nice peaceable, solitary luncheon while a photographer's studio made some copies of the photo. I also stopped by a telegraphist's to confirm my arrival at Selwick, leaving the arrival time vague so Ronnie's mother would not feel obliged to provide a car.

I'd been to Selwick Hall two or three times, brief visits that tended to be a flurry of social activities rather than leisurely days pottering about the countryside. Which was unfortunate, in a way, since the countryside was classically English Downland, with gently rolling hills and ancient patches of woodland. On a June afternoon, with no cloud in the sky, it would be no hardship to walk the two miles to the Hall.

The hedgerows were white with blossom, the fields scattered with new-cropped sheep. Twice I had to press into the hawthorn so as not to be run down by speeding motorcars, and twice laboriously peel my garments out of the thorns. Once my heart nearly stopped when a trio of partridges exploded up from the silent road, and once I spent an awkward couple of minutes trying to engage a sullen child in conversation before leaving him to his swinging gate.

I eventually turned down the drive from the lane, and made my way towards Selwick Hall.

The house was neither grand nor particularly large by Surrey standards, a redbrick, three-storey building with pseudo-Elizabethan chimneys and a slightly off-centre portico that emphasised the lopsided nature of the two wings, only one of which was deep enough for a series of rooms. It was the kind of house that called for a large and boisterous family, instead of individuals left behind by death.

Ronnie had grown up in the main house, but after her father died, his widow, child, and sister had moved into the side wing to make room for the Marquess. Ronnie had used the grand ballroom and formal dining room to celebrate her wedding to Miles Fitzwarren, but other than that, I gathered the Marquess kept to his side of the baize doors, and his sister-in-law to hers.

The reason for this long-standing and awkward arrangement had never been fully explained to me—few things are a more sensitive topic to an English person than finances—but I thought that despite his younger brother's financial acumen, the Marquess was fairly hopeless when it came to sensible investments. I suspected that nothing but the caution of previous generations had preserved the estate itself in Beaconsfield hands—although one might have wished that their practicality had extended to giving the women of the family a say in things, so that Ronnie was not faced with a choice of abandoning her home or pinching every housekeeping penny. So far, she had managed to remain in the London flat she and Miles had called home, but as the boy's costs grew, she might be forced to reconsider.

And so I left the main drive to follow the path to the east wing, and reached out to pull the bell beside what looked like a trades entrance. In a moment, I found myself looking at Ronnie's mother.

Tears seemed to be a theme for the day. Like her grandson, The Lady Dorothy had been weeping, although perhaps with less vigour and commotion than the lad, and more of a desire to conceal it.

She'd never been beautiful, no more than Ronnie was—they shared their short, verging-on-stout form and unfortunate pug nose, and neither had ever been able to do much with their mousy hair. I imagined looking at her mother would cause Ronnie some degree of despair, at what she would look like when she was in her middle forties. In fact, my friend's lack of conventional beauty had always been outweighed (at least, until motherhood took over) by her big heart and her eagerness to change the world; her mother's dowdy simplicity of spirit had been cramped only by a Victorian upbringing in what a woman did and did not do.

(Ironic, that, considering the entire age took its name from a Queen—who, come to think of it, might have been the physical model for the two Beaconsfield women, minus the black dresses, lace mantillas, and scowl.)

The countess had done her best to hide the redness of eyes and nose, so I pretended not to notice, merely greeting her as the old acquaintance I was. Lady Dorothy led me to a stifling sitting room, told the maid to bring tea, and embarked on a cheery conversation about the heat and the garden. The moment the maid shut the door, she sagged a bit—too well-bred to slump in her chair and blow a puff of air over her face, but that was the effect. She smiled, her first genuine expression since I'd arrived.

"It's very good of you to come, Mrs, er . . ." People who knew me before I married Holmes had difficulties with my choice of names—although my problem was nothing compared to this woman's, with her family links not only to inherited peerages and courtesy titles, but a granted position as well. It was the sort of tangle that only those whose male relatives sat in the House of Lords would be able to keep straight.

"Oh heavens, it's still *Mary*."

"Mary, then. Ronnie said you wanted to talk about Vivian's disappearance, although I'm not sure what she thinks you can do. We've searched all over for her—all the paths and trails, the corners of the house, up in the stables. She did not board a train, no one saw a strange motorcar. Edward even . . . even had the lake dragged."

"There's probably nothing I can do that you haven't, but I promised

Ronnie, she being a bit tied down. I hope you don't mind if I speak to the servants?"

"Of course not, if it can help. Not that it will take you long," she added. "There's only Lily and the cook, and a half-time gardener."

"Really? I'd have thought this sort of place would take a platoon of polishers."

"The main house has its own staff, of course. Although even it doesn't have as many as it should."

"I suppose these days country girls prefer work in a factory over life in service."

"Hmm."

My ears pricked at the sound: there was no agreement there, only her unwillingness to disagree—or, to admit to reduced circumstances.

"You must have brought in a lot of caterers and what-have-you to help with your brother-in-law's birthday last week. I understand it was quite a bash."

"That's not unusual. Edward hosts a lot of week-end parties. His political friends, for the most part. But it's true, this was busier than usual. Which is why we did not think much about Vivian's absence—we hadn't the time. Frankly, it was a relief to have her out of the way. She tried to be helpful, but even the silver she polished needed to be re-done after."

"I'm surprised the Marquess didn't bring in all the village women to help!"

Her gaze fell to her hands. "Yes, well, Edward's had some unfortunate investments of late."

"I see. Well, tell me about your sister-in-law. How was she, up to the point she left?"

Lady Dorothy looked relieved at my change of subject—easier to talk about the family lunatic than the family money. "*I* thought she looked marvellous! She'd had her hair bobbed, very fashionable. She'd put on a little weight, which was good since sometimes she looks positively skeletal. She mostly paid attention to the conversation, even held up her part of it. But that nurse—I don't know. At first, I'd have said

Vivian enjoyed her company, but looking back, I wonder if the woman wasn't . . . controlling her somehow. It couldn't be difficult to do, considering Vivian's state of mind."

"Controlling her, how?"

"Oh, offering up things to talk about, asking pointed questions, getting in the way of family affairs—the woman *claimed* that the asylum required her to stay in the room with Vivian every minute, which meant that she had to come to dinner with us—can you imagine? Once or twice I caught Vivian shooting these little glances over, almost as if she was afraid of her."

"Afraid?" I said sharply. "Physically afraid? Or as if the nurse might give a negative report on her?"

"I don't really know. Certainly when the two of them were alone—in the garden, walking by the pond—they seemed perfectly comfortable. But as I say, when we dined in the main house, Vivian scarcely said a word, barely touched her plate, sat and looked down at her hands. I wondered, afterwards, whether the nurse might have been so uncomfortable, dining outside of her class like that, that Vivian was afraid she'd have to pay for it later. You hear such dreadful tales about . . . those places."

It was a vivid and startling picture, the madwoman cowering in anticipation of her nurse's revenge over a petty scorning. "You are very fond of your sister-in-law, I think."

"I love Vivian dearly—I did, at any rate. Oh, Mary, you should have seen her before the War! So delicate and charming—the prettiest girl of her Season. And she *seemed* to adore it—the parties, the dancing, the spectacle and dressing up. It was only afterwards, when the talk turned sober, that she would fade and cower. The young men did not know what to do. She left early—it was barely July—and went off to Paris all by herself. Oh, with a maid, of course, she wasn't *that* bohemian. She knew no one, but that seemed to be what she was after. So odd. At any rate, she never married, and now she's become such a sad and fragile person, wrapped up in the most dreadful ideas and fantasies. The mind is a terrible thing, when it loses control." Ronnie's mother looked up, tears welling. "Please find her, Miss Russell. Help me keep her as safe as she'll allow."

"Do you think she may have . . ." I hesitated to finish the sentence, but she did not.

"Harmed herself? I think she could—I *know* she could. I lie awake at night and imagine her, putting on those heavy old jewels and dancing into the sea somewhere. But then, I also can imagine that awful nurse, looking at the weight of them and at the fragility of Vivian . . . She was Italian, after all."

I blinked at the non-sequitur. "Who? The nurse?"

"Yes! Those dark eyes, that skin, the black hair. Crime runs in their veins, doesn't it?"

"No more than it does in the veins of Englishmen, Scandinavians, or . . . Faroe Islanders."

"I hope you're right." But it was mere politeness.

However, the description tugged at my memory. "What was this nurse's name?"

"Trevisan."

"I met her, when Ronnie and I went to Bedlam—sorry, Bethlem—three years ago. Isn't she Cornish?"

"Is she? Odd, I could have sworn she was Italian."

The villainy of Mediterraneans knew no bounds.

I set down my cup of weak, half-drunk tea, and patted her hand, one of those meaningless gestures that seem to comfort some women. "Could I see your sister-in-law's rooms?"

"They've been tidied," Lady Dorothy said.

Well, I could only hope the overworked maid had taken a few short-cuts.

Chapter Five

....

I'M NOT SURE WHAT I EXPECTED OF A MADWOMAN'S apartment. Chaos, certainly. Clear signs of disintegration and terror. But either the maid had been particularly aggressive here, or I did not understand the impulses of lunacy.

Why had I never seen these rooms before? Had my brief visits coincided with times when Vivian was locked away? I'd always assumed that Ronnie's disinclination to invite her Oxford friends home was rooted in a faint embarrassment over her living situation and her mother's lack of intellectual gifts—but it could not have helped to know that a visitor might encounter an alarmingly erratic aunt.

Vivian's small private sitting room, in the upper reaches of the wing, was light and airy, remarkably free of clutter compared to the stodgy, dim quarters below. Books were neatly confined to a set of shelves, the bottom two given over to a series of leather-bound sketch-books. A simple, flat-topped desk stood beneath one window, with cups holding drawing-pencils and ink pens. Two chairs and a settee were arranged before the fireplace with a small table at their centre. They were upholstered in a soft green-blue cloth that reminded me of the ocean, and could not have been more than eight or ten years old. The wallpaper, similarly new, had a design so subtle as to appear merely texture. Its colour was a sort of faded terra cotta, with stronger touches of the same near-orange in the room's carpet and throw-pillows. Two carpets interrupted the polished wood of the floor, a small one under the desk, a larger one connecting the group of pieces in front of the fire—both of them thick, modern, and expensive.

The overall effect was somehow Mediterranean, redolent of clear skies, tile roofs, warm nights.

"Such a bare room," Ronnie's mother commented. "This happened after one of her first . . . fits. One afternoon she just started throwing things out of the windows, lamps and pictures crashing to the ground, and insisted that we have the stableboys up to carry out all the furniture. Every scrap of it, down to the walls and floor-boards. She slept on the bare floor that night, and the next morning came down with her gloves on and set off for Town. I was so concerned that I made her take one of the maids, to 'help her carry things.' When she came back that night, she began turning the rooms into . . . this."

Lady Dorothy's helpless gesture was a clear indication that, to her mind, these alien surroundings were proof positive of Vivian's loss of reason.

"When would that have been?"

"During the War—can you imagine? It was difficult enough to repair what one had, much less purchase things this . . . unusual."

"So this was after your husband died?"

"Not long after. Before the War, we lived in the central portion of the house, with Vivian. After . . . after he was gone, we moved over to this side so that Edward could return, just before Christmas in 1915. Vivian's fit would have been a few months later. Weeks, perhaps? At any rate, we'd scarcely settled in when—poof! Out of the window things went, and in came this. Heaven knows what she paid for it all. But she had her own money—still does, for that matter, although Edward is of course the trustee."

Of course.

I walked over to a cluster of seven nicely framed watercolours all of flowers, all by the same artist. "Are these hers?"

"She was so talented. Before the War, she used to take her paints out into the countryside. She'd be gone hours and hours—she'd wear a boy's trousers and put her hair under a cap. Still does sometimes, when she's home, though it makes Edward furious. I always thought it a sensible idea for a girl out alone like that, but never mind. She'd just walk, mostly, looking dreamily at the trees and hills, then stop for a while and do a sketch, sometimes a painting. She did an entire series of Selwick Hall itself—in the morning, at evening, in the winter. She had them framed on her bedroom wall, and they were the first things to be thrown out that day. I'll never forget the sound as they hit the stones." She shuddered, as if the shattering glass were also Vivian's mind going to pieces. "I rescued what I could of them. I have them in a cupboard downstairs. Perhaps I should have them framed again, if . . ." *If Vivian is not coming home.*

Before her eyes could start welling up, we were interrupted by a tap at the door: the maid with a question from the cook. I seized the opportunity and urged Lady Dorothy to go and deal with the problem, firmly shutting the door behind them that I might return to my study of the room.

To my surprise, I liked the madwoman's decor, very much. Which might mean I, too, was mad—although Holmes would no doubt have mentioned it. Or it could mean that Vivian Beaconsfield was mad only north-northwest. That when the wind was from the south, she knew her Axminster from her Art Deco.

Still, when the wind blowing through her mind *was* north-northwest, Lady Vivian was a woman who hurled her possessions from upper windows, assaulted her brother with a fireplace poker, and took a blade to her own wrists.

I began a methodical search of the rooms, from chair-cushions and floor-boards to picture-backs and the undersides of drawers. As always,

it was less a matter of actively searching for something than it was letting the mind passively notice the details and patterns of this woman's
chosen surroundings.

She liked soft textures rather than smooth ones, indistinct patterns
over sharp designs, and rich colours over pastels.

Her sketch-books drew me, and then drew me in. They amounted to
visual journals, with labels on the front covers giving their dates. Some
volumes spanned two years; others only months.

1910 and 1911 took up a disproportionate amount of shelf-space.
January to May opened with drawings of winter landscapes and interior
still-lifes, then abruptly gave way to startling splashes of colour and motion: a dance. This must have been her London Season, the time when
the country's chosen were trolled through Society in hopes of hooking
a likely mate. To my surprise, it appeared that she'd enjoyed the process.
Certainly there was pleasure behind the whirl of bright skirts on the
pages.

However, as one looked more closely— and as the sequence continued in the June to October volume—the emphasis shifted, from skirts
and gleaming candelabras to the faces of the onlookers: wrinkled old
women and smooth young men, both with expressions that were avid,
eager, and eventually oppressive.

One page, with a tiny date in the corner reading "9 July 1911," was
covered with disembodied hands, a nightmarish sea of grasping black-
and-white fingers.

With trepidation, I turned the page—and was looking at the Dover
cliffs receding off the back of a ferry.

She'd gone to Paris. Why did the verb *fled* come to mind? A few
pages of desultory Parisian scenes followed, dutiful sketches of Ver-
sailles, the *Tour Eiffel,* booksellers along the Seine.

Then the sun came up.

In September, to judge by the wealth of late-summer produce in her
drawings of outdoor markets, she'd gone south: Nîmes and Avignon,
Nice and Florence, Rome and Ravenna and Venice. She'd either spent

longer in that last, or been particularly fascinated by the canals, for there were dozens of small studies that experimented with the reflections of towers, flags, and passing gondolas.

It was startling to turn the page to a drawing of a man who could only be English, walking with his dog across a winter field that could only be Selwick.

The following pages were of him as well, and when one showed his face, I knew who it was: Ronnie's father, the artist's brother, Thomas Beaconsfield. He'd died before Ronnie and I met, but I recognised him from a photograph Ronnie kept on her desk. That face had also been a recurring theme throughout the sketch-journals, going back to Vivian's childhood. In all those images, her affection shone clear.

But it occurred to me that I had seen few of her older brother, Edward, the current Marquess. I pulled down one of the earlier volumes, labelled 1902, and indeed, there were only two that might have been he. I supposed that, being sixteen when Vivian was born, Edward had been off to University when his sister was tiny—plus, as Ronnie had told me, the heir preferred city lights to country pastures. Vivian had probably spent only brief holidays with Edward before he returned to Selwick after their brother's death. By which time the madness was creeping up around her.

Hers had been a typically protected childhood. Most of the figures in her earliest sketches were women of the household, with the occasional shift to groups of men working in the fields or stables. Children appeared sometimes, particularly one dark-haired girl who, to judge by the dates on the sketch-books, was a year or two older than Vivian. A friend? Or a companion, assigned the task of making sure the small, blonde daughter of the family did not get into trouble as she wandered the hills with her pencils?

I put the 1902 book back on its shelf (for a child of eleven, her drawings seemed remarkably sophisticated) and pulled down the last book on the shelf.

This one had no label, although as with earlier volumes, the occasional more detailed drawing would have a date in its corner. Here was

Ronnie, startlingly like she'd been when I first laid eyes on her. Several pages of wintry branches followed, with attempts to capture the look of ice. Then came a finished sketch from what would prove to be her brother's last home leave: Thomas Beaconsfield, wearing a Captain's uniform, stood behind his seated wife, hands on her shoulders. 12 February 1915. He had died the following summer.

I wondered if Ronnie knew the image existed.

The next pages continued wintry landscapes: snowdrops peeping out of leaves; bits of flaming log in a fireplace; a cat burrowed into pillows. The page after that was missing: torn out along the seam. I tried to think if I had seen any other missing pages, and thought not—although I hadn't studied every volume. Had some extreme of self-criticism led Vivian to remove this one? The pages that followed did suggest she'd been pushing herself to try something new: details dropped away, leaving quick, thin lines that at first glance were mere marks on a page, but soon emerged as studies of objects captured in a fast twist of the hand. As if someone had shown her a book on Japanese ink drawing—only these were faint, almost pointillist tracks of graphite that suggested an unfurling leaf, a blossom, a clutch of newborn chicks.

Then another page went missing, this one methodically picked away down to the fold.

After that second gap, an entire season had passed before Vivian took up her pencil again, to sketch a distant and solitary figure scything in a field. Then three acorns on the ground, so detailed that had they been in colour, the hand might have been tempted to pick them up. Two women in a large kitchen, backs turned as they worked on some project—the shape of the tins lying to one side suggested a Christmas pudding. And finally, another polished rendering, this one of Ronnie and her mother, before the fire. Ronnie appeared to be reading something aloud; Lady Dorothy was bent over some needle-work. The fire was lively, the scene speaking eloquently of love and warmth and survival.

This one was dated: *9 December 1915*. It was also signed: *Vivian Marie Beaconsfield*.

I frowned. Her framed watercolours were signed, but I could not recall seeing a name on any of the other drawings. Did she intend this as a finished piece, to go on the wall? If so, why was it still here? I turned the page, finding a curled leaf, snow atop a twig, and a shiny conker—none of them signed. After the conker came one final torn-out page, and after that: nothing. The remainder of the book held only blank pages.

Ronnie had told me that Vivian stopped drawing when her beloved brother was killed, but clearly she had not. True, she'd picked up her pencils less often, but with no less commitment to the process. Looking at those final pages, I could see no sign of what had to be building up in her mind. That single dead leaf, that lonely twig, might in themselves seem ominous, but not when compared with the preceding years of similar drawings.

Sometime around Christmas 1915, Vivian Beaconsfield had laid down her pencils, closed her last journal, and ceased drawing. A few weeks later, she flung her possessions out of the windows and stripped her rooms to the walls. And a few months after that, she had attacked her surviving brother and gone into care, beginning the cycle that finally delivered her to the gates of Bedlam.

The afternoon was drawing in, and I felt I'd exhausted the possibilities of the sitting room. I returned the undated sketch-book to the shelf, straightened the spines again, and went into the adjoining bedroom. It, too, was a bright space, with ivory curtains hooked back from the window. The bed was made up, the water carafe on the table filled—did the maid still come every day to tend to Vivian's empty quarters?

However, unlike the lightly furnished sitting room, this space was an Aladdin's cave of treasures. The bed-cover was lace-work over a creamy linen coverlet. The small wooden tables on either side looked German, each with an electric lamp with blown-glass bases and damask silk shades. A closely woven oval carpet next to the bed looked to be Turkish or Greek, as were the two pillows atop the coverlet.

But it was the wall facing the bed that drew the attention. Ceiling to floor, side to side, the wall was one enormous collage of shiny and curious objects, broken only by the mirrored dressing table set against its centre. All the objects were neatly hung and perfectly tidy within their allotted space, but the mix was idiosyncratic to an extreme: a curly twig here, a pyramid of buttons threaded through a hat-pin there, and between them a nosegay of long-dried flowers tucked into an infant's embroidered shoe. Six tiny, perfectly framed paintings of a rock—different views of the same rock, and hung with a compulsive's precision. There were scraps of cloth, a dog's collar, and a broken roof-slate on which was painted a track of bare foot-prints, like a miniature beach at low tide. I counted five masks—two Venetian, two African, and an oddity made from a turtle shell. A cameo depicted the Roman Colosseum; half a dozen silk flowers of different design and colour were scattered about. There were a dozen or so keys, modern to Medieval, from thumbnail-sized to as long as my hand, and as many antique photograph portraits of various sizes, some framed and others held up with a push-pin. One wizened object that might have been a plum lay inside an intricately worked straw basket three inches high; to its left, a bow tied of exquisitely delicate lace; to its right, a long, thin mirror with a gilded frame.

Dizzying, baffling, glorious: mad? I lay down on Vivian's bed, curious about what she would see from there, and found it oddly . . . composed. I removed my glasses to let the individual identities blur, and realised that if one imagined the objects as dots of paint, it made a modernistic, yet oddly comforting, overall impression. With two small flaws.

I put on my glasses and went to look. Yes, there were two places where things had been removed—one the size of my palm, the other of my outstretched hand. Both left tiny brass nails protruding from the wallpaper, suggesting that whatever had been there was considerably lighter than the slate or the mirror.

I tore my gaze away, to continue my search through drawers and under mattresses and carpets, atop curtains and under the stone sill outside the window. There was no clutter in her drawers and wardrobe, and all the clothing, somewhat out of date, smelt of cedar shavings or mothballs. The colours I found there were every bit as subtle as in her sitting room, and their fabric as pleasing to the touch. She liked velvet, and silk, and loose-knitted merino. And belts—she had quite a collection of new-looking belts. Perhaps to compensate for an institutional weight loss? Hanging on a hook, so as to avoid wrinkles, was a pale green evening dress, again rather out of date, that I guessed she'd intended to wear to her brother's birthday celebration. But there was also an assortment of male clothing—made to fit a short, slim figure.

Perhaps the maid had been instructed to provide Vivian with the means to go wandering through the hills again, in the gentle disguise of her childhood.

Other than that, wardrobe and drawers held nothing of interest. As I left the room, I paused to study the display.

The wall was mad, and therefore worrying. But it was also compelling, and therefore equally worrying.

No, I thought, turning away: Holmes would surely have let me know if my grip on reason was slipping.

Chapter Six

SHERLOCK HOLMES LOOKED AT THE BOOKS AND MUSICAL pages spread over his table in the Reading Room, and realised that in ninety minutes, he had taken in not a single word.

Two weeks they'd had this time: two weeks and one day since Mrs Hudson's case finished and she'd fled to Monte Carlo. Before that, he and Russell had nearly three weeks of calm between storms—although prior to that it was difficult to remember a time without demands.

Amusing to think that in his Baker Street days, boredom often drove him to a drugged stupor. When he'd ... married (interesting how, four and a half years on, the word still fit poorly in the mind) he had anticipated a life peaceably divided between his Sussex bees and her Oxford books, with the occasional piquant outing to the world of crime. Indeed, that's what they had, more or less, for the first two and a half years— until an acquaintance had called them to service, in August 1923. They had not stopped running since, racketing about the world, getting shot and taken hostage, with any number of threats thrown in their direction. During the past two years they'd had ... what? Ten quiet days at the end of 1923? After that, a handful of days here and there (mostly there) until the two weeks, and then three weeks, this past spring. They might have had two entire months to themselves during the autumn of 1924, but for Watson's little problem.

So much for retirement.

Still, it was probably all to the best—for him, at least. Lack of a challenge had always eaten at his spirit and his health. When he'd met Russell in 1915, he'd been on a downward spiral to the grave. At the current rate, he was going to live well into his second century.

Russell was a different question.

For her, the detecting life was less a demand than a choice. The young woman was quite capable of making a different life for herself— any number of different lives, come to that. Had she never encountered him on the Downs that afternoon, she would today be happily battling herself into a position of authority in the University, if not the Government. Marriage, normalcy—children, even: nothing was beyond her.

Instead, Russell had chosen to follow the path he offered.

She was content, he knew that. But he had also seen her eyes following the carefree young people the other night. He told himself that the slight softening of her eyes and mouth had been amusement, not wistfulness. He wished he could be sure of it.

He looked down at the books, and wondered if there had been a reason his musical studies had nudged him into the question of Johann Sebastian Bach's argument between formal and natural art. Or, one might say, between logic and passion, deliberation and mania ...

Pah. He slapped shut the aged volume, drawing looks of scandal from all around, and abandoned his table and his studies in favour of a missing Bedlamite.

Chapter Seven

....

HAD SELWICK HALL NOT BEEN TUCKED INTO THE FAR reaches of the county, I might have turned down Lady Dorothy's offer to stop there the night, in favour of returning to London. But I did want to speak with the servants, and I had no wish to tramp the lanes to the station after dark.

So I accepted, expecting a quiet meal before the fire with Ronnie's lonely mother. Instead, it seemed, we were to dine in grandeur at the Marquess' table. I'd met the man once or twice, most recently at Ronnie's wedding, and thought him an unfortunate product of the system of aristocratic privilege. Dining with him was not an enticing prospect.

However, it was difficult to refuse, since I'd brought one of those long, all-purpose skirts that (with a borrowed shawl) could pass as "dressing for dinner." And I did have questions for him. If I remembered his habits correctly, he might take enough wine to simplify that task—assuming I could control my own intake in his presence.

It's not that I object to self-assured men, not really. And although flirtation can be tiresome, I have learned to live with the fact that for a certain generation of men—men who've been schooled away from their sisters and mothers, and never learned how to converse with the opposite sex—hearty jests and an exchange of suggestive glances with any other male present was the best they could do. My habit was to remind myself that some men never got over the handicap of not being women, and keep my mouth in a tight-lipped smile.

Ronnie's mother had taken care not to underscore my own lack of satin and diamonds, although she had put her hair up, its silver threads winding like Nature's tiara amidst the dark background, and wore a necklace of small rubies that sparkled in the electric light.

She smiled, looking distracted, and reached out to straighten a fold in the silk wrap she had lent me. "You look very nice, Mary."

"I look like a bluestocking without a dress allowance."

"A very pretty bluestocking. Is that the gong?"

Distracted, or worried? For some reason, we were waiting at the end of a corridor, facing a plain wooden door. Lady Dorothy now reached for the handle and we passed into the main house as the gong's reverberations were fading. The long dining table was laid with three places. With a gesture towards the chair on the far side, my hostess took up a position behind the chair across from that one—and stood, her hands on the chair's back, waiting.

The Lady Dorothy—daughter of a duke, widow of an earl—waited in this oddly servile position as if she was well accustomed to it, but just as I was about to pull out my own chair and plunk myself down, The Most Hon Marquess of Selwick came through the doorway. The butler sprang to seat him, then came around and pulled out my chair while the footman pulled back Lady Dorothy's.

"Evening, Miss Russell," the Marquess boomed. "See you've fallen for this fad of chopping your hair. Pity, I remember it was charmin'."

And *I* remembered how he had found an excuse to touch it, at the wedding, claiming there was a bit of leaf caught in it.

"Oh, it got in the way when I was fixing the motorcar."

He looked startled, which was what I had been intending, but the look quickly gave way to something dangerously close to a leer. "You don't say. Fine figure of a girl like you, I'd like to see you bent over a fender."

Even the servile version of Lady Dorothy had to object to that. "Edward! Miss Russell is Veronica's University friend."

"But the gel's married, isn't she? Not too many blushes left to her."

His brother's widow stepped in before I could choose which verbal skewer to run him through with. "Miss Russell has come to see if she can find any clues as to where Vivian might have gone."

"Clues—hah! You make her sound like a Miss Christie sleuth."

I smoothed my napkin across my knees. "Not Baroness Orczy? Lady Molly, perhaps?"

His blank stare suggested he was not a fan of the Baroness' detective. My polite smile caused him to harrumph and reach for his glass.

Restored by drink, he attacked the soup that had been laid before him, not waiting for either of us to take up our spoons. I winced at his first slurp, and at every one that followed, wishing I had some crusty bread with which to drown the noise. As he clattered the spoon against the bottom of his bowl, I tossed out a topic of conversation, thinking he might chase it rather than the last scraps of carrot.

"I understand that felicitations are in order, my Lord. For your fiftieth birthday. I hope your party was satisfactory?"

"Have to do such things, it's expected, even if it costs an arm and a leg. At least my sister didn't pull her disappearing stunt beforehand, turn everything on its head."

Well, if the man was so obliging as to bring up the topic, I was happy to run with it. "So where do you think she's gone?"

"Probably on a ship to South America or something." He shoved his plate away, causing the butler to step briskly forward.

"Do you think she convinced the nurse to go along?"

"I do. And then tipped the woman overboard the minute they set off."

I shot a startled glance across at Lady Dorothy, but she was intent on straightening her silver. "Really?"

"Violent little minx, my sister. Looked like butter wouldn't melt, twist you around her finger, but she was a flirt when she was small and vicious when she grew up—she came after me half a dozen times, once with a poker. Bled like Billy-o! See the scar?" He parted his hair, although I could see nothing past the lumps and discolorations of his mottled scalp.

"Artists, you know," I said, keeping my irritation in check. "Temperamental sorts."

"Art? You mean her scribbles? Kept her out of mischief, I suppose—you gels need a hobby, don't you, until you're married? Not that she'd ever marry, what with Bedlam and all. But I never saw her do anything I'd want to hang over the fireplace."

I glanced down at the fork in my hand, idly contemplating what his scalp would look like with four neat holes to punctuate the bash-mark, but it would appear that the butler was well accustomed to the reactions of outraged guests, since he chose that moment to appear at my elbow and insert his dark arm into my field of vision.

I let go the fork, and dropped my hands to my lap as the oblivious Marquess drivelled on about a painting he'd helped a friend buy recently down in London, some Renaissance battle piece the size of a room with rearing horses and slashing swords, you could see the muscles and blood, now *that* was art, wouldn't you say, Miss Russell?

"So they tell me. Are you often down in London, my Lord?"

"I get down occasionally. Not as much as I'd like—I've let out the London house to a bunch of Americans. God knows what they're doing to the place, parties and whatnot with Reds and Negroes, bugger-boys and those idiotic Flapper girls. Probably using drugs and sticking their damned chewing gum on my Regency tables."

Lady Dorothy murmured a protest at the word *bugger,* but I nodded solemnly. "Yes, Americans can be tough on the furniture."

"Ought to be shot, all of them."

"What, Americans? That seems a bit excessive."

"No, the Nancy boys! Have you any idea—"

"Edward, *please.*"

The poor woman was so close to tears, I had to lay my teasing aside.

"I'm curious, my Lord, why did you let out the house if you prefer to live in London?" I knew why: he couldn't afford to keep it up. But I wanted to hear his reason.

"Responsibilities. Selwick needs a master. Place like this doesn't run itself, you know. Tenants need a firm hand. And there's Dot, here—she doesn't have anyplace to go. I'm guessing the gel and her boy will end up here sooner or later."

Dot, I suspected, would be as happy to be given free rein here, just as *the gel,* Ronnie, might have come back with little Simon long before this were it not for her overbearing uncle. As for the tenants . . .

"So what do you grow, here at Selwick? Not really wheat country, is it?"

"Um, well, some wheat. I think. Seem to be a lot of sheep."

"The Baileys make a lovely Double Gloucester," Lady Dorothy offered.

The Marquess brightened. "Yes, cows do fine, on some of the farms. And lots of pigs—nice bacon for the breakfast table, I'll say that for them. Rents keep falling, of course—farmers always complaining, but you don't see them starving, do you?" He laughed.

In fact, the children of farmers were the first to go hungry come drought, flood, or disease, although I bit back the remark.

Come to that, my topics of dinner conversation seemed to be growing as thin as my smile. We'd failed to find common ground in literature, art, or agriculture, and I refused to offer up my own interest in religion on the altar of his ignorance. What did that leave? The Fawcett search for a lost civilisation in the Amazon? Churchill returning us to the gold standard? The Scopes arrest? No, not that—I doubted this . . . person followed any news from America other than horse races and who was boarding a ship for Southampton.

Normally, given a choice between politics and sport, I would dredge up the names of some cricket players or make enquiry as to a preference for dry flies versus wet when it came to the local streams—but honestly, I could not be bothered.

"So tell me, my Lord, what's the political situation hereabouts?"

Ronnie's mother made a choking noise and reached for her glass. The butler and footman straightened a bit where they stood. The candles seemed to flicker briefly before they rallied—but the Marquess of Selwick looked first astonished, then ecstatic.

"The political situation? *Political* situation? A year ago I'd have called it somewhere between laughable and tragic—but at least we've got rid of that MacDonald looney and his Bolshevik friends, we can start pulling this country together again. Not that Baldwin's all that much better. He and his cronies have no idea what this country needs. Have you been watching—no, of course you haven't, women don't—but I tell you, there are some interesting things going on in Europe these days, things we could learn from. The damned League of— What's that?" He glared at his sister-in-law, whose objection to this curse had been marginally more assertive, but went on, regardless. "The League of Nations, they're going to bleed us dry. You ever heard such nonsense as comes out of that lot, tying us to what *other* countries want us to do? They can't even get the Krauts to pay the reparations they promised—ought to hand over some of their land to the Frenchies, if that's what it takes. Not that the French can run anything more complicated than a vineyard. But you look at Italy, now. That feller they got in there is going to pull things together!"

Dear God: could the man possibly be talking about Benito Mussolini? The self-declared *Duke of Fascism and Founder of the Empire*? Who had graced his inauguration as dictator back in January with a speech claiming responsibility for "all the violence"—including, apparently, one particularly brutal kidnap and murder of a political opponent by his Fascist Blackshirt supporters?

As soon as I had my breath back, I interrupted him, with a mildness that would have had Holmes edging warily back, but which went straight by this inbred peer. "He is a Socialist, you know?"

"What's that?"

"Mussolini. Or he was. First a Socialist, then an anarchist, and a Marxist, until he read Nietzsche and declared himself one of the *Über-*

menschen. He then tried to decide whether he was violently in favour of neutrality or violently in favour of war, but in the end he decided to declare a pox on both their houses and be violently in favour of himself and whatever struck Benito Mussolini's fancy at the moment."

The Marquess goggled, either at my argument or that the young female at his table had dared to make one, then rallied with typical male bluster. "Oh, I'm not saying he's the man for our own country—even Baldwin admits Britain's in no danger of falling in line behind a damned dictator. But the Italians are a Mediterranean race, hot-blooded in love and war. People like that want a strong man to control them. You know, talking about politics, I've been to a couple speeches lately, there's some of us here in this country thinking we could do worse than to take a page out of the Italians' book."

I found myself staring, open-mouthed at his naïveté. The response to a festering sore was not to extol its virtues, but to lance the thing and let the poison bleed out. The people of Italy would soon enough realise what they had, and set about lancing their *Duce*—one hoped before the poison spread beyond its borders.

Then my host went a step too far.

"But why the deuce are we talking about this? Granted, you women are like Italy, better with a strong man in charge, but politics isn't something you need to worry your head about."

Even the candle-flames shrank for a moment, such was the electricity gathering around the clueless man at the table's head. He gouged up a clot of potatoes with his fork and slapped it into his mouth while three of the other people in the room froze in their places and the fourth gripped her knife so hard the silver creaked.

I took a breath: remember, this is Ronnie's mother cringing across the tablecloth from me. Ronnie's mother, who was dependent on this . . . imbecile's good will. Ronnie's mother, who could be charged with collusion were I to drive this piece of silverware . . .

I forced my hand to open and leave the weapon behind. I placed my linen napkin on the table. I lowered my hands to my sides and felt the butler leap into place behind me, pulling out my chair. I rose, and addressed my laden plate. "Terribly sorry, I seem to have developed a case of the vapours, you'll have to forgive me, good night."

He scrambled to stand but I was out of the room before his chair had scraped back. I could hear Lady Dorothy's rushed voice behind me but in moments, I was on the safe side of the door to the east wing. When my hostess came in, two minutes later, she found me at the drinks cabinet with an already-empty glass in my hand.

I gave her a bemused look. "Do you know, I don't believe I've been that angry in a very long time."

"It's as well you didn't bring up the Suffrage question."

"I can imagine." I refilled the glass and asked if I might pour something for her.

"Oh, perhaps a drop of the pear brandy?"

I gave her a generous slug of the poisonous-looking yellowy-green substance, and retreated to a chair by the fire. When my pulse rate had cooled somewhat and the sharp edges of fury had been softened by three ounces of 100-proof solvent, I raised my eyes to her. "Why do you choose to stay here?"

Her gaze darted around the room, evidence that she was not prepared for bluntness. I drew back a degree, to say, "That is, it can't always be comfortable, to be around a man of such . . . strong opinions."

"Oh, but I'm not around Edward, not all that much. He and I have our separate realms here, and I only see him—that is," she corrected, opting for her ladylike reticence. "It is true that my brother-in-law and I are not always in agreement, but he's been quite generous, in permitting me to remain here."

"You could go elsewhere."

At that, finally, she lifted her head to face me. "This is my home, Mary. My husband loved Selwick above any place on earth. I feel close to him here."

What was it with the Beaconsfield women? Ronnie wouldn't come back to Selwick, where she'd grown up, because she and Miles had lived in London, while Ronnie's mother wouldn't go home to her Ducal brother because this was where she and *her* husband had lived. I was fond of my own situation in Sussex, the flint house that Holmes had lived in before me, but I couldn't imagine demanding to stay on there without him.

Or could I?

In any event, there was not much to say to her wish to remain here. And I was glad I had not responded in anger to the monstrous attitudes of the Marquess—although I would like to have driven my fork into him.

But the idea of stabbing the Marquess was a bit too close to a recent case of blood on my hands, and I moved towards less fraught ground. "Why did the Marquess never marry?"

"Oh, but he did. Goodness, that was ten—no, nearly fifteen years ago. When the old Marquess turned seventy, he more or less chose someone for Edward to marry. Nice girl, too young, I thought, and a bit . . . simple, but pretty enough, in a brunette kind of way. My brother-in-law has always preferred light-haired girls," she added. "Juliette was her name. Her people own a house up near Berkshire, so Edward knew her. She died in childbirth."

I made one of those vaguely apologetic noises, then asked if she thought the Marquess would marry again, adding, "Without a son, won't the titles lapse? I'd have thought that would matter to him."

"I'm pretty sure he will, yes. Lily tells me Edward's been seeing a fair amount of two or three of the neighbours whose daughters are of a marrying age. One must hope the wife he ends up with isn't *too* young."

Her mind was clearly taken up with thoughts of the consequences of the Marquess' theoretical marriage, causing her to forget the age difference in my own. Although in fact I agreed with her: if a young girl had to cope with marriage to a surly misogynist, there ought to be some bright sides to his personality.

I kept an eye on the level in my companion's glass, as we talked about nothing much. When she had put about an inch inside her, bringing colour to her face and relaxation to her shoulders, I gently turned matters to her sister-in-law.

"Thank you for letting me look through Vivian's rooms. Have you seen her sketch-books?"

"Those journals on her shelf? No. Or at least, not in some years."

"There's one drawing you might like to see. It's in her last one, the only journal that doesn't have a date on the outside. You could always tell her that I brought it to your attention, if she wonders how you came across it."

"A drawing of what?"

"You and your husband. He's in uniform."

Her face opened with a look of wonder. "Oh yes! I remember—we sat for Vivian, while she did it. It took ever so long, my foot went to sleep and Tommy kept making jokes and I would laugh and she would get cross with us moving. Such a lovely afternoon that was."

I could see the sadness about to overwhelm her, so I hastened to shove the conversation in a new direction. "Did you notice anything missing from your sister-in-law's rooms, after she left here? Apart from the jewellery?"

"I didn't really look. Lily made up the rooms afterwards; she might have noticed."

"I shall ask her."

"Do you mind—could it wait till the morning? I'd like to help, but I'm really very tired."

Vivian Beaconsfield had been gone five days now; another few hours would make no difference. So I spent the evening with a madwoman's sketch-journals, attempting to see the world through her eyes.

A most peculiar experience, and one that made my eventual sleep none the more restful.

Chapter Eight

LILY HAD A FULL BREAKFAST ARRAYED IN THE DINING room when I came down, to Lady Dorothy's consternation. Having eaten little of my dinner the previous night, I was glad enough for the solidity of the offering, and her mild protests faded as she watched the trays empty.

Afterwards, we took Lily up to the missing woman's rooms, and asked what she had found after the occupant departed on Friday.

"What do you mean, what did I find?"

Her wariness suggested that we might be accusing her of stealing, but Lady Dorothy reassured her otherwise. "We're only interested in how the rooms looked, Lily. Had Lady Vivian left anything behind? Or perhaps she took some of her things with her?"

"It looked pretty much like it does now—except for the camp bed, of course, that we'd set up for the nurse. Once we cleared that away, this is what it looked like—though naturally I cleaned everything, stripped and re-made Lady Vivian's bed, dusted all over."

"*Re*-made?" I asked.

"Yes. It was tidy, but she'd slept in it, so—"

"Do you mean to say that Vivian was making her own bed?" Ronnie's mother was surprised.

"Either she or the nurse did."

"Odd."

"It was like that most days. I'd thought it was maybe something she'd been made to do in . . . there."

"What about the clothing?" I asked. Vivian Beaconsfield went into Bedlam in 1921. The things I'd found in the wardrobe and drawers showed clear evidence, in odour and appearance, of having spent the intervening years packed away against the moths.

Lily looked sideways at her employer. "Mum, I didn't know if you wanted it all put away. I was going to ask you in a few days."

"That's fine, Lily. But did my sister-in-law take anything with her? There are empty spaces on the bar in the wardrobe."

"I left three extra coat-hangers, since I wasn't sure where the nurse would want to put her things."

"There are four here now," I pointed out, and stood back to let her hunt through the garments and identify what was not among them. Meantime, I looked again at the display-wall behind the dressing table, and drew the two empty spaces to Lady Dorothy's attention. She puzzled over them, agreeing that there had been something in each, but she could not tell me how long those particular nails had been unoccupied.

"She had ever so many little treasures hanging here. Some of them, like the masks, she'd mostly leave in the same place, but others she'd change all the time. I say treasures: some of them were pretty—her own little drawings, or an envelope with an exotic stamp, once a square of maroon velvet she'd found at the hat-maker's. But others were very peculiar, indeed. A dirty twig. A scrap of paper from a street-corner. Once I found the wing of a little bird she'd come across on one of her walks, all dried-up and gruesome. I made her take that one down, it was unhygienic. And some of the masks were very odd, too. Look at that thing—it's the shell of a turtle, if you can believe that, all stuck about with hairs and heaven-knows-what. And that African object! Would you want to sleep with *that* watching over you? Give a person night—"

"The mask!" Lily's exclamation cut off Lady Dorothy's litany, and we turned to her. "That's what's missing! That horrid half-mask with the moustache!"

"Oh heavens, you're right—how could I have forgot that?"

"There's a mask missing?" I asked.

"A most peculiar wall decoration, made by this woman in Paris who'd build realistic masks for soldiers who were wounded in the face. So the poor things could hug their children and go out in public without people staring."

"I've heard of them, though I don't know that I've ever seen such a thing." Even the concealment in *Le Fantôme de l'Opéra* looks like a mask, not an artificial face.

"It had a little moustache on it—heaven only knows where Vivian got the thing, but it's been up here for years, since . . . well, around when she began to get ill. Lily, you didn't take it down?"

"No, Mum. Though I was tempted to. Oh, but Mum? There *are* some things missing from here, after all. I'd put out one or two of her boys' outfits, in case she'd still want to go for one of her walks. That empty hanger held a pair of trousers and a coat."

That might explain how Vivian got away without being noticed: if one asked a ticket agent whether he'd seen a nurse and a small, blonde woman, he was not likely to talk about a dark-haired one and her moustachioed son.

Perhaps I could touch up that picture Ronnie had given me, to add a grease-pencil moustache?

Which reminded me: "This picture of Vivian—is that the missing jewellery?"

Ronnie's mother came over to see. It was a formal, posed photo of Lady Vivian at nineteen, her pale hair gathered behind a sparkling tiara, her low-necked gown framing the heavy necklace, a matching piece around the wrist of her long kid glove. All three looked too heavy for her delicate frame. From the fresh and hopeful expression on her face, I knew the picture had been taken early in her Season, before she realised that the only way the significance of those diamonds could be any clearer would be if her dowry were piled beside her in gold sovereigns.

"Yes, they were her mother's pieces. The Selwick jewels are, I'm afraid, mostly paste—good paste, and pretty, but still. My husband's grandfather was something of a gambler," Lady Dorothy explained, sounding apologetic.

"Ah, yes: Vivian's inherited money. Was there much of it?"

But that was going too far. "Oh, I wouldn't know," she said quickly.

Both of us were conscious of Lily standing across the room. Well, I could always track the mother's fortunes through Debrett's. "Did Vivian's mother have much of a family?"

"I'm afraid not; in fact, I believe the name has pretty well died off. There's a second cousin from one of the Colonies, New Zealand or perhaps Australia."

"That's too bad. Do you mind if I borrow this photograph? So we know what we're looking for?"

"Certainly. I have a copy in one of the albums downstairs."

I removed the picture, leaving the silver frame on the dressing table: three gaps in the wall now.

"And Vivian broke into the safe, I understand?" Only after I said it did I think this might also be something Lady Dorothy would not care to talk about in front of the maid, but she did not hesitate to reply.

"Yes, Edward was furious. It was—well, he was angry. Far more angry than he'd been about the jewels themselves. Perhaps he never thought of those as his. We don't know how Vivian found the combination, although since it's never been changed she might have known it all this time—or Edward might have it written down somewhere. He's not good with numbers."

"What did she take?"

"Well, that's what's odd, it doesn't sound like much. A hundred pounds or so, which is considerable but not compared to the necklace. And two or three small things that belonged to her mother and to Thomas—a

Fabergé egg, a Medieval locket, a funny little Roman creature that was dug up on the estate years ago. Knick-knacks, really, but just valuable enough that Edward didn't like leaving them around, in case they tempted strangers." *Or servants,* I thought, without looking at Lily.

"Was he fond of them, perhaps?"

"Edward? No, though Thomas loved the little Roman thing— probably a dog. Edward's just as happy to have the insurance."

"So why is he angry?"

"I don't know. She may have taken something else that he doesn't want to tell me about."

Now I did look at Lily, but could see that she did not know, either. Interesting.

"Lady Dorothy, is there anyone I should be sure to talk to? Anyone on the estate who was a particular favourite of your sister-in-law when she lived here? The cook, stable hand, one of the housemaids?"

"Most of the servants in the main house are new—such a turnover these days, isn't there? And Vivian never seemed to have much of an interest in the horses, so I wouldn't know about the stables."

"There was one girl in a number of her drawings—wait, let me find her." The two women followed me to the other room and waited as I paged through the 1902 volume to a drawing of the dark-haired girl. I then took down the one labeled 1908, done when Vivian Beaconsfield was seventeen. There was the same face, grown into womanhood.

Lady Dorothy placed a finger on the more recent image. "That's, um . . ."

Lily had no hesitation. "The Bailey girl."

"Of the cheese-making Baileys?" I asked.

"Their eldest," Lady Dorothy replied. "Ellen?"

"Emma," Lily corrected.

"Yes, that's right, Emma. I used to pay her a few shillings to watch the girls, from time to time."

"The girls?"

"Vivian and Veronica. Odd to think, but there's only eight years' difference between them."

"More like sisters than aunt and niece." I had known that, but only intellectually. "This Emma girl looks a little older?"

"Two or three years, as I remember. But she was . . . stronger, I suppose. A working-class girl who could take care of herself, and sensible enough that I didn't worry if she and Vivian were out all day. She moved away after the War, but it seems to me I heard she came home recently, to help her father."

"I should talk with her, see if Vivian went to visit. How might I find the dairy?"

"We have a motor—just tell Lily when you want to go and Freddie will take you over."

But first, I needed to do the rounds of the main house's servants, the estate manager, and the stable hands. That took me the rest of the morning, and at the end of it, I had added little to my store of knowledge about Vivian Beaconsfield other than their opinion that she was an odd 'un—an affectionate judgment, rather than condemnatory.

One of the lads told me the horses liked her, which seemed enough for him.

The estate agent told me, though not in so many words, that the master of the estate was spending his cash unwisely, and elsewhere.

The cook liked Lady Vivian. (*"When you find her, see if you can't get her to eat something."*) So did the head gardener. (*"Known her since she was a child. Only one in the Big House what knows the name of every flower here."*) And the Marquess' housekeeper. (*"She did the sweetest drawings for me every year, Christmas and my birthday."*) The butler and valet were new, hired by the Marquess out of London. Several of the household staff in his side were new, also, including one remarkable young woman with the shortest skirt, blondest curls, and heaviest makeup I'd ever seen on a housemaid—and the most impudent attitude. (*"Oh, that one! Loony of the first degree, she is, what she makes the Marquess put up with, you'd never believe!"*) I left the house torn between sympathy with Lady Vivian, and the uncomfortable sensation that bemoaning the Uppityness of This New Generation of Servants was a sign I was growing old.

———

I found Emma Bailey high on a ladder in a barn that contained all the evidence of cows apart from their actual presence. She was fiddling with a light fixture two feet above her head, a position that seemed alarmingly precarious. In other circumstances I might have cleared my throat, but I was afraid that startling her would make for a rapid end to the conversation.

However, either she'd heard first the car and then my footsteps, or she noticed the dimming effect of my person in the doorway. She spoke past her shoulder. "Yes?"

"Miss, er, Bailey? My name is Mary Russell, I'm—"

"Don't touch the switch," she warned.

"I shan't. Do I have the name correct?"

"That's me." She gave a final twist at some bit of wiring, stuck a tool into her trouser pocket, then pulled out a bulb and jabbed it into the fixture. She retreated a few rungs down the ladder. "Try it now."

The light went on without blowing fuses or exploding into flames. With a satisfied nod, she continued down the rest of the way, tipped the ladder back to collapse it, and swung it off the ground. She carried the heavy thing to the back wall and effortlessly boosted it onto a pair of hooks.

Walking back across the wide floor, she rubbed her palms together in a largely symbolic attempt at cleansing and stuck out her strong right hand for me to shake.

"Mary Russell," I repeated.

"Emma Bailey. I need a cup of tea."

I took the pronouncement as an invitation, and followed her across the tidy yard to the kitchen door of an equally tidy house. She stepped out of her rubber boots with scarcely a pause, pointed me to a chair tucked under a sturdy kitchen table, lit the flame beneath an ancient black kettle, and pulled two mugs from an open shelf: a series of movements as practiced and flowing as a dance.

"I'll be back in two minutes," she said, and left. I heard her stockinged feet trot up a flight of stairs, and obediently took my assigned position in the chair.

An orange cat wandered through the doorway and sat, tail around its front feet, facing the general direction of an empty bowl. I knew it was in fact studying me out of the corner of its eye, balanced between sudden flight and coming over to butt at my legs. Indistinct voices came from overhead, Emma Bailey's and a softer one. Floor-boards sounded. I followed the slow progress of creaks, a door opening and closing, silence for a time, then a sudden flush of water gave a clear indication of prosperity: indoor plumbing.

Considerably more than two minutes had gone by before I heard the sure feet descending the stairway. Her hands were clean when she came in, and she'd paused to run a comb through her hair. She glanced at the steaming cup on the table in front of me and down at the cat in my lap, but continued on to the sideboard.

"I didn't think you'd mind if I made the tea," I said. "Everything was there."

She didn't comment, merely filled her cup, adding sugar and milk. She bent down to pour a dollop from the jug into the cat's bowl—the cat having deserted me the moment she appeared—and carried her mug back to the table. I couldn't tell if she minded my presumption, which was interesting. People are normally easier to read.

"As I said," I started again, "my name is Mary Russell. I'm a friend of Ronnie Beacons—Ronnie Fitzwarren."

Emma Bailey's gaze shot up from the mug, locking onto me. Her eyes were deep brown with faint streaks of orange, and surrounded by thick black lashes under naturally arched brows. "I hear her aunt has gone missing."

"That's right. Ronnie asked me to come and see what I could find out."

"Why you?"

"Because it's not an easy thing to do with a small child."

"No, why *you*?"

"Because I'm good at asking questions."

Miss Bailey studied me from out of that impenetrable gaze. Whatever she saw, sitting across the table, seemed eventually to satisfy her. She took a hefty swallow and then sat back in her chair, the mug clasped between her hands. "Very well: ask."

"Did you see Lady Vivian when she was here last week?"

"No, I haven't seen either her or Ronnie in years."

"Why not? You were friends, weren't you?"

"Of a sort. Before the War, maybe. Not so much once she grew up."

"She used to make sketches of you, in her books. The last one I saw was done in 1909."

"That sounds about right."

"She came out—was presented in Court—in 1910."

"Around then."

"Then travelled to France and Italy for some months afterwards."

"That's right."

Her watchful attitude was remarkably like that of the orange cat, waiting for me to pass some undefined test, to prove that I might be worthy of approach.

I had been watching her in return, and now chose my words with care. "Vivian Beaconsfield was pretty, and had both money and a title, yet she never married. She didn't even seem to meet any men she particularly liked, either during the Season or when she was travelling in Europe."

Miss Bailey raised the cup to her lips for another swallow.

"Is there . . . a reason for that?" I asked carefully. "That you know of?"

Her eyes remained very still. After a moment, she supplied an answer that lay behind her words. "Perhaps."

"Ah. That would explain some things."

"Do you think so, Miss Russell?"

In fact, I did. In the Victorian era, upper-class families had been known to lock away their eccentric women, whether the sin was an illegitimate child, conversion to an extreme religious sect—or, being a lesbian. Granted, the disapproving wealthy were more likely to employ a private asylum over shameful Bedlam, but even a public institution knew how to hold secrets. Lady Dorothy's puzzlement over Vivian's lack of suitors suggested that she was an innocent, but it could explain some of the Marquess' eagerness to close the door on an inconvenient half-sister.

Particularly since he was clearly feeling a financial pinch, and the mother who had bequeathed Vivian her diamonds also left an inheritance.

So, should I simply let matters go? Let the madwoman slip away?

Reluctantly, I decided that no, I couldn't. Greedy uncles, dubious nurses, asylum superintendents lining their pockets at the expense of their inmates: there were too many questions whirling around one small pale-haired woman. I could help her—but I had to find her first.

The woman across the table had said something that the rapid firing of my brain had obscured. I looked up. "Sorry?"

"I said, I'm not bad at questions myself."

"Oh. All right, although I'm not sure how many answers I have."

"Have you met her uncle?"

"The Marquess? Yes, in fact I dined with him last night." At any rate, I'd started to dine.

"What did you think of him?"

With another woman, I might have shaded my response to the diplomatic. With this one, I was honest. "Pompous. Politically extreme. Socially offensive."

"Did you notice a blonde housemaid?"

"Yes, I believe I talked to most of the household staff."

"What did you think of that one?"

"Why?"

"You're doing the answers, remember?"

"I thought her a bit impertinent. Both rude and overly familiar in speaking about her employers. But that's not unusual these days, when girls have so many alternatives to service."

"Hmm. Do you know the sequence of Viv—of Lady Vivian's madness?"

This woman had a most peculiar style of conversation, composed of profound non-sequiturs. "Sequence? You mean, when it came on her? Well, her father died in 1914, when she was twenty-three. Her brother

Thomas died the following spring. Shortly after that, the Marquess came home and she, Ronnie, and Lady Dorothy moved into the east wing. That seems to have been the final straw, because The Lady Vivian started showing signs of increasing imbalance. She attacked the Marquess in the spring of 1916, and went into her first asylum. After that, it was a series of asylums, treatments, de-committals, and periods at home before things would go south for her again."

"And?"

"And what?" It was starting to prove irritating. "If you have something to tell me, Miss Bailey, just say it."

But instead, she grimaced and rose, setting her empty cup on the table. "I need to bathe and shave my father before I make him lunch. He's been ill, which is why I'm here. Give my greetings to The Lady Dorothy, would you please? And to Ronnie, she was always such a nice child."

And with that, she turned on her heel and walked out. I scrambled upright to protest. "I wasn't—can you at least tell me, is there someplace you know where she might have gone?"

"Someplace safe," she called down the stairs, and that was it.

I looked at the cat. Its pink tongue came out to pull the drops from its whiskers, before it settled to the serious business of bathing.

That word again: *safe.*

The word had stuck with me ever since Ronnie's aunt used it to describe Bedlam, three years ago. So if that looming grey monstrosity made for her idea of safe, what were similar alternatives? Would she have found a secure prison to check in to? A remote castle? A niche in some choking Underground tunnel? Perhaps we should be making the rounds of the country's other asylums.

Everything I had seen so far indicated that the greatest threat to Lady Vivian Beaconsfield lay in her own troubled mind. Even the obnoxious half-brother had never responded to her physical attacks in kind. Still, ultimately, any woman's safety lay in her income.

"Pawn shops," I told the cat. Its paw went still for a moment as it thought the matter over, then went on. Time for me to do the same.

Chapter Nine

....

THE PROBLEM OF TRUNK TELEPHONE CALLS FROM THE
depths of Surrey proving insurmountable, I ended up sending Holmes
a cable from the village: COULD USE YOUR HELP AM RETURNING TO
LONDON R.

If he was bored, this would give him an excuse to drop everything
and perform one of his miraculous self-conjuring tricks, that he might
be leaning with utter insouciance against a stanchion at Waterloo when
I got down from the train. If he did have something going on, be it
amongst the hives, in the laboratory, or buried in some dusty archive,
my choice of words told him it could wait.

Unfortunately, without Mrs Hudson, a telegram might sit for days
on the step before anyone took notice.

I used the post office's pen to mark up one of the photographs, and
on my way through the railway station, showed a pair of them to all and
sundry. One had Vivian *au naturel*. On the other I had drawn a moustache, darkened her hair, and coarsened her eyebrows, then cropped the
edges to make it feel like a different image entirely. The ticket agent

knew her, but he'd lived in Selwick a long time. A conductor thought he possibly recognised the young man, but it had been raining on Friday, so . . .

I found an unoccupied First Class compartment, and settled in.

When Holmes had a spell of thinking to do, he would build a cushion nest before the fire and work his way through a heap of his most disgusting tobacco. I, however, had never found combustion inspiring, and preferred to meditate on objects with more substance than a dart of flames or a wisp of smoke: a lengthy walk, the lick of waves on a shore, a solitary train journey.

The countryside went by: cropped grassland, farms, hedgerows, the back gardens in towns. For all the attention I paid, I might as well have been travelling through Stockholm as Surrey.

It is War time. A sensitive young woman is hit by two hard losses and a seismic change in the structure of her small corner of the aristocracy. Yes, the nation is in turmoil, but so is her private world: father and brother dead, her family's domestic arrangements turned upside-down. Her much older half-brother, frustrated by his reduced circumstances and its resultant life in the country, finds himself living cheek-by-jowl with a difficult young woman he barely knows. A flighty and fragile girl who turns out to be not only unbalanced, but—the family must suspect it—a lesbian, unwilling to be caught by a husband.

So, faced with this difficult yet financially solvent person, why *not* simply lock her away? As far as the Marquess is concerned, "the gel's" inheritance is rightfully his—after all, didn't her mother replace his as the Marchioness? Surely his stepmother's money should be regarded as part of the larger estate? She'd had no right to assign her money to the girl of the family, not when the heir was in need of it. In any event, Vivian was too mad to take care of her own inheritance, wasn't she? Perhaps everything would be simplified if she just . . . went away.

The rich June countryside gave way to London sprawl, my thoughts and mood growing as stained as the buildings that closed around me. It was a good thing that Holmes was not leaning against a stanchion when I climbed down from the train compartment. Had he been, I would surely have heaped my ninety minutes of dark thoughts upon his male head, as a convenient representative of his half of the race.

By the time he caught up with me that evening at The Vicissitude, my outrage had cooled—but it had also hardened into resolution.

"Why are you here?" he asked, looking around him at the smaller and more idiosyncratic of my London club's public rooms.

"When I got back from Surrey, I was in no condition to speak with Mycroft. Or you, for that matter. The Vicissitude seemed the best place for me."

The Ladies' club I had joined many years before offered temporary quarters for women on the move: in Town for a doctor, a colleague, or a research library, or passing through to a conference or political event in the bigger world. The women who took a room at The Vicissitude were not in London for a matinee or a fashion house.

Not, perhaps, the ideal setting in which to soften one's disapproval of the male gender.

My husband cast a dubious glance at the card propped up on the mantel—the sort of image an innocent viewer would take at face value, while a more sophisticated eye could not help noticing that the object in the Victorian lady's hand resembled a sharp dagger—and reached for his cigarette case. "They haven't forbidden men smoking here, I take it?"

"That is an ash-tray on the table, Holmes."

"Yes. And possibly, like most other amenities in this establishment, reserved for the use of women." Before I could give this the response it deserved, he cut in. "Russell, I can see that something has severely ruffled your emotional feathers. Perhaps you might tell me, rather than simply performing the surgical procedure the woman on that postal card is about to enact."

The patronising use of the term *ruffled feathers* nearly had me reaching for the heavy ash-tray—until I noticed the combination of wariness and determination in his grey eyes, and realised that he was deliberately pushing me towards the edge. There was only one possible response.

I dropped back against my chair and started to laugh.

Another woman would have missed the quick flash of relief across his sardonic features, since he hid it by the lighting of his cigarette. When the spent match was in the assigned container, he looked up at me. "It's your friend's aunt, I presume."

"Lady Vivian Beaconsfield. Mad and sad and betrayed on all sides."

"A stray chicken in a world of foxes," he murmured.

"Oh please, Holmes—enough of the references to *Gallus domesticus*. This Lady may be unbalanced, but she is not without resources, or apparently wit. And if she *has* been 'gobbled up,' she *will* be missed," I added, to show I was aware of his reference. "Unlike your Lady Frances Carfax, this is a woman who fought her way into a space that she could defend, even if that was only a patient's cell at Bedlam. A damaged woman who, I'm beginning to think, managed to hang on to enough self-respect and independence that she could seize the opportunity for escape when it came."

"Is this not a good thing?"

"Well, let's see what you think."

We were interrupted by the arrival of the tea-tray, which I had asked for when I realised we might be here for some time. I dropped the Privacy Please sign over the knob as the girl went out—for if The Vicissitude's residents overheard the conversation we were about to have, it might well set off a storming of the gates of Bedlam.

The traffic outside changed from daytime deliveries to evening homecomings. During the lag while London was at its supper tables, I finished my tale.

The ash-tray was half-full. The teapot was long empty. Holmes rolled the end of his last cigarette back and forth between thumb and forefinger, then sat forward to smash it into the mess before him. "We need to eat."

I blinked. Had I eaten that day? Breakfast, back in Selwick, yes— and a cup of tea with Miss Bailey. But to have Holmes be the one to suggest bodily attention was unusual. "I'm surprised you can summon an appetite. Doesn't the situation infuriate you?"

"Lady Vivian will not be better served by our malnourishment, Russell. And I have thrice heard footsteps hesitate over the sign on the door."

"I suppose we have monopolised the room a bit long. I'll get my wrap, we can take a walk."

Outside, Holmes tucked my arm through his, and donned an air of earnest attention. Relieved at his interest, I talked on, little noticing that his chosen path took us not into the open reaches of one of the parks, but before a series of cafés and bistros, each more tantalising than the next. At the fifth teasing wash of rich aromas, I grew suspicious; at the eighth one, I gave in. "Oh very well, Holmes, I will eat. You choose."

It was a Spanish place, unfamiliar to me although the waiters greeted Holmes as a long-lost friend, automatically guiding him to a private table at the back. Cold soup, warm bread, and a dark, harsh red wine arrived in moments, evidence that they either knew their customer's taste, or employed a psychic reader in the kitchen.

As always, food and drink took the edge off my sense of distress, permitting sensibility to surface. When we had our main courses before us—paper-thin cured ham buried under some kind of olive relish for Holmes, and a spicy *cabrito* for me—I took a mouthful, then shovelled in several more before I allowed my fork to rest.

"Holmes, what do you think I should do?"

"You're worried about the nurse."

"I'm worried about Vivian, because of the nurse. The women in Lady Vivian's family have been woefully blind—maybe even wilfully blind—but still, they do love her."

"Just so I am clear: do you wish us to bring her back, or let her go?"

I admit, I cherished that "we." Still, it took a while to reply. "Don't you suppose that will depend on what we find when we locate her? I thought I'd start retracing Ronnie's steps tomorrow. I know she telephoned to various hospitals and police stations, but—"

"Lady Vivian is not in London."

I blinked. "She's not?"

"Not unless she is better at the game than I."

"What do you mean?"

"I looked. Yesterday and today, all the places to which a woman of her position would gravitate, and many she would not. I am satisfied that unless she is disguised as a Whitechapel fish-wife, or has taken to the *gentil* suburbs, she is not in Town."

"Holmes, I thought you had . . . well, work to do."

"It seemed to me that your friend's missing aunt took precedence over my history of contrapuntal significance in Bach's cantatas."

I stared at him. It was one of the sweetest things he'd ever said, and the gruff abruptness with which he pushed away his plate and looked around for the waiter made it clear that he was aware of the slip.

Instead of the waiter, the owner came over, carrying three glasses and a naked bottle of some viscous amber liquid that cleared the sinuses and electrified the nerves. That and a table-spoon-sized cup of near-Arabic coffee and I was set for a day or six of unbroken labour.

Out on the pavement, I discovered that my body was in a most peculiar state: swaying lazily, yet my feet—and tongue—moving very fast. "So I was thinking, Holmes, that we need to do the rounds of the better-known pawn shops, jewellers, any place that would purchase an old necklace, really—Ronnie's mother gave me a fairly special—fairy pacific—a Fairly. Specific. Description. Of the necklace. Wonder if that's something Billy would do, if he's not still grumpy over Mrs Hudson leaving, not that we all aren't grumpy over that, though I do wonder how she's doing, that letter we had from her was not paricoloured—not Par. Tic. Ularly—forthcoming."

"Good idea." His voice seemed unexpectedly close, and I looked down to discover that at some point he had tucked my arm firmly through his, and our weaving progress had become a touch more linear. "I shall go to Bedlam, and interview the superintendent about Nurse Trevisan. I shall also ask to see Lady Vivian's records, although that may take official intervention, from—"

I stopped so abruptly his arm pulled away from mine. "But what if the Marquess has been paying Bedlam to keep her there?" To me, the Victorian scandals of imprisoned heiresses was a thing I had heard about. For Holmes, the 1890 Lunacy Act had been the morning news.

"Russell, did you not tell me that her commitment was voluntary?" *I'm safe here.* "True, but . . ."

"It would be easier to break into the headquarters of the Household Cavalry than into Bedlam. I could find someone to do it, given a few days. It might be simpler to have Mycroft issue a command that we be permitted a look at her records. Or Lestrade."

"Or *I* could break in."

He drew my arm through his again, to guide me down the pavement. "It would help to know where the records are kept," he continued as if I had not spoken. "We would not wish to give the superintendent sufficient warning to edit her file into the flames."

"I mean it, Holmes. I could break in. Not physically, over the parapets and through the bars. Do they have parapets in Bedlam? Walls, I suppose. No, I mean simply be brought in the front door. Nellie Bly did it, why can't I? Do they take new patients through the front door? There's probably a back entrance that the police wagons use."

"You wish me to commit you to Bedlam?"

I pushed away the faint stir of horror at the phrase, and looked up into his eyes. "Oh, admit it, Holmes: you've often been tempted."

Chapter Ten

....

IT WAS NOT A SIMPLE MATTER, PLOTTING ENTRY INTO Bethlem Royal Hospital. Nor was it a simple matter to prise specific dates and information from Ronnie the next day—particularly as young Simon was in an obstreperous mood, or growing a tooth, or something, which reacted badly against the pulse of morning-after pain that resided just behind my eyes.

However, I managed to extricate the necessary dates and details without causing alarm, by planting various suggestions that I would be going to each of the places her aunt had visited over the years. In any event, even friends are easily impressed with the solemn taking of notes, and willing to believe that it was all part of the investigatory routine.

The small centre of pain behind my eyes had grown considerably under the stress of our conversation, which mostly consisted of my question—"So, when was she sent to the Rawlins House private asylum?"—followed by Ronnie's "Well, it was either 1918 or 1919—no, it must have been the spring after the War ended because I came home from Oxford and Mother was trying to convince me that I could do a

Season even though I was already twenty and London was in shambles—
Simon, dear, don't pull the wheel off—oh dear, yes, sweetheart, it's broken now, don't cry, Mummy will fix it, see, all better—that I should do a
Season, which honestly, even she had to admit was not exactly a patriotic use of resources, remember we were still rationing some things—
petrol was it, or butter? Certainly we'd have had to re-make her old
gowns since you couldn't get silk for ages, so I said I wouldn't and—oh
yes, it would have been just before Easter because she was pleased she'd
been able to buy a new hat for the first time in years, and I remember
wishing Auntie Viv was there to back me up."

"So: Easter 1919, she was in Rawlins House. And how long was she
gone that time?" Which launched us off on another rolling barrage of
retrieved memories and exhortations to the offspring, punctuated by
full-throated protests from Himself.

Shattered, I crept away with my notes and a profound respect for the
mental tenacity of mothers everywhere.

It was something of an irony that I needed to collect myself before I
could plot my descent into madness.

As I remembered, Nellie Bly's journalistic exposé of the American
asylum began with her practicing bizarre expressions before a mirror,
then taking lodging in a boarding house while lacking the means to pay.
The act had begun when the police were called to evict her: by pretending to amnesia and continually bemoaning her nonexistent lost trunks,
she gave them little choice but to deliver her to the madhouse.

I suspected Bedlam might require more than that.

I also suspected Bedlam might not be easy to walk out of. Nellie
Bly's editor had promised to retrieve her, which seemed awfully trust-
ing. (But then, for a daring woman, Miss Bly could be remarkably naïve:
she thought "white slavery" meant going to a box factory and being paid
a pittance, rather than being locked in chains and sold to the highest
bidder.) Holmes agreed to come retrieve me in three days, if I hadn't got
out on my own by then—but unlike Nellie Bly, and even though it was
Holmes, *and* even though I'd pored over the floor plans of the place, I
thought a back-up source of rescue would be wise.

"Holmes, you might want to tell Mycroft where I shall be. That way, if you're hit by a bus crossing Oxford Street, I won't have to miss your funeral. And I did give you my notes and that photograph of Vivian's necklace, didn't I?"

"You did, although I may not be able to do much with either. I intend to be at the British Library all day."

"I would not wish to interrupt your research into polyphonic motets."

"What are you talking about, Russell? All motets are by definition poly—"

"Never mind, Holmes, just come rescue me if I get stuck."

"Have I not showed you the trick to strait jackets? One needs to expand—"

I left before he went looking for one, that he might demonstrate how Houdini did it.

Miss Bly's articles often described the difficulties she had in convincing people to believe her: too mature for one rôle, too good an accent for another, hands too clean or soft. But then, Miss Bly had not learned the arts of disguise from Sherlock Holmes.

In his days as a London detective, Holmes had painstakingly assembled a number of secret refuges throughout the great city, filling them with emergency provisions, reading matter, odd bits of weaponry, and all the necessary elements of disguise. Over the years, two of these bolt-holes had been swallowed up by the city: one to a Zeppelin's bomb, the other through renovations, when the building changed hands and the plans called for demolition of a wall behind which his narrow hideaway had been inserted.

Still, that left him—and me—with a number of options across the city, one of which I let myself into that afternoon. It was not one designed for long-term habitation, being every bit as cramped and insalubrious as I remembered, but at least there was a draught of air from some crack or other to keep one from asphyxiation. And the dingy walls pressing down on me could only help stimulate my appearance of madness.

The thought interrupted my rummage through cupboards that had been stocked before I was born, and I looked around me with new eyes. The madwoman's rooms in Surrey had been all soft edges and muted shades, which I supposed was restful if one's taste leaned in that direction. Holmes, on the other hand, surrounded himself with sharp edges and definite colours, preferring clear delineation over any degree of uncertainty. Would such a setting prove healing to a disturbed mind? I glanced down at the tangle of half-used tubes and makeup brushes, hair ribbons and cigarette holders.

Perhaps not.

An application of oil and talc turned my hair to straw. An irritant turned the eyes bloodshot, light grease-paint gave a patina of dirt to my pores, and a pot of lamp-black made my nails look like I had been mining coal. The final touch came from an innocuous-looking flask on the shelf, one mouthful of which, if one could manage to swill the vomitous mixture about the teeth and gums for long enough, would leave the mouth looking mildly diseased for three days.

A once-nice dress, good shoes in need of a shine, and mis-matched stockings. For a note of the eccentric (as well as warmth) I pulled on a pair of trousers under the frock. Then I removed one lens from my spectacles.

That in itself made me look somewhat mad, even without the red eyes and my rather pop-eyed stare as I squinted at a half-focussed world.

I looked like a lunatic from the middle-classes: not poor enough to be booted back onto the street, not wealthy enough to be coddled. Strictly speaking, I should have gone a few days without bathing, but I decided my outward appearance, my Oxford accent, and an air of genial confusion would be sufficient.

Holmes had also recommended that, if pressed, I ought to deliver a warning lecture on oysters.

I thought I had mis-heard him. "Oysters?"

"Correct. Clams are too symmetrical and mussels can be mistaken for their homonym—although come to think of it, that could add to the confusion. But oysters seem particularly symptomatic of mania. They certainly fooled Watson."

"Ah yes, I remember. And poor Mrs Hudson—the two of them were convinced you were dying."

"She was indeed rather cross. She increased our rent, as I recall. Mine, at any rate."

"She should have evicted you."

However, with his recommendation fresh in my mind, I did pause before leaving the bolt-hole to glance through the 1827 *Britannica*'s article on oysters, committing a few pungent phrases to memory.

I then settled my squashed hat onto my distressed scalp, and went off to prove myself crazed.

Chapter Eleven

··

IT TOOK ME A REMARKABLY LONG TIME TO FIND A HU-
mourless and unforgiving constable, and I located the one I did only by
noting his sore feet. He was not amused when I slipped up behind him
and tipped his helmet forward onto his nose, then skipped away out of
reach, giggling at his curses. I was faster than he and, as mentioned, he
was hampered by sore feet, so not until I feigned to stumble did he
manage to seize my arm.

I began instantly to weep, lest his meaty hands bruise me too badly,
and indeed, he was every bit as disconcerted as I might hope. He did
not let me go—but neither did he manhandle me too badly as he propelled me along the pavement to his station. I, meanwhile, alternated
snuffling moans with chipper queries as to whether he was taking me
home for tea, and if so I found his approach quite forward—but had he
seen my Gladstone bag anywhere? (Miss Bly, as I recalled, had used
"trunks" as a device on which to fix her attentions, but I changed it for
fear of coming across a literate copper.)

I was past exhaustion and well on my way to actual insanity by the time the police finally delivered me to Bedlam. I'd been wondering if I was going to have to bodily assault one of them, but close to midnight they grew tired of listening to my endless drivel and washed their hands of me.

Miss Bly had assumed an act of insomnia on her initial night of madness. Fortunately, the attendants who received me were sleepy themselves, and merely stripped and checked me, handed me a coarsely woven gown, and locked me inside a dim, narrow room. The door had no handle. The walls were grubby. The bed was a mat on the floor.

I examined the mattress and bedding as best I could, but they showed no signs of infestation, and when I lowered my face, the rough blankets smelt distantly of soap. I sat, considering the blank surface of the door. The sight made me uneasy, not only because I was trapped, but also because having no lock to pick was going to make it difficult to do what I had come here for. I took a slow breath, then another, then lay down and pulled the thin covers to my neck.

I can't say I actually slept, but I was startled when the door banged open to reveal a nurse in starched cap, apron, and a belt from which hung a chatelaine of keys, whistle, pen-light, and scissors. She remained in the doorway, which I thought quite sensible for a woman facing the unknown tendencies of a patient arrived by night.

"So, Miss, do you know who you are today?"

I sat up instantly, planting my back against the wall. "I'm . . . I, yes— I have no problems. Who are *you*? Where am I? I've lost my spectacles— and, Sister, what have you done with my Gladstone bag?"

"Never you fear, Miss, I'm sure Doctor will help you find it again. Now, are you going to get yourself up and dressed, or are you going to give us trouble?"

Since giving her trouble would clearly extend my time in this room without a door-handle—and risk the use of bonds or a strait-jacket— befuddled cooperation was clearly my best option. Perhaps I could convince them that I'd had a head injury and might come out of it soon.

"My head hurts," I whined. "I need my glasses."

"First a bath. Then you can have a word with Doctor."

I climbed into the shapeless, buttoned dressing-gown she handed me and let her propel me from the cell into a long, chilly stone hallway populated with trim-looking nurses and women in the same drab dressing-gowns as mine. Some of the latter were wild-eyed and twitching, shuffling along the passageway with a nurse's hand firmly around one arm. Others looked stunned, like the denizens of an opium den, while a few were as unkempt as if they'd spent the night under a bridge.

I allowed my nurse to direct me towards the end of a queue of belt-less dressing-gowns. All the nurses wore chatelaines of keys—on all of which, I noticed, one would be more brightly polished and hanging more readily to reach. Master keys, I thought, to ensure fast access in an emergency.

The more wild-eyed patients had nurses keeping firm hold of their arms, ready for trouble. Placid women were merely nudged into place and left to move obediently towards the bathing room. My own nurse deposited me in this queue, but then stood back to judge how I might react to this degree of freedom. I was grateful that she had said I was headed for a bath: from the sounds echoing down the hallway, I'd have anticipated a torture chamber.

Cold, disorientated, near-blind, and not having eaten for the better part of a day, it was not difficult to put on an act of fearfulness. Try as I might to convince myself that this was just like the Turkish baths, my shrinking skin insisted that I was about to be held under water until I confessed to some awful crime.

In the end, the greatest pain was the jerk of a comb through my tangled hair—and even that was as brief as the hair itself. When it was done, this assembly-line of bathing spat me out the far end, very clean, aggressively combed, and thoroughly humiliated.

This whole time, I had felt Sister's eyes watching me for any sign of rebellion, or even protest. I gave her none. With a nod of satisfaction, she gripped my arm again and propelled me back down the passageway.

I took great care to give no sign of the dread that filled me—though

when we continued past the cell where I'd spent the night, it was difficult not to sag with relief. But her hand noticed neither, merely directed
me onwards to a flight of stairs.

In Bedlam, up was good. I knew before I came that the basement level
was for the hard cases and the violent, while the top floor was for the
gentle and obedient mad. A rise in altitude could only be a good thing.

We came out on the main level, at the far end of a long, bright gallery that ran the full length of the women's wing. The nurse's hand
turned me towards the central hall, but I caught a glimpse of a room
across the way with comfortable chairs and writing desks. Then we were
marching down a long passage with deeply-set windows to the right
and a series of identical doors to the left, all with sturdy locks. The floor
had worn carpeting down the centre. The walls were regimented with
paintings and plants on the window side, paintings and busts on high
sconces between the doors. Shoved up against both sides, as if some
energetic adolescents had decided to create a bowling-alley, were chairs
both wooden and upholstered, side tables and etagères displaying vases
and figurines, glass display cases containing stuffed birds or silk flowers,
decorative (though empty) birdcages, potted palms that leaned towards
the light, and—yes aspidistras. The overall effect was slightly nightmarish, as if walking down an endlessly elongated sitting room belong-
ing to an aged Victorian aunt—an aunt confined to an abnormally wide
bath-chair. Disconcerting, but everything looked clean, and the predominant odour was one of polish.

We passed another set of stairs and a joining hallway briefer than
the one we had come down, then entered the area I had seen with
Ronnie—the public and office areas that were the literal centre of the
hospital, dividing the women's wing from that of the men. The room
used as a chapel, beneath Bedlam's oddly tall dome, stood just to our
right, explaining the faint scent of beeswax candles.

Here was the room where we'd met Lady Vivian. Right after it was
a door with a small plate saying PHYSICIAN'S ROOM.

The nurse knocked, waited for the "Come in," and pulled it open,
gently urging me through ahead of her.

Inside, there were many locked file cabinets, shelves with dozens of file-boxes, two desks, several chairs, and the promised physician, a slim young man in a white coat. Even without my glasses, I could see instantly that the doctor was very bright indeed. The nurse sat me in a chair across the desk from him and took a chair behind me. He introduced himself as Dr Rawlins, and began a review of my physical health, noting my excellent reactions, clear skin, lack of recent injuries, and rather unusual scarring. But when he went on to his diagnostic questions, so as to help determine my particular corner of Lunacy's map, my variation in response seemed to puzzle him. Some of my reactions appeared to be in line with what was expected of insanity, but others clearly did not ring quite true. My only advantage was his assumption that anyone trying to sneak into Bedlam must surely be mad enough to qualify for admission in the first place.

I apologised for not being certain as to who I was, and told him I had a head-ache. He gently circled back to the question of my identity. The third time he did so, I decided my name was Mary. No, I couldn't remember my surname, perhaps he could find it in my Gladstone bag? "It was taken from me. By someone. A man, I think? A large man with shiny buttons."

"The police constable?"

"He had a big black beard."

"Probably not, then. What was in this Gladstone?"

"My name."

"On a label, you mean?"

"Maybe."

"What else would it have been on, if not a label?"

"A case."

"There was a case inside the Gladstone?"

"There must have been, if it had my name on it."

"And what was in the case?"

Oh, the hell with it. "Oysters."

He blinked. "Oysters?"

"Pearls. A jewellery case must have had pearls, mustn't it?"

"Not oysters?"

"Why would it have had oysters? I don't even like oysters. Slippery, horrid things. Even the name is disgusting."

"Oyster?"

"Mollusc. Mollusc—one can't even pronounce it without grimacing. They eat by pulling in tiny creatures through their gills. The gills have mucous—there's another disgusting word. *Mucous, mollusc.*" I gave a delicate shudder. "The female expels her eggs by the million, did you know that? Million upon million of immature bivalve molluscs, coating the bottom of the sea. And they turn from male to female, did you know that? Shocking lack of continuity, eating the plankton and drinking the sea and lacking the energy to remain constant in their most basic of identities, and all so that they might be fetched from the bottom of the sea and set on plates for hands to seize—"

"Nurse," he interrupted, "has this patient been given anything to eat?"

Good Lord. I stared at him in amazement. The last thing I'd expected of Bedlam was a doctor with basic common sense.

Chapter Twelve

BREAKFAST WAS IN PROGRESS, SERVED ON TIN PLATES IN a room with long, bare wooden tables. I poked gingerly at the porridge, but it was in fact vaguely warm and neither burnt nor dotted with foreign objects—thus considerably better than some of my own culinary attempts. I did not count on it being of a quality that Mrs Hudson wouldn't have instantly fed to the chickens, but together with the coffee (lamentably weak, but most English coffee was) it would keep body wedded to soul.

However, my interest in the meal was less nutritional than informational, for here I could make contact with my fellow inmates. I chose quickly as I crossed the room, and aimed for a seat amidst a group of women with marginally more tidy clothing, and marginally less of the posture of wild things snarling over their meals.

Of the four women, three looked up as I sat. The woman directly across the table—a girl, really—was an elfin creature with shiny brown hair and a dusting of freckles across her charming little nose. She gave me a shy smile and said, "Pretty day, isn't it?"

This rather took me aback, since I had seen rain streaming down the windows of the long gallery as we passed through, but never mind, some people enjoy the wet. "I'm sure it will clear," I told her, and watched her good cheer fade into confusion.

But before I could reassure her, the woman to my right laid a hand on my arm and demanded, "Do you like shoes?"

Perhaps the best policy here was stout agreement? "Absolutely."

"I hate shoes. Shoes are terrible things. Footwear of all kinds that keep us from contact with Mother Earth, whether they're boots or brogues or Cuban heels or sandals or Wellingtons or espadrilles or Dutch clogs or riding boots or plimsolls or ballet slippers—"

("Pretty dancers, aren't they?" murmured the girl.)

I did not know what was more impressive, the woman's thesaurus of footwear or her lung capacity, but I thought it might be a kindness to cut her off before she ran short of either words or oxygen. "I once picked up a horrible splinter from Mother Earth. Limped for days."

The rain-lover and the shoe-hater stared at me, along with a third person at the table, a woman with some Orient in her ancestry. But the fourth one, who'd bent down to finish her meal—had that been a snort of laughter?

"I'm Mary," I told my companions, then hastened to add, "I think."

The Asian woman glanced at me from under plucked eyebrows, the girl assured me that it was a pretty day, while the shoe lady was distracted from her fixation long enough to enquire, "Don't you know?"

"Not really. I mean, Mary *sounds* right, although it might also be Judith, so I'm not entirely sure. But Mary will do for now."

"I'm Lesley," said the shoe lady. "That's Pretty, and Helen."

The shy smile came to life again. "Pretty name, isn't it?"

"Absolutely. And you?" The other woman—the woman I thought might have laughed—just gazed at me.

"She doesn't talk," Lesley informed me. "She has a tongue like a shoe's, hard and leathery, and all it does is sit there and shield her mouth from the laces. Not that all shoes have tongues. Take your Wellington boot, say. It doesn't have a tongue because—"

I tuned out this font of wisdom to focus on the last one, sitting on Pretty's other side. Dull greying hair coming loose from its thread bindings. (Perhaps hair-pins, along with ceramic dishes and pointed table-knives, were seen as dangerous?) What skin I could see was as untended as one might expect in this place, but her finger-nails were neat rather than chewed, and her hands and wrists did not indicate a life of physical labour.

"The nurses here don't seem too bad," I commented, in a voice low enough to ride beneath the footwear lecture. My reward was a faint twitch of the head, so I persisted. "I mean, considering the power they have, there's not as much bullying as one might expect. Even down-stairs. I mean, when I was in line for the baths there was a woman de-cided she didn't want to go, and it took three of them to bring her down. But even then they only did it as hard as they had to. Not vicious, like."

A faint shrug of the shoulders, so I kept on. "Tell me: I saw a room with some chairs and writing desks in it, at the far end of the wing. I don't suppose they have an actual library here?" Her head began to rise and then she caught herself, to retreat back behind her loosened wisps of hair. "If not a library, maybe the nurses have books that they lend out? I certainly hope so, even if they're just romantic novels or something. I can't imagine not reading at all, it would drive me, well . . ."

I saw her pull in a breath, then slowly exhale it. She laid down her spoon and straightened in her chair, causing Lesley's monologue to cut sharply off. And then the grey-haired woman turned her face towards me.

I was more or less ready for what she decided to reveal. That is, I had assumed there to be a reason she was hiding behind her hair—a reason beyond unreason, that is—but this . . .

Acid or fire? Something had taken half her features, leaving a mask of shiny scar tissue on the right side of her face. The eye was frozen half-shut, with a pale sightless cornea behind what had once been a lid. The right nostril was a shrunken hole, while the left was almost normal. The worst of the scarring ended above her lips, and although that side of her mouth was speckled with scars, I thought the muscles themselves still functioned, allowing her to eat and drink normally.

And to speak. She finished my thought for me: "Would drive you mad?"

The smile I gave her was as twofold as her own face: an acknowledgment of my poor jest, and of my sorrow for her suffering.

But that was all the exclamation of horror that I permitted to show. "Truth to tell, it might be better to pick oakum than read too many romance novels. What *is* oakum, anyway? Does one still pick it?"

At that moment, an enormous woman at the far end of the table rose and upended her laden plate over the head of a neighbour. The resulting uproar diverted the astonishment of our own neighbours at the grey-haired woman's lifting of her face, and various nurses leapt forward to break up the mêlée and to shift the breakfast gathering into whatever thrilling events were on the day's schedule.

I was returned to the office of the physician, but having been fed and watered, I was quite able to deflect Dr Rawlins' queries. After a brief conversation with my nurse over possible treatments—which seemed primarily to be a choice between a long soak in cold water, a long soak in warm water, or talk therapy—they decided to wait a day or two and see if my memories returned on their own. In the meantime, I could be put in with the general population—with limited privileges.

Since I guessed that "privileges" meant pacing up and down the garden like the inmates I'd seen from Ronnie's car that day, three years before, restriction was no hardship—until it stopped raining, at any rate. Or until I wished to make my escape over the wall.

I was even permitted to change my drab dressing-gown for slightly less drab day clothes—and even better, in a one-bed room with a latch on both sides.

The nurse then ushered me to the day room I had glimpsed earlier, a space now crowded with women in more or less normal clothing—although even the newer garments looked somehow dowdy. After studying the room, I thought perhaps it was a combination of their lack of makeup and jewellery, and also that their clothing all seemed too large for them, as if Bedlam had a rule against form-fitting dresses.

The women were scattered across the threadbare chairs and worn chintz sofas with a variety of occupations: needle-work, knitting (needles, apparently, not being considered as threatening as hair-pins), card games, and letter-writing (pens, similarly). One woman was reading loudly to a trio of ladies with wispy silver hair. Two women playing Mah-Jong sat beside a cluster of women with a book of crossword puzzles. An ill-tuned piano against the wall emitted pained groans from under the fingers of a dramatically positioned woman, accompanied by the harsh cries of some caged birds, the drone of a woman discussing her children with the empty chair at her side, and half a dozen ongoing conversations among the more corporeal. Three women plotted the offerings at an upcoming Musical Evening, a ward Sister cajoled women to sign up for a basket-weaving class, half a dozen retired schoolteacher types discussed a list of lecture topics, and a thin, nervous creature methodically tore illustrations from a ladies' fashion journal and placed them tenderly in a box labelled PATIENTS COSTUME DANCE.

And this was a place where the mad were intended to recover their equanimity.

I spotted my grey-haired neighbour at the far side of the room, sitting with her right shoulder to the wall. She was either staring off into space or listening to the conversation behind her—although, as I came close enough to hear, I decided it was the former, since I did not think a discussion of the relative dreaminess of Douglas Fairbanks and Ramon Navarro was to her taste. I pulled a chair around so as to face her. She acknowledged me with a swift glance, then looked straight ahead again.

In profile, her features were attractive—no, I decided: they were beautiful. Not in the current movie-star version of up-turned nose and baby-like roundness, but a more eternal idea of noble beauty, with high cheek-bones, straight nose, firm chin, arched brow. Had her hair not been grey, I would have thought her little more than thirty.

I had been among these people for a handful of hours, but one thing I knew already: the madder the woman, the more abrupt—blunt, even—

her conversation was apt to be. Well, I could be as rude as the next woman.

"What happened to your face?"

The eye that fixed on me was the blue of cornflowers. "Does it matter?"

"I think so. I mean, it's one thing if a spurned lover threw acid at you, and quite another if you were the one doing the throwing. If nothing else, it would mean I should take care not to irritate you when you're holding a cup of hot tea."

The eye blinked. After a moment, her body shifted away from the wall to gaze at me more directly, even though her right eye could not give her any additional information. After a moment, her good eye narrowed. "Were you making a joke?"

"Not a very good one, I know. I shall try better next time. So what did happen to you?"

"I worked in an acid factory and the floor overseer was practicing witchcraft. So I pushed her into her vat, and got splashed."

Good Lord. I felt myself draw back. "Really?"

"No."

It was my turn to blink. I studied the blue eye in the elegant half of the scar-masked face, and saw a gleam of intelligence looking back. "Were you making a—" but could not finish before laughter took me. She *was*—and the faint crinkle beside her unblemished eye confirmed it. I held out my right hand. "Mary R—Ruth," I told her, catching myself at the last instant.

"Isabella Powers. And I agree, Miss Routh: as I am led to understand these things, the nurses here are none too bad."

I kicked myself at the near-slip of the name: one would think that a person who had actually experienced amnesia would be better at feigning it. "I'm not sure if Ruth is my surname, or a middle name. They tell me I had a head injury," I explained by way of apology. "Things seem to be trickling back a bit at a time."

"What a blessing, to forget one's past," Miss Powers said evenly, then: "Have you chosen your make-work, Miss Routh?"

"Pardon?"

She raised her chin at the room, where one of the attendants was coming through to distribute an armful of needle-work projects among the patients. "Idle hands are considered the workshop of devilish thoughts, and the idea appears to be that applying coloured thread to woven fabric offers sufficient engagement for wayward minds. Ah, thank you, Nurse Abbott," she said, taking a half-worked square from the woman in the blue frock and white apron. "I shall get right to work on this."

Nurse Abbott looked down at my empty lap. "And what about us?" she said with the kind of hearty good cheer that makes the hands twitch with the strangling urge. "Would we like knitting or needle-work?"

"We would like simply to sit and talk, thank you."

It was as if I had not spoken. "Oh, we're the memory girl, aren't we? Well, until we're certain we know how to knit, maybe we ought to stick to needle-work. The tangles are less."

She handed me an eighteen-inch square of that stiff woven base cloth I had seen Mrs Hudson use, a large but very blunt needle with an eye a blind woman could have threaded, and three matted skeins of yarn in dull brown, dull green, and dull red.

I energetically shook out the length of the first skein, stuck one end through my needle, and set to working the entire length of it up and down the grid-cloth, wilfully overlooking the faint floral design with which the cloth had been printed. Miss Powers watched me for a minute, then resumed her own, rather more obedient, work.

"How long have you been here?" I asked her.

"Here in Bedlam? Or here in this ward?"

"There's more than one ward?" I asked disingenuously.

"Oh, dear child, yes. And I have been in nearly all—all the female sections, that is—apart from the Noisy Wing. I started out among the convalescents, and then moved in with the criminals. When time went by and I failed to show any further signs of violence, I was moved in with the incurables, although eventually, the chaplain went before the presiding physicians and pointed out that life in that ward had a certain . . . coarsening effect. Also, that if even were I not violently insane before, living with the incurables might push me in that direction. So I was transferred to the basement with the curable-yet-temporarily-uncontrollables. Last year, I was granted a space in the light and freedom above ground, amongst the palms and pianos. Hence, my willingness to participate in needle-work and tedious conversation. At least here, one can see the sky."

I considered asking what she had done, to land her in the criminal wing of Bedlam. Was that too blunt even for this place? Perhaps. "So how long have you been here altogether?"

"What year is it now? 1925, I think? Seventeen years."

I dropped the needle in shock. The woman had been here since 1908? "You must've been remarkably young."

When her damaged mouth smiled, there was just the slightest sag at the right-hand corner. "How seldom one exchanges compliments in here—I scarcely know what to do with it. I am thirty-seven."

Twenty when she was shut away behind the barred windows, for some act of obvious insanity that left her scarred. Had she been sentenced more harshly, she would have gone to Broadmoor instead, the permanent home for the criminally insane—filled with men and women who would have met the noose were it not for a humane judge.

I took up my work again, hoping like hell that Holmes was not flattened by a bus. And that he hadn't forgot to tell Mycroft where to find me.

Because if I tried to get out on my own, by admitting the truth? If I went before that pleasant white-coated doctor to say I was the wife of Sherlock Holmes and had come to Bedlam in the course of a case, so would he kindly let me go now, thanks very much—that truth would kick me directly over to the incurables wing, if not the padded room.

Chapter Thirteen

···

NO: BLUNTNESS WAS ONE THING, HONESTY WAS QUITE another. I came to an end of the drab brown yarn and threaded my needle with the drab red, doing the same monotonous running stitch: up, down; up, down. "Do you think they'll let you out, then? Eventually?"

"Well, I'm not still in with the incurables."

"And that's all it takes? Convincing the doctor that you're better?"

"Bedlam is an institution for those deemed curable, even if the progress is slow. In another year or two—less if I am very fortunate—I may be transferred to one of the upper galleries. And, if I pass that test of normalcy, sooner or later I shall be sent to Witley. The hospital has a farm there, where a patient may venture towards freedom."

Half her life inside Bedlam's walls: how would a person even begin to adjust to the modern world? "Do you have family?"

Isabella Powers' body shifted, returning her damaged side to the wall. I did not think she was aware of doing it. "None that would want me."

Friends? After seventeen years, that was unlikely. And if her family were denying her, there would be little support from them. So unless she had an inheritance . . . "Does the farm provide any sort of training, for jobs?"

Deliberately, she lifted her face, giving me a glimpse of that eerie pale eyeball. "Who would hire *this*?"

Neither makeup nor veil would be enough to let her move through the world—but wait. "A mask? There was an American woman in Paris, who made metal face-plates for wounded soldiers, beautifully painted to resemble their original faces. What about one of those?"

"This woman must be famous indeed," she remarked. "I'd never heard of her before, and now she's come up twice in the past few months."

The needle slipped and jabbed into my finger—which, though too dull to draw blood, nonetheless hurt. "Really? Had the other person been to Paris recently?"

"She won't have been recently, no. Though possibly some years ago."

Catching the scent of Lady Vivian made my heart speed up. "Is this a patient or a nurse?"

"A patient."

"What if you ask her to put you in touch with the American lady? See if she's still making them."

"That patient is no longer here."

"Discharged? Or just down at the farm learning to be normal? Because if so, you could—"

"She is gone. No one seems to know where."

"She *escaped*? From Bedlam? That can't have been easy."

"Not from Bedlam itself, no. She had a pass to travel home for a family event—a birthday, I think. She failed to return. Along with the nurse who accompanied her."

"What, the nurse left, too?"

"It's possible the hospital simply dismissed her. Losing a patient is presumably a firing offence."

"I should imagine so. Well, that's too bad—I'd have enjoyed talking with a patient who had travelled to Paris. I was there once." Damn:

another slip! "At least, I think I must have been. I have memories of the Eiffel Tower in colour, and the Seine, and the texture of baguettes in the mouth. My!" I exclaimed cheerily. "This conversation seems to be doing me a world of good: remembering one of my names, and that I went to Paris. The rest of it is sure to come soon, don't you think?"

"I should be careful what I wish for, were I you," she warned grimly, and threaded some sky blue onto her needle.

I decided not to make further enquiries of this woman, who would surely begin to suspect my motives if I kept after the missing patient and her nurse. So I finished working my three skeins of yarn into the stiff grid, then set about picking them out again, since pointless work seemed to be the goal of the exercise. Rain ceased to stream down the tall windows; the room grew a fraction lighter. Half an hour or so after it ceased, a bell tinkled, prompting various patients to rise and leave for some task or another. Miss Powers was one of them. I re-threaded my needle with the drab red and started on another pattern, one that had nothing to do with the inked flower on the surface.

A short time later, as I'd expected, I had my first visitor, who arrived trailing snippets of multicoloured yarn.

She was one of the participants in the Raymond Navarro–Douglas Fairbanks debate (this one a vehement Fairbanks-ite) who had lost two of her four companions to the call of the outdoors. Since that had left her at the mercy of two vehement supporters of Navarro, she soon looked for an excuse to be elsewhere, and seized on me.

"Welcome, my dear, you're new, aren't you?"

One might have thought me a church visitor after a Sunday service rather than someone dragged in by uniformed police at midnight. However, I nodded and gave her as much of my name as I'd retrieved to that point, adding, "I don't know if Ruth is my middle name or my surname. My memory seems to have a few holes in it."

My new acquaintance emitted a manic giggle, delighted at the opportunity to tell her stories to someone who hadn't heard them several times, and gave her name as Margaret Laine—"*Mrs*, that is, but you can call me Maggie, *hehehe*"—before leaping into revelations about the woman who had just left the chair. "Do you know Miss Powers? That is, you can't have met her Outside, of course (*hehehe*) but it's always possible you were here earlier and our paths didn't happen to cross ..."

"As far as I know, this is my first time here. And I just met Miss Powers this morning."

"Oh, well, she's one of our more (*hehehe*) what you might call *infamous* residents, had a child"—her voice dropped—"'out of wedlock,' and when it came about that her young man was already married, she was thrown out on the streets. After the child died—*starved*, I hear—Miss Powers got some acid and went to his house, but there was a struggle because she was too weak to throw it, so he lost his hand but she lost her *face*. They put her here instead of in Broadmoor. Can't imagine he's *comfortable*, knowing she may get out in a few years."

"Do people ever get tired of waiting, and simply escape?" I asked, helping myself to a length of rather pretty orange yarn from the tangle she'd arrived with.

"Ooh, that's not easy. Even a man'd find it hard to go over the wall— I've not heard of it happening. And a *woman*? Never. People don't *escape* from Bedlam—except (*hehehe*) if they're not *here*."

Hiding my smile, I urged her to explain, and heard the story concerning The Vanishing of Lady Vivian. It was mostly patent nonsense and wild speculation, with a climax of the lady holding a shotgun on her nurse and family and making away wickedly in the family's Bentley. But I nodded, and made occasional sounds of appreciation, and waited until she had exhausted the imaginary exploits of this feminine Scarlet Pimpernel.

"What about the nurse?" I asked when she had run dry.

"Oh, she never came back, she was *that* frightened by the whole thing. Sent in her resignation by letter. Or perhaps she wired it—in any event, no one here has laid eyes on her since the two of them left for Waterloo station." I drew breath to prompt her into a description of Nurse Trevisan, but a prompt proved unnecessary. "Just as well, that nurse was a most *peculiar* woman. Not bad, I'm not saying that, but she was all hoity-toity. Kept to herself, like. Though not with Miss

Beaconsfield—oh, I know she's *Lady* Vivian, but we don't have much time for titles and such here, the nurses usually called her Miss like everyone else. Nurse Trevisan seemed to like her just fine. The two of them would talk on by the *hour*. It was funny to see them walking, the one all tall and dark, the other tiny and pale."

"Do you think they might have gone off together?"

Such was the power of societal assumptions—a nurse would never side with her patient against an institution—that even the mad did not question it. And when they did, they leapt to a conclusion that I would not have considered the obvious one.

"You think Miss Beaconsfield *paid* her off, to help her escape? They do say she robbed her family *blind*. I'll bet that's what they did, *plotted* how to do it. That would explain all those long *talks,* wouldn't it?"

"Still, merely getting outside the walls wouldn't be enough, would it? If she paid the nurse to help her escape, where would the nurse take her? Did either of them ever talk about Cornwall, for example?"

"Why Cornwall?"

"From the surname—Trevisan. Isn't that Cornish?"

"Far as I know, she's a Londoner like me."

"But her family. Did she ever mention . . . I don't know, Falmouth? Newquay? St Ives, perhaps?" Weren't there loads of artists in St Ives?

But Mrs Laine was shaking her head. "I'd go to Paris, I would. They have caffs there on the pavement, sit and drink your tea—coffee, more like—and watch the world go by, nobody to know you. *Nobody* to find you and make you come back here, wash the dishes, make the beds, cook dinners out of nothing . . ."

Mrs Laine was not talking about Bedlam. Mrs Laine was talking about her own home, a place from which at least twice, to judge by the scars I could see at the edge of her sleeve, she'd made an attempt at a final escape.

I let her prattle for a while, about nothing in particular, until my lack of replies drove her in search of a more responsive audience. In the relative silence—the woman tormenting the piano had been taken out for her airing, the birds were dozing, and the room had settled into the buzz of a dozen conversations—I let my fingers perform their clumsy work while my mind nibbled away at what I had learned, and what I had not. As always, the latter began to loom ever larger, until finally I thrust the needle to a resting point and looked around for my next informant.

Instead, I saw a thin young girl sitting right up by the window, face turned to the brightness. Her head was covered by a snug, old-fashioned cap, tied beneath her chin. Her hands were similarly covered, not by gloves but by mittens, the padding too thick to permit her to turn the pages of the small book in her lap. As I watched, her hand came up to her temple, encountered the various layers of resistance, and dropped down. A moment later it rose again, this time to swipe the mitten cloth across first one eye, then the other.

I gathered my ladylike handicraft together and crossed the room to stand in the window near the girl. Her head came up. She gave me a vague and unfocussed smile. I returned it, then stood for a time looking out. Next to the building was a drying yard, rapidly filling with bed-sheets that had waited for the rain to stop. Over its head-height wall I could make out gardens, with lawns and gravel paths, flower beds and mature trees rising above the high surrounding wall at the back. Off to my left were the gates and lodge-house, with the men's side beyond the drive. Women with nurses were strolling the paths, while others—the securely non-violent patients, one assumed—were working their mallets through a soggy game of croquet.

Above the tree-line, even myopic eyes could see the hospital across the way, with the Roman Catholic cathedral behind it—dirty, blunt workaday buildings that made Bethlem look, somewhat ironically, like a green and friendly island loomed about by slums.

I took the chair next to the girl, startling her. She leaned forward to see more clearly. As I'd thought, the poor thing was nearly blind.

"No," I said, "we haven't met. I'm new—the name's Mary, though I'm not certain of the rest. They took your spectacles, too, didn't they? And honestly, what was the architect thinking, facing all the windows north? It's not like London ever has sun hot enough to roast the inhabitants. Perhaps he was afraid we'd get too excited if we had a few rays of sunshine. Would you like me to read to you for a bit? That's a book of poetry, isn't it?"

The thick mittens tightened over the small volume as if I had threatened to toss it in the fire. Closer up, I could see the reason for her bindings: the hair at her temple was gone, with nothing but a ragged fuzz. Trichotillomania was known to Aristotle, who placed it alongside nail-biting, coal-chewing, and paederasty. *For these arise in some by nature, and in others (such as those who have been the victims of lust from childhood) from habit.*

Not that I thought this girl would benefit from a lecture on Aristotelian ethics. "I could read something else, if you'd prefer. Or we could just sit. I'm working on a piece of needle-work here, although it doesn't seem to be coming out quite what the designer had in mind."

We sat for a time, me filling in the stiff fabric with blots of coloured yarn, her listening to my coarsely-woven sleeve go up and down. Her hands relaxed, and eventually the left one took clumsy hold on the little book and held it out in my direction. I laid down my art and took it from her.

"Emily Dickinson? Cheerful sort of woman. Did you know that nearly all her poems came to light only after she'd died? And they say she was a gardener. Shall I read where the ribbon is?"

The cotton-covered head nodded, so I pulled the ribbon aside to run my eyes down the page, becoming more uneasy with every line:

> *The Soul has Bandaged moments —*
> *When too appalled to stir —*
> *She feels some ghastly Fright come up*
> *And stop to look at her —*
> *Salute her, with long fingers —*
> *Caress her freezing hair . . .*

I could not help glancing over at what this girl had inflicted on her own hair. But she had an expectant look on her face—and she seemed familiar enough with the volume.

I cleared my throat and read aloud, through the goblin-sipping and the bomb-dancing, the shackled feet and the welcoming Horror.

Why couldn't it have been Wordsworth? Even the bee in this poem was *long-dungeoned* before rising *from his Rose*. I read down to the last words—*"These, are not brayed of Tongue"*—and turned the page, only to see what was clearly the beginning of the next poem.

"Hmm. That seems to be the end of it. Can it be a printer's error? Or is that actually how it ends? And you know, Miss Dickinson might have been a gardener, but she never studied honeybees. It's the females that do the work, not the males. Typical, males getting the credit."

The girl smiled, no sign of distress in her face now. I returned the smile, even though she probably could not see it, and turned the page to the next unsettling, agoraphobic, grammatically challenging poem.

Chapter Fourteen

THUS PASSED MY DAY AMIDST THE LUNATICS. BEDLAM was a most efficient machine: dinner at 1:00—perfectly edible, with several courses and vegetables that were not cooked to a pulp—followed by supervised airings in the garden, tea at half-four, then a poetry reading and group singing before our supper. The nurses counted every patient going outside, every patient coming back in, and every knife and fork taken from the locked cutlery box. The ward's scissors were kept at all times on the nurses' chatelaines, which made for multiple trips back and forth when a patient was working with something requiring much snipping.

All day, patients were kept fully occupied—if not with group activities, undemanding jobs, and outdoor time, then with water treatments, massage, and talk therapy. The nurses were watchful, and skilled at easing tensions, getting us through the day without bloodshed. Or at any rate, without anyone shedding someone else's blood. And the haggard woman with the heavily scarred arms only managed a small cut on her forearm before the nurse caught her, prising away the scrap of broken glass the patient had found in the flower bed during her airing.

(I surmised, from the tired exclamations of the nurses, that the place was still living with the results of a bomb dropped on the front lawn by a Zeppelin, which had destroyed every window on the north side. I also gathered that there were plans to move the asylum to the suburbs, down near Beckenham, a move that was much anticipated.)

By the time we sat down to our evening meal, I was exhausted, shattered of nerves, and craving strong drink, but I had managed three more conversations—sensible conversations, that is, not those that spiralled into personal delusion and fixation—concerning Nurse Trevisan. My initial impression of her was confirmed: she was competent, efficient, somewhat aloof, and had a soft spot for Vivian Beaconsfield.

When it came to Lady Vivian herself, the consensus was surprisingly sympathetic, despite the title tacked onto her name. She had been here since 1920, and was regarded as one of the permanent residents, the small number of women who were theoretically curable (thus not housed with the permanently damaged) but too refined to join the paupers in a county asylum.

She was melancholic, rather than manic. When she first came, she talked little and was liable to fits of silent weeping. Nurses had to urge her from her bed, urge her to place food in her mouth. They would lead her out of doors, and prompt her to move rather than stand in one place, head down. She was not permitted visitors in those early months, and when it was noticed that letters from home sent her back into her bed, those stopped, too.

Once the outer world had been thus walled away, the fragile creature began to make timorous ventures from her protective shell. A smile, a nod, the occasional brief conversation. She would actually choose a chair in the day room rather than wait to be placed in one, and participate in the arrangement of her hair, clothing, and room. Her equanimity faltered when Nurse Denver, one of her favourites, left to care for an ailing mother, but a few weeks later Nurse Trevisan arrived, and returned to the patient the sense of security she craved.

I was puzzled at the thought that Lady Vivian's continued presence at Bedlam was by her own choice. However, the view was unanimous:

many patients less balanced than she had been long since de-committed and sent back into the world. She looked to be here for life (or, at least, for as many years into the future as her family would pay).

If this was true, I was left with three possibilities. One, the doctors knew something about Lady Vivian that her fellow patients did not. Or, Vivian herself strongly wanted to stay here, where it was "safe." Third, that despite the laws and reforms of the Victorian era, Vivian's family— namely, Lord Selwick—was quietly paying the hospital to lock his sister inside walls.

I dreaded the first; I doubted the third. And if staying here was in fact Vivian's choice—at least, until the previous week—then I for one would have been happy to let her be.

I sighed down at the warped tin plate on the table before me.

However, she had not chosen to stay.

Thus, I needed another head injury.

I picked my nurse with care: one large enough to be somewhat clumsy, young enough to be inexperienced, and among those who had been there since the morning, that she might be going home soon.

I helped gather up my neighbours' plates, setting off with a precari-ously balanced armload towards the scullery window. As I came even with my chosen victim, I stopped dead, emitting a faint sound of dis-tress. I swayed; the tin plates rattled; and I fell—directly into the young nurse.

She collapsed beneath me with a shriek, hands pushing against my inert torso. By the time she rolled me off, I had what I needed—and as I made a dramatic recovery from my swoon, scrambling upright with the help of her skirts, I returned the chatelaine with the remaining keys back onto her belt.

Fortunately, it was late enough in the day that no one was eager to drag me off to have my skull x-rayed, least of all me. Doubly fortunately, I appeared hale enough that they returned me to my room and not to the sick wing.

My private room with the lock mechanism on both sides.

A mechanism that gave way to my stolen key—the one that had been bright with wear.

It was well after midnight when I put my head out into the dimly-lit hallway. Seeing no motion, hearing nothing but the hive-like chorus of many snores, I stepped out. Shutting the door noiselessly, I padded down the gallery towards the asylum's central rooms. But when I tried my key on the door to the physician's office, it did not work.

I'd expected it might not: master keys sometimes had their limits. However, a nearby room that I'd seen the nurses going in and out of did open to it. Inside, I found some comfortable old chairs, three small tables, a schedule on the wall showing the dates for upcoming concerts, poetry readings, and lantern-slide lectures, an ice-box, and a gas ring for making cocoa or tea.

Too much to hope for some meat skewers or old-fashioned hat-pins, but in a basket near the door I found a jumble of broken and confiscated items, including a choice of impromptu pick-locks. I helped myself to a sturdy hair-pin and a splayed paper-clip, and returned to the doctor's door, where I was soon inside. And as I'd hoped, I found the key to the file cabinets inside a desk drawer: male doctors did not wear chatelaines on their belts, nor did they spoil the cut of their clothing by loading their pockets with keys.

Lady Vivian's file was surprisingly thick for a patient who had been here barely five years, but it proved to include records going back to 1916: the admissions papers from her very first asylum. I read through them, then skimmed through the six other periods of hospitalisation that followed, from four different institutions. All the pages had words and phrases in common: *brought by family, voluntary admission, mania, violent outburst, certified insane, melancholia, delusions,* and *self-harm.* Again and again, Vivian would arrive in a state of desperation; she would slowly calm; she would return to normal; and she would be discharged as cured.

Except for Bedlam. Oh, the same words were there, but whereas the longest she had spent in any of her previous asylums was nine months, she had remained here since her involuntary arrival in 1920—becoming a voluntary boarder in 1921.

Towards the end of the file, there was a notation by the same young doctor who had interviewed me that morning. Dr Rawlins' handwriting read:

Patient asked if her certification had been rescinded and was told that yes, she was on the records as voluntary. Patient asked if that meant she was permitted to leave, and was told yes, given a 72-hour notice.

I looked at the date: a little over four weeks ago.

So, why had the dratted woman not simply given her notice and moved out? Or if her departure was a sudden whim, why not write a note to her niece and sister-in-law, to tell them that she had decided to fly away? Vivian was a woman of thirty-four, with an inheritance. Once Bedlam had pronounced her sane, she could go where she wished. So why not follow the brief formalities?

Possibly, because she had made no such decision. Possibly, because someone had decided that she should not return to the place she considered home.

I returned the file to its drawer and locked the cabinet. Where had they put me? I wondered. Under "A" for Anonymous?

I gazed across the office at "P," tempted to read about Miss Powers' acid attack, but I really had no right, nor even an excuse. Hers was no longer a criminal case, it was a psychological one, and no mere investigator could help her find a way through the labyrinth. In any event, it was getting late—according to the clock on the wall, in less than two hours the sky would begin to grow bright.

I replaced the file-cabinet key in its drawer, then put my ear to the door. I'd heard people moving about while I was pillaging the records, but they'd never come too close. I imagined that the wards for the more troubled patients would have been active around the clock, but this one seemed fairly quiet. I heard no one, and eased the door open to look: yes, the long gallery was empty.

Now came the tricky bit.

This central section of offices and meeting rooms made for the asylum's common grounds: the wings and wards all joined here—male and female, regular and violent—to make use of the visitors' entrance, the kitchen and laundry facilities, and the rooms that contained things all nurses would need close to hand. No doubt there were longer-term storage rooms at a distance, but with luck, the possessions of new patients would find a temporary resting-place somewhere here, on their way to being parcelled up and tidied away until discharge.

I avoided the hall beneath the dome—the palm-bedecked room used for chapel and holiday events—since I remembered that off that lay the porters' rooms. If there were night guards, they would be there. Instead, I opened various doors until I found one lined with shelves holding everything from fresh bedding and hospital clothing to bed-pans, hair-combs, packages of tea-biscuits, and one solitary strait-jacket. And a set of shelves holding various things that were clearly intended for more permanent storage, including a brown-paper-wrapped parcel with the label:

Female, mid-twenties, blonde—blue. NB: dress and men's trousers.

I did not need the confirmation of yesterday's date to know that here was my clothing.

I plucked off the twine and hunted through the garments until I found my spectacles—to which, I was pleased to see, some thoughtful nurse had restored the lens that she'd found in my pocket. I put them on, then exchanged my hospital wear for my own undergarments, trousers, and cardigan. As I threaded my belt through the trouser's loops, I paused. That was why all the inmates looked frumpy: in Bedlam, only the nurses were permitted belts.

Which explained why Vivian had such a collection of them in her wardrobe at Selwick.

I put the dress and hat back in the paper, along with the hospital's night clothes, tying the twine around it again before replacing it on the shelf—thinner now, but it might take them a while to notice.

By which time, I would be gone.

(I hoped.)

A glance at the window warned me that the brief summer's night was fast ebbing. I put on a motoring cap someone had left on a hook, dropped a packet of tea-biscuits into my pocket, then performed the ritual of the stealthy sticking out of head into the dim hallway again . . . only this time, the gallery was occupied. Very fortunately, she was walking in the opposite direction, and hadn't heard the faint click of the mechanism under my hand. I kept very still, and cursed to myself when she reached the far end and turned.

My head was back inside the storage room before her reverse-face was complete. With exquisite care, I inched the door all the way closed, turning the knob to permit the tongue to slide into the plate. I could not risk the noise of the lock itself, but fortunately, the night-watchwoman did not perform the constabulary act of rattling door-knobs to check the locks. Her heels thumped along the worn carpet, approaching, then fading up the side-corridor. I held my breath: would she continue through the baths and into the wing for the "noisy" (i.e., uncontrollable) patients, or would she return?

I pulled the door open a bare centimetre, ear to the crack . . . and heard her footsteps cut off with a *clank* from the bath-room door.

Again, I peered down the gallery: empty. I shut the door behind me and scurried along to the laundry—the stolen key did work there—and from there into welcome, blessed, open air.

I sat on the stoop to lace up my shoes, then looked down at the key beside me. Did I intend to come back? If so, a pass-key would save me time. On the other hand, I imagined that if hospital regulations called for the counting of patients and forks, so much more so a missing key. It had not yet been discovered, but surely a misplaced key would make for less trouble than a missing one? No reason to get the poor nurse fired. I stepped back into the laundry, laid the key next to a bundle of uniforms waiting for cleaning, and left Bedlam to its slumber.

Through the drying grounds, up onto the coal shed, over the wall into the gardens beyond. The drive ran past the lodge, which was sure to be occupied, but was there any reason for me to risk a set of noisy iron gates?

Instead, I trotted across the dark lawn, praying that there were no abandoned croquet hoops. The light from the street beyond showed me the large, ill-trimmed trees I had seen from the day room. I clambered up, then out onto a branch—only to freeze, as the bounce beneath me warned that the tree was considerably less mature than it had appeared.

Thinking very light and airy thoughts, I edged out, closer to the wall . . .

And stepped onto its top without breaking any bones.

A horse cart was coming along St George's Road as I dropped out of the heights. I peered closely at the rag-and-bone man, but when the startled old face did not turn out to belong to Sherlock Holmes, I tugged at my cap and strolled off towards the River and the city beyond.

Chapter Fifteen

....

THE ACTUAL SHERLOCK HOLMES AND I DID NOT MEET UP until later that afternoon, when I came blinking upright in Mycroft's guest room, dragged from slumber by the sound of the front door. I fumbled for the clock—then squinted more closely to see if it was still ticking. The curtains suggested dusk, but from the clock's hands and the sounds outside, it was merely a rainy Sunday afternoon. I donned my glasses and dressing-gown to walk into the flat, to be greeted by the aroma of coffee.

The eagerness with which I took the cup made Holmes' eyebrow rise. "Bedlam had a surprising number of positive features," I informed him, "but its cuisine was not among them." Without remark, he reached for a skillet and conjured up a meal more appropriate to a morning hour and a family of five, turning the whole mess onto a single plate and handing me a fork.

"Your lady does not appear to have pawned the necklace here in London," he said as I began to fling the plate's contents down my throat.

"However, I suspect that she may have visited her bank and withdrawn funds."

My own eyebrows went up in a question, although since his back was to me as he ran water into the pan, my silence alone communicated a request for more. Or perhaps he simply kept talking.

"The manager seemed disinclined to provide any details without the approval of some higher power, although his facial expressions as he examined various pages handed him by an assistant suggested that he had not been aware of the Lady Vivian's visit. I expect your Marquess down in Surrey will have had a telephone call to inform him that his half-sister made inroads into her own money, under her own power."

I paused with laden fork long enough to ask, "Have you any idea how much money we're talking about?"

"Enough to cause a forty-year-old bank manager to break out in a light sweat and suddenly recall an appointment that required my immediate departure."

So: enough for a solitary woman to live in relative comfort for a few years, though perhaps not enough to keep her in luxury. For that, she would need to sell the diamonds.

When the plate was bare, we filled our cups again and adjourned to the voluminous chairs of the sitting room. (Mycroft, once an enormous man, since his heart attack had become simply very large; his furniture reflected his former person.) While Holmes got his pipe going, I thanked him for his help, apologised for the interruption to his study of motets, then gave him a review of the previous days, from my visit to his bolt-hole and my evening's "arrest" to my eventual delivery to Bedlam, with all I had seen and heard inside its walls.

In all, I kept to precise detail rather than conjecture, there being little point in giving Holmes pre-digested data. As I went on, he retreated into his chair, sitting with his legs drawn up and his eyelids down, looking as if he had fallen asleep.

He had not. I came to a halt with the rag-and-bone man who was not Sherlock Holmes, and he remained silent. After a time, I stood and went back into the guest room, coming out twenty minutes later both clean and dressed.

He stirred, and reached for his long-cold pipe and a long-cold topic, one we had covered on Thursday. "A lesbian, you said?"

"Lady Vivian? I believe so. Miss Bailey confirmed it, more or less. And it would explain not only why an attractive young Hon managed to get through her coming-out Season without a ring, but also why some of her asylum doctors were so vehement about her fantasies that needed to be cured."

He shook his head, dropping the spent match into the tray. "One might as well condemn a cat for not being a dog, or a telephone's mouth-piece for not containing the speaker."

"But it isn't just that, Holmes."

"It's about the Marquess and his sister's money."

"Yes."

"The bank manager was remarkably chary of giving me details. As I said, he seemed unaware that she had been by—and I believe he was unaware of anything untoward in the handling of her account. But once I drew his attention to the records, he appeared to notice some, shall we say, irregularities? Hence his nervousness, and his need to dismiss me then and there. I intend to go back in the morning. Perhaps a night's uneasiness about the situation may have loosened his tongue."

"Holmes, surely asylums don't lock away women anymore just because their family aren't happy with them?"

"You don't think so?"

"It sounds positively Dickensian."

"There is a reason why Dickens remains popular amongst the lending libraries."

The possibility that the fragile, gifted woman I had met was locked behind bars because of a greedy and disapproving half-brother was bad enough. But now that she was out?

"Holmes, when I met Lady Vivian three years ago, she told Ronnie that she wished to remain in Bedlam. Her very words were, 'I'm safe here.' Do you think . . . ?"

"That she may have been speaking the simple truth?"

"That we should find her before the Marquess does?"

"I do. And you also need to ask your friend about her aunt's will. To see who inherits the money were she to die."

I listened to the word's bleak echo, and wondered what the odds were to her being alive.

Chapter Sixteen

···

IT WAS A RELIEF WHEN MYCROFT ARRIVED HOME. NOT that I was fully reconciled to my brother-in-law and his outsized rôle in the world of dark politics—I would probably never regain my early, naïve fondness for him—but time grants perspective, if not forgiveness. I had no trouble being cordial.

Holmes had told him about Lady Vivian's disappearance, and I filled in some of the details about my trips to Surrey and Bedlam.

But not over dinner: food was sacrosanct to Mycroft Holmes. He ate with gusto, Holmes and I less so, while we spoke of Percy Fawcett's Amazon expedition and the Scopes arrest, as well as a rumour Mycroft had heard of an invention called "radiovision" in America, which both men agreed sounded like a pipe dream.

Afterwards, Mycroft lit a small fire while Holmes filled glasses with our preferred varieties of *digestif*. Our host settled into the largest of his chairs, and began to talk about a recent problem that had come across his desk.

"Actually, it concerns a woman who made me think of you, Mary. Not that you're anything like her—mannish sort of thing, drove an ambulance during the War and never wanted to take off the uniform afterwards. No, what amused me was that when the woman was, oh, fourteen or fifteen, she signed up for the Scouts using just her initials so they'd think she was a boy. And when they found out and objected, she refused to be put off."

"She sounds like my type, all right. Did the Scouts let her in?"

"Her mother ended up forming the Girl Guides for her to play soldier in."

"Too bad, it would have improved Baden-Powell's boys no end."

"You may be right. But now the woman—Lintorn-Orman is her name, Rotha Beryl Lintorn-Orman, which sounds like a rather strained anagram for . . . what? *A northernly tribal moron? Not a nonthermal lorry rib? Rent a labyrinth or—*"

Holmes broke in. "Mycroft, was there a point to this?"

"Yes, namely, that the Lintorn-Orman woman has a bee in her bonnet—not that she wears a bonnet—about Reds and foreigners. That they're overrunning Britain, ruining the place, undermining the values of Empire, and we have to get rid of them. To a certain point she's right—none of us want to see the Bolshevik flag over Buckingham Palace—but having an entire policy of 'Us Good, Them Bad' does little more than create a magnet for trouble-makers. Most of my colleagues consider her just another flash-in-the-pan crackpot, and Labour openly laughs at the idea, but in two years, she's got thousands signed up as British Fascists, all of them eager to raise Cain about something."

"Didn't that group kidnap the Communist Pollitt?" Holmes asked.

"And marched on London during Empire Day."

I had to interrupt. "And this woman made you think of me . . . why?"

"It was a tightly limited analogy, I assure you, resting on the single point of her childhood antic. I cannot imagine you espousing a cause that lacks a carefully thought-out platform. This woman has nothing but her passions. So taken with the Mussolini people in Italy that she starts up her own party of Fascists—without noticing that if she tried to do anything of the sort in Italy, the Blackshirts would slap her silly and shove her back in the kitchen."

I nodded solemnly. "Alas, a lack of common sense is not an exclusively male prerogative."

Holmes stepped in with some question about Italy's Fascist lunacy, and I listened with half an ear as I thought about Rotha Lintorn-Orman. I had heard the name—it did rather stand out—and although I agreed that she sounded a bit maternally indulged, I also thought she was one of those who had tasted adventure and self-respect during the War, and fit poorly back into the status quo afterwards.

But, wasn't this the second mention of the Italian leader in as many days? I stirred, and spoke up without thinking.

"Ronnie's uncle the Marquess admires the Fascists, too. Oh, sorry—I didn't mean to interrupt."

Mycroft did not seem to mind. "I have begun to think this may be the direction towards which much of the country, if not the world, is headed."

Mycroft had been described, many years before, as a man who "audits the books in some of the government departments." Strictly speaking, this was true—except that the auditing he did was less that of sums on a ledger than it was the trends, costs, and vulnerabilities of international politics. If Mycroft Holmes saw movement in a political realm, it was there—or it would be.

But, Britain? This rational, benevolent nation in the hands of men like Mussolini or the Marquess of Selwick? Inconceivable. If it came to that, I'd rather be inside Bedlam.

With the thought of that great grey institution, I retreated again from the conversation, letting it break and ebb in the room around me like waves on the shore.

Bedlam had not been at all what I expected. I had ventured in, anticipating a cold stone mausoleum seething with the violent, the unrestrained, and the suicidal, kept under control by brutal and uncaring attendants. No doubt some institutions were exactly that—the county asylums, I suspected, were given considerably less money and little say in which inmates they could hand back to their families.

But when it came to Bethlem Royal Hospital, the word *asylum* was not entirely spurious. I had seen its inmates treated with gentle skill, given medical care and warm food by people who were willing to talk, and to listen. They were kept occupied with labour, but not too harshly. They were urged to test their own limits, but only by degrees. I personally would be driven to lunacy by the place, but would not a fragile mind benefit from the warm cotton-wool of placid activities and regular hours?

The one thing I regretted was that I'd left without seeing Lady Vivian's room. I had no doubt that, as a more or less permanent resident, she had accumulated both rights and possessions. None of her fellows had mentioned seeing her drawing or painting, although three years ago, she'd had both the materials and the dexterity to produce a charming Pierrot for young Simon. Perhaps she'd left a new row of sketchbooks on a shelf. Perhaps the images mounted on her wall would have given me a hint as to where she'd gone.

That last sketch-book back in Selwick, the one with the missing pages from the year of her beloved brother's death, had suggested that her art was going in some interesting directions. Mere dashes of the pencil to suggest an object emerging from the page, given substance in soft hints of colour …

I glanced at Holmes with a smile: straight-combed hair, perfectly knotted tie, deep maroon silk dressing-gown. Crisp lines down the front of his trousers; polish on his shoes. Mycroft was the same: there was nothing soft or uncertain in his entire apartment, apart from three chair-cushions and my own dressing-gown.

The two were going on about Mussolini again, the unexpected fervour with which his country had embraced him, how economic pressures and Great War losses could shape a country's wishes and expectations, how a harsh message of patriotic destiny and racial superiority could get a nation to overlook a brutal murder and clumsily staged cover-up. How his seizing of power did not bode well for the Adriatic region.

I found it difficult to imagine a Fascist march through the rich, rolling Italian countryside. Black shirts against the new corn; raised fists before the silvery leaves of olives. That blunt jaw of *Il Duce* against the soft . . .

I blinked as my thoughts stuttered to a halt. Blunt: soft. Crisp: velvets. Shapes appearing through the mist. Patterns began to rearrange themselves in my mind: a sketch-book in a time of retreat. Treasures pinned to a wall. A mask, a name . . .

A name?

I struggled out of my chair and hurried back to Mycroft's library, flipping rapidly through his enormous world atlas. When I found the page I wanted, I ran my finger west from the blue ink of the water . . . then stopped. Yes!

I looked up at the man in the doorway. Holmes in his crisp shirt and sleek dressing-gown.

"Trevisan isn't Cornish," I said.

"Very well."

"I know where she's gone."

"Lady Vivian?"

"Where she thought would be safe. There's only one place it could be."

He looked at the map, reading the name upside-down. "Treviso?"

"Not quite."

A place so soft, its buildings floated in the mist. A place where roads were water and pavements were bridges. An upside-down world with foundations of wood holding walls of stone, where power was soft and beauty hard, where superstitions were truth and truth was invisible. A place whose citizens were masked even when they wore their own faces.

Oh, Holmes was going to hate this.

"I think she's gone to Venice."

Chapter Seventeen

···

YOUNG MASTER BEACONSFIELD WAS SCREAMING AGAIN. The nurse had given notice and decamped for Brighton. Ronnie plopped him into the perambulator he'd long outgrown and we took to the streets.

It did quieten him. He sat upright, gripping the vehicle's sides and imperiously surveying the passing scenery like a maharaja in his sedan chair, around the Paddington Basin and down Sussex Gardens towards the park.

It calmed Ronnie as well—either the walking or the fact that her son was not voicing complaint. Or, I realised as we strolled along talking about inconsequentials, simply the chance at conversation with another adult. To judge by the state of her living quarters, she was doing without a housemaid or cook—and, by the look of her hastily-bound hair, unplucked eyebrows, and blunt-cut finger-nails, without her regular visits to the salon. All of which suggested she had put friends on the back burner as well.

She was probably sorely tempted to go home to Selwick—either that or beg for shelter in the unwelcoming Fitzwarren household. Both, clearly, were unpalatable—but pride did not pay the bills.

I nearly asked her outright: *Ronnie, aren't you lonely?* I had enough sense not to say it aloud, because of course she was: her husband dead, her mother far away, her friends put off by her own embarrassment. And now the lack of a nanny would keep her from looking for some kind of employment. She was, as were many women of her class, using no skills beyond the maternal.

It was an uncomfortable realisation, because I should have seen it long before. However, at least this was one problem I could solve. More troublesome was the question that had brought us back in touch in the first place. We crossed over to Hyde Park and were within sight of the Serpentine before I spoke again.

"I always forget that you and your aunt are so close in age."

"Yes, she's almost like an elder sister."

"It must have been so difficult when she started having problems."

"Vivian was always a bit odd. It was what I loved about her—that she wasn't like anyone else I knew. But seeing her in pain like that was hard. I was seventeen the first time she was taken away. And when she tried to kill herself . . . oh, Mary, it was so awful! I kept thinking, *There's got to be something I can do to keep her safe.* But there wasn't."

Simon had twisted around at the tension in her voice, a dubious expression on his face. But before the storm clouds could gather, I scooped up a branch with some ancient cypress cones on it and distracted him with it, then asked Ronnie the next sensitive question.

"Do you know anything about your aunt's will? Who is the beneficiary, and whether she's re-written it recently?"

"Her will? Why on earth would you ask about that? Do you think—?"

"Ronnie, I'm sure you've considered the possibility of her suicide. But if she *hasn't* recently reviewed her will, I'd say the chances are good she's just gone away."

Absurd, of course—and if Ronnie were thinking correctly, she'd never have given it serious consideration. Fortunately, mothers of young children rarely have sufficient energy to think correctly, so she took my reassurance at face value.

"She and I have the same solicitor. I'll ring him when we get back to the flat, and ask if she's made any changes."

"Good idea."

"It sounds as if you're no closer to finding her."

"Actually, I think I may be. Could she have gone to Venice, do you think?"

Forward progress stopped. "Good heavens, Mary—is that where she's gone? Oh, what a lovely thought! Auntie Vee *adored* Venice. When we were young, she used to tell me stories about it. That's why Miles and I went there on our honeymoon—she gave us the money for it."

I touched her elbow to keep us moving forward, lest His Majesty grow fractious.

"If she did go there, Ronnie, have you any idea where she'd stay?"

"I think she hired rooms in a palazzo—you do know this was a long time ago, before the War?"

"I saw the dates in her sketch-books, yes."

"She did arrange for an hotel for Miles and me—the Danieli—but I didn't get the impression she'd stayed there herself." The Danieli was the most expensive hotel along the open waterfront, a place foreigners picked when they had the money and wanted no risk of encountering a concierge who did not understand English—or, when they wanted perfection for a beloved niece's honeymoon. "I understand the Lido has become quite the hot place for night-life, although when we were there it was pretty quiet.

"So: how do you suggest I find her? It's summer, I can take Simon along, no trouble at all, but I'm not sure where to look."

Why is guilt such a powerful force? Guilt over an aunt's suicide attempt, guilt over a friend's unrecognised need. How could I compound it by letting Ronnie know how badly she'd failed to protect her aunt from the Marquess' greed?

The moment I'd looked down at Mycroft's book of maps, I knew what it would take to assuage my own regrets. I put on the very perkiest of grins and lifted my head.

"Good heavens, no. I've been dying for an excuse to go to Venice again. I have nothing going at present, so I'll just pop down on the train. I'm sure to come across her in a day or two—though it's probably best not to tell anyone about it, until we're sure. So, shall I bring you back a scarf, from that little place on the Piazza? Or a leather bag?"

Ronnie knew me well enough to see through the cheerfulness. But she also knew that she was in no position to turn me down. The look she gave me, of gratitude and camaraderie and hope, was sufficient reward.

"What about a toy lion, for the young man?"

Chapter Eighteen

 "SHERLOCK, YOU *ARE* GOING TO VENICE WITH MARY, I trust?"

"Why on earth would I do that? Russell is quite capable of travelling across Europe without an escort. And I have that case involving the Americans that Lestrade asked me to look into."

"I need you to go."

"Don't be absurd."

"Rome would be better, but Venice will have to do."

"I'm not one of your flunkies, Mycroft. You have agents to do your bidding."

"I know you dislike Venice—"

"With good reason, may I point out?"

"That was years ago, Sherlock. And the principals of that case are long dead."

"Am I not permitted my own preferences?"

"Not when I need you. Not when your country needs you."

"Mycroft, you cannot think that particular exhortation will work with me."

"Nonetheless, it is true—none of my people has your eyes. Or your experience."

"I am not one of your agents."

"No, you're my brother. And I am asking for your help with this. Look, Sherlock, you know how it goes. In the early stages of any case, be it one of your crimes or one of my political situations, there is no evidence upon which one can lay one's finger. What did you tell Watson—that it is like the trembling of a spider's web?"

"You know very well I was talking about Moriarty, not myself."

"You might as well have been referring to your own methods—or to mine. Sherlock, I cannot go, and I cannot yet tell one of my agents what to look for. I need you to go and get a feel for the place. I swear to you, these Fascists will be trouble—and it won't be confined to Italy."

"I admit I'm a bit surprised that you aren't more sympathetic to the Fascist message."

"If there were an actual message, you might be right, since one can talk to a man with firm principles even if one doesn't agree with him. But the *Fascisti* are less concerned with theory than they are with raw power. If one plays on fear, takes away any remotely complicated ideas, and offers people a sense of confidence and right, one's followers will beat to death any enemy they are pointed at."

"So where is their weak place?"

"I don't know. Which means I can't set plans in motion to counter them. You and I are both fully aware there will be another war before the century is out. I'd like to ensure that we survive that one, too. Preferably by a somewhat wider margin than the last."

"You think the threat will come out of Italy?"

"I think Italy signals the start of an epidemic. The Broad Street pump of politics, as it were. And I believe that the Fascists will be looking for those in power that they might infect."

"And you are the doctor who closed off the source of cholera-laden water. Does that make me the curate who assisted him?"

"No one believed Dr Snow, either, until he forced matters by removing the pump's handle."

"So now we're plumbers."

"Sherlock, I *need* you to go to Venice."

"Yes, Mycroft, I know. I know you do."

"You will find the city much changed."

"Venice hasn't changed in four hundred years, much less forty. The hemlines are further from the ground, that is all."

"But you'll go?"

"I will."

"Thank you. I'll have the files sent to Sussex."

"Don't do that. Have them here tomorrow. I'd rather Russell not know that I'm doing this for you."

"When is your wife going to get past this childish aversion to the realities of Empire?"

"Mycroft, has no one ever pointed out to you that name-calling can be extremely revealing?"

"Revealing of irritation, perhaps."

"Or, of a sensitivity over the truth. Brother mine, the power you wield *is* dangerous. The use you have made of it has *not* always been noble. Russell's objection to that troubles you more deeply than you admit, even to yourself."

"So you fling insults at me by way of revenge for the uncomfortable memories of Venice?"

"You may be right. I must be gone, I have an appointment with a burglar. Leave the file for me tomorrow."

"I'll put it on the dining table in the morning. And, Sherlock? Keep your head down, you and Mary both. There's violence brewing in Italy. I wouldn't want you—either of you—to become a target for Fascist boots."

Chapter Nineteen

....

"YOU TRULY DON'T NEED TO GO WITH ME, HOLMES." I eyed the laden valise, wondering if I ought to fill its last corner with another pair of shoes or a bathing costume.

His only reply was to flip closed the top of his own case and tug down its buckle. It seemed a remarkably small space for what would, I knew all too well, turn out to contain absolutely everything he needed, and in pristine condition.

I grabbed up the shoes—because honestly, why did I imagine I would have either time or inclination to lounge about in a bathing costume?—and wrestled the valise shut. Beneath it on the bed lay my pencil, now stabbed through a crumpled list of tasks:

~~Maps~~ (Why didn't all countries have Ordnance Survey maps?)
~~Beekeeper~~ (Fortunately, one was available.)
~~Tell Patrick we're away~~ (My farm manager would watch the place.)
~~Tell Exchange to route calls to Patrick~~ (Lest calls go unanswered)
~~Get Lira~~ (Enough to start us off in Venice)

Money for Ronnie

~~V's will~~ (I'd finally got the answer out of Ronnie's solicitor,
   although it took me a truly irritating amount of time and game-
   playing, but no, he had not received any notification of changes.
   The Marquess remained Vivian's designated guardian, but the
   actual beneficiary—this being the part the legal gentleman was
   loath to reveal, and only did so without saying it directly—
   would be Ronnie. If changes had been made, either they'd been
   done through another solicitor who had yet to register them, or
   Lady Vivian had made a holograph will.)

I looked up at Holmes, to ask about the item yet to be crossed off,
and found myself distracted by his moustache. Not that I minded it,
really. It was so thin, it practically blended into the line of his lip. Just
that with the dye in his hair and the darkening around his eyes, he
looked a bit . . .

Racy. As a disguise, it was oddly effective.

"Holmes, did your legal gentleman take care of the money for Ronnie?" Ronnie was familiar with my own firm, so I'd needed to keep their
name off of the correspondence.

"Tomorrow and on the fifteenth of each month, until such a time as
your friend sorts out her financial situation, one hundred pounds shall
be sent her from an anonymous 'Friend of Miles Fitzwarren.'"

I drew a line through that item on the list, and dropped it into the
waste-bin. Between consultations with Ronnie and buying detailed
maps of the lagoon and showing our photographs (doctored and otherwise) to half the railway personnel in England—to say nothing of searching out a neighbour willing to care for bees—we'd managed to delay a
solid week, with little to show for it. Although we could now be relatively
certain that Vivian had more or less emptied her bank account; that
Rose Trevisan was a London-born nurse with a spotless history of service; and that the two women had left London disguised as brother and
sister. Holmes had spent several of the days in London, about some unspecified business. I began to suspect his delay was deliberate.

"Holmes, I know how you feel about Venice, but honestly, I'm quite looking forward to this."

"Italy is not a comfortable place to travel these days," he said darkly.

"I know, but Venice isn't exactly Italy, is it?"

"I believe you'll find it has moved somewhat closer to the mainland. Well, perhaps Mr Mussolini has managed to get the trains running on time."

I turned to frown at him, and at the moustache. "Holmes, if that was meant to be a joke, I ask you to remember that his Blackshirts are dragging their enemies off the streets."

"Precisely. So kindly make an effort not to criticise the man in public, lest you be added to their targets." He picked up his bag and set off downstairs with it.

I followed more slowly.

Personally, I found Venice a delight. Venice was a place *between*— a fascinating blend of solid and liquid, of the West but Eastern in flavour, a place of tradesmen who dealt in magic. That one of its most prized industries was glass, a substance that went from liquid to solid through the use of fire and air, was no accident.

My first memories of the city built on water were as a child at my mother's side, when her laughter and incredulity proved contagious. I had been back five or six times since then—including a very brief stopover there during the spring, on our way home from Istanbul—but had never shed my amazement and affection for this city of stone laid upon the waters.

Of course Holmes would grumble at the idea of Venice: this was a man who clothed himself with sharp edges and clear colours, who valued cold facts and logical reasoning, whose entire career was based on tracing matters down to their base. One might as well introduce a British bulldog to a Siamese cat.

What I had not considered was that he might hate going there because of the danger it put us—put *me*—into.

Sixteen months earlier, in April 1924, Italy had held an election that put two-thirds of the Parliament into the hands of the Fascist Party.

At the end of May, a member of Parliament named Giacomo Matteotti—a vocal Socialist and long-time thorn in the side of the *Fascisti*—made a vehement speech protesting the growth of violence and criminal behaviour, accusing the Fascists of fraud in their victory, and demanding that the results be annulled. A book denouncing the Fascists was hurried to press. But shortly after his speech, Matteotti disappeared from his home.

He was neither the first, nor by any means the last, to disappear, but he was one of the most prominent and beloved. A country-wide search led to nothing but the blood-drenched car in which he had been taken, which proved to be owned and driven by the Fascist secret police—close colleagues and friends of the Prime Minister himself. When Matteotti's body was finally discovered in August, crowds lined the funeral route. Anti-Fascist posters went up on walls. All fingers pointed at Mussolini. The world waited gleefully for Italian Fascism to crumble under charges of conspiracy and murder, and another would-be tyrant to fade away behind bars.

Yet it did not. Instead, the thugs succeeded. Newspapers critical of the cause were shut down. The Italian king decided that he feared the country's Republicans and Socialists more than he did the Fascists, and refused to dismiss the Mussolini government.

And a few months later, in January of this year, Benito Mussolini stood before his nation to declare himself absolute ruler of his country, and to take proud responsibility for the violence that had put him there. As he put it, "Italy wants peace and quiet, work and calm. I will give it these things—with love if possible, with force if necessary."

The trains would run on time.

As I vaguely remembered from the half-heard conversation in Mycroft's flat, my brother-in-law had been saying that the April election did indeed show any number of irregularities, from Fascist intimidation to disappearing ballots, and that at the time of his death, Matteotti had in hand documents suggesting that *Il Duce* and his cronies had pocketed a great deal of money from a sale of their country's oil rights. Mycroft had also heard, from his grey inside sources, that Mussolini himself had hesitated over making himself dictator, until his fellow Fascist leaders threatened to take over themselves if he did not.

Once the tail was wagging the dog, Italy was doomed.

Up until now, I had not really made any link between my soft, floating-world memories of Venice and the brutalities taking place in the rest of the country. But clearly Holmes had.

In centuries past, the Venice lagoon had been a moat that kept the world at bay. Would it still, in this harsh modern era?

Chapter Twenty

....

THE TRAIN CAME TO ITS END ON SUNDAY, TWO DAYS AND four nations after we'd stepped out of our Sussex door.

The ideal approach to Venice is from the sea, standing at a ship's rails as the faint traces of buildings take form through the mist. She resembles (and I must agree with tradition here: Venice *is* feminine) a queen seated on a throne in a wide, flat field. Solitary and regal, she waits in patience for those who would come to do homage.

Instead of that entry to *La Serenissima*, we puffed across two miles of water on hundreds of stone arches, waited while the customs men came to check our hand luggage, and climbed down into the cacophony of any railway station on the planet. The salty air churned with the sounds of shouting porters and crashing equipment, customs inspectors and street urchins, the hiss of venting steam and the slams of compartment doors, the cries of greeting and the occasional shriek of a traveller seeing her bags vanish into the crowd.

And yet, this was different. There was no stink of idling taxis, for one thing, no clop of hooves or rumble of motor lorries or whine of motorcycles. We were in a port city, yet there was no sign of heavy-goods traffic. Groups of laughing foreigners suggested a resort town, yet bright holiday clothing was more than balanced by workaday garments. Uniforms of various kinds put the crowd into order, funnelling traffic from iron rails to waterborne craft.

I watched the familiar scene with pleasure, until my eye was drawn to an oddity: two black-clad figures created an eddy in the swarm, in a way that even the customs officials did not. Most of the people giving them wide berth seemed unaware that they were doing so, but even the laughing tourists subsided a touch as they approached the Blackshirts, and their laughter resumed only when they were out of earshot from the two Fascist representatives.

I shook off the creeping awareness of the outside world and turned my mind to our next moves.

The previous Friday, when Thomas Cook & Co. had proven a broken reed and failed to come up with adequate rooms, I had dredged the name of an hotel from the depths of memory and sent them a wire. We had left Sussex before any response could arrive, and since the tourist season was clearly well under way—despite heat, Fascists, mosquitoes, and the stench of summer canals—I only hoped that someone had recalled my mother's name with enough affection to offer us a servant's room under the sweltering eaves.

As I prepared to join the milling crowds heading towards the water and thus the Venetian equivalent of a taxi, I became aware of a person standing before me, very still and quite close. I adjusted my eyes, and found a trim young man in hotel livery, with a name in fancy stitching on his breast:

Hôtel Londres
&
Beau Rivage

"Signor and Signora Russell?"

"Yes," Holmes said. Thanks to Mycroft, he even had a passport in the name of Sheldon Russell, an ebony-haired gent, pampered and well glossed from the tips of his shoes to the teeth behind his pencil-thin moustache. Thin disguise, but along with the change in his stance and the languid air he wore, even someone who knew him would hesitate, wondering, might this be a cousin . . . ?

"The keys to your luggage, please? I shall see it through Customs. Come, your boat is just here."

I followed his pointing finger, and saw a sleek steam launch with a man in the same uniform. I held out the keys and my valise, but told him, "We'll walk, thanks. It's been a long train ride. Oh—and tell the maid not to unpack the bags. We prefer to do so on our own." And had, ever since the day one inexplicably thorough hotel maid had happened across a hidden compartment, dutifully removed the contents for cleaning, and sent a bullet whizzing through the next room.

The hotel man bowed, cheerfully acknowledging our English eccentricity, accepted my tip, and trotted to the hotel launch with our valises. While he explained to his colleague, hands gesturing, that these mad English guests wanted to walk to the hotel, the even sleeker launch beside it drew in its gangway and let out a belch of steam. This one bore the name Hotel Excelsior, and it turned away with an air of disdain, as if to show that *its* guests did not need to wait along with *hoi polloi*. The launch went serenely off, ignoring the gondolas, cargo transports, fishing boats with furled sails, many varieties of shallow-hulled canal boats, and one lone rowing skiff.

Holmes scowled at our own waiting launch. "Do you suppose we shall ever see our possessions again?" he asked me.

"It's quite a good hotel, Holmes."

"All the more reason for a thief to pick their jacket out of a laundry."

Was I being naïve, gullible—touristic? I did not think so. "Venice has little serious crime, and a very clear sense of honour."

"Amongst thieves," he grumbled, so I slid my arm through his and urged my husband and partner towards the foot-bridge linking the modern world with the timeless city known as *La Serenissima*.

This most unlikely of cities grew out of the waters centuries ago, a refuge from chaos following the disintegration of the Roman Empire (another power that kept the trains running, metaphorically speaking). Its residents expanded their literal footholds in the lagoon by driving trees down into the mud and perching buildings on top. Before long, its ships ruled—and plundered—the known world.

In the process, Venice gave rise to an idiosyncratic, oddly democratic, and utterly ruthless system of government. The Doge and his Council were absolute rulers, and yet a constant and precarious balance of power ensured that no one man—or even family—could establish a permanent authority over the others. A Doge's salary was small, forcing him to maintain his interest in healthy commerce. After a Doge died—and the number of Doges who failed to succumb to natural causes served as a cautionary tale to each successor—his estate was reviewed, and pillaged if any trace of misdoing was found.

This inborn system of stalemate proved popular with the Venetians themselves, since it allowed them to carry on the business of business while the government squabbled and bickered and compromised itself into stability. It also, incidentally, laid the groundwork for America's three governmental branches, designed to frustrate each other into tiny increments of progress.

For eleven centuries, the Venetian system held—until Europe on the one hand took to the seas and cut out the Venetian middleman, while the Ottomans on the other side grew powerful enough to block the formerly bottomless stream of trade from the East. When Bonaparte passed through Venice in 1797 on his way to a more important enemy, he decided, like any lesser tourist, to ship home his pick of the city's riches. "I shall be an Attila to the state of Venice," he thundered. Since the Venetian Navy consisted of but a dozen galleys, its Doge abdicated, and a thousand years of Republic quietly ended.

Under the Bonaparte régime, *La Serenissima* lost her independence, her authority, her vast agricultural hinterland, and a great deal of her art. (Most of which, to be honest, had been stolen in the first place.) Stripped and powerless, she was thrown to Austria in the peace accord.

But her stones remained. Like many other cross-roads of trade—Jerusalem, Cairo, Tokyo—the wealth of the city lay indoors, hidden from passers-by behind inscrutable faces.

As inscrutable as the faces of the residents.

"Venetians seem to have a very clear sense of Us and Them," I mused. "Or rather, Us and You. Anyone who isn't Venetian is by definition a customer, brought for the express purpose of having money removed from their pockets. But like any people who spread out across the world, they're not fussy about how people claim residency. If you eat at a restaurant three times, you're part of the family. If you hire a gondolier for a season, you're expected to hire him the next time you show up, or God help you."

As we walked, as my reflections on Venetian history eventually brought me back to the idea of our luggage sailing off with a clever thief, I felt Holmes glance down at me in growing consternation. Finally, he dropped his arm.

"Russell, how are you so familiar with this place?"

It is very seldom that one can achieve superiority over Sherlock Holmes, but I concealed my gloating expression behind a serenity fitting of our locale.

"I'm sure I've told you that my mother adored Venice. She only brought us here twice, and I was a child, but we were here for some time, and she often talked about it—and, about this."

This was an island like any other in this tight conglomeration of islands, an irregular shape composed of a nondescript *campo*, or open plaza, framed by a single row of buildings whose backs overlooked the surrounding canals. The London equivalent of the *campo* would be a square of lawn with a fountain, crossed by paths and flower beds, with streets separating it from the facing houses. Here, the lawn was paving stones, the fountain was a well, and its landscaping amounted to a few trees and one hanging basket of parched-looking geraniums. Children played, dashing in and out of the doors of houses that opened directly onto the *campo*.

And not only of houses.

"The word 'ghetto' was coined—quite literally—at this place. The word comes from the Venetian dialect for metal—Jews were given the right to run foundries and pawn shops. Odd combination, isn't it, metal and old clothes? The Jewish quarter was shut every night, and patrolled to make sure its residents stayed in. And, one must admit, that Christian trouble-makers stayed out. Venice always regarded its Jews as a sort of business partnership, and even after Napoleon, they've continued to feel a sort of contractual obligation." I looked up at the building before us. "This was the synagogue we attended."

After a bit we left, over the bridges to the more polished and maintained districts.

Venice is small. A brisk and direct walk would have a recent arrival stepping off its far end in less than an hour. Not that one can walk directly—or even briskly, once one hits a tourist path.

But with a directional compass (internal or actual) and a pair of decent shoes, one quickly develops an instinct for which tiny cramped lane ends at a door, and which connects to another lane that goes through a *campo* to another passageway that debouches onto a minuscule *campiello* that . . .

Holmes and I made our way through the city labyrinth with darkness at our heels. When we stepped out into the relative vastness of the Riva degli Schiavoni, remnant of an ancient wharf-side marketplace and now the only open waterfront in this crowded city, it was momentarily dizzying. I blinked a few times, looking around to get my bearings, and was ridiculously pleased to find that I had overshot my target by only two bridges.

What's more, when we were shown to our rooms—a prime suite (the manager assured me, clasping my hand and exclaiming over how *perfetto* it was to see me again) rather than a baking garret beneath a tile roof—there sat our possessions, demure as if they had never even considered running off with the man in the steam launch.

A quick inventory confirmed that no one had discovered the secret compartment in the valise. I re-fastened its clasp and wedged it into one of the wardrobe shelves, as indication that I did not want it taken to the hotel's storage room.

The next order of business was a long soak in a great deal of hot water.

Chapter Twenty-one

WHEN I EMERGED FROM THE STEAMY CHAMBER, THE grime of travel scrubbed from my pores, I found Holmes on the dark veranda. He had clearly made use of the shower-bath in the suite's other bath-room, and dressed for dinner.

I sank into the other chair and watched the lights sparkling off the water: the public gardens far down to our left, San Giorgio Maggiore directly across from us, the Giudecca and the Salute down to the right, and bustling back and forth at our feet, a hundred varieties of water-craft. Just visible through the evening vapours was the twinkling Lido, with its stretch of fun-palaces, sanitoriums, and Adriatic beaches. And just to the side, halfway across the water, another island—what was that one? Not the cemetery island, that was to the north. A hospital?

Holmes shifted forward to crush out his cigarette, moving into the light from the room behind us. As far as I could see, his white shirt had only the faintest hint of a wrinkle. My frock, even after hanging in steam for the better part of an hour, had a sharp crease across the mid-dle. Well, it didn't matter, I would soon be hidden by a table.

At the thought, my stomach gave a growl. Holmes set his hands on the arms of the chair. "Shall we go down?"

I beat him to the door.

We had asked the manager to reserve us a table, and when we walked in, we were instantly whisked away to a candle-lit alcove.

Holmes watched the maître d'hôtel's eventual retreat, bemused. "Your mother must have made quite an impression, considering that she could not have been here more recently than 1912."

I smoothed the linen napkin on my lap. "Ronnie and I may have added to that impression, a bit."

"You and—ah. I did not know that you had come to Venice while you were at Oxford. This was after the War, surely?"

"Well after. And after Oxford. It was when Ronnie first learned she was pregnant. Miles was in Ireland, and she needed distraction. Since you were off in Baluchistan or Albania or somewhere, I thought, why not?"

"And you never mentioned it?"

"Well, did you think to mention Baluchistan?"

"It was Macedonia, and I did tell you."

"As you walked out of the door."

At the time, Holmes and I had been married for half a year, yet he had not hesitated to pack a bag without consulting me. If I'd happened to be away that morning, I'd have no doubt walked in to an empty house and a scribbled note. I was newly wed, and I'd found this cavalier attitude . . . irritating. When he returned, I took care to drive home the message that I was no longer his apprentice, but at the time, his blithe disregard had driven me to a secret of my own.

He protested, "Mycroft needed—"

"Of course. And when you got back, I told you I'd been off with Ronnie."

"I believe you said that you'd gone to see her."

"That's more or less the same thing."

"It is not at—"

"Yes, I would like a glass of wine, thanks." I smiled up at the gentleman lingering behind Holmes' shoulder, by way of reassurance that we were not about to start flinging the crockery.

Sensibly, once we had chosen a wine (which took some time) and ordered dinner (which took considerably less), Holmes did not return to the topic of unexplained travel. Instead, after some tiny adjustments to his silver and an application of butter to bread roll, he asked if I had any further thoughts as to a plan of action.

We had debated just this question all the way across Europe, without coming up with a firm outline for action. Granted, Venice was a small city, in acres and in citizens. And granted, it had a clearly delineated population of foreigners. However, simply to wander the *calli* and canals looking for Vivian Beaconsfield did not seem an efficient use of our time. Might as well take up a table at Florian's and wait for her to walk past.

So as I had done at various points along the train route here, I ticked off on my fingers the things we knew about Ronnie's aunt. "She's English. She's blonde. She's a lesbian. She's artistic. And she's more than a little unbalanced. Together, those make for a Venn diagram with a narrow point of overlap. Someone will have noticed her."

"Perhaps," Holmes mused, "I might take the 'artistic' sub-set, rather than the lesbian?"

"Agreed. Unless you brought along a woman's wig and clothing?"

"I did not anticipate an invitation to a *Carnevale* party, no."

"Pity."

Once upon a time, *Carnevale* took over the streets in Venice building up to Lent, but that was one of the things dragged away by Napoleon's conquest: forbidden by the humourless Austrians, forgotten under decades of economic malaise, and banned again during the Great War. Venice still held the occasional masked ball, but these were private affairs, beloved primarily by foreigners.

Perhaps, considering Lady Vivian's fondness for masks, I should add a sixth area to our search: the knick-knack souvenir shops of San Marco?

Waiters arrived with our courses, soup and fish and beef for me, with a curious variety of non-kosher sea creatures for Holmes. The restaurant began to fill, with voices in several languages setting the chandeliers a-quivering. The table closest to ours held our generational opposite: a dowager with a young man whom I did not think was a grandson or indeed any kind of blood relation, although he was most attendant to her needs and rewarded all her quips with a hearty laugh. Beyond them a quartet of Germans prodded suspiciously at their plates. The table on our other side was more interesting, two bronzed young Englishmen and a woman of perhaps sixty, whose beads-and-feathers costume suggested she was heading for one of those *Carnevale* parties. She spoke little, but lit up a series of thin, dark cigarettes at each break between courses. I bent my head to listen to them, curious as to her nationality, and caught the word *Fenice*.

"That trio is talking about La Fenice," I told Holmes. "You should go to the opera, while we're here."

"Is Lady Vivian a devotée of opera?"

"Not that I know of. But you are. Feel free to go, if you like."

"Thank you," he said, a trace sardonically. He knew me well enough not to suggest two tickets.

The taller, darker-haired, and marginally less sun-burnt of the young men was also the drunker. His voice continued to rise as our courses came and went. Just before the maître d' went over to invite him to lower his voice, he was embarked on a raucous and somewhat raunchy tale of a woman who held a party out on the Lido that involved a melonseed-spitting contest between a renowned pansy (his word) and the city's chief Fascist.

"'We'll settle the question of which tongue is stronger, or my name isn't Elsa Maxwell.' 'Cept the way she said it, the Fascist didn't even see that she was being rude about him and clever about the pansy-boy, d'you see? You know, like, the boy's tongue—"

Fortunately or otherwise, the maître d' swept up to the table and hushed the diner's suggestive remarks.

However, my mind was neither outraged nor amused. Instead, it had snagged on the woman he had mentioned.

"I swear I know that name," I said to Holmes—but from where? Long ago, far away . . . ah. "My mother! She used to know a Mrs Maxwell who had a daughter named Elsa, back in San Francisco. They worked together on some money-raising projects in the early days of the War, Mrs Maxwell being one of the few people who believed the War would last long enough for America to get involved. Although she may have simply been playing up to my mother. At any rate, her daughter was, shall we say, larger than life? Too large for the society of the Bay Area, at any rate. That story about the melonseed-spitting sounds precisely the sort of prank that Elsa Maxwell would have pulled."

Had I actually met the woman? My sense of her was oddly incomplete. Which suggested that either I had encountered her just before my brain was rattled by the accident that took my family, or that she was one of those people so distinctive in the words of others, one begins to think one has actually met them.

I suspected that we had in fact never come face to face. Still, my impression of her was vivid. Perhaps because at fourteen, one's sensitivity to unspoken judgments and the secret knowledge of adults is at a peak, and everything that was said about Elsa seemed to resonate with double meaning.

Looking back, I thought I could guess why.

"Holmes," I said, keeping my voice down, "I may go over to the Lido tomorrow."

"Good heavens. The play-ground of the rich and infamous? Why would you wish to go there?"

"Because among other things, if it is the same Elsa Maxwell, gossip had her as a lesbian."

"Are you suggesting there is some sort of a . . . a guild?"

"Of course not. But there may be a community of the like-minded."

Before we could go further with the thought, the drunken young man's voice rose up again. Holmes dropped his table napkin beside his glass. "Shall we take some fresh air?"

This time of night, and particularly on a Sunday, the majority of strolling was done up in the Piazza San Marco, with any pedestrian traffic here either on its way back from the public gardens, or on its way home to the working quarters near the Arsenale. The evening air was soft, with the largest noise a gentle tap of waves against stones and wooden boat-hulls. Light danced off the water. I tucked my arm through his and we strolled, paces matching, along the flat waterfront in the direction of the gardens.

It happened in an instant.

One moment the evening was quiet and warm and touched by the magic that inhabits all islands. The next moment, a slim figure hurrying out from a narrow passage walked straight into a pair of men headed in our direction.

All three staggered back, but none of them fell. I anticipated laughter—if they happened to be acquaintances—or else a rapid exchange of furious Venetian ending with growls and grumbles as all went back to their former paths.

What I did not expect was to have the man who had been walked into, a dark shadow of a figure, take a step forward and smash his fist into the slim man's face. The offender bounced hard off the wall and collapsed to the pavement—only to have his attacker step forward to kick him, then again. The sound was terrible, even fifty feet away, low thuds followed by mewls of pain. I started to move, but Holmes grabbed my arm.

"Holmes! That man—"

"Wait." Something about the urgency of the word stopped the protest on my lips. My eyes sought out the figures again, fearing further attack—but instead, the two dark figures stepped around the man on the ground and disappeared into the alleyway from which the victim had so precipitously dashed.

The grip on my arm loosed, and I hurried forward.

The man was already on his feet, head down and shoulder propped against the wall. Blood poured from his nose, but he ignored me completely until I had summoned enough Italian to ask if he was hurt. He shook his head, though that had to be untrue. But when he turned aside before the contents of his stomach surged forth, and he did so without crying out in pain, we were reassured that no major damage had been done.

He remained standing—supported, but upright. Then at my use of the word *polizia*, he gave me a sickly smile and shook his head again, making an effort to step away from the wall. After a moment, he shambled away. We watched him go.

"He was lucky, Holmes."

"Yes."

"But we should tell the police."

"Those were the police."

I gaped at him. "What? Those . . . thugs?"

"Did you not notice, there was no gleam of white shirt beneath their jackets?"

"Blackshirts?"

"Yes."

The dark alleyway seemed to crawl with threat and the sour stench of vomit.

"I believe I've had enough fresh air for tonight, Holmes."

Chapter Twenty-two

....

BETWEEN THE HEAT AND THE DISQUIET, NEITHER OF US slept as firmly as I might have hoped. We were on our balcony at dawn, watching the city creep into existence.

Shapes emerged from the darkness, shy, deceptive. Across the San Marco Basin, the pale front of Palladio's San Giorgio took on substance: a domed outline, the tower. Off to my left grew the hump and jumble of trees in the public gardens, their organic shapes foreign in a city where *soft* referred to marble and lead. The pale curve of the Riva degli Schiavoni described the water's edge before its route veered towards the Arsenale, that centuries-old ship-yard that had been the base of Venice's immense power. Venice was full of that kind of invisible pull, with patterns and shapes that only a knowledge of history would explain—and even then, mere explanation was rarely sufficient.

It was a city with a feminine face over masculine muscles. Where larch pillars sunk in mud held up palaces of Istrian stone—stone that itself was a product of the sea. A place where one's main floor was above the ground, where a thousand years of work could be wiped out by a wave, where a city ruler could be felled by an anonymous note or a labourer's family sleep beneath a Tiepolo fresco.

Venice begged for metaphor, and at the same time, defied any attempt at reducing it to words, notes, or pigment. For centuries, Venice had fascinated artists of the ineffable, keeping Tintoretto and Titian and Veronese busy with one attempt after another at capturing the essence beneath its surface beauty. The city was a poem one never truly understood, a piece of art that kept pulling the eye. This must be what music was to Holmes: a surface texture that suggested a deeper meaning.

The island across from me shimmered beneath the growing dawn. I could now see masts from the marina at San Giorgio's base. Closer in, a gondolier plied his way towards the Grand Canal, and I became aware of his voice, greeting the rising sun with song: "*O sole mio . . .*"

And with cliché, the magic shattered and I laughed aloud.

Chapter Twenty three

RUSSELL'S EAGER RUSH TO DEFEND A CASUAL VICTIM THE previous night had troubled Holmes, and rode his mind as he sat on the hotel balcony waiting for the kitchen to awake and produce tea. It was still dark, but at least the majority of mosquitoes had retreated to their niches, leaving a stray few to be repelled by pipe smoke.

Holmes was realist enough to recognise that he himself had not perhaps given Mycroft's warnings sufficient weight. But why would he? Mycroft's own government supported Mussolini. The Chancellor of the Exchequer openly praised *Il Duce*'s strength—although one should not overlook Churchill's history of party-changing and self-aggrandisement.

Keep your head down, Mycroft had urged. Perhaps now Russell might beware of the dangers.

The city coming into view off the terrace railings had always been a slippery place, as unsuited to straightforward investigations as it was to motorcars. No direct lines of sight, no firm foundation underfoot, not a simple Yes or No to be had. Façade here was treated as reality. A casual conversation would take a turn that landed a foreigner into a mire up to his waist.

What irritated him most was how it made him feel like a blustering Englishman, harrumphing over the antics of the blasted foreigners.

Startled, he looked across at his young wife, who had just broken the dawn's stillness with a full-throated laugh.

Chapter Twenty-four

....

HOLMES ASKED WHAT I WAS LAUGHING AT, BUT I JUST shook my head and asked him how he intended to pass the day.

He cocked an eyebrow at me. "Are we not here to find your friend's aunt?"

"I mean—"

"Russell, how do you propose to divide up our search area? There are three districts north of the Grand Canal, and three to the south. Further afield lie the Giudecca and San Giorgio Maggiore, followed by the Lido and Murano and Burano and several dozen other islands scattered across the lagoon. I should prefer not to be here until Easter."

Why did I feel as if this were a test—one in which I was not performing very well? "Unless Vivian has found herself a deserted island, she'll want a place she can blend in. We could begin with the San Marco area and work out, on this side of the lagoon, and at the northern end of the Lido on the other."

"Showing her photographs to gondolieri and pawn brokers."

"Well, she has to get around somehow, and she might need to sell the necklace, so yes to both. But also I'd say places with night-life. She used to love parties, and if she's re-visiting her youth, that may be part of Venice's appeal."

"If night-life is her joy, she should have gone to Paris."

That was certainly true: by last night's evidence, most of Venice still took to their beds well before midnight.

"The wealthier visitors, Americans especially, have taken to hiring palazzos expressly so they can hold parties into the wee hours. I could speak to an estate agent and see about holding a few of our own. Tempt her to come to us."

He did not quite shudder. "Those parties must endear them to their Venetian neighbours."

"Or we could sail up and down the Grand Canal at night, peering through windows?"

"I shall begin with San Marco, and keep an ear out for the sites of festive affairs."

He was being remarkably amenable. Suspiciously so. "Holmes, you don't generally volunteer for the tedious parts of an investigation."

"To search here through winter would leave me crippled with rheumatism."

"Fine, though do feel free to take in the odd matinee if you like. And I shall go and build sand-castles on the Lido."

"Metaphorical ones, I trust?"

"Not necessarily."

After breakfast, I went for a quick raid on a series of tourist shops near the Piazza—and, I will admit, some touristic sight-seeing. After lunch, I boarded a lagoon steamer for the Lido, donning my dark-tinted spectacles and holding my new wide-brimmed hat clapped down against the wind. The straw shopping basket on my shoulder held a book, a beach towel, and a packet of cigarettes that I hoped I wouldn't have to smoke. Nothing that I wore or carried was the least bit frilly or girlish. On the other hand, it stopped well short of bluntly masculine. I was not trying to look like a lesbian. My attire was merely . . . practical.

The Lido is a long, narrow sand-bar of an island that vaguely resembles a femur warped by rickets—slightly ironic, considering that large portions of it were devoted to Germanic hospitals and spas for skin diseases. In Shelley's day, it was a stretch of sand and thistle, inhabited by lizards, useful for a morning gallop with one's aristocratic poet friends. Now, to judge by the maps and what people said about the place, it was not likely that a poet could get his horse to a gallop without smashing into trams, pigeons, and sellers of lemon ices.

The Lido's eastern shore, facing the open Adriatic, was where its beaches lay, and where expensive hotels had been built to house visitors like those two bronzed young Englishmen. For those staying in Venice proper, a *vaporetto* remedied the problem by flitting directly from the Riva degli Schiavoni to the Lido, without having to bother with any of the islands between. When we had tied up, eager beach-goers jostled past me towards the electric tram, which crossed the narrow patch of land before trundling down the waterfront to the Hotel Excelsior, one of the most expensive establishments in all of Europe.

I did not join the surge, choosing instead to stroll along the shops, gardens, and cafés towards the shops, terraces, and cafés of the public beaches. There were not only trams on the Lido, there were cars—and delivery lorries, vendors' carts, bicycles, and all manner of transport that Venice itself lacked. It was busy, and noisy. The streets were crowded—and when I reached the shore, I found the beach even more so. Come August, the sand would be hidden beneath a pulsating mass of burning flesh, swimming costumes, and straw hats. As the road and tram-lines turned south, so did I: down the serried backs of a kilometre of bathing-huts, the sea visible in brief glimpses between them.

Then the road and tram-lines gave a jog, accompanied by a sharp division between the four-lira-a-day hired huts and the wide luxury cabanas that came with a room at one of the most fashionable hotels in Europe, where a night's stay cost more than twice what Holmes and I were paying across the *laguna*.

The Grand Hotel Excelsior was the Queen of the Adriatic, a vast Moorish pleasure palace, the darling of the modern set. Cupolas and colonnades, tennis courts and cabaret, cocktails and fireworks, sun and sin—and although June was early for the English contingent, the London Season still being under way, I thought the Prohibition-racked Americans might be eager to start things early.

Today's venture was by way of reconnaissance, since I anticipated that—despite the well-tanned skins of its two representatives at dinner last night—the Lido set would be more night-owl than sun-lark. I stood before the domes, flags, and minarets of the Excelsior, trying to make myself into the kind of person who would stay there.

It might have been simpler to walk up to the desk and ask for a room. However, if it turned out that the hotel was full, I risked being recognised as a non-resident in future visits. Anonymous enquiry was one thing, but for today, I would depend on attitude . . . along with a blatant but casual flaunting of wealth.

I reached down to adjust the heavy bracelet I wore: a sizeable cluster of emeralds and gold, that was actually a necklace left me by my mother, wrapped several times around my right wrist. From a distance, it looked like an amusing piece of costume jewellery. Up close, when the quality came into view, my blithe display of something that would pay for a London terrace house could not fail to impress. The shock lay in the attitude.

No one questioned me as I strolled into the hotel's vast and wind-swept foyer, my right arm reaching up as I passed through the beams of sunlight, green sparks blazing in all directions. I continued across the space to the beach-side doors, where I stood outside for a moment as if searching for a friend.

The beach-front play-ground before me was made up of groomed sand, substantial bathing-huts, bright canopies—and a strong wire fence down into the water that marked the southern border of the hotel's property. The private beach had been raked clean of seaweed and looked to be as much broken shell as it was sand, making a pleasant sound underfoot. The cabanas with their striped awnings were arranged in a semi-circle, and it was easy to see that the closer one came to the water, the more luxurious the fittings and attentive the service. The northern border of the beach was a long, well-maintained pier, while directly off-shore was moored a floating island, occupied with lounging figures. All up and down the coast-line, I could see a number of long, thin jetties stretching out into the water, to provide for diving-platforms and, more prosaically, to eke a few more grains of sand from each passing wave.

When I saw a quartet of crop-haired women dressed in brightly-patterned silken pyjamas and bejewelled sandals walk laughing out onto the beach, I knew I was in the right place.

At the third display of daytime pyjamas, I looked down at the frock I wore. Time for another set of shops.

I am not sure who was the more startled when I returned to the Beau Rivage that evening: the concierge as I came through the lobby, or Holmes, when I walked into the room.

Both, being gentlemen, hid their consternation behind one minutely lifted eyebrow, but only to Holmes did I explain myself.

"Adaptive plumage, Holmes."

"Ah."

"But also surprisingly practical as beach wear. The only sun-burn I have is along the tops of my feet." I gazed admiringly down at the peacock hues of my voluminous and assertively expensive silk pyjamas, light and loose as a personal tent. "They say beach pyjamas will soon be all the fashion."

"Russell, are you quite well?"

I laughed. "I know. But in fact, once I had these on, no one thought to question me. I spent the day flitting from one group of bright young things to the next—many of whom are hardly young, and most of whom are none too bright. Still, that made it all the easier to make an impression."

"To what end?" Holmes asked, then added, "And by the way, I hope you do not plan on wearing . . . those down to the dining room?"

I spread the outer seams of the twin tents, which between them could have given shelter to a Bedouin and his flock of goats. "A tad informal for the Beau Rivage, I agree. Let me go scrub off the sun-oil. I'll be right with you."

I was working the sand from my toe-nails when the bath-room door opened and Holmes entered with a pair of slender glasses. He set one on a small table beside the marble tub. Tiny bubbles suggested the Italian sparkling wine called Prosecco, dry on the tongue and perfect after a day in the sun. I took a deep swallow, then submerged entirely to remove the salt from my hair.

When I broke the surface, Holmes spoke. "Do we cross to the Lido tonight, then?"

"Actually, Holmes, I don't think so. Neither of us has the appropriate plumage to make an impression on the beau monde. You need at the very least a bright waistcoat, and I need . . . I don't know what I need, but I know it's not yet hanging in the wardrobe."

He made no attempt at hiding his look of relief at the stay of punishment.

"What was your day like?" I asked him.

"I'd thought it was tedious, until you trumped it with yours. I did establish with some certainty that Lady Vivian has not pawned or sold the necklace here in Venice." He had done so in a typically Holmesian fashion: by assembling a platoon of Venetian Irregulars. "The gondolieri are a proud and independent confederation. They go everywhere, see everything, and tell no one but each other—and their families. But if one makes them a proposition that appeals to their pride and their sense of humour, and particularly if one brings their sons and daughters into the matter, they can be an invaluable source of inside knowledge."

"You offered a reward for information about the necklace?"

"I did. What's more, I offered a reward for a lack of information as well."

"Really? How much will that cost us?"

"In money? Very little. In pride and laundry costs? Potentially a great deal."

I studied his downcast eyes. "You made a bet? With a gondolier?"

"I may have offered a small wager."

"Do I want to know what it involves?"

"Probably best not to concern yourself yet."

I sighed, and drained my glass.

When I was dressed, considerably more soberly than peacock silks, we made our way downstairs—but instead of heading for the dining room, we continued through the lobby, strolling arm in arm along the wide promenade to dine beneath the stars, where the pigeons had gone to bed and even a plague of tipsy tourists could not spoil the night.

We sat at a small table before the basilica, a scene that had not substantially changed since the day Marco Polo sailed off to meet Kublai Khan. Holmes shifted his chair beside mine so we could hear each other over the band's fin de siècle tunes, and we began to review our invasion of Venice.

"If Vivian did come here," I began, "then she brought enough money to live in adequate, if not Grand Canal–palazzo, comfort. If she came with her nurse, and if Nurse Trevisan does have family ties in Venice—and yes, there are far too many uncertainties here—then they would probably either stay with family or let a house, rather than go to an hotel." I waited for Holmes to nod, then continued. "Once here, she could do the sensible thing and live anonymously in one of the working-class quarters, where no one would notice her for years. Or, she could decide that having made it this far, she was safe. After all, she's broken no laws—the jewellery and money were hers to take, and the other small things could be debated. Now, I can't claim to know the woman, but I suspect that someone in her state would be pulled between the two. She would want safety, but she'd want to taste her freedom as well."

"Agreed."

"The Lido is a logical place for us to look. It's frenetic enough during the day, I dread to think what it's going to be like when the sun goes down. And if she and Nurse Trevisan are lovers, it would be a lonely life indeed if they did *not* reach out to women like themselves. Some of whom, I imagine, would be drawn to the foreigners-on-holiday atmosphere on the Lido."

"So you feel we may find her over there?"

"I was thinking we might take a room at the Excelsior for a few days. As you pointed out, the only things moving around Venice at night are bats and felines."

"And Americans."

Something in his voice caught my attention. "What have you found?"

"Less *what* than *whom*."

"But someone who might be useful?"

"Possibly."

"Holmes . . ."

"Do you know the name Cole Porter?"

"No. Short for Columbine? Is she a lesbian?"

"Not exactly. She is a he, and he is a young . . . song-writer, I suppose, rather than composer. I happened upon his work four years ago, in a musical comedy playing at the New Oxford Theatre. Dreadful rot, by and large, but the young man does have a knack for clever melodies and rhythms. The sort of thing audience members hum as they go out of the door."

The sort of thing Sherlock Holmes generally turned up his long nose at. "He must be doing well if he can afford Venice in the summer."

"No, he comes from money, and married a great deal more of it. The Porters have become regulars in Venice—they are among those wealthy Americans who hire palazzos on the Grand Canal and wear on the neighbours' nerves. According to my *Irregolari*, their guests have a habit of spilling out noisily across the city in the wee hours."

"And you think Vivian would go to those parties?"

"Perhaps not yet. But I hear that in Paris, most of Porter's house-guests have titles to their names."

"You propose that we'd have better luck there than with Elsa Maxwell and the Lido crowd?"

"I believe *I* would."

"Coward." He said nothing, merely taking another bite of his *risotto nero*, but I could see the crinkles beside his eyes. "Would you like to set this up as a wager? Since you seem to be playing the odds today. Your second of the day?"

"If you wish."

"For what prize?'

He looked off into the plaza for a moment. "What about, the next tedious task that comes along?"

That covered a wide variety of undertakings, from the boring to the disgusting, although the word *tedious* at least ensured it would fall short of life-threatening.

"And what precisely defines a win?"

"Finding the door that leads to Lady Vivian Beaconsfield."

"You're on."

He laid down his silver and put out a hand, and we shook in agreement. For a moment, I considered asking him bluntly just what it was he was doing in Venice—but it was such a nice evening, I hated to spoil it. Particularly when it was no doubt something I did not want to know. So instead, I returned to my earlier point.

"Agreed. And if you believe there's a chance we may find her over here, I won't startle my accountant by bills for a week at the Excelsior. However, assuming we find that door, we have to be well prepared to walk through it. In style."

He sighed. "You are suggesting that I submit to an eye-sore of a waistcoat."

"It'll be nothing compared to what I shall be forced into, Holmes."

That wince, I noticed.

And so, safe in the anonymity of the middle-class tourists from Dubuque and Berlin, we finished our meal beneath the warm misty sky, and strolled back through the peaceful evening, to prepare ourselves for battle.

Chapter Twenty-five

ON OUR WAY BACK THROUGH THE BEAU RIVAGE, I HAD paused to consult with the manager about my sartorial needs. After breakfast the following morning, I presented myself downstairs for the attentions of his chosen expert, a trim and intense young woman with his same green-grey eyes and reddish hair, whose gaze undressed me the moment I appeared (in a clinical manner, that is: less admiration than measuring-tape).

I told Signorina Barbarigo that business matters (unspecified, but with hints that they were substantial) required me to dress in a way that would impress the chic set over on the Lido. I told her that cost was no barrier. Then I said I'd need it by nightfall.

Her kohl-painted eyes blinked rapidly half a dozen times as she made an abrupt reassessment of possibilities. I braced myself for protest, for the wringing of hands, for sighs and wheedling and a lack of enthusiasm—but instead, got merely a question. "So, how do you say, off-the-rack rather than bespoke?"

I liked her already. "I'm afraid so."

"Bring your cheque-book, Signora."

We dove into the labyrinth of streets, her quick-moving, child-sized Cuban heels leading me through passages too narrow to walk abreast, along green and stinking canals and among the tables of diners and, several times during the day, in and out through the ground floors of palazzos. We paused but three times, to restore our energies—and, that I might engage her in conversation. Over coffee and hard little biscuits, I heard about her family back to the Seventy-fourth Doge, Agostino, who had built the plaza's ornately magnificent clock-tower (which she told me all about) and lost a number of key Venetian ports in a war with the Ottomans (which topic somehow did not come up). Over a lunch (fortunately taken at a table with a cloth long enough to conceal my feet as I slipped off my shoes) made up of risotto, meat, salad, fruit, and wine (which left me wanting a siesta with the rest of the city), I learned all she knew about the Lido crowd. This was not much, and mostly consisted of rumour and newspaper reports, since she was a good girl and disapproved of the foreigners' wild parties out there.

Finally, late in the afternoon, we settled behind a small table in a tidy little *campo* and ordered restorative food and drink. Across the pavement, a group of boys in juvenile Blackshirt uniforms were enthusiastically drilling, make-believe rifles across their shoulders.

I glanced at my companion. Her face was closed as she watched the lads, the oldest of whom might have been fourteen, but I took her lack of smile—either approving or amused—as an indication of her leanings. "Boys too young to remember the War," I murmured.

"Some of them will remember the fear. Venice took a lot of bombs."

And in ten or thirty years, when the resentments and unresolved issues of the War built into another one, these lads would no doubt be the first to urge their fellows to punish those who had made them lose face. Their mock drill ended with them setting down the butts of their wooden guns with a chorus of cracks, then raising their hands in an odd, straight-armed salute and shouting some unintelligible chant. Guns up again, they marched off down one of the *calli*—only to come backing out in confusion, ejected from the narrow passage by two men carrying a large set of drawers.

Our Camparis arrived, followed by a platter of fried objects. I took a grateful swallow, chose something from the plate that did not have too many appendages, and turned my mind from a dark future to a matter closer to hand: to see what my informant could tell me about Venice's lesbian *demimonde*.

"I had a cousin who adored Campari!" (Need I say that I had no such cousin?) "She used to bring a bottle of it when she came to visit, although I was too young to be permitted more than a sip. I wonder what happened to good old Sylvia? Last I knew, she was living somewhere in Italy. And she did adore Venice, I remember that."

"You should try to find her," *la signorina* suggested in her charming and perfect English.

"I really should. The problem is, she's . . . shall we say, she's rather the dark sheep of the family. Do you know that phrase—dark sheep? She developed a . . . a sort of friendship. With another woman. Sylvia always was a bit too easily influenced. I never thought she was particularly fond of that woman, and I figured that sooner or later, she'd come to her senses. But when the family wrote her off, it meant—well, where could she go? Poor thing! I wonder if the time has come to, I don't know. Make contact again?"

Signorina Barbarigo, though disapproving, was clearly taken with the prospect of rescuing this fictional Campari-loving cousin from the clutches of a wicked lesbian.

I looked up from my glass of blood-red liquid, eyes going wide. "Say, I don't suppose you have such a thing as a . . . a bar or cabaret that caters to that kind of person, here in Venice? Not that you'd have been there personally," I hastened to add, "but you seem to know the city so well, you might have heard of such a place . . . ?"

She had not. But the way I presented the question saved her from taking offence—and me from appearing to have a personal interest in lesbian cabarets. She told me she would ask her friends—and now, we had an hour before the shops began to close, what did I think about shoes?

When my stern taskmistress deposited me back at the Beau Rivage, she was every bit as energetic as she had been that morning, while I longed only to soak my sore feet and sleep.

And when I attempted to pull out my cheque-book, she would not let me.

"It was my pleasure, Signora," she said. "I will return in a day or two and see if the things meet your approval. And," she lowered her voice, "to tell you if I have any information about . . . the other."

And with a *click-click-click* of the precarious heels that she had not slipped off all day, she was gone.

Surveying the garments in the privacy of our rooms, I honestly had no idea what to make of them. That they were expensive, I had no doubt. That they fit me, I could see in the mirror. But were they what the Lido set would consider fashionable?

Not a clue.

Fortunately, the Signorina had provided me with a written list of what dress, or perhaps garment, was to be worn with which shoes, bag, hat, or scarf. As I puzzled over it, I wondered if she had got them mixed up—but no, she had taken scrupulous care over noting the precise details of each item before permitting the shop-keeper to bundle it up for delivery. Her instructions were such that even I could not mistake them, no matter how much I might wish to.

So yes: that long, silken orange-and-umber scarf was to be worn with the grey-and-umber dress—not as a scarf, but as a belt, so low upon the hips as to feel near to falling off. And the scarlet frock with the fringe hem? In the shop I had not realised that it was essentially a tunic with tassels, and that the moment I walked (or bent down, or sat—or breathed, really) my legs would be extremely . . . visible.

There was one I rather liked. What was more, I thought I could wear it without being overly self-conscious or uncomfortable. The fabric was a blue and silver lamé, the same blue as my eyes, and it was deceptively generous in its coverage, permitting mere glimpses of skin to slip in and out of view in slits along the half-sleeves and hem, but with sufficient fabric on the top that my various scars were out of sight. With it, she had assigned me an intricately beaded bandeau with a pert sprig of feathers, in various shades of the same tone.

Low black heels for the feet, a small black beaded bag for the wrist, and a silky wrap that she'd assured me would be warm enough even on the boat back—plus a touch of powder, kohl, and lipstick—and I was set.

An unattached woman in a Lido hotel would be a conundrum, no matter how I played it. My goal here was to play it to the mysterious hilt, with the object of establishing myself as the sort of puzzle one longed to solve.

As for the spectacles, well, those could just be another idiosyncrasy.

Holmes had not appeared, which might mean he was having trouble ingratiating himself with the Cole Porters. Cheered at his failure, I tripped through the hotel and across the promenade to the *vaporetto* stop, piling on board with an assortment of tired workers headed home and excited partygoers headed for the bright lights. Night was fast approaching, and we grabbed for hand-holds as the waves of another boat jostled us up and down. I smiled at the girl standing almost on my toes, who looked fourteen beneath the paint of a thirty-year-old. I firmed up my grasp, checked that the bag was still swinging from my wrist, and looked out at the busy water. A similar vessel approached, headed towards the city proper, this one filled with comprehensively burnt beach-goers, tired workers headed home to supper, a trio of brightly-dressed girls, and by way of grim contrast, two men in the unrelieved black of the Milizia Nazionale, their wide faces betraying how over-heated they—

I lunged forward so hard I nearly sent the painted child overboard, elbowing people aside, forcing my way to the *vaporetto*'s railing to lean out over the passing waves, trying to see . . .

But I was too late. If I'd jumped over and swum to shore in the other steamer's wake, I would still have been too late.

It couldn't have been he—merely a trick of waning light on a half-seen face, a silly consequence of my preoccupied mind. I apologised to my fellow passengers, settled my wrap, tugged at my lacy gloves. Impossible.

In any event, what would he be doing here—and of all things, dressed as a Blackshirt? It was a different man. A man who just happened to resemble Edward, Eighth Marquess of Selwick. Ronnie's uncle, Vivian's brother.

Must have been.

Chapter Twenty-six

SHERLOCK HOLMES, ONE SHOULDER HOLDING UP THE wall of the balcony, watched his young wife and the Venetian girl bustle away into the morning. Russell looked remarkably cheerful for a person who claimed to loathe shopping for clothing. He smiled, and took out his cigarette case.

To his surprise, he had become mildly interested in the situation—Mycroft's situation, at any rate. He'd come here thinking that a report on Italian Fascism was a task any journalist could have done, but moving through Venice the day before, he'd begun to realise the delicacy of the matter. Who was the Fascist here? The Blackshirt, yes—but what about the *Carabinieri*? The *polizia*? The mayor, the gondolier, the waiter overhearing conversations, the greengrocer around the corner from Fascist headquarters?

If a Blackshirt felt free to beat up a clumsy passer-by, what act could six Blackshirts goad each other into? And what might they do to an inquisitive foreigner? In his thirties, Sherlock Holmes might have welcomed an opportunity to match physical skills with a bully, but he'd found himself less eager as the decades went by.

He wished he understood the world's fascination with Venice. The city had long shed any position of import in the world's affairs, becoming an ornate and empty picture-frame, a crumbling play-ground for the rich and romantically deluded. Were it not for the sure knowledge of what was to come—knowledge available to any student of history, or even of basic psychology—he might even have some sympathy for the Fascist desire to clean the place up.

He did agree with his brother, that there would be another War. And he was beginning to think that the *Fascisti* would be at the front of things—although it was difficult to predict whether Italy or Germany would set the first match to the tinder of post-war bitterness and economic loss. Perhaps in the next War, more of the bombs would come down away from the canals and lagoon, and free up a bit of real estate, as the Zeppelins had done for London.

In the meantime, he had promised his assistance to both members of his family, and he did not think either missing aristocrats or loose-tongued Fascists would pass beneath his balcony and save him from looking. He crushed out the half-smoked stub and checked his watch: that third pawn shop he'd been to the previous day would open in an hour. Plenty of time for a visit to the steam-baths near La Fenice, to indulge in a nice, close shave.

Two hours later, he was back in the room: clean, pounded, chin shaved, moustache trimmed, and the owner of a new violin.

It was not a particularly good instrument, and in a dryer climate might set his teeth on edge. Here, the warm damp air softened the wood enough to give the sound shape. And once he had replaced its worn steel strings with proper gut . . .

The result was surprisingly full. Satisfied, he settled in to reconstruct Mr Porter's tunes—first, one he'd heard at the Winter Garden four years before, then the one that stood out in the New Oxford the following year.

Ghastly shows, of a sort he'd never have submitted to of his own will, but now he was just as glad that he'd been forced to follow a long-time (and now, long-behind-bars) quarry into those depths of human endeavour, the music halls.

Were Mr Cole Porter to raise himself up above that level of entertainment, the young man might have something to offer the world.

He put away the instrument when the sun had passed its zenith, and went to occupy his afternoon with Mycroft's tasks. Once, coming out of an antiquarian bookseller (a man whose brother was in the Milizia Nazionale), he heard a familiar voice and looked down the zig-zag alleyway at his wife. Russell was laughing at something her diminutive companion had said. She did not spot him, although he followed for a few minutes until the two women stepped into a purveyor of silks, and he left them to it.

He returned to the Beau Rivage in early evening, to leave the books and fetch the violin. Before they'd boarded the train in London, he'd known that Russell's chosen hotel would probably not serve his purposes—not even those that Mycroft had thrust upon him. Were this a British establishment, he'd have surreptitiously negotiated with the staff to come and go through a back door, but here, it was simpler to buy one's invisibility outright. So yesterday, after he'd set the gondolieri to their necklace-hunt, he'd continued into the darker, less salubrious corners of the city. There he found a room costing precisely one-tenth the tariff of the Beau Rivage, with approximately a twentieth the square footage and no amenities whatsoever—except for the invaluable one of relative anonymity. Not that people here would not talk—but the tight neighbourhoods of Venice meant that talk would take longer to spread.

His trip through the pawn shops had furnished the room with an entire change of clothing, hat to shoes—perfectly acceptable clothing, but of a sort that would have caused the concierge of the Beau Rivage to direct him towards the kitchen entrance. The suit was a touch old-fashioned, the shoes a trifle worn, the clothes more suited to a commercial traveller than a touristic one. Or, perhaps, to an itinerant musician.

By dusk, he was entertaining the diners at a restaurant very near the Grand Canal, waiting for a signal that the Cole Porters were passing by.

Chapter Twenty-seven

THE STEAMER THREW ITS ROPES OVER THE BOLLARD ON the Lido dock. My impulse was to turn immediately back, in hopes of catching some trace of the man who looked like the Marquess of Selwick, but that would be a fool's errand. Instead, I let myself be swept ashore with the rest, again by-passing the trams in favour of walking an indirect route across the sand-bar island. As I went, I tried to force the dark preoccupation from my mind. It was a face like any other. The man would not have dropped everything and come here. It had not been him.

I gave my thoughts a hard shake and shoved them ruthlessly away. Time to don my mask for the gilded set.

I have spent most of my life an outsider, both by nature and through the circumstances of my history. Divided between England and America, Jew and Christian, wealthy and not—even before meeting Sherlock Holmes, I'd had a lot of experience with forging identities to fit a given situation.

Sometimes, the best approach was that of a social chameleon, echoing a group's behaviour from vocabulary and accent to gestures and bodily stance. Intense and rapid research is key, and the higher the status of a group, the more precarious the act: one small class-related slip—a misplaced phrase, a moment's uncertainty over a choice of fork—and the switch of disapproval is thrown, forevermore.

The other approach is that of coquette. Not that simple eyelash-fluttering and the tapping of a boy's sleeve would suffice here: a crowd that included the wealthy and the politically dominant would be wary of, and amused by, any attempt at open seduction.

No, coquetry here would need to play on the weakness of this specific group. Namely, these people would not believe that any person might consider them inferior. Thus, they would be unable to resist someone who apparently did.

Because any woman who found the smart crowd dull must be fascinating indeed.

I directed my steps down along the backbone of the Lido, feeling the excitement build around me—and the closer to the great hotels, the more focussed the energies.

It had just gone ten o'clock. The guests were moving from dining room to Chez Vous, the Excelsior's cabaret that opened into the gardens. As I found the day before—and as I counted on tonight—no one seeing my garb and attitude questioned my right to be there. However, when it came to paying for the drinks I intended to order, that might be another matter. Not drinking would be a mistake; cash payments would stand out; I required a . . . sponsor, shall we say. Albeit an unwitting one.

So as I passed through the noisy crowd, my little beaded bag happened to slip from my wrist. I stooped to retrieve it—and came away with the key I had seen protruding from a rotund gentleman's pocket.

His attitude and that of his companions said they were in for a long stay. I found a seat at a tiny table, waved the key in front of the harried waiter to prove my room number, and we were off.

Three times over the next couple of hours I left my table to go admire the fountains or use the Ladies'; three times I came back to a new place, each one closer to my targeted group. I never looked bored, never looked lonely, never gave the least indication that I was uncomfortable with being by myself. I ordered drinks from the waiters, smiled into the flashes of hotel photographers, and nodded encouragingly at the band. I put on an attitude of contented self-sufficiency, as interested in my surroundings as any South-Seas anthropologist was in her tribe. Twice, I even took out a tiny note-book and wrote something down.

The most difficult part of the act was the young men who came buzzing like wasps around a lunch-tray. None of them knew me, since I had kept my face firmly tucked beneath my hat during the day, but all of them pretended to. Why do young men never believe that the world will go on nicely without them? A dozen times before midnight, a figure in a dinner jacket would appear in my field of vision, make clever conversation, and linger for a while. It was, in part, because I wore my wedding ring on my right hand, but even shifting it over did not dislodge the persistent. My second table-move and trip to the Ladies' was the only way I could free myself of the attentions of one particularly drunk and disbelieving baronet.

However, when I wandered back into Chez Vous, a couple was rising from the very table I wanted, and my programme of patience and bland ruthlessness paid off: the table was mine before my rivals could claim it.

I moved the chair a few inches, enabling me to see the dance floor—and more important, giving my target a clear view of my profile. I asked for another glass of Prosecco (of which, truth to tell, my palate was growing a bit tired) and concentrated on the dance floor with an academic eye. The table behind me—tables, rather, since several of them had been pushed together as the numbers swelled—was raucous, but unlike most by this hour, the merriment they gave off was not merely drunken blare. Actual conversation was being made—or attempted, at any rate—and although none of what I managed to catch was particularly profound, nonetheless it sounded a considerable step up from the gossip and back-biting I had heard amongst the beach chairs.

I smiled to myself, at the thought that this was the table I might actually have chosen to join, were I left to myself.

Perhaps that smile was what did it. The Gioconda sensation on my face had scarcely faded when a chair scraped back and I saw a figure rise to his feet and move in my direction. Just before he reached me, I stretched out an arm for my little bag on the table. My fingers worked its ornate clasp, slipped inside, began to draw back—only to have a hand with a sleek gold cigarette lighter appear before my face. A flame snapped to attention. I looked at it, then let my eyes travel up the slim, beautifully tailored arm to the shoulder and face framed by dark curls with sun-burnt ends. I summoned the enigmatic smile.

"Terribly sorry, I don't smoke." So saying, I finished withdrawing my arm, and waved back and forth the little note-book with its delicate silver pencil clipped to the cover.

His face was priceless. He let the flame detumesce. The table behind me erupted in laughter, but before he could turn away with embarrassment, I laid a hand on his sleeve. "It was very kind of you to offer, though. Thank you."

His flush faded, and after a moment, he gave a grudging chuckle. "Well, I can see you drink. Buy you one of those?"

"Thanks, but I'm married."

"That's all right." The flush returned as he realised how that could be taken. "That is, I'm not—look, I was asked to see if you'd care to join us. If you're tired of sitting by yourself, that is . . ."

I took pity on him. "Who is doing the asking?" I half-turned, to run a quick eye across the gathered strangers as if anticipating a known face among them. Thank heavens, there was not.

"Miss Maxwell." When I did not respond with the proper awe, he ventured, "Miss Elsa Maxwell?"

"I don't believe I know a Miss—wait. Elsa? Does she happen to be American? From San Francisco?"

"That's her." He beamed, pleased as punch to have hit the ball at last. I swivelled again to survey the gathering. Every set of eyes was focussed on our little tableau, even those who had been facing the opposite direction. This time, I permitted my gaze to pause on the face of the unlikely woman at the centre of the group's regard.

She stuck out like a bull in a herd of antelope: an unlovely woman in her forties with a large nose, three chins, untended hair, and a pair of huge and hideous diamanté earrings. She wore an exuberant sequined dress that made her bosom look vast, and a smear of carmine lipstick that might have been put on in the dark. But in that unfortunate face were a pair of dark eyes that saw every person and thing in the room. I felt her gaze eating up all the details of my life, seeing through the act, seeing beneath the assurance to the outsider—and caught myself: that gaze was a tool. The woman would know nothing about me that I did not wish to give her.

I turned to tuck away the note-book and pen, then permitted the young man to guide me around the conjoined tables. He proudly handed me over to his American hostess, who summoned a chair to her side and patted its seat. I perched on the cushion, and put out a hand. "You're Miss Elsa Maxwell? Of San Francisco?"

She was clearly accustomed to being recognised, but was less prepared for the second half of my question. "Originally, maybe. Not any longer."

"I believe our mothers worked together during the War, raising money to buy aeroplanes for the RAF."

The sharp eyes took on a degree of warmth, and more than that, of humour. "If your mother managed to get some money out of mine, she musta been a powerful talker."

"I think she may have been more interested in your mother's energy than her cheque-book."

Elsa Maxwell laughed—and that was all it took for Mary Russell to become one of the Lido set.

I was very glad that the mask I wore was so close to the face beneath: somewhat aloof, rather sardonic, impatient with idiots, and with a clear, academic interest in everything around me. I was also glad I hadn't tried to suggest I was a lesbian: those Maxwell eyes would have seen through that in an instant, and rejected me out of hand. Because—as I was soon to learn—Miss Maxwell was amiable with the shallowness of those around her, and only mildly impatient with drunks, but when it came to fakery, her rejection was scathing and absolute.

I would also learn that once a person had made it into Elsa's good graces, they were intimate friends for life.

The night passed in a blur of the powerful, the talented, and the simply beautiful. I danced, I drank, I even flirted (mildly, and a touch nervously: who knew when Holmes' face might appear amongst the crowd?). To my surprise, I had fun. Near to dawn, the band packed away its instruments, yawning waiters began to trade the night's linen for breakfast settings, and Elsa Maxwell's dozens of intimate friends drifted away to their rest, separate or together.

I got to my feet, numb and dishevelled, yet more content than I would have believed possible at the end of an all-night affair. I squinted out over the still-dark ocean, and wondered how long I should have to wait until the *vaporetti* started crossing the *laguna*.

I adjusted my drooping bandeau and held out a well-mannered hand to the lady in the sequins—who seized my arms instead and gave me a smack on the cheek with her garish smear of lipstick. "See you around?"

"Perhaps. Though I have to admit"—I checked for lurking waiters, then lowered my voice—"I'm not actually a guest here." I pulled the stolen key out of my bag and laid it on the table, tucking some lira beneath it to cover the drinks I'd used it to purchase.

My new best friend Elsa thought that was the funniest thing she'd heard all that long and merry night. When she had her breath again, she gave my arm a shake.

"Honey, you come back tonight. Anyone who can bring the Honourable Terrence Shields-McClintock to heel like that has my vote."

The Hon Terrence stood, grinning and tired, at her side. His father was the seventeenth-richest man in England, and Terry (as I had been instructed to call him) planned to stand for the next election. Elsa, chuckling, started to turn away, then paused. "Say, if you're not staying here, do you have a way home?"

"The steamers will go—"

"Terry, run her home, that's a darling. You'll sleep better after anyway."

His easy acquiescence made clear that when it came to an Elsa Maxwell command, one might as well argue with an avalanche.

Chapter Twenty-eight

....

OF COURSE, WHEN IT CAME TO ARGUING WITH AVA-lanches, I had far more experience than the Hon Terry. Had the man been inebriated, unwilling, or simply hard on the nerves, I'd have shed him the moment Elsa's back was turned.

But he was amiable, and easy on the nerves (and frankly, eyes). He was even relatively sober. Of greater interest, however, was that he'd been a Lido regular longer than Elsa herself: I was not about to let this one go without picking his brain.

First, though, I was required to pay homage to his boat. It was, in-deed, admirable, a long, sleek wooden vessel with two open cockpits, fore and aft, separated by a flat portion of what I took for decking until I realised that the engine lurked beneath it.

"You like her?" the Hon Terry asked proudly.

"It's beautiful. Is it yours?"

"Indeed she is. It's a Runabout. American. I had her shipped out a couple years ago, costs a small fortune keeping her up over the winter but it's nice to have her when I'm here." I permitted him to hand me on board, then watched him go back and forth turning on the running lights, which he managed without fumbling or falling into the water. He did seem to stumble as he came on board, his trailing foot lingering a moment on the docks, so I kept an eye as he stepped down behind the wheel and bent to adjust the mixture, quite like a motorcar. He did so without hesitation—and when he pushed the starter and set his hands on the wheel, I looked up to see that the little push his hesitation had given now brought our prow into precisely the angle of a clear path out. I grinned in appreciation, and listened to the throb of a well-maintained engine.

"That's a big motor," I said.

"Six-cylinder Packard, two hundred horses. Get you to Ravenna in a couple hours. Pretty mosaics there, you know?"

"So I understand." I watched him edge the controls up, threading a path through the hotel's small harbour into open lagoon.

To my relief, once out, he was content to putter his way towards the city itself, standing at the wheel so as to keep an eye for stray gondolas and packing crates, going just fast enough to ruffle his curls in a manner that would have tempted the fingers of most young women—but not enough to make speech difficult.

I did not run my fingers through his Byronic locks. I didn't even look at him, only rested my forearms on the wind screen (my wayward bandeau securely looped around a wrist) and used the remnants of my strained voice to interrogate him. The dear boy imagined I was being friendly.

"You seem to know Venice well."

"Been coming here since I was in short pants. I was a sickly thing. Weak lungs, you know? The Mater took me here and there, Switzerland and Spain and all over. Ended up on the Lido, and the old bronchials seemed to be happy at last. So we'd come here most summers, to set me up for another English winter." There was no sign of congestion there now—certainly his broad chest gave no indication of chronic infirmity.

"You must have spent your childhood longing for June. When did you meet Elsa Maxwell?"

"Interesting creature, what? Few years back, three maybe, she and Dickie showed up, just when things were getting a bit monotonous. Walked in, looked us over, and came up with a party. She likes parties with what you might call themes. Pretend murder, find the culprit—or alphabetical treasure hunt—alpaca scarf, bottle of gin, champagne glass, dog collar. Another time she sent us on a scavenger hunt, nuttiest list of things you ever saw. 'Course, things do tend to get a bit out of hand, so she likes to keep a few friends with cheque-books to cover bail and repairs."

"She doesn't regard that as her responsibility?"

"Oh, Elsa hasn't a sou. Well, maybe one or two, but not any real cash. All she has is energy and ideas. And you've met her—she's contagious, wouldn't you agree? There's a rumour the hotel tears up her bill because she's so good at bringing in the customers. I hope you're coming to the party she's getting up on Saturday? Ah, I say!" He reached down and switched off the big engine, which coughed in protest. "*We are even now at the point I meant, said Maddalo.*'"

He was looking at me expectantly. After a moment's thought, I came up with a phrase. "*And bade the gondolieri cease to row*'"?

He beamed in approval, and swept his arm at the night. "*A windowless, deform'd and dreary pile, and on the top an open tower, where hung a bell.*'"

I peered out at a darker presence in the darkness. "*What we behold shall be the madhouse and its belfry tower.*' So is this the lunatic island that Byron showed Shelley?"

"The very same. Creepy, ain't it?"

San Servolo was nothing but a faint presence—and far from iron-tongued bells or the prayers of maniacs, the only sound was the patter of tiny waves against wood.

"Hmm. Does it make a difference to know that a lot of the madness they dealt with—still do, for that matter—is because of pellagra? That as soon as the patients began to eat something other than maize, they got better?"

He thought for a moment. "That should help, but I don't know that it does, much. Poor blighters."

We rocked and listened to the night for a minute.

"There can't be any city in the world quieter than Venice," he said in a soft voice.

"Once one gets away from the Lido."

"Does rather bang at the ears, doesn't it?"

"Hard to think of Byron and Shelley riding horses along the beach."

"Vaulting the chaises and dodging the balloon-men? One can still ride, though further down, past all the hotels. I'll take you one morning, if you like."

"I'm not much of a horsewoman."

"They're not much of horses."

"We'd be well matched, then."

"What about breakfast? You hungry?"

"What, now? I'm not sure that there's anything open in the city."

"Sure to be, down at the port—but no, I was thinking of Chioggia."

"Isn't that at the far end of the lagoon?"

"Be down there just as the cafés open. What do you say?"

"Terry, sorry dear boy, but my husband . . ."

"Yes, of course," he said instantly, and reached down for the starter. The engine sputtered, nearly caught, then to my relief, started cleanly. The Hon Terry spun the wheel in the direction of San Marco and raised the speed—but I touched his arm lightly. "No need to rush. This has been a lovely night—and we wouldn't want to come across any modern-day Byrons swimming towards the Grand Canal."

He looked aghast at the thought and immediately backed down, eyeing the water ahead as I resumed my gentle grilling. He talked happily, on all manner of topics from the Bridge of Sighs to the making of masks to his fears that the *Fascisti* would sooner or later clamp down on the freedoms of visitors, and that would be the end of the Lido set. He'd met Cole Porter, went to a few of the Porters' affairs the summer before, but hadn't seen him yet this season.

"Swell chap, you'd never know he's from someplace like Iowa or Missouri. And his wife's a sweetheart—a little older than him, but what a beauty she is. She gave her first husband the bum's rush 'cause he used to beat her. Can you believe that? Even if you're stinking blotto, you don't hit a girl. Should have bumped the snake off, not divorced him. Still, the old gal hit on a prize with Porter. Clever devil, and tinkles a sweet keyboard. Pity about the socks, though."

"Socks?" It was a challenge to follow his American-flavoured slang.

"White cotton things. Ugly as sin. Makes him look like some kind of health nut—Naturist or vegetarian or something. Still, at least he doesn't wear 'em at night, or I'd have to write him off as a bounder."

I laughed, causing him to protest that Venice was filling up with nuts, Americans in sackcloth and sandals, greasy hair and all.

"Terry, I haven't seen a single greasy-haired, sackcloth-wearing American since I got here."

"They're about. Or they were. Come to think of it, they're fewer on the ground than they were. You suppose that's Mussolini's doing? Points to him. Which reminds me, I wonder if that Mosley chap will be here this year? Bet he'll be happy about things."

"I don't believe I know Mr Mosley."

"Oh, you must know Tom—Harrow's MP? Well, he was, I hear he's gone over to Labour now."

"You mean Oswald? Oswald Mosley?"

"That's right, but they call him Tom. He and his wife, Cimmie—Lady Cynthia Curzon that was?—come here sometimes. Not a bad sort, but Lord, don't get him started on economics! He and Duff Cooper don't exactly see eye to eye, which makes it smashing fun to watch Cimmie and Diana—Cooper's wife?—be polite at each other."

As a long and involved story unspooled, it was driven home to me that August would not have made a good time to come here. I can't say I moved in those circles (I can't say I moved in any circle, really) but in a country as snug as England, I'd had dinner, drinks, a dance, or a class at Oxford with half the names he mentioned. In August, I would not get ten feet before someone recognised me.

He finished his story—"And the topper is, the scampi was bad, and the next day he was sick as a dog!"—just as we entered the San Marco Basin. The city's lights gathered us in, the Riva degli Schiavoni looking oddly naked without its crowds. I pointed at a pier just along from the Beau Rivage. When he had brought our side up against it, I stepped ashore before he could switch off the motor or toss a mooring line.

"You don't need to come," I said firmly. "My hotel is just there." I gave a vague flap of the hand in the direction of half a dozen doors.

He raised an invisible hat to me. *"And soon the Runabout convey'd her to her lodgings by the way.'"*

"Thank you for the ride. I enjoyed it, very much."

"Any old time. Will we see you tomorrow?"

"If not tomorrow, then soon."

"I look forward to it. Sleep well, Mrs Russell. My salutations to your husband."

I let myself into a room that purred with the sound of gentle snores, and fell asleep with the dawn, surprisingly happy with my lot in life.

Chapter Twenty-nine

....

HOLMES AND I TOOK OUR BREAKFAST AT AN HOUR CLOSER to lunch-time, even here in Italy. My voice was hoarse from the previous night, despite some litres of scalding tea. Holmes, too, had been out late and was not yet dressed, his pyjama-ed legs propped on an empty chair, his cup and saucer balanced on his chest.

"What did you accomplish yesterday, Holmes?"

"I went shopping."

"Really?"

"I bought three books, two very old musical scores, and a violin."

"A violin."

"Yes."

"A nice one?"

He took a sip of his coffee. "Not particularly."

Instead of playing his game, I decided to tell him about my own day. It took quite some time, even though I omitted a few things for later consideration, or in case I needed to tease out of him why he'd bought a violin.

We'd moved on to buttering rolls and ordering more coffee before I finished.

"Interesting collection of influential people at that table," he commented at last.

"Yes, it's a good thing you didn't go—better to stick to the Americans, who might not recognise you. And I gather that Duff and Diana Cooper and your friend Churchill and his wife, and Diaghilev and Nijinsky and Coco Chanel and, well, half the names of the social pages come over in August. It is a sort of modern-day, round-the-clock *Carnevale*, with makeup instead of masks, and—with apologies to the Christian calendar—Miss Elsa Maxwell as the Lord of Misrule. Her forte is the organising of parties. Her art form, you might say—to bring together an unlikely group of people and give them something even more unlikely to do. Childish parlour games with a touch of sin. Tremendously popular with the rich and bored. Why a violin?"

"To attract Mr Cole Porter."

"And did you do so?"

"I did. In fact, I am to audition today for a party he is holding on Saturday night in Ca' Rezzonico."

"That's their palazzo?"

"This year it is. A Baroque pile even larger than it looks from the water."

"Wait, isn't that . . ."

"The one in which Robert Browning died? And John Singer Sargent worked? Indeed."

"Good Lord. What must that cost?"

"Eighty or ninety thousand lira a month, give or take. Plus hiring a few dozen gondoliers on retainer, and the servants, and the parties. One year they created a floating dance-hall with a jazz band—although, lacking a lavatory, it was short-lived. I imagine the Porters' summers here contribute a million or more lira to the local economy. To say nothing of what his guests leave behind."

"I can see why the authorities put up with a little noise at night. Is it his money, or his wife's?" Terry hadn't said, not directly, but one suspected that a woman who dumped her abusive husband did so with a cushion.

"He had money, she had more. She may not support him financially, but she does so in every other way, from social to professional."

"Well, our Saturday looks to be a busy one, Holmes."

He lifted an eyebrow.

"Elsa Maxwell, too, is having a 'bash' that night. In full costume."

He returned his attention to the bread roll, concentrating on an even layer of apricot preserves. "I refuse to attend in deerstalker and calabash."

"I believe it's to be *Carnevale* themed. Somewhat more glittery than a houndstooth Inverness. Not that you'd find one of those in Venice."

"One clear point in the favour of this city," he grumbled.

"Holmes, why is it you so dislike Venice?"

"It is a place of masks over masks. Only in the subcontinent does one find a people so cavalier about facts, where a Yes is so apt to hide a No. It is . . . inefficient."

"You prefer to keep the *vaporetti* running on time." To my surprise, his face closed up. "Damn it, Holmes, what is it—what does Mycroft have you doing? It's something I'm going to hate, I can tell."

For a moment, I thought he would not answer, and I felt my anger stir. Perhaps he felt it, too, because he put down the untasted roll and took up his linen napkin, methodically rubbing nonexistent crumbs from his fingers. "My brother wishes me to break into the town's Fascist headquarters."

Frankly, I hadn't thought he would reply, or I wouldn't have taken an irritated bite of food. As it was, I nearly choked before I convinced it to go down. "*What?* Dear God, Holmes, has your brother gone *insane?* They're a trained militia! Is he picturing the Blackshirts as some geriatric Volunteer Corps, marching along the cliffs with—"

"Russell."

"—wooden rifles or something? What does he think, they're going to let you waltz through their files-room?"

"Russell! I did not agree to do so."

"But you didn't outright *refuse*, either. Did you?"

"I merely promised to keep my ears open. And—*and*," he repeated firmly to interrupt my protest, "I did tell him that if breaking in were required, I would send for the assistance of some younger, and no doubt fitter, agents."

"Really?"

"I should not wish to be the cause of my brother's murder at the hands of my wife. Or, widow."

"Holmes, that's the most sensible thing you've said for days. But honestly, is that why you came? Because Mycroft wants a report on Fascism?"

"Kindly do not permit your voice to carry down to the pavements, Russell. Yes, my brother anticipates trouble in coming years from the followers of *Il Duce*. But since the rest of His Majesty's government find nothing wrong with an Italian dictatorship—and indeed, are following the movement with considerable interest—Mycroft requires a reason to start up an open enquiry."

"A reason such as, some fact his brother happened to come across during a completely unrelated trip to Venice?"

"More or less. In any event, breaking into the Venice headquarters would be absurd, since any important memoranda would surely be immediately sent to Rome." He resumed eating his roll. "Tell me about your admirer, the young man with the speed-boat."

"Speed-boat, yes; admirer—well, Platonic, perhaps. It's fairly clear the Honourable Terry's preferences run firmly in the other direction. He has a nice boat and pleasant manners, and more to the point, he let spout with a few rather predictable passages from Shelley that reminded me: the Venice lagoon has its own island madhouse."

He grumbled something too low to hear, no doubt along the lines of all Venice being a madhouse. I ignored him, pointing off at the water where an island stood between us and the Lido. "San Servolo is a lunatic asylum. I wonder if it's worth asking if a former Bedlam nurse has shown up there looking for employment."

"Not at San Servolo."

"Why not?" I responded, trying not to give way to irritation.

"Because the patients there are male. For a madwoman, one needs look to San Clemente."

How on earth did he learn these things? "Very well, I shall look to San Clemente."

"I shouldn't bother, they have neither admitted an Englishwoman nor hired a nurse since April."

I glared at him. "It's your gondolieri, isn't it? You got them talking."

"Gondolieri are the cabdrivers of Venice. They are everywhere, at all hours, crossing the lagoon even when the steamers have ceased operation. And when waiting for fares, they have nothing to do but smoke and gossip, like housewives around the village well."

"That and ogle passing girls."

"And not one of them has noticed a small blonde Englishwoman with a tall dark-haired companion."

"Holmes, Vivian and the nurse can't have been here for much more than a week."

"Still, it is suggestive."

"In the sense of suggesting she's not here? You may be right, but we've only begun to look. In her position, I'd have gone to ground for a time. And besides, your taxi drivers may have missed something. What if the two women have their own boat? What if they walk everywhere?"

His eyebrow twitched, one of his more maddening habits, and he shifted as if about to rise.

"Something else, Holmes." He subsided. "On the steamer last night, going over to the Lido, we passed an incoming boat with two Blackshirt passengers. One of them looked remarkably like the Marquess of Selwick." Before he could calculate the timing or ask the question, I gave it. "I'm afraid it's possible, just. I saw Ronnie on Monday. And I had to ask if she could think of any place in Venice where her aunt might have gone. I did tell her not to mention to anyone that I'd asked, but I didn't stress it because . . . well, I couldn't bring myself to say outright that her uncle might be stealing from Vivian. Might even be a threat to her. So

Ronnie knew we were coming here. And I'm afraid that, being Ronnie, she might have mentioned it to her mother."

"Who in turn could have told her brother-in-law."

"It's *possible*. And if he left immediately, he could have been here for nearly a week."

"How certain—"

"Not at all. It was dusk, it was a momentary glimpse of the side of his face, and his body was mostly hidden by other passengers. He only caught my eye because the two of them looked so out of place, but he was already in the process of turning away."

"Did he notice you?"

"I don't see how he could have. My *vaporetto* was even more crowded than his—and it could as easily be pure imagination, since he's been on my mind. But I did want to tell you, just in case."

His steepled fingers tapped at his chin a few times, then he stood. "My appointment with Mr Porter is at noon. He wishes to challenge my violin skills, to see if I am up to his needs for the Saturday party."

"Have fun, Holmes." I followed the sounds of his dressing with half an ear, staring out over the busy waterway. Steamers coming and going, gondoliers shouting, laden boats of all shapes and sizes weaving comfortably along—and closer in, along this singular section of waterfront promenade, a cross-section of the world's peoples.

For a thousand years, Venice was a cross-roads for commercial and military power. When it fell to Napoleon and became a pawn in the game of empires, the skills of that millennium did not die, but slipped beneath the surface. Its people, like any conquered group, learned to hide their true faces from rulers and clients alike. Outwardly welcoming, warm, and inclusive, in fact they were as insular and tribal as the inhabitants of any mountain fastness.

The gondolieri would take Holmes' money, they would give him good value for it, but they would not mistake contractual arrangements for family loyalties. They would sell him truth, but an edited version of it, appropriate to an outsider.

Some questions were better asked directly, of a person whose reactions one could see.

I spent some time with my maps and guide-books, then dressed, pushing aside my bright new costumes in favour of the wardrobe's more conservative contents. I added sensible shoes and a wide-brimmed hat and left the hotel—but rather than cross the Riva degli Schiavoni and hire one of the waiting boats, I joined the tide washing into the Piazza, and from there, into the shopping streets with the men out front waving bright goods and spraying us all with scent. I stopped in the place with the brightest window-decoration between the Piazza and the Rialto Bridge, and ordered three more beach costumes that I hoped Holmes would never have to see me in.

After that, I retreated into the nearest *calle*, to search out one of the clans of gondoliers that gathered along the inner canals.

The Venetian gondola was a form of transportation, yes—but by 1925, it was equally a Romance. Invariably, the more handsome the oarsman and the better his singing, the more substantial his tips from giggling visitors. My first congregation of men in the distinctive wide hat and blouse-like shirt of the gondolier was unsuccessful: every one of them eyed my approach with something resembling a leer, and despite my sensible dress, whistles followed my retreat down the *fondamenta*. The second such gathering was the same, underscored with a sotto voce joke that triggered male guffaws. At the third, I had to brace myself to walk in the direction of the half-dozen loitering figures—but then I saw my ideal: short, ugly, untidy, and built like a fire plug, with all his mass at the top.

He looked up in astonishment as I passed by his physical superiors to stop in front of him, assembling a question in hesitant Italian. *"Parla inglese,* Signore?"

"I spik some Englis', Signorina."

"Good. You look strong enough to row the lagoon, yes?"

"No problem, Signorina. I go to Lido, Burano, Mestre—Chioggia, even, with two."

"You have a partner, then? Er, *il compagno?* For a second oar?"

"*Si, si—Carlo, la signorina ha bisogno di un secondo.*"

"*Scusi,* it's Signora,*" I told him.

"As, Signora, so young! Carlo and me, we take you far and fast." Carlo was one of the less Adonis-like loiterers, young and tall but wiry rather than muscular.

"Not too far, and not that fast, but I'll need you to wait. Um, *aspettare*? While I am talking to someone?"

"*Si si,* no problem. We go now?"

"We go now. And your name?"

"Madame, I am Giovanni Govesi, at your humble service."

And with that noble declaration, he and his comrade-in-oars bowed me onto my cushions in his shiny black gondola, and we pulled away from a set of handsome faces wearing the sour expressions of men who realise they have missed out on something.

"You wan' the Lido?"

"In that general direction," I replied, unwilling to be specific while ears were still nearby. When we had wound our way out of the city "streets" and into the highway of the Grand Canal, I turned about in my seat to tell my driver where we were actually going.

"Signor Govesi, I would like—"

"Please, Signora: Giovanni. I am Giovanni."

I inclined my head by way of acknowledgment. "Signor Giovanni, I need to go and speak with the people on San Clemente."

The oars drifted to a halt.

"Is that a problem?"

Carlo and Giovanni exchanged a troubled look, then resumed their grip and their rhythm, with considerably less enthusiasm than before. I studied the older man's face, then decided to ask. "Signor Giovanni, I know what is on the island, and I do not want to cause you distress. *Dolore,* yes?"

"No, Signora, is no problem. Is only, the island, it is a sad place, *capite*?"

"Yes, I understand. I won't be there very long."

"It is fine, Madame. Fine."

I settled back into my seat, allowing the two men to get on with their rowing. As I'd hoped, my clearly demonstrated lack of their language encouraged them to talk easily together over my head. And although much of what they said was Venetian rather than Italian, there was enough of an overlap that I could make sense of portions.

"Do we really have to go there?" the younger, Carlo, asked.

"The pay will be good, think of that. And we'll be gone before dark."

"What if *she* is there?"

"Why would *she* be there, at the landing? Hot day like this, she'll be inside, or under a tree in the garden. Just don't tell her on Sunday that we came by without seeing her, it'll be fine."

I took care to keep all awareness from my face, staring off at the palazzos and waterborne craft.

"Just so *he* isn't there."

"When does *he* ever go to see her?"

In a chorus, both men hawked and spat over the side. I allowed my gaze to come up, with a vague smile, then went back to watching the movement around me.

But neither man continued with his thoughts about either the loathed *him* or the worrisome *her*. Instead they talked about one of their fellows who had been kicked out of his house by an irate wife when she'd discovered his second family—a story that gave me quite a few new vocabulary words and helpful insight into how a Venetian held secrets (namely, by storing them over on the mainland in Mestre) but which had nothing to do with San Clemente or its inmates.

The gondola skimmed past the Salute and across the San Marco Basin, ducking into the canal that crossed the Giudecca and into open water again, then straightening for a run at one of the larger islands ahead of us.

The Isola di San Clemente was (according to the maps) a teardrop-shaped piece of land with (according to the guide-book) a varied history: monastic community, pilgrim hospice, then quarantine island during various plagues, which supplied it with both hospital and burial grounds. After Napoleon, the island's religious were kicked off to make room for a military garrison, until finally, the hospital was converted to a place for the area's lunatic women.

We put in among the marking pillars, and I let Carlo help me out. A man appeared from one of the buildings, bare-headed and jacket unbuttoned. His arm came up as if in friendly greeting—but a swift motion at the corner of my vision cut him off sharply. The upraised arm descended; the man came to a halt. As I approached, I saw him look doubtfully between me and the two gondolieri behind me.

"*Buongiorno, Signora.*"

I returned his greeting, established that he spoke enough English for my purposes, and continued in slow and simple phrases. "*Signore,* my name is Mrs Russell."

"Amadeo Albanesi, *Signora.*" We shook hands.

"Signor Albanesi, I have a friend. She came to Venice in the last one or two weeks. She has spent time in a lunatic hospital in England. You understand?"

"*Un manicomio, si.*"

"Right, thank you. My friend travels with a woman, a nurse, who may be from here—from Venice, I mean—who is not quite so tall as me." I held my hand up on my forehead to indicate Nurse Trevisan's remembered height. "Brown hair, brown eyes, small . . . er, mole? Here?" I touched my jaw-bone.

"*Il neo? Si. No, Signora,* I have not seen one like that."

"What about my friend? She is small." Again the hand came out, this time at my chin. "Light hair."

"*Bianchi?*"

"Well, I wouldn't call—that is, I don't know if it is white. Pale blonde."

"*Biondi?* No, we have no new patient *con i capelli biondi.* Hairs of the blonde."

"But you do have one with *white* hair? A new patient with white hairs—hair, I mean?"

"Six, seven days new, *si.* Not English. Or, maybe. Not . . . anything. *Non parla, capisce?*"

"Lei non parla affatto? Neanche un po'?"

Signor Albanesi looked relieved at this shift into something resembling his own tongue, and proceeded to inform me that although, yes, they had a new patient, she wasn't blonde, but white-haired, and that they didn't know if she was English or German or what, since she hadn't spoken a word since she was brought in nearly a week ago.

I glanced at the doorway behind him. "Signore, may I be permitted to meet this patient?" I hurried on as I saw refusal on his face. "Or just to see her, for a moment. I could solve your problem, of who she is. Her family has money," I offered.

His dark eyes studied mine, then looked behind me towards the lagoon and city beyond. I could see him consider my request—which offered not only the solution to a puzzle, but a possible relief of some financial burdens, institutional or personal. He seemed about to speak— and then his face shifted, drawing in with what looked like dread, or even fear. I started to turn, but before I could see what attracted him he grabbed my arm, dragging me out of the light and towards the depths of the building. *"Venga, Signora—presto presto!"*

His urgency was such that I went along with him. Once inside, he by-passed the first door to yank open the second, trying to shove me within. That I resisted. "Why? What is wrong?"

"Signora, please, *cinque minuti* only, maybe ten is all, of silence. Here. Then I will take you to see your friend. But *per favore la prego, silenzio!"*

The door shut in my face, but did not lock. I heard him scuttle into the adjoining office, then hurry out again. When I edged the door open, I saw him walking briskly down to the *manicomio*'s pier, adjusting his official hat and doing up the buttons of his uniform.

I also saw my two companions scrambling to row away before the fast-approaching motor-launch smashed their delicate craft into the boards.

At the sight of the man who stepped off the launch, I drew back my head like a threatened turtle.

It was—no, be honest: it *might* have been—one of the men from the *vaporetto* the previous evening. I had seen both men from the side, and this could have been either—or someone else entirely. In any case, the newcomer, too, wore black: black trousers, black belt, black shirt, and a black neck-tie—with incongruous splashes of white in the shape of spats on his fashionable two-toned shoes. Shiny buttons and glints of silver on his collar suggested this was an officer's uniform, but he was hatless.

He must also have been hot in the sun, because he stormed impatiently past the island's ... guard? Greeter? Head nurse?—towards the shade. I retreated instantly, holding the door just a fraction clear of the jamb, my ear pressed to the crack.

The fairly one-sided discussion that followed was more comprehensible than that of my gondoliers, being Italian rather than Venetian, although portions of it were swallowed in the newcomer's rapid-fire speech and his use of words I did not know. It seemed that his appearance here was a regular thing—daily, apparently—albeit one he liked as little as the island's employee did.

His presence was due to a patient by the name of Dalso or Dalser, newly arrived and (according to Signor Albanesi) creating a tremendous uproar over being separated from her young son. "She screams, *Capitano*. All night and much of the day. There will be questions."

"And you people cannot deal with questions? *Bah*, these are women, slap them and they shut up. Are you all——that you suckle at your mama's tit?" I missed the word, but could tell it was a rude one.

"*Capitano*, I am married with three sons!" Ah: it meant *homosexual*. "But she is a woman, even if a mad one. She longs for her child. And I understand the boy is only ten years old."

"It is being seen to," the Captain snapped—at least, I thought that was what he said. In any event, it seemed to relieve Albanesi, who gave unctuous thanks—retreating thanks, as it turned out: the five minutes he had promised me were over. I just hoped my gondolieri hadn't abandoned me entirely.

Albanesi stood more or less at attention until the motor-launch was halfway back to the Giudecca, at which point his shoulders slumped and he pulled off his hat to mop his brow with a handkerchief.

Returning inside, he gave me a sickly smile and dropped into the chair behind his desk.

I sat down across from him. "That man is a *Capitano* of the MVSN?"

He blew a puff of air over his sweating face. "The *squadristi* of *Venizia* are decent men, most of them. When we receive one from *Roma*, well . . ." His shrug was eloquent.

"I heard him say he brought a patient here? Signora Dalso?"

"Dalser," he corrected, then stopped, the sickly look creeping back onto his broad features. "You did not hear that name, Signora. *Onestamente*, it will be better for you to forget that name."

"Who is she?"

"*Per favore*, Signora Russell. *La scongiuro.*"

I tipped my head, which he could take as an agreement if he wanted. "So, tell me instead about this nameless pale-haired woman who came last week. May I see her?"

He was more than eager to substitute one wayward lunatic for the other, although it took some time to make an arrangement with the actual staff of the *manicomio*. While he went off to do so, I went out to check the docks, and was pleased to see my two gondoliers, stretched across the cushions, chatting and smoking.

At least I wouldn't have to emulate Lord Byron's swim across the lagoon.

After a bit, a nurse came to inform me that the nameless patient had taken her lunch and was being led to a bench beneath one of the trees in the garden, where I was invited to go and look at her. I asked if I might be permitted to speak to her, and although it was irregular, the nurse had to admit that since no one else had succeeded in making any contact with the woman, my attempt could not harm anything.

But it was not Vivian.

The garden was a patch of dry grass and spent flowers. A dozen women clustered in the shade beneath the trees, talking—with themselves or others—and reading or gazing out over the lagoon. Birds fluttered about in a tall cage, their chatter and squawks not quite drowning out the manic speech of a couple of women and some cries from the windows overhead. The solitary figure the nurse led me to was, as the guard had suggested, white-haired rather than blonde. She was almost thirty years older than Vivian and with the looks of the Mediterranean—Iberian, I thought, rather than Middle Eastern. I settled onto the bench beside her, feeling her eyes flick up as far as my chin, then go back hurriedly to a study of her clasped hands. They were not the hands of a woman of the highest classes, and her teeth were in need of attention, but she felt to me like a person of a certain amount of education. I began with English. "Your family is wondering where you are."

No reaction, although she did not seem to be deaf. So I repeated the phrase in German, then in Hebrew, and again in one language after another, stringing them together to make it sound like one friendly and conversational monologue. There was a slight twitch in her fingers when I recited it in Spanish, so after a couple more tries—Hindi, Latin, and a rough facsimile of Japanese—I said it in Portuguese.

I got no further than, "*Sua família se pergunta—*" when her head snapped up. To my surprise, she looked not relieved, but terrified.

I shot a glance around the garden, hoping the nurse wasn't watching too closely, then hurried to reassure the woman in a mangled but apparently comprehensible attempt at her language. "*Senhora*, is there anything I can do for you? The nurses here, they don't know who you are. They only want to help. I won't tell them you're Portuguese, if you don't wish it."

She went still after that last reassurance, her gaze eloquent with question. "All right," I told her, "I won't give you away. But do you wish me to get a message to someone outside?"

A minute shake of the head.

"Very well. I shall leave you here. Although," I added as a thought occurred to me, "*Senhora*, I wonder if you've heard of another new patient, named Dalser?"

Her ageing eyes flew wide, then fluttered up past my head before she leapt to her feet and scurried across the sun-scorched lawn. I made no attempt to go after her. The poor creature was clearly terrified of something; I had only made matters worse.

But before I left the garden, I studied the building in the background—the building the Portuguese woman had stared at in horror before running away. Its windows were barred, some standing open to catch a little sea breeze, but from somewhere up there came a madhouse sound that tied this place to Bedlam: a long, thin keening noise with neither direction nor word. Like an animal in pain—or a woman separated from a young son.

No: I was not likely to forget this patient named Dalser.

Chapter Thirty

HOLMES TOOK A *TRAGHETTO* ACROSS THE GRAND CANAL, landing on the wrong side of a small waterway from the Porters' Ca' Rezzonico. However, a circuitous walk brought him to a bridge and the palazzo's gates. As the servant led him up a ceremonial staircase and through the stunning, high, light-filled ballroom beyond, Holmes reflected that this was a house built to make lesser mortals feel that the gods dwelt among them. The family motto might as well have been *sumptibus parceretur*, as clearly no expense had been spared: a site on a magnificent sweep of the Grand Canal, its architect the greatest one available, with a bottomless purse to tempt all the Names of the Baroque to decorate its many surfaces. Putti and tapestries, frescoes and *trompe l'oeil*, gilt and marble and crystal, a ballroom that could host hundreds—there was even a garden the size of a decent *campo*, unheard of in this tightly-built city. Ca' Rezzonico was a massive, magnificent, mind-boggling temple to excess, the cost of which could have comfortably set up entire nations.

Today, its occupant was a small man at a piano.

When Holmes was shown in to the inner room, just after midday, he found Cole Porter at a grand piano that in any other house would have been impressive, but here looked mildly apologetic. The pianist was making rapid-fire notations on music sheets propped on its rack, at his elbow a *pietra dura* table like a tapestry half-buried under a sprawl of newspapers, empty coffee cups, an overflowing glass ash-tray, and a cat.

The cat poured itself onto the floor and departed. The man kept writing, left-handed, wearing a dressing-gown and stubble despite the hour. His right hand stole along the keyboard as if under its own guidance. The melody reminded Holmes of something . . .

Yes: a song from that 1919 musical play. Was Porter even aware that his hand was picking out the notes of "I've Got Somebody Waiting"?

"You know what they call this floor of the house?" the younger man demanded without salutation, his slightly pop eyes squinted against the smoke from his dangling cigarette.

"In England we call it the first floor. Here it would be the *piano nobile*."

"Exactly. The noble piano, and here we are, in my cosy little corner of the palazzo." He plucked out the cigarette and stood to shake hands with his would-be violinist. "Morning, Mr Russell."

"Mr Porter. So tell me: did this noble instrument come up the stair-case, or was it raised by pulleys from the canal?"

Porter laughed. "The stairs—and they got this far and decided they'd have to take it apart to get it any further. But, how'd you guess it didn't come with the place?"

"If it had, the tuning wouldn't be going off."

He grimaced. "I know, I got a guy coming this afternoon—always seems to take a couple weeks for the wood to settle down. Bring your fiddle?"

Holmes moved a silver candelabra off the stunning table, trying to ignore the drips of wax across a glorious lapis columbine, and set his case there instead. "I did. What are you working on?"

"Can't call it work—I'm the laziest guy in town. And anyway, song-writing is a mug's game. You give 'em your best, and they knock 'em to the side, one by one. No, songs are a good hobby. I play for my friends and they don't complain."

"You're a bit young for retirement."

"People like me are born retired. Anyway, I was just playing around with some ideas. A musical, you know? About a kid who shocks his family by falling for a Paris actress. What d'you think?"

"It sounds the sort of thing for which Broadway is known."

"Think so?"

"Perhaps a bit . . . light."

Porter crushed out his burning stub in the Murano glass bowl, spilling ash across a king's ransom of inlay work. "Yeah, well, I wrote a nice serious piece—'Within the Quota.' Lotsa yawns. Didn't even cover its costs."

"Perhaps a satiric commentary on America's repressive 1921 immigration law would have translated better into opera than it did a ballet. A modern-day *La Bohème*."

"You *know* it? Jeez. I bet you've been talking to Linda. Did she tell you she had me doing fugues and symphonies with Stravinsky? At the Schola Cantorum?"

"Linda is your wife? I don't believe we've met."

"She'll be back soon, I'd guess. Yeah, those fugues nearly killed me—I used to sneak out to the Folies Bergère for some fresh air. No, I'm better at snappy love, the music and lyrics. Oh, and college fight songs—I'm hot at those. If only Broadway wanted football-love ballads. Catchy, finger-clicking music. You know?"

As the composer talked, Holmes had taken out his violin and set it beneath his jaw to check that it hadn't lost its tune—so he replied to Porter's question by dashing the bow into a climbing progression leading to the maudlin opening notes of Porter's song "Old Fashioned Garden." The younger man threw back his head in laughter, then pounced on the keys, adding flourishes of ridiculous complexity as he warbled the words to a tune that had sounded out of date when it was new, six years before. His voice was nasal; his playing was flawless.

At the end, his supple fingers continued on into another run of notes, uncertain and unfinished. "Problem is," he mused, "I get tired of shallow music. It's like people who are pretty on the surface but have nothing below." His fingers pounded a march down the keys, dull feet descending a staircase. "So booorrrriiing. Give me a song with layers to it—or a person who's pretty on the surface but smart or clever or even vicious underneath . . ." The illustrating tune shifted to a light but minor-chord tinkle, the sort of music to warn an audience in a picture house. "Now, *that* kind of person *does* something to me."

Violence, perhaps? thought Holmes.

"Of course, a pretty face with a brain behind it—like Linda—or a song that sounds simple until you start to think about it . . . those are worth spending time on."

"That is true for many kinds of art. Poetry certainly. Japanese prints. Fairy tales."

"You're right about that last. Some of those fairy tales—all very well and good till the lights went off and then, *wow!* Used to give me nightmares. Red Riding Hood's grandma gobbled up by a wolf. Sleeping Beauty poisoned by her own stepmother. I remember lying awake in my bed wondering what the hell Goldilocks was doing in the woods all on her own."

"Along with Hansel and Gretel, it is one of several variations on the Babes in the Wood story."

"Babes in the wood, eh? Catchy."

"Two wealthy orphans are given to a greedy uncle, who decides to have them killed, only to have the soft-hearted hired murderers abandon them in the forest instead."

Porter reached for his cigarettes. "And some creature finds them and raises them, so they can grow up and take their revenge, right?"

"Actually, in the original story the children die and the woodland creatures cover their bodies with leaves."

The cigarette lingered, unlit. "Not sure I don't like it better my way."

"Broadway would," Holmes said dismissively. "Now, have you decided what sort of music you want on Saturday? Porter? Mr Porter?"

The pianist absently discarded the unlit cigarette and picked up his pencil instead, pawing through the sheet music for a blank page.

Half an hour later, having filled his eyes with Tiepolo and Colonna, with Allegories and gods and the family pope, Holmes heard his name echo along the *piano nobile*. He made his way back through the live-in museum to the composer, who was still on the piano bench, looking cross. "I thought you were here to work?" Porter demanded.

"I was allowing you to think," Holmes replied mildly. "Shall we continue?"

They worked—if *work* described it—for a couple of hours before Cole's wife swept in, tut-tutting at his unshaven face and silken gown. Linda turned out to be American, too, with a well-tended Kentucky drawl and an air of brooking absolutely no nonsense when it came to her husband's comfort or his work.

It was instantly clear that Cole adored her—worshipped her, needed her, and consulted her on everything. Including, or so the gondoliers' rumour had it, his liaisons with pretty young men. "Mr Russell, you know my wife?"

Holmes rose as Linda came into the salon. "I have not had the pleasure."

"What? Linda, there's someone in this fair city you haven't laid claim to? Linda, this is Sheldon Russell, fiddler supreme—you'll find he has lovely manners. Mr Russell, Linda Porter, the queen of my heart, the tyrant of my schedule, you'll come to love her despite her frightening abilities—all my friends fall in love with her, don't they, dearest?"

"Good to meet you, Mrs Porter. Mr Porter, I'll be off now, let me know if you'd like me to—"

"Oh you can't go, I forbid it, we've hardly started."

"Cole, dear, lunch is in nine minutes, Gerald and Sara are starving, and that strange little prince fellow who followed you in yesterday is here. And before you ask, no, you can't come to lunch in your dressing-gown."

"I'm running, see me go? But surely we can throw another plate on the table? Mr Russell and I are having such a good time."

"Oh, I wouldn't think of—" Holmes began.

"Don't you dare put that violin away! No, Linda, I'm not going up until he's agreed to stick around, even if Gerald starves. Mr Russell, you must stay for a musical afternoon. Ignore your commitments, fling your proper behaviour to the wind: I require your strings."

The young man's pop eyes made him resemble a puppy begging for a treat, and Holmes, amused in spite of himself, appeared to relent. "Very well, let us misbehave. Although I've—"

"Hah—yes, Linda, I'm gone!" And he was.

"—eaten quite recently," Holmes finished, turning a quizzical look on Linda. The wife merely shook her head in affection, so he laid his instrument down and stepped forward—but instead of shaking her outstretched hand, he bent over it at a courtier's nicely judged distance: to actually touch lips to fingers would be the act of a sycophant or gigolo, while too many inches' distance carried a threat of disdain. Her quick smile as he straightened told her he'd read her correctly. She pulled a cigarette from Cole's enamel case, allowing him to light it.

"Mr Russell, what have you and my husband been getting up to this morning? No good, I hope?" She settled decoratively onto a brocade settee, leaving him to perch at the edge of its matching chair.

"We ran through some songs that may crop up on Saturday, but he kept getting side-tracked into ideas. I understand he's working on a Broadway revue."

One perfectly shaped eyebrow went up. "Is he?"

Holmes made haste to back-pedal, lest he be seen as encroaching onto her sphere of influence. "Oh my, I hope I'm not giving away something he was planning for you. You'll act surprised, I hope?"

Her ruffled feathers went down a bit. "I'll try my best."

"In any event, I expect that 'working on a revue' is an exaggeration—more like exercising his fingers. I was actually wondering if he didn't want to try something more classical."

This led to Linda's deprecating story about how she'd tried to convince Cole to work with Igor Stravinsky and a description of his successes at the Schola Cantorum (placing rather more weight on the school than Porter himself had), followed by her husband's short, politically-inspired ballet, which had been a rather greater success in Paris than it was at home.

Through her chatter, Holmes took great care not to appear that he was trying hard to please her. He countered some of her points, kept his laughter polite rather than effusive, and made it clear that when it came to Cole Porter, this visitor was interested only in a musical friendship.

Then Porter came back, shaven and sleek, and kissed his wife and took his new accompanist out to the palazzo garden for luncheon. By the end of the afternoon, Holmes had received the royal warrant of appointment to the Porter household.

The next step would be to see the Porters' list of invitations for Saturday night.

Chapter Thirty-one

....

AS WE SURGED BACK ACROSS THE LAGOON, MOVING WITH more enthusiasm than on the way out, I covertly studied the second oarsman, young Carlo. The shirt he wore was of a sufficiently coarse weave that it retained its shape even when damp—unlike the light and clinging upper garments worn by his more preening brothers. Nonetheless, the boy had muscle. More than that, he had the knack of motion, a quick beat at the end of each stroke that powered the craft forward. A gondola was entirely different from a punt—a lithe enamelled craft rowed by long oars rather than a blunt and heavy canal boat propelled by pushing with a pole—and yet, there was a similarity in the finial gesture of expertise.

Watching Carlo brought to mind Holmes' mention of a wager with his gondolieri Irregulars—and that gave me an idea.

I gathered myself on the cushions to look behind me at Giovanni. His position at the stern of the gondola was the command one; the second oarsman provided more power. I studied his stance, his easy steering, the positions of his arm—making him nervous indeed. His rhythm faltered as he gave me an uncertain look, then consulted word-lessly over my shoulder with his junior.

"Signora, is there a problem?"

"No no, not in the least. I'm just interested in the way the gondola is rowed. In England, we sit in the centre with two short oars. We also have long, shallow boats—you understand 'shallow'?" I held my hands fifteen inches apart to illustrate the depth. "We call them 'punts,' but because we use them on rivers that are not very deep—sometimes canals—we use a pole, a long stick, to push off the bottom."

"Ah, punt, yes, I have heard of this. Young boys take their girlfriends, yes?"

"Sometimes. And often fall in." Both men laughed, and their strokes picked up again—until I made my request. "May I try?"

The rights of women had not made it as far as the Venice lagoon. Giovanni looked shocked. Behind me came a spluttering sound. But I had chosen my time with care: we were in the lee of Santa Maria della Grazia. There were few boats here at present, and no gondolas visible through the haze off the water. I stood, taking care not to rock the vessel in the least, and stepped over the seat-back, holding out my hand for Giovanni's oar.

As usual with men, be they Boy Scouts or gondoliers, he had no defence against a woman who assumed command. He drew back as if I were infectious, causing me to grab for the precariously balanced oar. He seemed to be waiting—for me to admit I was kidding, or to erupt into shrill giggles, or perhaps simply to tumble with a shriek over the side, I don't know which. Instead, I braced my feet in the same places his had stood, and positioned my hands on the long oar.

I glanced up at him. "You might want to sit."

When he had edged past me to the cushions—Carlo, too, hastened to ship his oar and abandon the vulnerable standing position—I tried out the oar. The first stroke pushed the boat's nose around like the hands of a clock, causing the professionals to *tsk* even as they looked relieved at my incompetence.

I crabbed the oar a few times before I managed to return the metal cock's comb at the prow in the right direction. Without looking down at my bemused passengers, I presented my offer. "Let us make a wager. If I manage to get us to San Giorgio without mishap, you will tell me about the woman you know on San Clemente."

The two exchanged a look that was a mix of uneasiness and disbelief. "And, Signora, if you do not?"

"Then I shall double the day's fees."

After another wordless consultation, Giovanni nodded. "*Si.*" Amused now, he turned to take up his regal position on the seat, mocking the attitude of a proud tourist.

And I started rowing in earnest.

It was slow, at first. The high perch was more like the Cambridge style of punting than Oxford's, and my hands were slow to perfect the delicacy of the steering process. But the weight of two men in the gondola's belly helped stabilise our course, and after that it was more a matter of muscle power.

In minutes, my arms were burning. The upright peg used to brace the oar for its push offered little control, turning the craft's lithe darting into a clumsy forward shamble. The intended snap of power at the end of the stroke deteriorated as my forearms gave out, leaving the work to the less flexible but more authoritative shoulder muscles. Sweating, quivering, and parched, I plugged methodically on. San Giorgio inched slowly closer. I thanked all the gods of Italy that the tide was not on its way out, for we'd have been flushed back past San Clemente and into the Adriatic in no time at all. Onwards, aching, cramping, numb . . .

Finally, Giovanni took pity on me. Or perhaps he spotted the approaching gondola and dared not risk the mockery of his fellows, I don't know, but he stood, wordlessly gesturing me to stop. I did so, my hands beyond feeling the wooden grip.

And he smiled.

He helped me back into my rightful place, dropped a stoppered bottle of warm water into my lap, and resumed his position. Carlo, too, rose to his oar. In moments, we were skimming towards Venice proper.

My fingers managed to extract the cork. I poured water down my throat. I sat as we slid between San Giorgio and the Giudecca, and out into the San Marco Basin. Just before I stirred, to remind him of our bet, Giovanni spoke.

"My sister, the mother of Carlo, she is there in that place. Her husband"—both men paused to hawk and spit over the side—"came into money. Not a lot, but money. And so he has a pretty young girl, in Mestre, and my sister, she gets a little angry one day as she is making ravioli and hits him with her ravioli pin. He shout, the *polizia* come, and my sister, she keep hitting, and so . . . We think, San Clemente a good place to rest, to be calm, *si?* But her husband"—again the noisy demonstration of disgust—"he pay to keep her there. The judge agree, because she hit the *polizia,* and because the judge a friend of her husband"— it seemed as automatic a gesture as the sign of the cross—"she stay there."

"For how long?"

"Two year, three month."

"Good Lord. Can't you get another judge to hear the case?"

"He will not. Her husband"—hawk; spit—"is now member of Milizia Nazionale."

A Blackshirt. Was that him on the launch? No—the *Capitano* was too young. Still, the mere sight of his clothing would explain why they had hurried to get out of its way.

Near the entrance to the Grand Canal, Giovanni asked where I wished to go.

I pointed ahead of us, just past San Marco. "I'm staying at the Beau Rivage."

He corrected our angle, and soon put in amongst the forest of pilings. Carlo held us against the dock as Giovanni handed me up and out, waiting politely as I retrieved money from my purse. I added a dignified sum on top, to make up for the blow his masculinity had suffered in turning his boat over to a woman, then paused, purse in hand.

"Giovanni, would you like to work for me for a few days? *Esclusivamente?*"

The negotiations took a while, and had they been written down would have had enough codicils and amendments to satisfy an Inner Temple barrister, but in the end, I had a pair of taxi drivers available to me day or night, at a daily rate that would be added to depending on how much and at what time I required their service. I handed over the first day's fee and wrote down his instructions on how a message might reach him, day or night. We three shook hands, and parted amidst the consternation of half a dozen more handsome and more decoratively dressed gondolieri, who were clearly wondering what I saw in these two poorly-turned-out examples of their breed. And though I hadn't specified that their contractual obligations included complete discretion, I thought I might have gained it, regardless, if for no reason other than their pleasure of keeping secrets from their fellows.

Back at the hotel, I called for food, drink, and a large bowl of ice for the swelling in my pained hands. I sated my gut, soothed my hands, sluiced the day's soil off the rest of me, and finally stretched out to read what Mark Twain had to say about Venice. Three lines in, I fell into a dark and bottomless hole.

Chapter Thirty-two

HOLMES DRAGGED ME FROM THE DARK HOLE NO MORE than two minutes later. I cursed him under my breath, then gasped as I tried to shift the huge weight of my body on the bed: somebody had lit me on fire.

"What is wrong with you?" My unfeeling husband had crashed in, thrown what sounded like a full drum set onto the marble floor, and set off a Niagara in the bath-room taps.

"Oh God," I wheezed. "I've strained every muscle in my body." Even the arches of my feet felt pulverized.

"What was that?" His huge bellow echoed through the room, or perhaps just through my skull. I moaned. When he dropped onto the edge of the bed so as to hear me, the reverberations made me whimper. "Russell, are you injured?"

To give him credit, he did by now sound a bit concerned, although less than he might have been if he'd actually seen blood on the floor. Cautiously, I worked myself up a little on the pillows, trying to ease my burning neck and shoulders. "Holmes, have you ever rowed a gondola?"

The heartless scoundrel actually laughed. "Oh, yes. It makes use of muscles one didn't realise one had. Let me add some more heat to the bath."

He dumped a hefty dose of brandy into a glass and placed it in my hand. When it was gone and the bath-tub filled, he helped me stand, helped me cross the room, helped me into the water.

More brandy; two aspirin; heat.

Twenty minutes later, I thought I might live.

The shower-bath next door ran for a while. He came back in, gleaming and shaven, carrying a third dose of painkiller, and turned on the hot tap for a while—too long a while, in fact.

"Stop, Holmes—I feel like the entrée in a cannibal feast."

He closed the tap. "How far did you row?"

"From Santa Maria to the start of San Giorgio."

"Then I imagine you're more than ready for dinner. Shall I have it brought up?"

"I just ate a platter of sandwiches. Wait: is it dark already?"

"It has been for some time."

I'd slept for considerably more than two minutes. Long enough that dinner on our terrace, without having to struggle into formal dress, sounded an excellent idea.

From soup to nuts, I slowed down only as I approached the *zabaglione*. The waiters, who had been in and out serving the various courses, poured our coffee and left us to the night.

I felt nearly human.

Holmes propped up his heels and balanced his coffee atop his thighs, a manoeuvre that would have me leaping up from the scalding liquid in my clothing. I set my own cup on the table beside my chair, and enjoyed the lack of pain.

"You appear to have missed the last *vaporetto* to the Lido," he noted.

"Not tonight. And lest you think it's because I'm exhausted, I decided against it *before* the day's adventures. Best not to appear too eager." Or—yes—to collapse face-down on the table. And before I did so here—"Holmes, can you get a coded message to your brother?"

"Rather than a trunk call?"

"I may be a touch paranoid, but I don't imagine dictators would hesitate to listen in on international telephone calls. And when it involves the lives of innocents . . ."

"What do you need?"

"There's a woman named Dalser in the San Clemente asylum who has something to do with the Fascists. I don't know her first name, but the mere mention of her makes the residents sweat with terror. And, there's a militia Captain who comes all the way out to the island for a daily report on her."

"Suggestive."

"And while you're wiring to Mycroft, could you also ask him to check on the whereabouts of the Marquess? I don't really think it was Lord Selwick I saw, but still, I'd be happier to know he's in England."

Without comment, he set his cup on the table and went to find paper and pencil, to compose a coded message that seven hundred miles and three languages' worth of telegraphist could not render impenetrable.

In sympathy to the cause, I forced my body to stay upright and vaguely conscious until he went off to send it.

I did not hear about Holmes' day until Thursday morning, as we sat on our balcony watching the modern-day Canaletto come to life on the San Marco Basin before us. It was still reasonably early, and I'd soaked the residue of stiffness from my shoulders before the rattle of our breakfast tray roused me from the bath.

"I was too weary last night to ask about your day." I concentrated on manoeuvring a large dollop of grapefruit marmalade onto a crescent roll.

"Unlike yours, mine was harder on the liver and lungs than on the muscles. I spent most of it at the Cole Porters', in occasional musical interludes intruded upon by a constant tide of rich and titled visitors, American and European."

I'd caught a whiff of his discarded clothing when I opened the wardrobe, its fabric ripe with cigarettes, strong drink, and—oddly—women's perfume. "I hope for your sake the music was bearable." I aimed the laden bread at my face.

"Much of it was not to my taste; however, it was eminently bearable."

My mouth being occupied, I could only look a question at him: Holmes tended to be unforgiving when it came to music. Also when it came to much else in life, true, but particularly music.

"Mr Porter, despite being a remarkably talented young man, wishes nothing better than to write light musical pieces for the theatre. Songs, rather than sonatas. And he chooses to build those songs around the stuff of infatuation: champagne and shining hair, a longing gaze and a bit of witty repartee."

I replied, somewhat stickily, "We can't all be gloomy Germans, Holmes. Especially not young men married to wealthy and indulgent women."

"Yes, it's easy to think of Porter as a dilettante—and indeed, he pretends his interest is superficial. However, I've seen a slavey put less effort into scrubbing her steps with the housekeeper looking on than Porter does when no one's in earshot. And though it is true Linda encourages him, it is more than mere indulgence."

"That's his wife? Linda?"

"Yes. An interesting relationship. One of considerable affection, and yet, by all appearances and much local gossip, the marriage is a 'lavender' one."

I coughed on a bit of bread—I wouldn't have imagined he even knew the phrase. "An arrangement of . . . convenience?"

"Hmm."

"Does she suspect?"

"Oh, I'd say she is quite aware of his outside interests."

"Good Lord. Oh, the poor thing."

He stirred his coffee as he considered his reply. "Russell, I imagine that you have had any number of acquaintances make assumptions about your marriage to me."

I was so startled, I could only stare at him.

"In fact, the permutations of marriage are wide and many. One such is that of the Porters. On the surface, theirs appears a façade, convenient to both but ultimately sterile. However, having spent the day in their company, I saw nothing but affection and respect. I saw two people for whom solitude is loneliness, and loneliness is horror. So, together they face the world, and amuse one another when the world is elsewhere."

"I see." Although I wasn't entirely sure I did.

"I would also say their social life stands in for the kind of shared interests that bind more conventional couples."

"Parties are their children?"

"The guests are, certainly. Pampered and groomed, their preferences considered, their entertainment paramount. The Porters' guest lists are closely discussed for balance, size, and personalities."

Did I hear a point coming, out of this most unexpected conversational detour? "Are you talking about their invitations for the party on Saturday?"

"I am. I have not yet seen it in detail, but I am to understand that it includes not only the cream of Venetian aristocracy and American wealth, but key members of the new Italian power structure as well."

"Fascists?"

"That is, after all, where power currently lies. One can hope there are enough footmen to keep them away from the Socialists."

"You think a rich American homosexual would invite Fascists to a drunken bash?"

"Until one has seen Blackshirts kicking a man, Fascism may be merely a political party. I imagine that, unless something comes along to remove Signor Mussolini from power, most high-ranking Italians will join the party, at least in name."

This cheerful morning conversation was interrupted by a rapping at the door—my new beach pyjamas, each one proving more exotic than the last. Holmes gave a polite shudder and went off with his new violin. I chose the garment I judged least likely to cause a riot, packed it into my bag alongside a small set of binoculars and a large map of the lagoon, and put on normal clothing to go hunt down my gondolieri.

As I mentioned, the Lido is a long, thin sand-bar that keeps the Adriatic away from the calm lagoon waters. Tides rush in and out through a series of channels, three of which are suitable for ships. The oldest, and for most of Venice's history the only deep channel, is in the centre, called Malamocco. Halfway between it and Venice proper—and thus ideally situated both to serve incoming ships and to be a first line of defence against a seagoing enemy—stands the island of Poveglia.

It, too, had spent some time as the quarantine place for suspected plague ships. It, like San Clemente and San Servolo, changed purpose as Napoleon closed the houses of religion, as the plague faded—and, as roads provided an alternative route to invaders.

My detailed map of the lagoon showed Poveglia as a patch of some fifteen or twenty acres divided into three sections. A foot-bridge joined the two northern parts. The small southern bit had the octagonal shape of a military fortification.

That was the full extent of my knowledge of this island—that, and it was haunted.

Not that spirits weren't commonplace throughout the Venice lagoon. Even that most populated of tourist sites, the Piazza San Marco, has an entrance that locals automatically veer around, since the space between the two columns (stolen from elsewhere, like most of Venice's landmarks and treasures) was long used as the city's execution ground. Suspect islands ranged from San Servolo's *"windowless, deform'd and dreary pile"* to the wailing surrounds of San Clemente and the long-time leper colony of San Lazzaro. Further out, where lights and bustle gave way to swamp and mists and tidal mutters, there were places where fishermen hesitated to cast their nets, where the stoutest of gondoliers would not go even by day.

And chief of those, it would appear, was Poveglia. Which was why it seemed a good place for a closer look.

My chief gondolier did not agree.

"No, Signora, no no no, you do not wish to go there. There is nothing on Poveglia. Ruins and ghosts, evil things. No, it is a bad place. Very bad."

Sounding better and better.

"You may be right. Still, I'd like to look at it, even from a distance."

"The *vaporetto* to Malamocco," Giovanni decided firmly. "It goes past. Very, very close. But there is nothing to see, nothing but ruins and mad things."

The last phrase caught my attention, but Giovanni's growing agitation made it obvious he was on the point of ending our arrangement. Since I doubted that any of his prettier colleagues would prove more stout-hearted, I stepped away from my insistence, gave them an alternative assignment, and made my way to a steamer that meandered its way down the Lido.

The day's haze was just beginning to rise from the water as we chugged near to the haunted island. I raised the field glasses, propping my shoulder against the boat's cabin to keep them steady.

The northern island was solidly framed by a sort of hedgerow composed of small trees and large shrubs, its interior hidden from anything short of an aeroplane. Vegetation leaned over a narrow waterway, then resumed on the other side. In this middle section, buildings could be seen above the greenery: vine-draped roof-lines, a derelict church tower. Then came the octagonal section I had seen on the map, its sloping sides made of tightly fitted stones that would hold it above the winter storms.

As we approached the Malamocco dock, I asked the *vaporetto* man if this boat continued south, or turned back up the Lido. He gave a brusque nod in the direction we had come, so I resisted the disembarking crowd and went for a word with the man at the wheel.

"Signore, I would very much like to go back by way of the other side of Poveglia. Just for my interest. Perhaps . . . ?" He glanced down at the lira I was slowly passing from one hand to another. I paused, added another, paused. At the third, he nodded and the bills vanished.

"*Grazie mille, Signore,*" I told him, and returned to my position at the starboard railing.

The island's western side was something of a duplicate of its other half: octagon, water, middle part with buildings, a second canal with a foot-bridge, then hedgerowed wilderness. However, the buildings were not as ruined as the eastern passage had suggested: there was a closed boat-house with a new door, and fresh tiles in the roof of the long building facing the octagon. At their back, a glimpse of bricks and wheelbarrow suggested active renovations, although I saw no one moving. I could feel my fellow passengers watching me, with a figure at my elbow in the colours of the *vaporetto* company's uniform, but not until Poveglia was receding from view did I lower the glasses.

The passengers turned away; the uniformed man did not—clearly, the helmsman had told him of our change in route. "I was interested in the island," I said—truthfully enough.

"*È un luogo maledetto,*" he growled.

"*Perché?*"

Either his vocabulary was insufficient or his emotion too great, because rather than explain why the place was malevolent, he grumbled for a while in the Venetian dialect, then stumped away.

However, a gentleman who had overheard the exchange volunteered some information. "Tens of thousands of souls died here, Signorina," he explained. "Of the plague, primarily. They say the soil is made of bones and hair."

I nodded. "My boatmen wouldn't bring me here."

"They may be wise. There are sounds at night here. I have heard them, over the noise of the motor. And . . . smells, smells that linger on the offender."

"It looks as though people live there."

"Two, three years past, a doctor came, with . . . followers?"

"You mean patients? A health resort?"

"No, Signorina. More like *un culto.*"

"A cult? Like, Naturists? Or Spiritualists?"

"*Folle, tutti quanti.*"

"*Credulone? O pazzi?*" Did he mean the man's followers were foolish? Or insane?

"Both, I think, Signorina. But not friendly."

"I see. Thank you."

He nodded and faded back into the other passengers, rather than risk having to talk further about it.

Had it been a new lunatic asylum under construction, or even a health resort, I might have looked more closely, but I could not imagine Lady Vivian coming under the influence of a religious charlatan while she was in Bedlam. And although it could conceivably have been Nurse Trevisan's doing, I could not fit the idea of that nurse's calm and sensible demeanour into a community of religious dupes.

For the moment, I would file Poveglia under "Possible But Unlikely."

Chapter Thirty-three

TO HOLMES' IRRITATION, THERE WAS A MARKED LACK OF piano music and laughter coming from the windows of Ca' Rezzonico as his *traghetto* plied across the Grand Canal. At the entrance, the servant who came to the door confirmed that, yes, Signor and Signora Porter had left for the day, gone to Murano with Signor and Signora Murphy and some other friends, or possibly Burano since the Signore and Signora had not decided and they wished to send both glass and lace home with the friends, and possibly they did not know the difference between the two islands—but in any case, *mi dispiace molto* but they are not here. What, the Signore wishes to come in and use the music room in the absence of Signor Porter?

But of course—this way, Signor Russell.

The maid's attitude being, If this English fellow wants to steal the silver, well, those mad Americans can afford it.

When he left two hours later, Holmes carried away not silver, but something of greater interest: a copy of Linda's guest list.

Chapter Thirty-four

BY THE TIME I REACHED THE MAIN LIDO STOP, IT WAS well after noon. I paused in the Excelsior to change my clothing, and on the beach found some dedicated partygoers only now edging towards consciousness. Others had been out on their padded chaises for hours, either under the candy-striped awnings or baking their well-oiled skin in the open. Attendants scurried about with drinks and ices, a few children played in the surf (nowhere near as many as in the public areas), and people in swimming costumes danced to gramophone music out on the floating dock-island. Desultory talk flitted back and forth across the sand.

Need I say, it was the talk I was after, rather than ices and sun?

However, I did begin with a swim—walking all the way down to the water before I shed the garish pyjamas, diving rapidly in before anyone could focus on the scars visible around the edges of my costume.

I was a strong swimmer, well practiced with Holmes along the rugged shingle beach near our home in Sussex. This water, though open sea rather than lagoon, was calmer than ours, and warm. I swam past the dancing couples and turned to follow the line of the beach: half an hour down, then slightly more back again.

Pleasantly tired, I waded out and flung my towel around me—again, quickly, before curious eyes could focus—then walked back up the beach.

A voice from one of the shadowed huts called my name. I veered aside, greeting my friends from Tuesday night. "Hullo, Elsa. Good afternoon, Miss Fellowes-Gordon."

Her companion—I had not yet been asked to call her Dickie, so I used her mouthful of a double-barrelled surname—gave me a languid nod, and Elsa patted a chair. "Honey, you must need a drink after all that exercise."

"Sounds lovely, but first I need to rinse off the salt. You planning on being here for a while?"

"Nothing doing until dinner, so sure."

I bestowed an absent-minded smile—the sort that indicates vague friendship without an exact recollection of names—on those gathered around her, and went to find a shower-bath. As I walked away, it occurred to me that Elsa was the exception to the beach's class structure—that she and Dickie should have been located in a cabana nearer the water. Was this because she had more personal magnetism than money? Or was it by choice—that she wished to be nearer the cross-roads of action?

It was probably both.

When I was clean and cool, I returned to my good friend Elsa and settled onto the chaise she indicated. I told her pet attendant what I'd have to drink and eat, and exchanged greetings with her various actresses, politicians, aristocrats, and the simply wealthy. Then I faded into the scenery, listening to conversation. I picked up some titbits about Elsa's past and her plans for the autumn. I paid attention to a brief exchange about the local Fascists, listening to whose voice held approval and whose doubt. I asked about interesting night-clubs in Venice, and noted the names—but the consensus was that Venice had none, and the Lido's best was right here.

Someone mentioned Cole Porter. His name brought knowing chuckles and some affectionate remarks, although one of the girls did not much care for his wife, Linda. I murmured that I'd heard she and Porter both had their side-interests, hoping that the idea of Linda Porter as a lesbian might give me some direction to follow, but no one pounced on it. Two of the younger women, mutually anointing their skins with cocoanut oil, were speculating about the necessity of aiming the sides of their bodies towards the sun, or whether the sun reached down the curvature of the limb to do its work, because it would be dreadful to have a tan that was not uniform.

"Someone needs to invent a sort of human rotisserie," I commented. "Slowly spinning a person around and around."

This caught the imagination of about half the people there—those who weren't asleep or reading a novel—and soon the suggested invention had been expanded to include an automatic misting of oil and the regular raising of drinks—attached to long straws, one of them suggested, so as not to disturb the continuity. But when this progressed to its logical conclusion—what did the rotisseried human do when the drinks caught up with the bladder?—the eruption of giggles and guffaws startled our fellow beach-goers.

I smiled benignly, having established myself as a Good Sport and a Clever Girl, and stretched out an arm for my glass.

That Thursday afternoon and evening with the Lido set went much like Tuesday's: the smells of salt air and cocoanut oil and perspiration, the sun beating down, nothing on the schedule except food, drink, flirtation, and endless talk about nothing at all. I could see why everyone drank so much. How else to bear the monotony of gossip, card-playing, and magazine-reading? How else push aside the suspicion that a responsible adult did not while away entire days playing games or paddling in the water and pushing servants around?

I should leave, I thought. *I'm finding precisely nothing about Vivian Beaconsfield.*

But if she had come to Venice, wouldn't she show up in this group, sooner or later? This was what she had enjoyed, in her Season: not the serious business of finding a mate, but the colour and buzz, the silliness and whirl, the dancing and the masks.

One more day here. If I'd heard nothing by tonight, that was it: I'd have more luck scouring the coffee-houses on the Giudecca.

So I lay, surrounded by *marchesas, principes,* Ladies, and Sirs who drank Prosecco and champagne, nibbled lemon ices and hunks of watermelon, and discussed matters no more pressing than the dinner menu. These were people who could put together a revolution—and certainly bankroll one—yet here they lolled with no more purpose than a beach-full of sea lions.

Perhaps, I wondered as the Excelsior's shadow crept with infinite slowness across the sand, the fault is mine? Maybe after so long running flat out, I'd forgot how to relax. Holmes and I had been on the road and on the case for ... well, years now, and any muscle so long tensed takes time to stop its clenching.

Perhaps my twitching boredom with the titled and the rich was the mental equivalent of a cramp in an overworked muscle? If so, my fretting was not going to reduce the cramp any. Instead, give the muscle—or the mind—some form of exercise, however pointless.

So, with little better to do, in between casting delicate hints about small, blonde Englishwomen and taller, black-haired women with moles on their necks, I devoted the remainder of the day to perfecting my persona, stretched upon my divan with the other lords of the realm. The Miss Russell I'd begun with was something of a cipher; she now edged into outright mystery: interested in those around her, but oddly aloof. Widely travelled, but not in these circles. A person more apt to be polite to a bar-man than to a baronet. Who understood even the most suggestive of double-entendres, but seemed to find them ... disappointing? True wit caught her imagination, but the ersatz left her untouched.

Was I wealthy? And how. Educated? No doubt. Was I a prig, a prude, or a bluestocking? Absolutely not. But was I hetero-, homo-, or nonsexual? Hmm: now there was a question.

In between listening hard for any trace of Vivian Beaconsfield, and dropping oblique remarks into various conversations, I set out to vamp the Lido crowd. I did not aim for Elsa Maxwell herself—too obvious, and fortunately, I didn't appear to be her "type." Instead, I took some care in turning the attention of others back onto her, subtly but regularly.

The result was an invitation to dinner, informal and private, with Miss Fellowes-Gordon-oh-please-call-me-Dickie and a handful of others—including, I was delighted to see, my young man from the other night, the Hon Terry, who'd spent the day with chums in the town.

I claimed the chair beside him, ruthlessly elbowing aside a daughter of Count Volpi. On my other side was a remarkably brown young Tory MP who (as the evening went on) proved to be great friends with Winston Churchill and more or less married to a duke's more or less daughter. That is, they were married but he spent his life straying, and his wife bore a striking resemblance to the duchess' paramour.

Introductions made, I turned back to Terry with a question about the upcoming masked ball—which theme, I had been told, was, "Come as your true self."

"Tell me, is Elsa's 'do' on Saturday night actually a ball?"

"No, that's just what the old girl's calling it. There'll be a band and dancing and food, of course, but—well, now that I think of it, I guess that does make it a ball. You are coming, what?"

"I haven't been invited."

"Invited—hah! Elsa!" The American looked up from her conversation with a white-haired woman I'd seen in a cabana so high in status, it nearly touched the water. "Haven't you invited Miss Russell here to the bash on Saturday?"

"Of course I have, honey. She's one of my intimate friends, why wouldn't she come?" And with a twinkle, she turned back to the old lady.

"So, Terry, what's your 'true self'—what costume are you wearing?"

"Oh, mustn't tell. That's what the masks are for, to keep people guessing."

"The costume balls I've been to, it was pretty easy to see who people are."

"Sure, sometimes. Depends on the mask, of course. Mine—well, you won't have much of a problem. But sometimes between the mask and the paint and the feathers, it's hard going. And of course, there's always a few newcomers, so just when one is about to say, 'I know you!'—one looks down the line and sees the person one thought one was talking to."

"I'd imagine Elsa would be pretty hard to disguise."

He chuckled. "She'd need a pretty substantial costume, that's true. And for you, it'll be tough to hide your height. Like the girl who came last week—only the other way 'round, of course."

"Who was that?"

"Dunno. We called her 'Cinderella' 'cause she disappeared around midnight. Itsy slip of a thing. Pale hair, pinky mask, said almost nothing, danced all night—then *poof!* She was gone."

Good Lord: I'd endured an entire day baking on the beach and here, all along . . . Terry frowned. "Er, did I say something wrong?"

"Oh, sorry, no. I was just . . . reminded of a thing. That I have to do tomorrow. Sorry. But about this Cinderella girl. She sounds like someone I know—I don't suppose she had a companion? Tallish, darker? Has a mole on her jaw?"

"Well, there was a fella she danced with a lot, he had a mole—he didn't say much, either, but not a bad mover."

"Did you by any chance see which way they went, after they left? I mean to say, they're not staying at the Excelsior?"

"*I* didn't, no. But you might ask Bongo—he was madly taken with her, moped around for days when he couldn't find out who she was."

"Bongo . . . ?"

"James is his name. James Farquart-Sitherleigh. Big fellow, small head?"

"I don't believe we've met."

"He's around—maybe not today, he had something going in town."

"Might 'Bongo' be back tonight?"

"Anything's possible."

After an interminable meal, punctuated by the MP's hand on my right knee (Why did I keep expecting Holmes to walk in the door?) and

Terry's blithering about American sports in my left ear, we adjourned to Chez Vous. There, I found many of the same faces, a few new ones—but not, unfortunately, that of James-Bongo Farquart-Sitherleigh. As the night wore on, alcohol flowed, music pounded, and drugs made their appearance, discreet at first and then less so. It became harder to shake off intrusive hands on the dance floor, as daytime flirtations became the more urgent decisions of the night.

It was exhausting. And when a mass exodus occurred halfway through the night—a slow time for the Chez Vous band coincided with the rumour of an American Negro jazz band at the Grand Hôtel des Bains down the way—I started off with the rush, only to gratefully duck away.

My head spinning, my face aching with hours of smiles, I stumped tiredly across the island. There I found my faithful gondolieri, as requested many hours before, waiting and ready. I let Carlo wrap me with a travelling rug, not even contemplating its potential for fleas. We pushed into the dark, quiet waters, and flew, pulled by the city's lights and two men's expertise and eagerness. As we went, I found myself humming low, *When daylight is fading, Enwrapt in night's shading, With soft serenading, We sing them to sleep* . . .

Giuseppe and Marco—no, those were the operetta: *Giovanni* and *Carlo*—slid into place before the Beau Rivage. They walked me across the wide quay to the hotel door, tipping their hats to me and murmuring that I should pay them tomorrow, tomorrow.

So grateful was I for their silence and their skill—and so firmly planted in my freestyle Lido persona (also, yes, maybe a little drunk)—that I nearly kissed them both, right there on the hotel steps. Fortunately, I caught back the impulse in time. Not only would they have quit instantly, but the night manager would have had my bags packed and in the lobby before morning.

Chapter Thirty-five

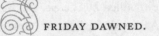 FRIDAY DAWNED.

Little point in rushing over to the Lido before noon, since my chances of finding Terry's friend with the idiotic pet name that early were minuscule. Instead, I settled down to another morning of a warm tile balcony, another view of a living Canaletto, another breakfast of bread and jam. One could get used to this, I supposed.

Again, I gave Holmes a distilled version of the previous day: sun, drink, boredom, and a quick and fleeting glance of what might be Vivian Beaconsfield, in the guise of Cinderella. "I hope to find this Bongo fellow today. And you? What news from the Fascist front?"

The moment I said it, I heard the echo of a boot in flesh, that inhuman mewl of pain. "Oh, God, Holmes, I'm sorry—the attitude of the Lido set seems to be contagious. I meant to say: did you find out anything about the Porters' guest list?"

"No need to apologise, Russell, I of all people can understand the dangers of a prolonged act. Yes, I did see it, under the nose of the servants."

"Anything interesting?"

In response, he dug in his pocket, dropping a quarter-folded sheet of expensive writing paper on the table. I put down my cup and undid it, finding it covered top to bottom with his pinched scrawl: names, scores of them. Nearly all of them with check-marks by their sides.

"Good heavens, Holmes. You looked into all these people in one afternoon?"

"And evening. I had assistance."

"Your waterborne Irregulars?"

"And a variety of garrulous shop-keepers, fishmongers, butchers, and delivery boys."

I placed the sheet down on the table. "Well, you certainly had a more productive day than I did. Any conclusions to be drawn?"

"Your Elsa Maxwell may be disappointed to lose some of her prizes to the Porters this week. There were many names whose importance lies in their titles: the director of La Fenice opera house, the director of the Biennale international art exhibitions, the director of the . . ."

I waved away a wasp buzzing the jam-pot, wondering when Holmes would reach the point of his recitation.

". . . including three Francolettis."

A glance at the list confirmed my memory, that the very last name on it was just that. Holmes reached out to refresh his coffee, forcing me to ask. "Very well: who are the Francolettis?"

"Francoletti is an old Venetian family. As with many such, over the centuries their fortunes receded, and one by one they sold all of the important holdings that generations of marriage and acquisition had brought in all over the country—leaving the Francolettis with a mouldering palazzo, a venerable name, and a handful of worthless properties, including a stretch of swamp on the nearby mainland. Their sons were educated and scattered to the humiliation of earning a living. The palazzo slipped into further disrepair. And then, shortly after the War, Count Giuseppe Volpi looked at precisely that swath of worthless land on which to build a new deep-water port, a project aimed at transforming the economy of the entire Veneto district. The Francoletti palazzo is no longer in disrepair, and the family are on their way to becoming extremely wealthy indeed. The third brother's name is Renato. He is fluent in English and has recently been brought back to Venice, having lived in Rome most of his adult life."

At the name of the city, I looked up. "Is this brother by any chance a member of the Milizia Nazionale?"

Holmes smiled. "More than a member. Renato Francoletti is a *Capitano.*"

Yes, he could have led with that revelation, but I could not begrudge him his little drama. Although it did make me very aware of the terror of a certain San Clemente guard, and the thud of heavy boots. "Good to know. But do make sure there are plenty of people around if you ask him about Vivian."

"I imagine, given the surroundings, it would be no difficult thing to turn the talk to mad English-speaking visitors."

"Take care, Holmes."

"Don't I always, Russell?"

"Frankly, no."

I sat for a moment, thinking over what the last two days had brought us.

I now had: an entrée to the Lido set, and with it an American party-organiser and a number of new acquaintances with varying degrees of money, wit, social rank, sobriety, and sexual conformity. A trip to San Clemente had added to my store two gondolieri; a confirmation that Vivian was not in that particular *manicomio;* an unsought mystery woman with Fascist connexions; and a greater appreciation for the homely Oxfordshire punt.

Holmes, in the meantime, had assembled: one weathered violin; a platoon—if not a company—of waterborne Irregulars; an introduction to Venice's Milizia Nazionale; a growing intimacy with the city's by-ways; and what could only be called a friendship with an unusual young musician. My mind did, I admit, stick a bit on this last one.

"You seem to like this Mr Porter."

"He interests me. And he is remarkably talented, if he can find a way to keep his temptations under control."

I studied Holmes: aquiline features, expressive hands, a slim and wiry figure that belonged to a younger man. "Er, Holmes. Do you think . . . I mean, this Porter fellow is fairly . . . notorious. Is it possible he—that is, I assume you made it clear . . ."

"That I am not, as they say, 'interested'? Yes, Russell, the man does seem capable of mere friendships. He is under no delusion that I will fling down my violin and shower him with—"

"Holmes, stop, for God's sake!" Of all the images I did *not* want in my mind's eye! "I simply wanted to be sure you weren't . . ."

"'Leading him on'?"

"Holmes, your well of English threatens to be permanently defiled by the Porter crowd—but yes, that's what I meant."

"No. Music is our shared language, one in which he is remarkably fluent."

"Fine. Just so—oh, never mind."

"I must go. Will your admirer with the speed-boat be returning you again tonight?"

"I may ask my two other gentlemen admirers to bring me back, rather more sedately, Giovanni and Carlo."

"Have a charming afternoon," said my husband, to all appearances utterly unconcerned by the growing list of gentlemen at his wife's beck and call.

Chapter Thirty-six

....

THE FRANCOLETTI PALAZZO, LIKE MOST OF ITS TYPE, had two entrances, the one on the water being its more ornate and ceremonial. As Holmes walked past the workaday back doors onto the *campo*, he noticed that they stood open, revealing a housemaid scrubbing the aged tiles of the ground-floor *portego*. He continued into the *campo*, vexed—as he generally was in this most uncooperative of cities— by the choice of exits on which to keep watch: water landings and terrestrial doorways were invariably on a building's opposite sides. However, in this case, the *campo*'s end (as his map had suggested) was open onto the waterway. A motor-launch stood at the palazzo's landing, with a liveried attendant to suggest a possible imminent departure.

To his pleasure, there was even a *caffè* convenient to his task of keeping watch, which provided not only a view of the canal and a tiny jolt of espresso, but the previous day's *Messaggero* as well.

He settled to the headlines: Amundsen's North Pole flight crews had, against all expectations, survived, dropping out of the sky in Norway; the Fascist Party Congress was claiming many triumphs in Rome;

the Geneva Protocol now prohibited the use of weapons such as tear gas. Before his cup was empty, the palazzo's door came open and discharged three men wearing the black of the Milizia. One stepped casually into the waiting motor-boat, the other two were less confident. Strangers to Venice.

The launch—which had either come in from the other direction, or been laboriously backed along the narrow waterway—started up. As it passed the *fondamenta* on which the tables had been set out, Holmes raised the paper and listened with care. The Venetian native was speaking excellent English, but slowly. One of his companions—the one leaning towards him with a frown—was less fluent in the language.

"—will be most impressed with what we are building on Marghera. We will be able to bring in the very biggest ships, and Venice will become . . ."

As the boat negotiated a turn in the canal, sunlight fell upon the object of Francoletti's lecture: a burly and distinctly English face, paying avid attention to claims of a grand future.

The Marquess of Selwick. *The Fascists will be looking for those in power that they might infect.*

Such as an ambitious and impatient aristocrat, sympathetic to the Fascist cause, who has reason to come to the Fascist homeland. Naturally, he gets in touch with the local authorities to help locate his sister. But if, once there, he is met by a powerful and like-minded colleague? If the two men look at each other and see enormous potential?

Then Mycroft's prediction becomes correct: Fascism gains a foothold in England.

There was little point in racing to hire a boat and follow the men: they would be gone for the rest of the day. Holmes finished his coffee and the newspaper, thumbed a coin into the saucer, then walked off through the by-ways in the direction of Ca' Rezzonico.

The house was just waking, but Holmes was amused to find that "practicing for Saturday night" had almost immediately been swept aside in favour of, "Say, what do you think of this?" Holmes began to realise that, at home in Paris, where he spoke the language, Porter had a whole community of musicians to call upon. Here in Venice, if he wanted company at the piano, he had to make do with a near-to-elderly amateur violinist.

For in the Porter household, "company" was paramount. Cole Porter did not let his musical hobbies get in the way of his social life. And yet Holmes could see that a portion of the man's brain worked even as he drank and laughed with his unending stream of visitors—and while he slept, probably. The man seemed to spin words and music as a peasant woman spun her thread: at all spare moments, in all circumstances, without appearing to be aware of it as labour.

Take Holmes' jocular agreement, on their previous meeting, to a suggested afternoon of irresponsibility. "Let us misbehave," Holmes had said, and instantly regretted the phrase, less for its sentiment than for its jarring discord with the personality he was putting forth.

Neither Porter nor his wife seemed to notice, which was all to the good—and he had taken greater care to act the easily amused elder statesman at the luncheon and musical afternoon that followed. But clearly the phrase had stuck in the man's ear and, over the past twenty-two hours, been harvested, cleaned, combed, and was now in the process of being spun into thread.

The stilted suggestion was now an informal encouragement: "Let's Misbehave." Of course, the saucy lyrics that followed would never find a publisher, much less a stage anywhere in the vicinity of Broadway or the West End, but it was a rough first attempt, and Holmes suspected that Porter would keep tinkering with it until he had a song whose language would pass in mixed company, even if its sentiments would bring a blush to the cheeks of a sexagenarian detective.

(And what might the man do with a song based on the Latin numbers—*quart, quint, sex, sept* . . .)

Holmes caught himself, cleared his throat, and said, "Now, as to your guests tomorrow night: I would imagine that some of them might find the tunes of the 1890s more familiar than those of last year's, er, 'hits'?"

Chapter Thirty-seven

....

MY MORNING DRAGGED, NO EASIER ON THIS SIDE OF THE lagoon than the other. I dawdled, I bathed, I tried to read, I drummed my fingers, and I finally took the Excelsior's launch over to the Lido.

Where I dawdled, drummed my fingers some more, and finally went for a long walk down the island and back up again.

Upon my return, about a third of the cabanas were occupied, including that of Elsa Maxwell.

"Hello there, darlin'," she greeted me. "You're up and about early."

"Oh, I don't sleep a lot."

"I know the problem, dearie. Have a drink."

"Thanks, maybe some coffee. I don't suppose you've seen Terry yet?"

"Oh, we probably won't see him for a while; he went off with somebody pretty last night."

Not, I thought, a girl. I hid my deep sigh and asked the hovering attendant for an espresso, settling in for another useless day among the lotus eaters.

But shortly after midday, a most unexpected sight came marching down the row of cabanas: a young man's legs in a swimming costume, the upper part of him hidden behind a pair of long Alpine skis balanced across his shoulders. Elsa's cabana fell silent. Her film star turned to see what had caught our attention. Soon, all eyes were on the approaching figure. The legs came to a halt; the long wooden objects swung down to rest on the sand. It was the Hon Terrence, my admiring boatman, grinning hugely.

I wondered if he might require a nice calm rest period amongst the San Servolo lunatics.

Elsa spoke first. "Terry, dear, you're a few hundred miles and a whole lot of clothing away from using those things."

"No, dear thing, I ordered these 'specially. Have you any idea how hard it is to buy a pair of skis in the summer? I heard about this American who's skiing on water. Just tie a rope to the boat and hold on, and Bob's your uncle."

"Sounds like a great way to break your neck," Elsa commented, but not everyone was of the same opinion. In two minutes flat, Terry was headed towards his speed-boat with three other handsome young men, none of whom was named Bongo. The women around me watched the mass retreat, sighing.

"Such a pity," one of the girls murmured, and returned to her sun-worship.

Thus the afternoon was enlivened by the sight of Terry's speed-boat practicing brief bursts of speed just beyond the swimmers—very brief bursts of speed, for the most part. One time a figure managed to stay upright for nearly three triumphal seconds before shooting head over heels into a great gout of water, and the big engine cut again.

After an hour and a half of abortive and no doubt cumulatively painful efforts, the sleek boat turned for shore, tying up at the splendid Excelsior pier that stretched out into the sea. The four men walked down the boards and up the beach, three of them rubbing aching shoulders, all of them looking glum.

Their welcome was none too sympathetic. What, had they thought that since snow was water, skis would work on the wet kind, too? And had anyone actually seen this American alleged to have done it? Well, walking on water had always been something of a miracle. Maybe they'd start selling floating boots so people could walk over to San Marco instead of waiting for a *vaporetto*.

And so on.

I, however, had been watching with an eye to the physics of the problem, and finally took pity on the poor Hon Terrence. "You know," I pointed out, "if you leaned back far enough, it might force all the weight onto the flat of the skis. It's when the tips dig in that you get in trouble."

Four handsome young faces stared at me, but only one with an expression of hope. "You think so?" Terry asked.

"One would have to be strong enough to fight the pull. And the person driving the boat would need to control the speed, too. That's a lot of factors to balance."

To my astonishment, he took the remark as an offer. He reached down and seized my hand, yanking me to my feet. "Great! Let's try it."

I snatched back my hand. "Oh no, I'm not risking two dislocated shoulders, thank you very much. And I was hoping to see your friend Bongo."

"Oh, he won't be here for hours. And I'll do the skiing. You can drive."

"I've never piloted a boat before—well, not one like yours."

"You can drive a car, can't you? Bright girl like you, we'll be zipping all over in no time."

He seized my hand again—so I grabbed my hat and let him pull me along.

Terry was, in fact, a clever teacher, with little of the patronising attitudes one becomes accustomed to in a lesson involving males and machinery. Perhaps he was merely so eager to get on with the challenge of skis on water, he forgot he was showing the details of ignition, throttle, and acceleration to a girl.

I killed the engine only once.

Out on the water, I practiced a series of gradual accelerations. When I was satisfied that I understood the sequence, if not the actual speed required, I let him jump into the water with his two wooden planks and the length of rope.

The first failure was mine, when I took off too fast for him. The second was his, when he failed to lean back. The third attempt saw him teeter upright, hold for a count of one, two—then make a spectacular somersault with both skis flying.

He was laughing in exhilaration when I brought the boat past him again, and grabbed the trailing tow-rope.

Half a dozen more attempts, and he was skiing, on the water, upright, in the centre of twin sprays taller than he.

Water-skiing had come to the Lido.

I made the Hon Terry stop before he drowned of exhaustion. He couldn't make it on board without my help. As I made for the Excelsior pier, he lay belly-down over the motor-housing, chin on forearms, telling me what he'd learned and how Buff and Jiggles had been doing it wrong and how it might be easier with a wider ski. When he finally ran dry, I ventured a question about Bongo.

"Bongo?"

"Yes, your friend, remember? We were going to ask him about the Cinderella from the other night?"

"Right! Yes, Bongo—oh, I think he's gone." I came a hair's breadth from wrapping the anchor rope around his neck and shoving him back over the side. Fortunately, I delayed long enough for him to finish the thought. "No, that's next week, Puffer's the one leaving today. Bongo had to go hold the hand of an aged aunt, or a bank manager, or something. He should be back—ah, wait. Yes, you've conjured the devil!"

I followed his gaze to the Excelsior's decorative wharf, where a dozen or more nicely endowed young men leapt about, arms waving in wild approval. Terry sat upright—stifling a groan—and swung his feet onto the passenger seat, both arms slowly rising up for a return salutation. One of the greeting committee was indeed remarkably tall, and his head noticeably under-sized.

"Oy!" The boys at the dock having come into shouting distance, Terry shouted. "You lot see that? I told you there was such a thing—all you need's a brilliant driver!" And to me he added, "Go ahead and take her in here; they'll move her into the harbour before dark."

As the Runabout nudged up against the structure, Terry jumped stiffly out—to be boosted onto the shoulders of his mates and carried in triumph down the boards. They'd have carried me, too, had I not clung to the wheel and threatened to dive over the side. I watched them go, keeping a close eye on the elusive Bongo—at which point Terry won my undying love and devotion by catching his friend's attention and sending him back to me.

Bongo loomed. I felt like climbing up onto the engine housing to keep from getting a crick in my neck. But Bongo was a simple soul, the kind of retriever-dog, country-house, tweed-and-shotgun Englishman one did not expect from (I had gathered from the gossiping hordes) the son of three generations of mine-owners.

"Terry said you wanted to talk to me?"

I introduced myself and stuck out my hand. He eyed it, causing me to wonder if he'd ever shaken a woman's hand before, but gamely wrapped his paw around mine and let me move his arm up and down a few times. "Lovely to meet you, Bongo, thanks for coming back. Yes, it seems a friend of mine was at the 'do' last Saturday. Terry said you'd spotted her—you called her 'Cinderella'?"

"You *know* her?" His face took on a look of such pleasure and longing, it was painful to witness. "Oh, she's the most . . . I saw her and thought . . . I couldn't believe such a creature . . ."

"Terry said you followed her when she left. Did you by any chance see what direction she went in?"

"Oh, I tried, I really did. When I saw her, I . . . Oh, it took me all night to . . . I'd just worked myself up to going over and seeing if she'd dance with me when I realised she was gone. Gone! I ran out of there so fast I knocked over a couple of waiters, and started grabbing people until they'd tell me which way she went. I got to the harbour just as she was pulling away, she and that dark girl in the evening suit. I ran—and

I run fast—but when they got to the water and opened up, I lost them. It was dark," he explained sadly, as if to say that had it been daylight, he'd have followed them across the lagoon.

"Which way did they go?"

His left hand came out, pointing to ten o'clock. Which, although it eliminated only half the lagoon, still helped.

But first: "Um, Bongo—James: About this Cinderella. I'd forget about her, if I were you. I don't think she's really interested in men."

"Oh, I know. A creature like that, she floats above the world. But even girls who float on air sometimes need a fellow to, you know. Buy them dresses and pet kittens and whatnot. She'd come to love me, I know she would."

All I could do was thank him and send him back to Terry's procession of triumph, now a beach-full of cheering strangers. As the dock's attendant tied off the ropes of the pretty little Runabout, I reached out a hand to run it idly up and down the polished wood.

What a grand afternoon. All that practice would make it so much easier, when the time came to steal my new friend's boat.

Chapter Thirty-eight

....

AT HALF-FOUR IN THE AFTERNOON, AS HOLMES WAS longing for tea (and, he suspected, the American for a cocktail), Linda walked in. Not that she hadn't been walking in and out all day, along with half the people, pets, and servants in the palazzo, but this time she was alone, and this time her face was uncertain.

"Cole, dear, there's a . . . gentleman wanting a word."

"He can't have one, he'll have to take a sackful," Porter said, then noticed her face. His hands came off the keyboard. "What's wrong?"

"Nothing, nothing at all. He's perfectly polite, charming even, just—" She gave an embarrassed laugh. "Well, those outfits they wear, they're a bit . . ."

"Intimidating?" Holmes provided.

"Exactly. The *Fascisti*, dear. You know, black, black, black. As grim as New York in January."

"I'll come down in a minute."

"Actually, Cole, do you mind—that is, I thought I'd bring him up. If that's all right?"

Even Holmes could see that Linda Porter did not want this intruding Blackshirt mingling with her guests as the cocktail hour got under way. He was not surprised when Cole stood up and said, "Oh, it's time we were stopping anyway. Bring him along."

But not, it seemed, into the music room. Instead, Cole wandered slowly after Linda, Holmes on his heels, as far as the *portego*, the connecting room and general reception hall that overlooked the Grand Canal. A room filled with art and dignity, where even a large man felt small—and a small man could feel large, were he the master of the house.

The Fascist was following Linda up the stairway, and there was no mistaking the direction of his eyes as she climbed. His gaze lingered on her skirt as she moved into the room, shifting at last to take in the two men waiting for him: tall and old; short and young.

He looked between them. "Signor Porter?" As if a man in a suit gone shiny with age might be paying for a summer at Ca' Rezzonico.

Cole put out his hand without hesitation, although Holmes could see tension in his jaw.

The newcomer did a sort of click of the heels as he shook hands. "Renato Francoletti, *Capitano* of the Milizia Nazionale, at your service. I wanted to thank you for your invitation tomorrow night. And to ask your indulgence, that I might bring a guest as well?"

Porter produced a charming smile that did not quite reach the eyes. "Sure, no problem. It'll be enough of a crowd that one or ten more won't be noticed."

"Oh, not ten—ah, but you are making the joke."

"Might be."

"Thank you, Signore, I am sure he will enjoy the evening."

Porter's eyes flickered briefly at the pronoun as he considered, then instantly dismissed, the chance that the man was hinting at his own interests: no, his guest was more colleague than friend.

The *Capitano* was not finished. "This is an important gentleman, from England, who is in a position to do much for the city and for *Italia*, in the eyes of the world." And, it was clear, for one *Capitano* Renato Francoletti.

"We'll do our best to keep him entertained."

"And if I may, I also wished to suggest a further . . . indulgence, for the future."

"And what is that?" Looking on, Holmes was amused to see that Francoletti was one of those who could not tell the difference between friendliness and good manners.

Linda could. She moved around beside her husband so that the two faced the Venetian militia man, shoulder to shoulder, for all the world a pair of welcoming householders.

Francoletti lowered his voice to confide, "I am told that *Il Duce* may be coming to Venice, later in this summer. *Il Presidente,* yes?"

"Mr Mussolini, I know."

"He finds an interest in Americans, and he does enjoy music. I would be most happy if you were to come and meet him, if he honours my house with a visit. And perhaps to play an American song for him."

"Oh, I'm no professional, not at all. There's loads of better people around."

"That may be, but he finds you of interest. You and the delightful Mrs Porter, of course." Captain Francoletti inclined his head, his glance lingering on Linda's bust as it went past. Linda's face took on the kind of gracious smile that Southern ladies wear just before the knives are drawn, although the Captain did not appear to notice. "You have become such a force in Venice, these past years. Many of us in the city feel that we should make note of that, in some way."

In other words: *The two of you throw around so much money, even the President of Italy wants to get on your good side.*

"Well, then, I'd be honoured to do a song or two, if you don't mind that I can't sing worth a damn." Porter's smile had grown a touch more genuine, as the opportunity of performing for honest admirers presented itself.

"Good, then. I will let you know when *Il Duce* is considering a visit here. And I will look forward to our time tomorrow night."

Porter started to extend his hand for another shake, but the *Capitano* paused. "Oh, but one suggestion. Both for my . . . colleague tomorrow and for *Il Duce* later on. You perhaps should play nothing too . . . pansy."

Both Porters went as still as the *portego*'s statues. Eventually, Cole's head tipped a fraction.

"I beg your pardon?"

"Maybe I use the wrong word, *pansy*? Modern music, it's often not masculine, but *Il Duce*, he is most masculine person. And of course, my English friend. It is perhaps an American taste, I do not know. But you will remember this, please, when you play for them."

The *portego* was, for a long moment, suspended from the real world. The air ceased to stir, no tumult rose from the Grand Canal, the cat in the balcony doorway held itself very still. Linda was the first to draw breath, straightening to her full height as she did so. Her eyes blazed, her shoulders went back, her mouth came open—

And she stopped. Holmes, standing to the side, had seen the tiny motion: Cole Porter's hand had moved, one finger touching his wife's arm, ever so lightly.

After a moment, she tore her outraged eyes from the *Capitano* to look at her husband. He gave her the tiniest shake of the head, the most silent of warning looks.

She held his gaze, an argument of a thousand words taking place in utter silence and in the space of four seconds. Her eyes suddenly glistened, and she turned abruptly away.

"Terribly sorry, gentlemen, there's something I've forgotten." Her heels hurried across the *portego* tiles, nearly running by the time she hit the stairs.

Cole drew a breath of his own, and raised his pale features to the burly man in black.

The *Capitano*, satisfied, thrust out a hand that was like a contract.

And slowly, unwillingly, Cole Porter took it.

The two men watched the *Capitano* walk away, watched him disappear down the stairway. The outer world crept back into the palazzo.

Holmes did not want to look at the young musician. He knew what he would see there, knew that he'd never be forgiven for seeing it: shame as a husband, resentment as a proud man, gnawing disbelief as a person with civilised manners.

Humiliation, that he had not had the servants throw Francoletti in the canal.

Self-loathing, that he had abjectly received a heap of casual abuse as a thing he had to eat.

Even a man with his money, his gifts, his joy in life—even such a man.

Holmes took a deep breath, blew it out deliberately. "By God, Porter," he said. "I hope to hell you've got some alcohol downstairs."

Porter's choked laughter told Holmes he'd got it right: that if a stranger's insult could be borne, then so could a friend's having witnessed it.

Chapter Thirty-nine

························

DESPITE MY LONG SILKEN GARMENTS, AND DESPITE HAV-ing worn my hat securely tied down, my hours at the wheel of the Run-about had left me fairly comprehensively burnt. I tried to reassure myself, as I eyed the glowing person in the bath-room mirror, that in spite of my hair-colour, sun-burns tended to fade to a tan fairly quickly. Still, for the next twenty-four hours, I was going to resemble a freshly cooked lobster.

Holmes did a double-take when he came in. "Did you fall asleep in the sun, Russell?" He went to the drinks table, and handed me a glass.

"I had a rather more active day than that. I was helping a young man to water-ski."

One eyebrow quirked. "Skiing on water? Like those young men rid-ing the surf near San Francisco? I shouldn't have thought the Adriatic waves high enough for that."

"They're not. No, this involves standing on skis and holding for dear life on to a rope attached to the back of a fast boat."

He winced as he tried to picture it. I laughed.

"I remained firmly at the wheel. Even so, Holmes, I am starving. I could eat a horse—a kosher horse. And then we may have a little project."

"I shall dress quickly."

We took our meal down in the dining room again, ignoring the maître d's injured expression as he ushered us in, pointedly welcoming us back to "our" table.

However, perhaps our absence from his dining room since Sunday served to warn him that we were culinary Philistines, unwilling to take the proper time over a meal: our courses arrived without delay, and none of the staff lingered to offer their advice. Which tonight was precisely what was required.

When we were alone, I lowered my voice. "Holmes, do you have anything going tonight?"

"There will be a round of festivities *chez* Porter, but I am not required to attend."

"Would you like to come and help me commit grand larceny and trespass instead?"

"What, no battery and assault?"

"I'm hoping it doesn't come to that."

"Just as well. Italian prisons are not places of comfort. I should be honoured to assist in your felonious pursuits, my dear Russell."

"If we're lucky, it will only be trespass."

"I have never found 'luck' a dependable companion," Holmes noted calmly, and tucked into his soup.

In between intrusions from the waiters and the passing-by of other diners, I told Holmes about my day and the discovery of Bongo Farquart-Sitherleigh's beloved Cinderella.

"I think it's Vivian and Nurse Trevisan."

He frowned. "How does this involve your proposed felony?"

"The young man was smitten by her. When I finally tracked him down this afternoon, he told me that he'd run after her, and saw her boat pulling out of the harbour. But he was interested enough to follow as far as the lagoon, so he saw what direction she was going."

"And you think that narrows things down?"

"It's worth a shot."

"We need to ensure that she goes nowhere near Ca' Rezzonico on Saturday. No, she's not on the list, although there are various names that could be she. However, the *Capitano* has asked permission to bring a guest. An English guest."

"The Marquess?"

"The name was not provided, merely the nationality."

"If it is him, the last thing we want is for Vivian to walk in. But she's already been once at the Lido, chances are she'll be there again tomorrow night instead. Oh, *why* haven't we heard from Mycroft?" I complained. "I suppose this means you'll need to remain there the whole time, rather than come by the Excelsior first."

"It would be difficult to watch Ca' Rezzonico from the Lido."

"Even for a man of your skills. And you're certain the Marquess doesn't know you?"

"We have not met in person, and my present face does not look like the images that have been in the press."

He'd touched up his hair again, to an even sleeker black, and his moustache was so precisely shaped it might have been drawn on with ink. He'd also done something to his eyes that made them seem darker.

I pulled my thoughts back to the task at hand. "Shall we have coffee?"

"I suspect we will need it, before this night is gone."

"And what about your day, Holmes? Was it a success?"

"I am not certain that word describes it, but yes, I have a considerable amount of information to hand over to my brother."

"So we may not need to commit a second dose of trespass there?"

"Compounded by breaking and entering? Into the Fascists' headquarters? Perhaps not."

Looking better and better.

After dinner, Holmes and I went for a stroll up the Riva degli Schiavoni, leaning over a canal for a time while he smoked and we both thought our thoughts. We saw no Blackshirts. On our way back through the hotel, I wrote out a message to my intrepid gondoliers and gave it to the bellman to deliver. Then Holmes and I retreated upstairs to change into dark clothing.

We left the hotel just before eleven o'clock, silken burglars' masks and small electric torches in one pocket, pick-locks in the other.

Giovanni and Carlo were waiting.

I introduced the three men, then took my seat on the cushions. Holmes settled beside me. Giovanni and Carlo hung dim lanterns on either end of the craft, and we pushed out into the darkened San Marco Basin. I was pleased to find a slight breeze up—not enough to affect their rowing, but sufficient to clear the mist. Another pair of visitors to *La Serenissima* might have found the quarter-moon overhead romantic; we found it useful.

Shortly after midnight, we stepped off the gondola, walked a short distance in the direction of the Excelsior's wild racket, and peered into the little harbour, half-full of expensive boats of many sizes. When I spotted our target, I pointed it out to Holmes, then worked my way through the shadows while he went to create a small diversion. When he joined me, I hit the ignition and eased away, as the night-watchman dealt with a very minor and easily extinguished blaze at the other side of the gardens.

Out in the lagoon, Holmes switched on the lamps and I turned the Runabout's prow towards the quarantine island-turned-cult-headquarters, Poveglia.

Going south along the Lido, we passed through a series of distant cacophonies: jazz from Chez Vous; a Gershwin band from the Grand Hôtel des Bains; something sedate from one of the lesser hotels; and finally, women's shrieks, men's laughter, and the indistinct gramophone crackle of "Yes Sir! That's My Baby" from the veranda of a house on the lagoon.

Then even that died away, and the low beat of the motor was the only thing to be heard above the breeze.

Keeping well back from the island lest our motor attract attention, I described a circle around Poveglia. Holmes peered through the field glasses. It was mostly dark, other than some navigation lights, but when we rounded the hexagonal part at the south, we saw lights from one of the buildings inland.

Before leaving the hotel, Holmes and I had studied the general maps and my slightly more detailed sketch of this tripartite island. The boathouse, on the southern of the two dividing canals, faced the abandoned military hexagon, but was close to the area where I had seen signs of work—precisely the area where we now saw lights from behind a shuttered window.

But I kept us moving, as slowly as the big motor would permit, until we had circled around to the northern end again. "The eastern side?" I suggested, and felt more than saw his assenting nod. We doused our running lights, and by the thin glow of the moon steered towards the opening of the upper canal. I shut off the motor and reached for a paddle. When we were close enough, Holmes scrambled to shore with the tie-rope, fastening us to a convenient tree.

He led the way down the narrow stone path along the edge of the island, which was light enough to show in the night, but a dozen steps down it I slowed, then stopped altogether. "Holmes, I smell something very dead. Do we want to risk walking through it?"

"I'd rather not use our torches."

"Can we try the other direction?" That was where the buildings lay, but on the other hand, the place was hardly overpopulated.

We doubled back, to walk the canal-side path-way as far as the footbridge. To our left a wide path stretched into the island's centre, which, as the other had been, was little more than a lighter area of ground in the darkness. This one was wider, and went in the direction of the building in which we had seen lights. We took that, pleased to find it firm and silent underfoot. Ahead, a black tower against the night suggested the church; to its right, a faint glow, well above the ground.

It proved to be a couple of upper-storey windows, shuttered against the night. I leaned against Holmes' arm, to breathe. "I don't see any way to look inside, do you?"

Again came the sensation of his shaking head, and we moved on.

The path widened to a sort of tree-dotted *campo*, or maybe orchard, but we kept to the left and found a smaller way circling the church end of the long building. As we came around it, I heard the patter of water against hard stone: this was the small canal that divided central Poveglia from its octagon.

The surface became firmer beneath the weeds. Best of all, the light spilling out from the far end of the building clearly came from ground-floor shutters. We crept past the church, then the high middle portion that had three or four storeys. Dim rectangles glowed above us—suggesting either heavy curtains, or lights from an adjoining inner room.

Then came the third section, the portion with only two floors. Thirty metres away, narrow stripes of light spilled from two windows, revealing wall, weeds, overgrown path, then sparkling water. We stood for a time, listening to the night: the sough of the wind; a susurration of water against moss-draped rock; the whine of a mosquito in search of blood. As I raised my collar against that last, I heard a sort of gulping squawk from farther up the island, followed by the faint, high thread of noise that was the voice of a bat.

No machinery, no gramophone records. Trams with iron wheels might have been a thousand miles away. Only the vague aroma of wood-smoke suggested that the building beside us was inhabited by human beings.

Holmes' shoe gritted against the path as he moved forward. I followed, all senses alert. A bat darted through a shaft of light, hunting the attracted moths. When brightness lay at the very toes of our shoes, we stopped again to listen. Something large moved behind the shutters. A small metallic clatter was followed by a muttering voice.

Calf-high weeds lay between the path and the building, but nothing large enough—or sharp enough—to keep us from peering through the cracks. I allowed Holmes to continue to the far window, then together we crept forward.

The air smelt odd, the closer I drew to the lighted room, of chemicals and burning paraffin. Taking care not to touch the wood itself, I leaned forward to squint into the dazzle between the shutters.

A heavy line obscured the left-hand side of my vision, but beyond it was an array of glittering glass shapes and, oddly, some kind of chart on the wall. I gingerly moved over a step, to a spot where a gap between two boards offered a narrow horizontal view of the room.

Another heavy upright—and because I had recently spent a night in a room framed by precisely that view, I recognised it instantly: an iron bar, set into the window-frame between the closed shutter and the now-open glass pane behind. The glittering shapes were laboratory equipment: test tubes, flasks, alembics, and retorts—a Kipp's apparatus stood to one side, identical to ours in Sussex, and as with our laboratory, the shelves held everything from homely baking soda to stoppered apothecary bottles whose labels wrapped halfway around the sides. Everything not on a shelf was lined up across a high wooden work-bench, along with an old-fashioned microscope, an electric desk-light for close work, several kinds of mortars and pestles, a Bunsen burner (currently unlit), three different sizes of mounted clamps, and various objects whose use I did not know. My gaze lifted to the back of the room: the charts included one of the blood flow in a human body, one with the muscles in a human body, and a third showing all the organs in a human body.

This would have been quite ominous enough, considering that Poveglia was an island from which passers-by heard shrieks and wails. But then I inched a bit farther over and what came into view froze me in my tracks. An autopsy table. It had draining troughs around the edges, an array of lights overhead, and a set of shelves with metal trays holding all the requisite scalpels, bone-saws, and mallets needed to open a corpse—everything but, I was extremely grateful to see, the corpse itself. The table held nothing but a crumpled rag.

Dear God, what was going on here?

When a white shape crossed my field of vision, it so startled me that I stepped back, catching my heel on a stone and nearly sprawling onto the ground.

I did manage to keep my own madhouse-shriek firmly behind my teeth. I took a deliberate breath, let it out, and brushed myself off—not looking to see if Holmes had noticed—before returning my eye to the crack.

It was a man in a doctor's white coat, ill-shaven and haggard. His hair needed cutting—and combing and probably washing as well. The coat was riddled with unsavoury smears; its breast pocket bulged with writing implements and scraps of paper; one side-seam was torn up from the hem. His hands were nicked and discoloured, like Holmes in the throes of a chemical investigation. If I'd been told the man's name was Moreau, I would not have doubted it for a moment.

He had crossed the room to mix something in one of the mortars, taking the stopper from a glass storage bottle and measuring out a scoop of some brilliant green powder resembling chromium oxide. I watched for a while, but despite having a first in chemistry, I could make no sense of what he was doing.

Perhaps Holmes would know.

In any case, the doctor appeared satisfied with the progress of his mixture. He abandoned it on the work-bench. Wiping his hands on the front of his coat, he went back across the room to the autopsy table. He pulled a tray from one of the shelves, removed a couple of instruments, and bent over the rag on the table.

Except it was not a crumpled rag. It was a creature, slightly larger than my fist—and when he picked it up to position it better under the lights, the long naked tail identified it.

A dissected rat is less troubling than a human autopsy, but still.

The man bent to his work. As he did so, a sound rose in the night, a sound that took a moment to identify: the man had begun to hum beneath his breath, a tuneless buzz of noise that, along with his nonchalant dabs and slices and flicking aside of scraps, set my skin to crawling.

Chapter Forty

....

I'D HAD ENOUGH—AND SO, I WAS GRATEFUL TO SEE, HAD Holmes. We left our spy-holes and continued to the end of the building. No windows here, no autopsy tables, no rats, nothing but the sultry breath coming off the lagoon.

I gave an exaggerated shudder. Holmes started to reach for his cigarettes before he caught himself—he, too, appeared to have found the room troubling.

"Holmes, what the hell was that?"

"Curious, I agree."

"Not the word I'd have used. Creepy, yes. Macabre? Disgusting? Just plain weird? God, yes."

"Some of his equipment was remarkably out of date," Holmes mused.

"Not that autopsy table," I objected. It looked precisely like the one I'd tried to avoid the last time Lestrade dragged us into a murder investigation.

"True. And one of the graduated cylinders was made by the Corning company in America within the past ten years."

I didn't bother asking how he knew. "Holmes, we *can't* leave Vivian here. Not with that going on."

"Frankly, I am not sure precisely what *was* going on in that laboratory."

"Creepy stuff? Autopsies?"

"Merely a necropsy. Unless you propose that a human might have a tail like that."

Not unless that really was Dr Moreau—but I did not say it aloud. "I'm not sure it matters. Whatever he was doing, I doubt Ronnie and her mother would be happy to have Vivian anywhere near it."

"You suggest we storm in and remove her forcibly from the premises?"

"Don't you? Holmes, I know you brought your gun with you." The care he had taken in keeping that side of his jacket away from me on the gondola and in the Runabout had made it obvious.

"Russell, your friend's aunt has been here for some days—perhaps as long as a week and a half. Wouldn't you prefer to approach her on, as it were, neutral territory? Miss Maxwell's party is less than eighteen hours away."

I counted wavelets for a while, watching the shimmer of light across the water. Then I sighed. He was right: Vivian might be here against her will; however, to be suddenly and violently wrenched out of her bed by an armed rescuer would be traumatic even for a woman of unquestioned stability.

"All right. But, Holmes—if she doesn't show up at the Lido tonight, we're coming here first thing Sunday morning to carry her out."

Chapter Forty-one

WE RETURNED TO THE EXCELSIOR'S HARBOUR IN MUCH the same way we had left: I paused to let Holmes off at its mouth on the lagoon. He created another distraction (not a fire this time) while I steered the valiant little boat up to its allotted berth. Somewhat short of petrol, true, but I hoped the Hon Terry would check the gauge before he ran it too far out from shore.

I met Holmes (slightly out of breath) and we woke our snoring gondolieri, who rowed the distance from Lido to Piazza somewhat more slowly than they had on the way out. We took to our beds as the sun was turning the mist to warm pearl.

I woke to a faint sound. I remained face-down, vaguely trying to decide if I could ignore it or if I needed to leap into a posture of defence—and then Holmes, whose thoughts had clearly been running the same sleep-clogged track, identified the noise and rose.

It had been the whisper of an envelope slipped beneath our door. I patted the table for my spectacles, and sat up on the pillows to watch him walk across the room, ripping the flap of the telegram. He read the message without reaction, then handed it to me on his way to the desk telephone.

Mycroft had not bothered to put his reply in code, writing simply:

NAME IS THAT OF INCONVENIENT FIRST WIFE OF
ITALIAN DUKE STOP YOUR LESSER ARISTOCRAT LEFT
ENGLAND TWO DAYS BEFORE YOU DID STOP M

I read it a second time, my brain cells wrestling to attach the words to knowledge. At the third attempt, potential meaning took hold.

"Could he possibly mean the Dalser woman is *Mussolini's* wife? That the President of Italy has locked up a woman in San Clemente?" I exclaimed.

"'Duke' does translate *Il Duce.*" He spoke into the telephone: *"Buongiorno, Signore. Vorrei il caffè, per favore. Si, per due. Si. Grazie."*

"Mussolini. Good Lord, if the papers get wind of this ... No wonder a *Capitano* is willing to go out every day to make sure she's still there! And by 'lesser aristocrat' I suppose he means the Marquess? If so, the man must have left England—oh heavens, barely forty-eight hours after I talked to Ronnie. It's my fault, for not making it clear that she shouldn't tell her mother."

"True. Although it does serve to confirm the location of all the players in our game."

"I'd have been just as glad to leave the Marquess out of it."

"I trust that whatever costume you have for tonight, it will permit you to take your gun?"

He'd eyed the boxes that our costumes had been delivered in, but not enquired further. I grinned. "Oh, yes."

Coffee, breakfast, newspapers, food, and our toilettes took up the remainder of the afternoon. When Holmes came out of the bath, rubbing the towel on his jet-black hair, he stopped dead, glowering at the garments lying across the bed. For him, the Porters' invitation had said: *Come as a hero.* For me, Elsa's instructions were: *Come as your true self.*

"What is that?"

"Your costume, Holmes. Surely you know Zorro? Douglas Fairbanks? No? Never mind, put on some eye makeup and you'll look perfect—and you can hide behind the hat if you need to. You'll also find it a lot easier to play the violin in those than in some of the costumes the shop had on offer."

His gaze travelled to the other set of clothing. "That looks like a man's suit."

"It is. But not just any man." I put on the flesh-coloured half-mask attached to a pair of spectacles, over-sized circles I'd scoured the city to find—and which I'd then had fitted with actual, ground lenses, paying a small fortune to have them done overnight. Seeing no recognition dawn, I added the straw hat, then an expression of bland stupefaction. "Harold Lloyd? That's all right, Holmes, everyone else will recognise it."

It took some convincing for him to don the voluminous pirate's blouse of heavy blue-black silk, the snug trousers, and the rakish scarlet sash that tied around his waist like a lopsided bustle. The hat was not exactly right, its brim being a touch too narrow, but he set his foot down at the red kerchief. "Russell, that is something Mrs Hudson would wear for attacking the cobwebs."

"Well, I suppose you can just keep the hat on. And that moustache you've grown is close enough. Let's see if we need to make adjustments to the mask." Doing so cost him some hair, when he attempted to pull off what I'd tied snugly in place, but the eye-holes were sufficient. More or less.

"You might want to push the mask out of the way before you go down any flights of stairs, Holmes," I suggested. "Especially if you're wearing this."

With a flourish, I pulled the pièce de résistance from its scabbard, slicing the bed-cover as I did so. I looked down in dismay. "Oh, dear. When I told the man to clean it up, I didn't mean to sharpen it as well."

My ageing Zorro came around the bed to gingerly take both rapier and scabbard. In his hand, the grip seemed to nestle into place, the length of shiny steel looking more like an actual weapon than a film prop. He tried it out in the air, quick flicks of the wrist that caused the metal to sing as it had not for me. "This is not a bad piece," he said in surprise.

"No? Well, just make sure you don't leave it lying about. Some drunken idiot could disembowel someone with it."

When he was dressed for the night, his eyes darkened and hair sleeked back, he looked extraordinarily—yes—dashing. The only incongruity was the violin case. Knowing Holmes, once the instrument was tucked under his chin, it would seem a natural part of the Mexican hero's costume.

I, on the other hand, looked like somebody who only had to walk past a house to have it fall on him, who would straighten up just as a beam swung past, who would walk out his door in a new white suit and bump into a child with a chocolate ice-cream cone . . . I gave the looking glass a smile of vacuous innocence, and ambled away towards the *vaporetto*.

Chapter Forty-two

HOLMES WALKED DOWN THE RIVA DEGLI SCHIAVONI AND through the Piazza San Marco. He wore the Spanish don's flat-brimmed hat, although the mask was tucked in the scarlet cummerbund—masks on public streets had been outlawed during the War, anonymity being seen as an invitation to crime, and there was no sign that the Fascists were good-humoured enough to lift the ban. A tourist might get away with nothing more than a stern warning, but an obscured face still attracted the kind of attention he did not at the moment wish. If the police were to stop him for the infraction, they would surely notice that the sword he wore was real. They might even go on to find the gun.

Better to invite the humour of passers-by and look like a damnable motion-picture player. Even the police didn't take a middle-aged Zorro seriously—especially one carrying a violin case.

On he walked, across bridges, through the Piazza, winding through *calli* and *fondamente* and *campi* to the Grand Canal, where he paid double to have the *traghetto* cross the busy waterway *trasversale,* to drop him on the Ca' Rezzonico steps.

The festivities would not get under way for another hour, but the palazzo was humming with activity—hanging up lanterns, mounting torches, taking delivery of trays and boxes. Six swarthy gentlemen, none under six feet tall and all with superbly defined muscles, stood ready to receive guests arriving by water. All six appeared to have climbed from their beds with their sheets clutched around them, although as Holmes drew nearer, he decided their dress was intended to be a sort of toga.

The night's theme was "Come as a Hero," but if these were intended to be gladiators, they were missing their swords.

"*Seite romani?*" he asked the large man who hauled him onto the mossy steps.

"Sorry, mate?"

Not Roman: Australian. "I was asking if you were meant to be ancient Romans?"

The man looked down at his skimpy cotton folds and the hairy knees below. "The lady said we was s'posed to be Greek."

Ah: the brief garment was meant to be a Greek *chiton*, pinned at one shoulder. "Very handsome," Holmes told him.

The large man tugged at the skirts, clearly uncomfortable with the fact that he was standing a good foot above the eye levels of the approaching guests. A gust of wind would be revealing.

Abruptly, the six men betrayed a shared military past by snapping to attention and all but clicking their rope sandals together. Holmes turned to find Cole's wife, Linda, in the doorway, her beautiful face wearing a professional smile. She was wrapped in a silken dressing-gown, makeup on but hair still pinned: either she was to be a hero of the boudoir, or she had yet to finish her own preparations. "Mr Russell, there you are—Cole was wondering if you were going to be late."

Linda ran the household with an iron hand: being late, he had been informed early on, was a mortal sin that condemned a man to the eternal punishment of being removed from the Porter guest lists.

"I wouldn't think of it," he assured her.

She gave him a quick and dismissive nod, then addressed the smallest of the six would-be Greeks. "You may light the torches. You all know where the buckets are, in case of mishap?"

Six hands instantly snapped out to point at their nearest fire-buckets. Linda nodded, peered up and down the Canal in satisfaction, turned—and gave Holmes a surprised look, evidently having expected him to be on his way to report for duty. She slid her arm through his in a manner both friendly and decisive, moved him into the damp ground-floor *portego* as far as the workaday, non–ceremonial staircase, and launched him on his way. He continued upwards, smiling to himself. He liked Linda Porter, but as seemed to be the rule amongst Cole's friends, thought it wise not to cross her.

He found Cole in one corner of the huge ballroom, wearing an open-necked shirt, twill trousers, and soft shoes over his customary white socks. The piano had been moved in and now sat on a low stage, along with an assortment of band equipment, from banjo to megaphone. Porter was playing a tune Holmes hadn't heard before, jaunty on the surface but with an intriguing thread of melancholy. He paused, frowning at some technical problem Holmes couldn't begin to guess, but when he reached for his cigarette, he noticed he wasn't alone.

"Hey! That's a dashing outfit."

"So I am told."

"Linda will love it."

"I saw her downstairs, making certain the torches were lit. I think she was going upstairs to dress."

"Lord, that time already?" Porter mashed out his cigarette and stood. "I won't be long, go ahead and get a feel for the room."

The sun was nearing the horizon. It was an hour at which Holmes (to himself if no other) would admit a grudging admiration for the centuries of communal effort that had gone into shaping this peculiar city—especially when the view was filtered by the watery effects of eighteenth-century glass. He gazed across the red-tile roof-tops for a time, then turned to the wishes of his current employer, undoing the clasps on the case and tucking the violin under his chin. He moved about the room, his gaze rising to the frescoed ceiling, twice the height of the other rooms on the *piano nobile*. There, the chariot of Phoebus battled the dimming glaze of two centuries of smoke from fires, tobacco, and candles—a touch ironic, considering that the god's name meant *brightness*.

The old violin began a cantata—the piece that had been the subject of his aborted studies in the Reading Room, a mere two weeks ago. The notes were Bach; the words addressed the question of good art versus bad, with Phoebus and Pan arguing their respective cases amidst a whirlwind of supporters and critics. As he walked up and down the ballroom, the instrument found certain spots where some combination of architecture and decor caused its voice to sing, brightening the dusk and giving polish to the stained frescoes. He was not surprised that the best place of all was where Porter had located his piano.

At the whisper of motion behind him, he edited the Phoebus aria to bring it to an end. A pair of hands began to clap, and he swung into a bow of acknowledgment.

"Good old John Sebastian," Cole said.

"Did you know the librettist for that cantata was a lawyer?"

"Picander? No, I hadn't heard that. I was at law school myself for a while, before I fell in with that old seductress, music."

"Were you?"

"Yes indeedy. Nearly killed my grandfather when he found out I'd left the straight and narrow. Just think, I could be running the business today if I'd just played my cards right." His homely face broke into a grin.

"A great loss to the world of commerce, I'm sure."

Porter's garment was similar to that of the muscle-men at the palazzo's entrance, although while theirs had been coarse cotton in the brief servants' length, his came to the ankles and was of a luxuriously heavy silk, subtly woven, with a geometrical border of rich golden threads. It also covered more of his upper body, which was just as well: the pianist's muscles were no match for an Australian stevedore's.

As the young man crossed the ballroom, Holmes noticed that the border of his tunic was echoed by a golden aura around his dark hair: a laurel wreath, crafted from exquisitely thin gold leaves, so light he seemed to have forgot he had it on. The delicate shapes shimmered with his every move. It should have looked ridiculous, atop such a physically unprepossessing figure of a man: it did not.

Although it did stretch his dignity nearly to the breaking point when he dropped onto the bench and began to warble, "Yes, We Have No Bananas," not waiting for Holmes to catch him up. At the end of the chorus, he shifted into C minor, and with the darkening of keys, his words shifted as well.

> *Yes, we have no girls for you,*
> *We have no girls for you today.*
> *We've nice lads and ladies*
> *And old tarts with scabies—*

The words grew ever more suggestive and tinged with shades of blue, although typical of the man, they never descended to raw obscenity. They also broke off the instant Linda appeared in the doorway, returning to the more prosaic chorus of Greeks and bananas followed by a triumphant piano crescendo and violin glissando. The two men held . . . then cut off.

Linda clapped politely, then swept into the ballroom, followed by three guests who wore the awkward expressions of people realising they're the first at a party. Porter instantly leapt to his feet to welcome them, and somehow ended up making them feel as if they'd done him a special favour by coming before the rabble descended and robbed him of the chance to talk to these, his true friends. Holmes, meanwhile, gritted his teeth into a smile and settled into the task of playing as background texture to the sounds of people having fun. He had resigned himself to Rossini arias and Verdi melodies, along with some girls' school music from Vivaldi. Once the noise rose he might get away with a motet or two from Monteverdi.

Twenty minutes later, the windows were dark, the ballroom was filling nicely, and the noise level had rendered the violin all but redundant, even from its position of greatest authority near the piano. Holmes had seen several familiar faces, enough to be glad for the wide don's hat which, together with the status of Paid Entertainer, rendered him invisible. When he came to the end of his current slice of Vivaldi, he ended with a flourish—and no one noticed.

Except Linda. She materialised from the crowd with a glass in her hand, holding it out with a smile of exceptional warmth. He transferred the bow to his left hand, took the glass, and raised it in a gesture that incorporated both thanks and a toast.

She leaned forward to have a word, a curiously intimate gesture from this formal woman. "The band is just finishing their dinner; you can have a rest."

"It has been a pleasure." And the champagne was not only proper Champagne, it was perfectly chilled.

"You are very good, Mr Russell, for an itinerant musician. I couldn't think what Cole was doing, inviting you to play, but I should have trusted his judgment. Why aren't you in an orchestra somewhere?"

"Oh, Mrs Porter, I am naught but an amateur."

"A gifted one. But if you weren't professional, what did you do?"

"This and that, and some of the other." Linda Porter was of the class who did not expect a man to have a profession. "A bit of consultation, from time to time."

"One of those clever devils who look at a business and see how it would be run better?"

"Something of the sort. And I hope it will not seem forward if I were to say that I cannot imagine any way to improve on your efforts tonight."

The compliment pleased her. She stood beside him for a moment looking over the big room filled with men and women in heroic dress. There were various Roman-type costumes that might have been Marcus Aurelius or Caesar—or Alexander the Great, for that matter. He saw two versions of George Washington, a Florence Nightingale, three

Emmeline Pankhursts, a Harriet Beecher Stowe, a Robert the Bruce, half a dozen versions of Pocahontas or perhaps Sacagawea (two of them male), one remarkably fit and blond Mahatma Gandhi, several equally well-endowed versions of Achilles, a man with the moustaches of Louis Bleriot, and more Ernest Shackletons than he could count—although he'd seen Linda send their various dogs (some of them taxidermy) out to the garden.

"Mr Russell, you seem to be our only Zorro so far."

"And you, Madame, the only true Hero."

At that, the lovely face dimpled. "You caught it!"

"What, that you and Cole are Hero and Leander? Of course."

"No one else has."

"Mrs Porter, you see before you the product of an outmoded educational system, which is based upon beating Latin and Greek into a boy's mind before he has a chance to meet the penny-dreadful."

"Poor you."

"Indeed. Though it does make one remarkably well suited to games of charades." He took another swallow of the rather nice champagne, listening to her lovely laughter rising above the hubbub—but then the room's ambience seemed to shift, and go a touch dark.

Literally so, with the entrance of two men dressed entirely in black.

Ebony suits, shirts, shoes. Black neck-ties and belts—Holmes wondered idly if their undergarments and pocket-handkerchiefs had been dyed to match.

Linda, following his gaze, made a small noise that might have been a curse, instantly stifled. The two men at the entrance to the ballroom looked large and implacable and out of place amidst the bright colours and happy noise. The one in the new-looking suit—older, larger, and standing slightly to the fore—was clearly the other's trophy: proud proof that the junior man was entering a new and influential world.

The foreigners among the guests looked somewhat puzzled; the Italians looked either approving or uneasy. Some among the latter found reason to fade back into the room.

Cole appeared at his wife's elbow. The Porters exchanged an eloquent and resolute glance, then donned brittle smiles of social cordiality to step down from the low stage and move towards the entrance.

Capitano Francoletti and the Marquess of Selwick had arrived amidst the Caesars and Shackletons, both of them dressed in the fashion of their Fascist hero, Benito Mussolini.

Chapter Forty-three

I WONDERED HOW HOLMES WAS GETTING ON, ACROSS the lagoon in the civilised atmosphere of Ca' Rezzonico. Long before my *vaporetto* reached its stop on the Lido, I began to hear the Excelsior's band above the chug and chuff of the motor. As I walked across the narrow island, the very air seemed to reverberate: if there was a tinkling piano—heavens, if there was a full men's chorus—one could not hear them.

When the cupolas and flags of the Excelsior were before me, I stopped to fit the Harold Lloyd spectacles through the mask. Settling the hat more firmly onto my slicked-down hair, I crossed the road to the cabaret.

I walked into a maelstrom. Gyrating figures, dazzling lights, the blare of trumpets and pound of drums, merged with the beach-resort tang of sweat and salt and alcohol and smoke of many kinds. It was dizzying, the wild pound and motion pulling at one's blood in an effect that was primitive, overwhelming, and impossible to resist. The intentions I'd carried across the lagoon blew away like a wisp of eiderdown.

In the face of this, any attempt to remain aloof and alert was preposterous. One could either flee, or join the frenzy.

And I was not permitted to flee.

I paused just inside the Chez Vous door, struggling for a point of balance between the hot pull of the cabaret and the cold needs of working a case. Committing myself to that dance floor would make it impossible to keep a careful eye out for the arrival of Lady Vivian and her nurse companion. But standing back and watching would put me outside of the crowd I needed to blend with.

I took a deep breath, and plunged in.

Many years later, I would participate in an aquatic event known as white-water rafting, a sort of half-guided fall down a long series of dangerously fast and boulder-strewn rapids. On that distant day, as I reached for a balance between pure terror and a desperate attempt at control, I would find the same attitude that saved me that night on the Excelsior dance floor: a small, cool voice directing an endless tumble through an irresistible force, with the one goal of not actually going under. Time and again, the pull that nearly drew me down—the temptation to just throw it all away and accept that I was going to wake up the next day under a table, or on the beach, or in someone's bed—instead heaved me to the surface again, and I would see my hand reaching out for an olive- or fruit-bedecked glass and deflect it to the one containing only water.

The thin voice of sanity remained, overwhelmed but attending to my surroundings. And so, when a small figure flashed by my fast-moving eyes, I continued circling my partner about—one advantage of being the male partner—to look again.

A diminutive figure in a cloud of warm colour: loose gold dress, turquoise belt and shoes, terra-cotta-coloured plumes in her bandeau; a woman with pale hair and a beautiful gold-and-blue mask; a woman dancing with a figure in evening suit and simple black half-mask—a figure who had a dark mole along the jaw-line.

When the song ended, I bowed to my partner and abandoned her, making my way to the bar area at the less frenetic edges of the cabaret. As Harold Lloyd, I could have access to Vivian Beaconsfield simply by inviting her out onto the floor—but first, I wanted to watch. The band started up again. Vivian and her partner obeyed its call, while I eyed the two of them over the top of my glass.

I saw no trace of the dull, subdued woman I had met in the grey surroundings of Bedlam three years before. This cloth-of-gold creature was a swirl of light—loose frock, dancing fringe, a blur of colour from the plumed crown. She sparkled from head to toe. She even seemed taller than that dull, hunched figure who'd been brought to the asylum's visiting room. With her heeled shoes, she was only three or four inches shorter than Nurse Trevisan.

And the nurse. The half-mask obscured her eyes, but she never looked away from Vivian, never stopped grinning. Her arms—positioned in the man's rôle—were both supportive and encouraging. Some men bully their partners, others use them to show off: Rose Trevisan encouraged her partner to move wherever she wanted.

The two women leapt and shimmied with hundreds of others, in and among the *contessas* and *principes,* the sons of railway barons and the daughters of newspaper titans. And yet the pair were in a world of their own. There was affection in their stance and the touch of their hands—more, there was . . . trust.

Every inch of Vivian Beaconsfield shouted her joy.

I would have been very happy to walk away from the Lido then and there, leaving the two women to their dancing and their Venetian lives. Wherever they were hiding, here in the lagoon with their Dr Moreau, they had found what they wanted, and deserved.

But . . . the Marquess was in Venice, too. I could not go without warning Vivian—and without seeing what I could do to set the situation right. It was my carelessness that led Lord Selwick here, and put her back into his reach.

When the song ended, I set down my glass of champagne and took a step out onto the dance floor.

Only to have the sky explode overhead.

Hundreds of sweating faces craned upwards; hundreds of throats emitted a chorus of *Oohs.* Hundreds of masked faces turned blue and then red with the bursts of the Excelsior's fireworks. And although they were going off right overhead, most of the dancers began to move towards the beach and gardens, so as not to have one scrap of trailing ember hidden by the hotel's roof-lines.

The plumed head-dress was tall enough that I could glimpse it across the crowd. I kept back, not wanting to alarm Vivian's keeper when they were a brief dash from freedom: time enough, when the fireworks ended and they came back into the cabaret, to speak to Ronnie's aunt unmolested.

The sea of people gleamed and flared and shifted colour. Exclamations rose at any spectacular or intricate burst of light. Even the band musicians came out to watch. A few explosions later, I noticed the Hon Terry, shoulder to shoulder with a very handsome young Venetian. He caught my eye, and we traded grins above the intervening heads.

The pops and booms from overhead built to a crescendo, until the last sparks were floating down towards the Adriatic. Reluctantly, the enthralled masses lowered their chins and looked around for the next thrill. The band stamped out their cigarettes and returned to their instruments, but to my surprise, the flow of the crowd divided, with some marching back for the dance floor, while an almost equal number drifted away in the direction of the beach-side doors. For many, the sky show marked the end of an exhausting and satisfying night, leaving the Chez Vous population much diminished.

I took a step towards the hotel—and had to grab the back of a garden bench to keep from keeling over. What was this? I'd been drugged! Someone had adulterated my drink, I must . . .

No, my brain patiently informed me. In between a handful of glasses containing nothing more than mineral water, I'd also consumed a great deal of champagne, punch, and heaven only knew what else. *Just pause a minute and breathe deeply; your feet will start working again. And your brain.* Did I really want to speak with an already nervous woman while I was in this condition?

I peered into the dance-hall, and there she was, happily fox-trotting across the floor. On the far side of the dancers—with space now between them, one could see—the Elsa Maxwell table had resumed, with some of the less fit individuals sitting and talking enthusiastically about something or other.

So I, too, sat for a while, on a garden bench overlooking the water. I took off the mask, rubbing at where it had irritated my nose and temples, then laid it beside me on the bench. This was one of those times I wished I smoked, to give my hands purpose—but when I became aware of a growing disinclination to rejoin the dancers, I fitted the mask on again, got up, and directed my feet back into Chez Vous.

However, the fireworks display that had signalled an end to the day for many seemed to have had the opposite effect on those I was with—or perhaps it was the diminished state of the dance floor. It was then I learned how much of an understatement the Hon Terry's comment was, that a Maxwell-generated affair tended to "get a bit out of hand." An Elsa Maxwell "do" was less a planned party than a lit fuse: shape the charge, point it upwards, then stand back to watch the fireworks. Unfortunately, I was only halfway across the dance floor when this one went off.

Miss Elsa Maxwell rose grandly to her feet and swept towards the entrance, pulling with her a flood of others, giggling and guffawing and grabbing their hats, wraps, and discarded masks.

Amidst the gabble I heard an alarming series of words: *Porter* and *Cole*, *Grand Canal* and *boats*—and belatedly, figured out what was going on.

The Lido set was gate-crashing Ca' Rezzonico.

A riot spilled from the Excelsior, washing out onto the road and stumbling with hilarity over the tram-tracks. Any faint hope I might have had that their intentions would be stymied by the lack of late-night *vaporetti* vanished when they headed, not for the public docks, but into the manicured gardens and down to the yacht-strewn inlet. Every boat-owner in the crowd had his own mob of best friends; money was pressed into the hands of strangers to commandeer their resting vessels into taxi service; motors started up, women shrieked, men shouted.

And I was ruthless in fighting my way to the side of the Hon Terry, whose boat was sure to be the fastest there.

Except that we were third out of the little harbour. And the Hon Terry was both safety-minded and distracted by his handsome Venetian friend.

The *laguna*'s speed limits are set for good reason. Between floating débris and the chance of late-night gondolas and swimming poets, out-distancing one's front lantern is an act of murderous irresponsibility.

But the boat ahead of us held a small, blonde-headed woman and a figure with a black half-mask.

So I took a resolute breath, and elbowed Terry out of the way.

At least I had the sense not to instantly push the boat into water-skiing speed, setting off a drunken race. Instead, I veered away, maintaining our sedate progress but in the direction of the lagoon's southern reaches. Protest rose up, voices calling for Terry to take back the wheel, that we were going wrong, that we'd never—

But the moment I'd put San Servolo between us and the others, I shouted a command to hang on, and hauled the controls all the way up.

When the two boats came back into view, we were not only at a distance, but at an unexpected angle. And since I did not immediately roar up to the front of the pack, but instead kept well to the side, I became a different boat entirely, a curiosity instead of a challenge.

I took the slim canal between the Giudecca and San Giorgio Maggiore at a marginally slower pace, then instantly resumed our breakneck speed the instant we emerged into the channel. Whoops and cries rose from my passengers, although the Hon Terry looked more and more alarmed as we approached the mouth of the Grand Canal. The sleek boat leaned on its side as I swung around *la Salute*. Courting couples and insomniacs propped against the railings of the Accademia Bridge leapt back in terror as we roared beneath their feet.

Only then did I pull back on the throttle, wondering which one was Ca' Rezzonico. I expected the equivalent of the Lido noises, tumult and a blare of music, but either the Porters' festivities had finished early, or the ballroom was back from the Canal—then at the next kink in the canal it became obvious: who but a pair of obscenely rich Americans would adorn their entrance with brilliant flaming torches and an array of Greek wrestlers?

I glanced back along the Grand Canal. When I saw no lights approaching, I let out the breath I'd been holding since San Servolo: we were here before Vivian. I came in to the palazzo a bit firmly—Terry let out an anguished protest—but the instant our rope was in the hands of the resident Greeks I waved my cohort forward, commanding, "Go! Hurry up! This party's just getting started!"

Laughter and shrieks resumed as if a switch had been turned. The puzzled Greeks sprang to help these late arrivals, but when the man holding our rope moved to tie it, I told him not to, that I'd move the boat over myself.

Terrence made to take the wheel, but I clung on hard. "Oh, you two go ahead in. I'll just make sure there's room for the other boats, and be up in a minute."

My calm demeanour convinced him, along with his new friend's eagerness. But before they got out, I said to Terry, "Oh—and would you look around for a violinist dressed as Zorro? Please? He'll want to know I'm here. Thanks."

The next boat chugging along the Grand Canal held our fearless leader. Elsa Maxwell disembarked grandly into the muscular bare arms of the Greeks, followed by an extraordinary number of passengers in a sort of circus clown-car effect. I made the Greeks (they weren't Greeks, they were a mix of dock-workers from all over) tie that boat down at the far end—which meant that the third boat to arrive would put in beside the Runabout.

By this time, rumour of the gate-crashers, or perhaps of my dramatic arrival down the peaceable waterway, seemed to be percolating among the Porters' guests, a few of whom had come out onto the balcony—which had strings of electric lights rather than torches—to view the entertainments below.

I kept my Harold Lloyd mask in place, and waited for the next boat and its small, golden passenger.

It came at last, lumbering down the waterway, barely nosing out the fourth in our procession, which had left the Lido on our heels. The two would dock nearly simultaneously. I could not take a chance at it being the wrong side.

I clambered out to jump onto the slippery forecourt, grabbing one substantial biceps to keep from going down. "Hold this rope for a minute," I ordered, and pushed between his fellow Grecian stevedores to await the next invaders.

The lumbering boat slowed more, turned its nose, and came into the light, directly in front of me. I stepped onto its prow before any of its passengers could move.

She'd taken off the golden mask, her naked face staring up at me as I dropped down beside her.

"My lady—Vivian—wait here a moment."

She jerked back, terrified at the sound of her name from a concealed and unknown man. The nurse's arm came forward—and with a curse under my breath, I shoved up my bespectacled mask. "It's me, Ronnie's friend, Mary. Mary Russell, remember? We met at . . . at Bedlam."

Three years before, I'd had long hair gathered atop my head, steel-framed spectacles, and the pallid complexion of an Oxford undergraduate. Vivian stared, one timid hand reaching out for the support of her friend. At last she glanced sideways, by way of consultation, and I let the mask drop so as to restore my vision. "I'm terribly sorry about this," I began, but my explanation was cut short when her gaze flicked upwards to the Porters' official guests, gathered along the upstairs balcony.

Her mouth dropped open, a rictus of pain underscored by a high-pitched moan. Her hands snapped up, her body bent away, and the nurse wrapped strong arms around her, searching for the threat.

When I looked up, I saw it staring down, caught in a flare of the fiery torches.

Edward, Marquess of Selwick.

Chapter Forty-four

....

"COME!" I SNAPPED, PUTTING ONE ARM AROUND THE smaller woman and half-lifting her into Terry's boat. Nurse Trevisan hesitated, not having seen the Marquess, but faced by Vivian cringing in terror and a stranger in a Harold Lloyd outfit offering escape, she decided to go now and sort it out after.

I'd left the boat's motor running for precisely this reason, and slapped it into Reverse, nearly yanking my Greek attendant into the Canal. The instant our prow was clear of the other hulls, I spun the wheel and shoved the handle into Forward. The throaty engine bit into the water, nearly obscuring the shouts from behind—but when I looked back, I immediately took it out of gear and let the nose drift towards the side.

The dark figure racing along the narrow frontage tore off his mask and, as our two paths coincided, he simply took to the air—to come crashing against the rear passenger well just as two figures in black burst out of the palazzo in pursuit. I waited until my new passenger's legs had drawn up towards safety, then slapped the motor into gear and headed for the mouth of the Canal. A backwards glance assured me that he was in—and that one of the pursuers had gone down on the slick stones, the other man stopping to help him.

But the boats at the palazzo would all have their keys in them, so I pressed on the speed, and flew as fast as I dared over the dark water.

I felt his presence at my back, and shouted over my shoulder. "Welcome aboard, Holmes."

"Had I known that Zorro would be required to take flight," he answered, "I'd have rigged a line from the roof-top."

We were under the Accademia Bridge when a woman's voice came. "Slow down, and turn here."

Nurse Trevisan. I throttled back, and followed her directions into the side canal.

"Pull to the side up there, just after the *sandòlo,* and shut down the motor." Figuring she meant a kind of boat, I pulled into the only gap I saw. As we slowed, she clambered onto the Runabout's front to shut down the forward light, then retrieved the dripping rope, stepping onto the *fondamenta* to pull us in. Holmes turned off the aft light and took hold of a cleat set into the walk-way. Our motion stopped. There was not enough light down here to reveal us—unless they, too, came down the canal.

We waited. And waited . . .

Two minutes, three—and a boat roared past the mouth of the canal.

I let my shoulders slump with the relief of tension, but I made no move to get us going again. Instead, I asked Holmes to see if there were any travelling rugs under the back passenger seats. When he found one, I waited until the nurse had wrapped it around Vivian's shoulders against the night.

And then I asked the woman to walk away out of earshot.

She looked to Vivian, who hesitated, then nodded. The boat bounced as Nurse Trevisan's weight left it, and I waited until her footsteps faded before I spoke, keeping my voice low.

"Vivian, this is my husband, Sherlock Holmes. We're here because I promised Ronnie and her mother that I'd find you. But before I can explain any further—and certainly before I can decide what to do—I need to know what is going on. Why did you leave England so suddenly, and steal the necklace, and not tell anyone where you were going? Didn't you realise it would look as if something had happened to you? Am I right in thinking you've been hiding on . . ." I heard my voice rising, and forced myself to stop. We could sit here all night while I pelted her with questions—and that was before I tried to explain how her brother came to be here.

First things first: "Vivian, I simply need to know who's in charge of your life."

She had looped the ties of the mask around her left wrist, and played with it now, its ornate surfaces gleaming in the faint light. "I am sorry . . . I intended to write Dorothy and Ronnie as soon as I could find someone to post a letter from some town far away. I do understand how concerned the two of them must be. But in truth, Miss Russell, I took nothing that was not mine to begin with. And there is nowhere I wish to be other than here."

"All right, well, let's begin with that last. I'm guessing you're on Poveglia, right? Look, last night Holmes and I went out there and we saw that . . . that doctor, who lives on the island. He's doing some dreadful things there."

Vivian looked amazed—but then, to my astonishment, she burst into merry laughter. It was a startling sound, one I had never heard before—one I'd not expected to hear ever, much less in reply to a question like that.

"I believe I should invite you home," she said, and raised her voice a fraction. "Rose?"

Nurse Trevisan's footsteps returned out of the darkness, until she stood looking down into the boat.

"We shall have guests," Vivian told her.

The nurse looked from me to Holmes, then nodded and went to light the front lamp. Holmes did the same to the rear one, and I nursed the big engine into a slow crawl up the narrow canal.

Near its end, Nurse Trevisan had me pull aside and wait while she walked up to the Giudecca Canal to look for our pursuers.

When she came back, she asked if I dared cross the water without lights.

"It would not be the first maritime sin I've committed tonight," I told her. This time, I went slowly, so as to give our hull a chance against large floating objects. Holmes moved up, sitting on the decking that covered the motor and dropping his feet onto the empty seat behind where I stood. Nurse Trevisan also remained standing, watching the water first in one direction, then the other.

Drawing near the other side, she directed me into a narrow opening, and we passed through that canal as well, the throb of the engine echoing off the high buildings. At this one's end, she repeated the manoeuvre of walking ahead and looking.

When she stepped back into the Runabout, she said, "Let's light the lamps but go slowly. If they're out there, they'll be looking for someone in a hurry."

So I took my leisurely time, tucking our passage in beside the string of islands as closely as I could. The night grew chill; Vivian leaned against the other woman's legs, for warmth and companionship, her feathered bandeau dancing in the breeze. Holmes waited for a hidden patch to light a cigarette, and smoked it behind sheltering hands. Santa Maria della Grazia, then San Clemente, with its mysterious Portuguese woman and its inconvenient First Lady, followed by Santo Spirito—until finally, Poveglia lay before us.

"Turn off the motor," said Nurse Trevisan, the first words spoken since we had emerged from the last canal.

I silenced the boat and we lay, bobbing gently, straining to hear the sound of a motor above the breeze. Nothing.

Our engine coughed into life and I eased our valiant and twice-stolen craft in beside the other vessel in the narrow boat-house, trying to ignore the spill of lights from the macabre ground-floor laboratory. The nurse tied up, shut the boat-house doors, and pulled out a tiny pocket-torch to lead us towards the inner side of the long building.

This side was the *campo*, or perhaps derelict orchard, that Holmes and I had passed through the night before. Keys rattled into a lock. A click of mechanism turning; a door wheezed open.

Inside was a dimly-lit foyer that joined the middle of a long institutional corridor with many doors on either side. A small light bulb burned directly overhead in this cross-roads, with another over the stairway we climbed. The layout on the upper floor was much the same, although the walls here were covered with fresh-looking wallpaper rather than the dingy paint below.

The nurse went through the first door to the left. As we filed in, she set about lighting a paraffin lamp, then crossed the room to make sure the curtains were drawn. This was a communal sitting room, with chairs and settees that would accommodate twenty or more people, arranged in three casual groups. A large fireplace occupied the inner wall, clean and bare for the summer but for a vase of dry grasses.

Nurse Trevisan said, "I need a cup of tea. Vee?"

Vivian had sat in what seemed to be a favourite chair, which in the daytime would be next to a garden window, and was in the process of unpinning the plumed crown—slightly the worse for wear—from her blonde head. "Oh, yes thanks."

"And for you two? Tea, coffee, cocoa? A drink?"

Holmes and I were both happy with tea. She nodded and walked out, crossing the hallway to an open door on the other side: the run of water; the scrape of a match, and the puff of gas igniting. I exchanged glances with Holmes, who followed the nurse. Vivian placed the head-dress, mask, and a small pocketbook on the low table at the centre of her chosen circle of chairs, then kicked off her shoes and tucked her feet under her on the wide cushion.

"Which is your room?" I asked.

"Why?"

I did not answer, but after a moment she nodded as if I had. "You want to know if there are bars on the windows. Back into the hallway and to your right, it's the fourth one on the right after the stairs. Take a lamp. And kindly be quiet, Miss Russell. Women are sleeping."

The hallway was plain, its floors of tile cracked here and there but clean to the edges. The walls had fresh wallpaper; the fourth door had been recently painted. And it was clearly her bedroom: the first thing that caught my eye when I held up the lamp was an odd flesh-toned half-mask with moustache, precisely the size of one of the gaps on her wall in Selwick. Hanging beside it were two photographs, both taken in the Selwick garden. One was of her brother Thomas, which from his carefree stance was taken before the War. The other was more recent, showing Thomas' wife and daughter. This one I could date with some precision, because Ronnie's pregnancy was just beginning to show. She glowed with happiness.

The room was even more sparsely furnished than the rooms she had made for herself at Selwick. It could be simply that she'd only just arrived. Still, its walls had been freshly painted, and in the same colours as the other: warm terra cotta, cool turquoise. Which, I suddenly realised, were the very colours of Venice.

There were no bars on the windows. Her wardrobe held colourful new clothing, from skirts to shoes to four brand-new belts. A pretty bowl on the table held an assortment of fresh fruit. A tiny, pitted bronze figurine—probably Roman, probably a dog—stood beside the lamp on her bed-side table. Inside the table were some papers and two small jeweller's boxes. The smaller one had a Medieval locket on a modern chain; the larger one held an exquisite lapis-and-gold Fabergé egg. I looked carefully at the papers, and as I shut the drawer, I could not help thinking that the bed itself was plenty wide enough for two people.

Smiling, I went back towards the communal room. I could hear snores, and the voices of Nurse Trevisan and Holmes from across the hall, though not the words. I set down the lantern and closed the door, then took a chair across from Vivian, pulling off the Harold Lloyd mask at last. It took some time to disentangle the spectacles, but I did not rush: the nakedness of a face that normally wears glasses is disarming, and I wanted Vivian to feel herself in a position of strength. I finally dropped the mask beside hers and donned the spectacles alone, wrinkling my face to settle the unfamiliar nose-rests into place.

I sat back in the chair, returning her scrutiny.

Why did I keep thinking of Vivian as older than she was? In part, I supposed, because the aunt of a contemporary is usually of the previous generation, but also because when I'd seen her she'd seemed as small and bent as a geriatric. Lady Vivian Beaconsfield was in her early thirties. Tonight, she looked it.

Her hair, artfully tousled by the bandeau, might have belonged to any Young Thing on an Excelsior chaise longue—though her skin was not as tanned, and her eyes were considerably clearer. She'd spent a night dancing followed by two fraught hours in an open boat, and yet she looked less exhausted than I felt.

Time to see how resilient she actually was.

"You came to Venice to get away from your brother."

She winced, but did not retreat. "That's right."

"You used his birthday celebration to get your hands on the diamonds, then took advantage of the confusion not only to slip away, but to take out the money in your bank account." She nodded. "You took a chance with the safe."

She said nothing.

"You wanted a couple of things it held."

"They belonged to my mother's family, not to Selwick."

"Where are the diamonds?"

"They're too valuable to leave around. I had Rose put them in a bank vault in town."

"I'd have thought the egg would go there, too."

"You're right, I should put it there, but my mother loved it so, I wanted to have it for a little while."

"And then, there was this."

I took from my pocket the third thing I had found in the table: a shot in the dark, but I could see it hit home.

She looked at the unsealed envelope without reaching for it. "Did you read it?"

"I merely glanced at the opening lines."

Vivian sighed. "Go ahead."

So I did. I read it with care, looking back at portions and holding it up to the light. I returned it to the envelope. I laid the envelope on the table before her.

"When a person is the subject of a commitment order," she said, "elements of her ... legal status change. When I went into Bedlam, five years ago, my brother Edward was appointed my guardian. That gave him the right to handle my affairs, particularly any financial matters. The most recent order of commitment was revoked two years ago, but when I went to get my mother's Fabergé egg from the safe in his office, I found that."

"It wouldn't take precedence over your official last will and testament."

"No." She raised her gaze at last, and gave me a sad smile. "Not if I was alive."

The document amounted to a new will for The Lady Vivian Beaconsfield, giving the bulk of her possessions to the Marquess of Selwick, "*in recompense for the considerable expenses incurred by the Selwick estate over the lengthy illness of The Lady Vivian.*" That its beneficiary was also its signator, as her named guardian at the time, might be the basis for a legal challenge—if Ronnie and her mother wanted to take the Marquess to court over it.

"When you said you were safe in Bedlam, that day when Ronnie and I came to visit, was this what you meant?"

"No. I was not aware this existed until I saw it two weeks ago. My fears were ... not about that."

"But once the commitment order was cleared, why didn't you simply leave Bedlam? I've been there—it's not the most comfortable place in the world, and you have both family and money. Were you afraid he ... afraid that something might happen to you, on the outside?"

Her eyes closed. When they opened again, her face wore the gaunt, aged look that I had seen there, three years before. "Yes. Except I *knew* it would happen. Eventually. He ... Edward is my *brother!*" she cried. "I ... I loved him, when I was small. I revered him. When he came home for the school holidays, I would treasure any time he deigned to give me—reading a story, building a fortress. He was my big brother, who lived in another world, but occasionally would visit.

"Not like Tommy. Tommy played with me as if he were close to my own age, never made me feel like a child. When he died, my world ended. And when Edward moved back home the following spring, my world . . . turned upside-down. He was unhappy, deeply so, and he . . ."

Her voice faltered, and stopped—but in fact, I had scarcely heard a word after her first cry.

Edward is my brother*!* Four words, but with them, the edifice that I had built, all my conclusions about money and greed and political machinations, everything shifted, to reveal the shape underneath.

That shape had been at the back of my mind for days—weeks, now. The sequence of Vivian's life and madness, the dry notes of the asylum doctors, the cheeky maidservant at Selwick. The dairy-woman, Emma Bailey, had known, and told me across her kitchen table.

Dear God. Those who have ears to hear, let them hear.

The shape had been pushing at me, I think, since the train back from Surrey, when I seized on the clean and straightforward answer of money. I had been loudly irritable with Holmes, so eager to condemn the male race, to condemn the Marquess of a lesser crime, because I could not bear facing the awful knowledge whispering in my ear.

"Your brother molested you."

Her eyes snapped up. "You *know*?"

I was ashamed to tell her how long it had taken me.

Chapter Forty-five

....

I WAS OF COURSE FAMILIAR WITH DR FREUD'S THEORY, that a claim of incest reveals the sex fantasies of an hysteric. But "hysterical" is the modern's cry of witchcraft, its punishment incarceration instead of burning. As a woman—and as a student of Sherlock Holmes—I should have used William of Ockham's razor to cut to the truth: that some claims of incest were in fact just that.

Not that I was certain Vivian Beaconsfield had openly made such a claim. Emma Bailey's suggestion had been far from overt. The notes of a dozen different mental doctors had employed cautious language and faint distress over these accusations made against a man of his rank.

Of course, if she had made those accusations in the open, would it have done her any good? Even I, trained in Holmesian cynicism, had managed to squirm out from the unpleasant hypothesis that Emma Bailey, medical records, and Vivian's own personal history had pushed into my face: namely, that in 1916, Lady Vivian's surviving brother, resentful at being forced out of his lively home in London by the War and financial straits, looked at this pretty and vulnerable twenty-five-year-old near-stranger and saw not a sister, but a woman. And like all women, she was there for his convenience—even if some young housemaids might believe that his interest was personal.

Looking across the table at her, sitting here on this island of the mad, I could not avoid the hardest truth of all: this poor creature had been betrayed, first by her blood, then by those whose job it was to heal her soul. Time and again, she'd been granted asylum; she'd been fed and rested and declared healed—and then, like a shell-shocked soldier, sent back to precisely the situation that had driven her to insanity.

How many women locked inside Victorian asylums, I had to ask myself, were there because they had offended their doctors with disgusting, ungrateful, and obscene "fantasies" about the male relatives who controlled their lives? The crime here was not the theft of a diamond necklace. It was the theft of a woman's person, her security, her very mind and spirit.

I'm safe here, Vivian had said. And she was speaking nothing but the truth. I forced myself to continue.

"You showed no real sign of problem before your brother moved home. But within weeks, you had stripped your rooms to the walls and thrown your drawings of Selwick Hall out of the window. Your only acts of physical violence were against him. When you were away from him, you got better.

"And no one believed you. Not even the doctors."

If she'd been startled before, now she was stunned. "How . . . ?"

"I read your case file, at Bedlam. One doctor after another wrote, 'She's an hysteric, making wild accusations against the man who has done everything to help her.' You would talk to them; they would make their notes; you'd realise it was leading nowhere and go silent; and they would happily declare you cured and send you home. To *him.*"

Tears glistened in her eyes.

"Dr Freud has many insightful conclusions about the human mind," I continued bitterly, "but when it comes to women, he might do better investigating the male sex's preoccupation with cigars."

To my astonishment, she let loose with a snort of astonished laughter. A moment later, the rattle of cups signalled the arrival of the two who had been waiting at the door. Vivian dashed the moisture from her eyes and swept our masks and the envelope off the table.

Strong tea, fresh milk, hastily cut triangles of cheese sandwich, a plate of delicate almond biscuits. Truce, and silence, for a couple of minutes—during which Holmes eyed Nurse Trevisan with curiosity, Nurse Trevisan eyed Vivian with concern, and Vivian eyed something no one else could see. Then she looked up at the other woman.

"Rose, I think it's time to introduce Miss Russell and Mr Holmes to your cousin." Rose didn't look altogether convinced. "They've been here, they've already seen him. And they want to help."

The two women continued the wordless conversation for a time, until Rose put down her cup. "Come on, then. But keep quiet—people are asleep."

Holmes and I followed her down the stairs and along the corridor to its end. We came to a halt at the last door on the southern side—the room where we had seen the mad doctor. Light shone from beneath it. The door was fitted with a sturdy hasp and padlock. I frowned, trying to remember if I'd seen other padlocks as we came along.

Holmes, however, was in no doubt. He made a *Ha!* noise, indicating sudden revelation—always irritating, if one hasn't yet made a connexion—and raised an eyebrow at the nurse. "Your cousin?"

She, too, kept her voice very low. "My mother's brother had a daughter and two sons; this is the younger. He was a doctor, who came back from the War badly damaged. Some men get over it; others do not. He, I believe, never will. Do you need to see him? Strangers make him ... troubled."

Holmes shook his head, and although I was not sure I agreed, I was willing to go along for now. As we made our way back towards the stairs, I thought of the island where the Hon Terry had stopped our motor, the outline of the bell-tower in the night.

"Was your cousin held on San Servolo?" I asked.

"No, it was a dark and terrifying asylum on the mainland. They kept him chained, though he's never been violent."

"Yet you leave him in a room with slits in the shutters, where trespassers are sure to peer in and see ..."

"We give him the toys he loves, and what work he is capable of. Some of which is surprisingly helpful."

Holmes stopped dead on the landing. "Cadaverine!"

I stared at him, caught up by one of my more vivid laboratory memories—then started to grin. "No! Is that what we smelt? The rotting corpse I thought we were about to step into?"

"On the path, yes."

"The fellow on the *vaporetto* even told me that people found the island's odours unnerving."

"I imagine they did, particularly as it tends to linger in the pores."

"Lysine and sodium bicarbonate. Good Lord."

Nurse Trevisan nodded. "We only put it out when we're having problems, since we then have to live with it for weeks." I could well imagine: Holmes' demonstration of the stuff, some years back, had been the impetus for one of Mrs Hudson's longer trips away.

"And in the meantime, your cousin provides the island with a mask of madness. Helping to promote your neighbours' belief that the place is haunted. Ingenious."

Back in the sitting room, Nurse Trevisan took the chair beside Vivian, while Holmes and I sat across the low table from them.

"So, what?" I asked. "You live here on an island you pretend is haunted?"

"Oh, none of us doubt it is haunted. Yes, we encourage the belief with the odd wail and the occasional walk along the front wearing an old bed-sheet—and we've found offensive smells particularly effective in discouraging both children and courting couples. But how could this place not be haunted? Centuries of plague victims died here. The north side of Poveglia—across the foot-bridge—appears on older maps as 'the burning grounds,' since that is where generations of the dead were incinerated. The soil there is lovely and rich. And the wild place on the other side of the church? That is given as 'the plague field.' They tried to start a garden there but had to give it up—apparently the number of skulls and scapulas was a bit disheartening."

"Who is 'they'?" I asked.

"Women, of course."

"Women like us," Vivian added.

"Meaning ... Sapphic?"

"Some. Not all."

The nurse explained. "Some of the women here have spent time in insane asylums. Others were merely fed up with the world of men. You, Miss Russell, would be quite welcome," she added solemnly, "were you to become tired of your current situation."

Holmes and I laughed—his, it must be said, was a touch hollow. "But you can't be planning on hiding behind a ghostly veil for long?"

"There's a bit more to it than bed-sheets and ghostly wails," Rose replied. "Poveglia is in fact a registered mental asylum—'asylum' being a word that to the outside world means a place to lock up lunatics. But to those inside, it can indeed mean shelter. A place to lock the world *out*. My cousin downstairs is listed as the asylum's doctor, though he arrived with a diagnosis of *dementia praecox*—what is now called schizophrenia. Since he came, two years ago, I'm told the number of illicit visitors has fallen dramatically. Poveglia's neighbours seem quite content to leave its madwomen to the care of a mad doctor."

"A new kind of plague island," Holmes commented, "offering quarantine against the insanity of the world. While the inmates are free to come and go to the city."

"And to the Lido's cabarets," I added.

The woman had a most unexpected dimple in her right cheek. "We have a storage room filled with appropriate dress."

"But who is in charge?" Holmes asked. "Who started it all?"

Nurse Trevisan turned on him a rather pitying look. "Sir, those are two very different questions—although they take the same answer. No one person started it, and no one person is in charge. All work, all vote, all perform different functions. Some voices receive more attention, either because that woman brought more money with her or because she suffered more to get here, but in the end, each vote is equal."

"How long have you been here?" I wondered.

"Me, personally? Ten days. I was born and raised in London, and would come to Venice on family visits. But one of my cousins—her brother is the man downstairs—moved here in 1920, the year after it started. You know what happened to women everywhere as soon as the War was over, when the men returned? Three Venetian war widows were among those faced with the realities of what is called 'normality': one was told by her father that she must marry a wealthy but crippled returning officer; another's brother-in-law assumed he'd take over her husband's business that she had been running; and the third was threatened with committal to San Clemente if she did not make room for her uncle and his large family in the house she and her husband had built. The three women were friends, and together they found another way.

"The woman with the business happened to be a partial owner of Poveglia, which at the time was deserted but for the nets of fishermen drying on the path-ways. The other two women scraped together enough money to buy out her brother's interest in the island, and the three of them set up a sort of camp here. Others heard of them, and came to join. The only rule is that there can be no long-term residency of children. It is not fair to them—and besides, families may be willing to rid themselves of spare women, but they do not feel the same over their young."

"How many women do you have here?"

"Thirty-two or -three—one is trying to decide."

"And only one man?"

"My cousin, yes. Shall I tell you how that came about?"

"Please." Holmes sat back, fingers on lips, while Vivian curled up on the chair in the attitude of a child settling in to hear a favourite story.

"As I said, this community began a few months after the War ended, when all was in confusion and people were only slowly returning to the city. My cousin Emelia came eighteen months later, when Poveglia had a population of fourteen.

"They knew even then that it could not last. Women, trying to live by themselves on an island? They were armed, yes, but all it would take was one boatload of drunken men and it would end. In fact, when I came back to Venice to celebrate my great-grandmother's ninetieth birthday one December—this would have been 1922—they'd just had an incident where a fisherman tried to force his way into the building. Two of the women threw on men's clothing and chased him off with sticks, but they were worried, rightfully so.

"I was working at Bethlem hospital, and I happened to tell my cousin Emilia how surprisingly little trouble the hospital had with the neighbourhood ruffians. That the reputation of Bedlam appeared to keep them out."

I stirred. "When I met you—when Ronnie and I brought little Simon to Bed . . . Bethlem—you told me something of the sort. That an evil reputation could be a protective wall."

"True with stone, and all the truer when the walls are of water. My cousin was interested, and so they found ways to strengthen those walls. Sympathetic family members spread rumours, reinforced by the bed-sheets and strange noises."

"And your resident Dr Moreau."

Rose Trevisan's face was attractive, when dimpled into a smile. "A clever piece of theatre, is it not? Emilia arranged for him to come here the following summer. He seems happy. And there's no doubt, having a man—a licensed physician, at that—to hide behind has proved terribly convenient."

Holmes pulled at his lip in thought. "Why did you decide that Poveglia might be a reasonable place to bring a Bedlam patient?"

Vivian sat forward sharply. "She didn't—"

"No," Nurse Trevisan interrupted, "it's a valid question. You are quite right: if Vivian had been an actual patient—committed by doctors, in need of treatment and a carefully controlled routine—it would have been hugely irresponsible of me. And I would have been professionally negligent to have entered into any sort of a personal relationship with her. But by the time we met, Vivian was no more insane than you or I.

She was there voluntarily, behind those walls, putting up with its boredom and bad food and discomfort over the very real perils of living outside."

"When Rose told me about Poveglia, it was I who wanted to come here," Vivian said. "I who planned our escape. Most of it."

Holmes sat with his fingers steepled in thought. I met his gaze for a silent consultation, knowing that he, too, was envisioning a searching boat with a Blackshirt *Capitano*. Both of us were thinking how easy it would be to lock thirty-two additional patients into San Clemente alongside my gondolier's sister and Mussolini's inconvenient wife.

And both of us could imagine all too well the complete and final disappearance of the sister of the Marquess of Selwick, allowing for a more permanent transfer of the woman's inheritance.

I turned my gaze to the two women: the nurse in her man's jacket, the golden fairy in her sparkles. Vivian's feet were again tucked up on the chair, although it now seemed less an expression of comfort than one of making herself small.

Which was not difficult. Even now, all the parts of her seemed child-like, from her delicate hands to her tiny feet. How did she find women's shoes? I wondered, considering . . .

A faint, tiny voice of a thought spoke into the back of my mind. Not a plan, not even a fully fledged idea, just an awareness of similarities.

I'd met someone else in recent days with child-sized feet in Cuban heels. Someone who had not struck me as particularly fond of Fascists.

Chapter Forty-six

....

HOLMES AND I ABANDONED THE LADIES OF POVEGLIA long before sunrise, having made certain there was someplace Vivian could hide if the Marquess came looking—and having extracted a promise that she would be there when we returned.

We putted sedately across the silent, dark water, at a speed that threatened to clog all the valves in the big motor. Rather than risk a third surreptitious entrance to the Lido, we retraced our route to the Ca' Rezzonico landing. There we found the palazzo silent, but the other boats still tied up. The torches had burned out, and only one of the Greeks remained, snoring mightily as we came and as we left. The palazzo's lights were burning, which suggested that either the partygoers were in a similar stupor, or they had moved to yet another venue.

The *traghetto* stop was deserted, so Holmes led me down a narrow path that opened onto a marginally larger passage that kinked around and came eventually to the Accademia Bridge, which took us through more lanes and *campi* to the Piazza San Marco—where we found the remainder of the conjoined party, their mad-sounding whoops ringing off the stones of the Ducal Palace. Somehow, they'd managed to get someone to open a café—not Florian's—and drag out a piano, on which a small man wearing a sort of toga was currently pounding out dance tunes, while around him heels flew and costumes disintegrated. Sometimes, I had heard, local residents protested the disturbances of foreigners with stones and sticks, but tonight the only onlookers were two waiters in ill-buttoned uniforms leaning, half-asleep, against the wall.

"Is that your Mr Porter?" I asked Holmes.

"Yes. His wife is the one dancing with T. E. Lawrence." Not the actual Lawrence of Arabia—unless the hero of the Arab War had somehow grown ten inches since we'd last met. I pointed out one or two of the *dramatis personae* from my side of the lagoon—Miss Maxwell and her companion Dickie; the Hon Terry and his Venetian friend; and Bongo, dancing with a small dark-haired woman and clearly no longer pining over the loss of his Cinderella.

However, there were some among the rowdy gathering who would instantly recognise Holmes beneath the Zorro costume. A duke, a High Court judge, two former Cabinet ministers—adults, it would seem, among the children at play. I chuckled at the idea of my twenty-five-year-old self thinking of men twice my age as children—then shook my head at Holmes' inquiring look and addressed the question of how we might reach our beds.

"Shall we take to the back streets, Holmes?"

The wild rout was gathered mostly at the foot of the clock-tower, leaving the Piazza's wide colonnaded sides dark and deserted. At the closest point to the Porters' impromptu cabaret, the passageway would be hidden by the campanile—so, no: we did not have to turn back. We did walk briskly, and kept close to the darkened windows of shops and cafés, blending into the sea of chairs waiting to be scattered across the paving stones for morning seekers of coffee. At the end of the Ducal Palace, we clung to the walls until we were nearer the water, then made a straight run at the Beau Rivage.

We even made it to our beds without being pounced upon by dancers, or benighted sun-worshippers, or the city's prowling black-clad Fascist Milizia.

Far too early on Sunday morning, bells rang. And rang and rang again. Not the harmonious peals of the English bell-tower, but the frank, flat clatter of Roman Catholic Europe, which required only a loud and no-nonsense call to prayer.

The words I spoke into my pillow might have been construed as a prayer, in different tones and settings, but the insistent noise did have one of its desired effects: I rose from my bed.

And once upright, the demands of the day came rushing in.

Coffee; bath; more coffee; breakfast. And when my tongue would work without my tripping across it, a conversation with Holmes.

I told him what I had seen on the Lido. He told me about his evening at Ca' Rezzonico, how deeply annoyed Linda Porter—and hence, Cole—had been at the repressive presence of the *Capitano* and his English guest. We discussed the oddities and utopian dreams of Poveglia's Amazonian settlers, and agreed that the likelihood of the women's utopia surviving the *Fascisti* régime was lamentably slim. We talked about Vivian and Rose Trevisan, and agreed that, given the circumstances, it was not the unbalanced nurse-and-patient relationship it might have seemed on the surface.

And then I gave him my faint, tiny voice of an idea, based on the similarity in the shoe size of Vivian Beaconsfield and my guide to the city, Signorina Barbarigo. He listened; nodded; put down his cup and picked up his cigarettes, smoking as we watched the traffic build over the lagoon. At the end of his cigarette, he proposed a variation on the beginnings of a plan that I had suggested.

"Huh." Now it was my turn to reflect. "Do you think he'd do it?"

"He might."

"Well, then."

And Holmes smiled: a wicked little curve of the mouth such as I'd rarely seen there. What's more, I could feel precisely that expression taking hold on my own face.

It is a precious thing, to be in agreement with one's husband, particularly when it comes to misbehaviour.

Chapter Forty-seven

THAT NIGHT, WE ATE EARLY AND RETIRED BEFORE THE sky was fully dark.

Midday on Monday, as the exuberant noon-time clatter and boom rang out from the various churches, I stood in the queue for the Lido steamer, watching two muscular young men in black Milizia garb swagger up the Riva degli Schiavoni. As they went, they stared hard into the face of every person less than five and a half feet tall.

At the Excelsior, I walked down the shell-strewn sand to Miss Maxwell's cabana, and asked if we might have a private talk. Since there was little chance of that on the beach, we adjourned to the Turkish Bar where, surrounded by the furnishings and attitudes of the seraglio, I described what I needed, and why.

Elsa Maxwell was a practical woman, and had little income of her own. She was also a proud woman with clear lines when it came to acceptable behaviour—so I had to take great care not to make it sound as if I wanted to hire her services. Rather, I wished her assistance, and I was happy to pay for it: a very different thing.

Fortunately, she also had a great sense of humour and a personal experience with injustice, so she did not take a whole lot of convincing.

I slipped her an envelope—"for expenses"—and repeated my plea for secrecy, to which she assured me there was no problem, honey. We drained our coffee cups and went back down to the seaside, pleased with our little conspiracy.

I spent the afternoon behind the now-familiar wheel of the Runabout, lengths of twine holding my hat on my head and my sleeves to my wrists, as the boat pulled a series of young men and a few women up, down, and mostly into the Adriatic. My calm competence at the wheel soothed Terry's nerves, until I could see him wondering if he'd imagined my breakneck stunt across the *laguna* on Saturday night. He had, after all, been rather drunk . . .

Back under the shade of the cabanas, drinking vast quantities of liquid and listening with half an ear to the exaggerated exploits of those who had attempted the skis, I spotted another pair of Blackshirts making their way along the pavements before the Excelsior. One of the girls—a Senator's daughter from Manhattan, doing the modern version of the Victorian Grand Tour—was watching them as well, and glanced over at me.

"I've been here two weeks and never seen any of those Fascist guys over on this side of the lagoon. Now that's the third pair I've seen today."

"They must be melting in those shirts."

"And how. Black does make a guy look dreamy, though. I'd like to spoon a little with that sheik with the 'stache."

"If you don't mind a cloud of male sweat." Still, the girl had a point: there was a reason romantic heroes wore dark colours. Like, for example, Zorro. Mussolini's followers seemed to have figured out how to capture their public's imagination.

I crossed the lagoon early, before the evening's drinking got serious, and again, noticed the increase in black shirt-fronts and ties.

Holmes had seen it, too.

"You think the *Capitano* called for reinforcements?" I asked him.

"They are clearly not native Venetians. In fact, some of them appear to find the city confusing. They tend to stick to the Piazza, the train station, and the Riva degli Schiavoni."

"Good. How are things going on your side?"

And he told me, with satisfaction.

Any stage play is a delicate mechanism dependent on the smooth working of all its parts. Actors, props, stage, script—all must be lubricated with the oil of practice, since one failure, one dropped piece or ill fit, can reduce matters to chaos. The simpler the mechanism, the less risk of catastrophe.

What, however, if catastrophe is one's aim?

That night, we put the final touches on our plans.

Tuesday morning, the clockwork shifted into motion, as we sat on our balcony writing letters—anonymous, in the ancient Venetian tradition of letter-borne accusations. Each missive suggested a different location for a certain blonde English visitor. In the afternoon, Holmes slid the letters into various post-boxes and hotel collection baskets, then made the rounds of our many and varied gondolieri, giving each a coin and a topic of conversation that they might drop into various ears during the course of their day. Meanwhile, I went over to the Lido with quite a bit of money in my bag. There I spoke again with Miss Elsa Maxwell, followed by a series of brief talks with the hotel's waiters, barmen, and photographers—those with film cameras rather than old-fashioned plates. On the return *vaporetto* trip, my purse was considerably thinner.

On Wednesday, when the number of Blackshirts had reached its height and their frustration was at a peak, Holmes went to deliver a parcel, while I packed several bags and set off, one last time, for the Lido.

The curtains began to lift.

Chapter Forty-eight

....

DARKNESS HAD FALLEN OVER OUR STAGE, NAMELY, THE Excelsior cabaret. Our actors, none of whom had seen the full script of the play they were about to enact, were busily engaged in restoring their flagging energies with alcohol. The jazz band held up a relentless beat; Elsa Maxwell held court and a glass of champagne; I held off the attentions of a would-be suitor; and beneath the table the Hon Terry held the hand of his new Venetian friend.

To my relief, the sound of Holmes' whistle was loud enough to cut through the rising tumult. At the signal, I shot to my feet, caught the eye of the bar-man, and shouted in a voice that reached all my neighbours and half the waiters, "Hey, everybody—today's my *birthday*! Let's have some *fizz*!"

There is nothing like champagne to stoke the flames of a party— especially since I had paid the bartender beforehand to have a hefty supply waiting on ice. In an instant, two hundred people made a fast shift into the top gear of party mood. Glasses were emptying, pulses were pumping, the band upped its beat—and Miss Maxwell sent a trio of recent New York arrivals out onto the floor to demonstrate a bizarre rhythmic contortion (What had they called it—Raleigh? Charleston? Some town in the American South) that involved much kicking of heels and spinning of torsos, with the occasional tipsy falling-over on unaccustomed foot-wear.

The hotel's photographers had been contracted (and again, paid) to aim their lenses at everything in sight. Time and again, the sudden flares of their magnesium flash-trays lit up Chez Vous like a monochrome version of Saturday's fireworks. My co-conspirator, Elsa (who *thought* she was directing this production), looked over the pulsating scene with approval.

By the time the seven black-clad figures—whose arrival had triggered Holmes' whistle—stormed through the door from the hotel, they found a riot in progress.

A riot composed of notably delicate men and oddly muscular women, all of whom wore masks, and all of whom were drunk as Lords and spinning like dervishes.

In moments, waiters had pressed glasses into the hands of the seven newcomers (another of my instructions). The men looked somewhat taken aback, although only one followed his *Capitano*'s lead and put his glass down untasted. I gave them thirty seconds to study the room before I rose, pasting on a series of expressions: first puzzlement, then recognition, and finally uneasiness.

Because I had chosen a table very near the hotel's entrance, the Marquess spotted me the moment I got to my feet. He also noticed—could not help to notice, so exaggerated were my amateur dramatics—how I took a hasty step to the side, obscuring the person behind me at the table.

He turned to shout into the ear of the *Capitano*, who had been surveying the room with open disgust. The Fascist's eyes came around to me, a still point amongst the whirl, then dropped to the silk-stockinged ankles visible behind my trousered legs. The *Capitano* gave a triumphant smile, and gestured commands to his underlings.

The two younger Blackshirts he sent to the left, to block the exit into the gardens. The two older ones went around the right side of the crowded floor, to a place where the dancing spilled onto the forecourt to the beach. And the remaining one—the man without champagne on his tongue—the Captain set down at the doors to the hotel.

I edged closer to the silk stockings, then glanced behind me to check that all my players were on their marks. Towards the garden, the two young Fascists had already attracted admirers, male and female. On the beach side, a sort of can-can line of mixed sexes was distracting the two older ones. All four men were looking a touch confused as it occurred to them that not all the attractive women pressing up against them were quite what they seemed.

Holmes loomed into view then, working his way across the crowded floor, his arms wrapped around a load of equipment to protect it from high-kicking heels and outflung elbows.

When I turned to face the entrance again, the *Capitano* and the Marquess were bearing down on me, elbowing away would-be admirers—literally, in one case, causing a pile-up of legs and shrieks across a table.

I blocked the Marquess by thrusting a bottle of champagne into his hands—and so ingrained were the habits of an English aristocrat that he took it. "Lord Selwick!" I shouted. "I never thought to see you in a place like this. I didn't even know you were in Venice! I love your costume, so realistic! Is this a friend of yours? How d'you do? Mary Russell!" Having freed a hand, I thrust it out at the man I'd seen terrifying the asylum guard on San Clemente—and such were the habits of a native Venetian that he accepted it.

But the Marquess would be distracted no longer. He thrust the bottle at a nearby set of willing hands and wrenched me aside, stepping forward in my place so as to stare down at the person I'd been hiding.

The slim figure was all golden: gold shoes, sparkly stockings, short gold dress, golden bracelets around one wrist. As the dark trousered legs pushed past me, the sitter noticed them. The feathered bandeau dipped, pausing with gaze averted. The golden shoulders rose and fell with a deep breath, and then the entire figure began to turn in the chair, and rise to face the accusing Marquess. Only at the last moment did the downward-facing head come up, the feathers thrown back as the golden arms shot out to embrace the startled Englishman. The Marquess stared into the pop eyes for a small eternity (one ... two ... three ...) and then Cole Porter turned to his enthralled audience with an exaggeratedly coy grin, all but fluttering his eyelashes. At that precise instant, a photographer's magnesium flash briefly washed all colour from the scene. The Marquess struggled to pull free, but I was right there, getting in his way, and Porter's arm had him in a death grip. The small musician used his free hand to yank off the bandeau and wig he wore, gave a glance at the *Capitano* as if to check that he was in a position to witness this—then rose up on his toes to plant a kiss directly on the mouth of the Marquess of Selwick. A second flare, accompanied by a roar of laughter.

The third flash came when Porter, arms still locked, turned to meet his wife's eyes across the table, his face given over to a grin composed of pleasure and jest and the hard, cold triumph of revenge.

The Marquess finally managed to throw off the embracing arms and stagger away. A fourth camera flared, the crowd cheered, the *Capitano* looked appalled—and the band played on.

Late the following morning, Holmes returned with prints of the photographs. Within minutes of the previous night's fracas, all four photographers had had cameras ripped from their hands and smashed to the floor by the *Capitano*'s Blackshirts; however, since all four of those cameras were the cheap replacements Holmes had carried in, no real harm was done—to our plan or to their livelihood.

When the Blackshirts had retreated, it was a moment's work to retrieve the devices from beneath their concealing tablecloths. Four rolls of film were retrieved, four cameras returned to their owners, four photographers paid off and told that they should go home, now.

Each of their pictures was crisp and clear and perfectly timed. The first appeared to show the Marquess of Selwick in the embrace of a woman in a shiny dress—albeit a woman with rather hairy arms. The second, however, was clearly the Marquess kissing a man. In the third, Cole Porter's ecstatic face and tousled hair revealed just the right amount of the Marquess: enough to identify him, but not to show his expression—although that on Cole Porter's homely features was interesting. Something personal there, more profound than mere exultation at a successful prank.

The fourth, taken by the photographer closest to the door, showed laughing onlookers and the Marquess pushing back in disgust—but that one could be discarded, along with the ambiguous first one.

Yes: the second and third photographs, put side by side, would be quite enough for our purposes.

I hoped not too many people suffered from the after-effects of the previous night. Things had, in the Hon Terry's phrase, got a bit out of hand after the Blackshirts' brutal destruction of cameras sent a ripple of protest through the inebriated crowd—many of them Americans who'd shouted for a photo to send to the folks back home. The dissent was good-natured at first, but when the *Capitano*'s men smashed the third camera, revolt became more open.

Then the Milizia made the mistake of shutting down the band. As the wrangling continued, the romantic appeal of black costumes began to turn, along with the mood of the room.

No one saw where the first flying orange-slice came from, but in an instant, bits of alcohol-soaked fruit and booze-sodden olives filled the air, soon joined by bar-snacks of devilled eggs and rolled salami. At the slap of the first thrown oyster against his forehead, the *Capitano* turned and fled, with the Marquess on his heels. Having only five men—and having enough sense not to draw his weapon on the Excelsior's guests—he retreated to call for reinforcements. By the time those arrived, the party had broken up.

In the confusion, Holmes and I rescued the precious cameras and slipped their rolls of un-wound film into the dark pouch of his beaded handbag.

Yes: *his*—for I see I have neglected to mention the details of my Monday conversation with Miss Elsa Maxwell.

I'd been told how the lady liked to hold themed parties—scavenger hunts, come-as-you-are balls. It was also common knowledge that she depended on the kindness of others when it came to paying the bills. So when I offered to under-write the bar tab for a party with a specific theme, she was all in favour. The theme? Come as Your Opposite.

Girls were to dress as boys, and boys as girls—but to further stir the pot, women who preferred trousers were instructed to find themselves a feminine dress, while boys whose preferences were . . . of a lavender tint, were invited to come as he-men.

Holmes, believe it or not, had walked into Chez Vous wearing a pair of my neon-toned beach pyjamas.

I wore his evening suit with its cuffs turned up.

Linda Porter also wore an evening suit, although it had been tailored for her sleek figure, and there was no mistaking her for a man.

And Cole Porter? He was dressed in Vivian's golden costume.

The Marquess had seen his sister wearing it, outside Ca' Rezzonico on Saturday night. Because it had a loose fit, and because Porter was not much taller than Vivian, we had only to scour the city for a blond wig and a pair of gold shoes.

Vivian herself kept well clear of the Lido—because over the past few days, the Milizia Nazionale had received a dozen letters and a score of tips from gondoliers and shop-keepers: a small, blonde English-woman was sure to be at the Excelsior cabaret on Wednesday night.

I realised that both Holmes and I were studying the third photo-graph, the one showing Cole Porter's full face.

"He looks like a man who's just won a hard-fought game of tennis," I remarked.

"A hard-fought battle in a war, more like."

It was true: Porter did not look as if he'd been playing a game. Or if a game, it was an important one. "I'm glad we could make it worth his while. Although I hope there aren't too many repercussions—from the Italian government, I mean. Did you have much trouble talking him into wearing the dress, Holmes?"

"Porter, no. His wife took longer to convince. She's extremely protective. On the other hand, she likes to make him happy, and she could see how badly he wanted this. Men such as Porter put up with a lifetime of snubs and insults. He's learned to take his revenge indirectly—through a third party, say, or by means of clever and convoluted jokes hidden inside his songs. Not many people notice the sharp edge behind the fluff. In any event, Linda let herself be convinced that playing along would make her a 'good sport'—because it also meant the two of them could extract a revenge on the *Capitano*, through his all-important British guest, for the open contempt he'd shown them both."

I picked up the fourth picture again, the one that showed mostly the table and the crowd of dancers pausing, mid-flail, to watch. Porter's face was blurred, little more than grinning teeth, but the camera had caught a slice of Linda's face. This was a woman who'd married a homosexual—knowing what he was—and who had just watched him give a man a hard kiss on the mouth. Yet there was no anger there, no hurt. What I saw there was distinctly pleasure—not arousal, but . . . yes: pride.

I imagined that Mrs Porter, too, experienced few victories in her married life. The insulation of riches could go only so far.

As for the Marquess, there was no mistaking him, either: dressed as a Fascist, in the full and affectionate embrace of a transvestite man. The Italian Fascists' disapproval of homosexuals was in fact relatively low-key, and Cole Porter himself could certainly laugh the picture off as a bit of fun at a fancy-dress party—but the Marquess? For Edward, Lord Selwick, evidence that the pictures had survived would come as a shock—and a threat. Proclaim his innocence as he might, these photos would end his political dreams. The British establishment might overlook homosexual behaviour—might even practice it—but it could never forgive a man who'd permitted himself to be made a laughing-stock in the papers, caught *in flagrante* by the light of a photographer's flash.

As we'd left Chez Vous, film in hand, we had heard the two men arguing. The Marquess was insisting that, yes, it truly had been his sister that night outside of Ca' Rezzonico—after all, it could not have been Porter, now, could it? But the outraged *Capitano* was not open to argument. The outraged *Capitano* was barely open to English, swearing in a furious mix of languages that his new "friend"—the word was accompanied by the exact *Pah!* spitting gesture my two gondoliers used—had thrown him into a position of ridicule, *public* ridicule! That he'd be lucky not to be demoted to patrolling the Alps! Imagine, starting a brawl—in the *Excelsior,* of all places! Filled with Americans and English and French and— (The words that followed were unintelligible and probably Venetian.) Now the foreigners would all be writing home to say they'd been *threatened*—by the Milizia! What if they all decided to pack their bags and stay away, go to the Riviera next year instead? What would *Il Duce* say about that, eh? Venice was his showcase, and did the Marquess know how much the Excelsior alone brought in every year? As far as the *Capitano* was concerned, the Marquess could board the first train out, and take his *disruption* home with him. (*Pah!*) *Italia* was very fine without the help of England, thank you very much.

I smiled, there in my suite in the Beau Rivage, as I picked up the two photographs. One look at these, and the *Capitano* would be chasing after the Marquess' train with a rifle.

"You know, Holmes," I said as I slid the two prints into an envelope, "I never realised how satisfying blackmail could be."

Chapter Forty-nine

SHERLOCK HOLMES WATCHED THE TWO CRISP IMAGES
disappear into the envelope, but he was thinking about the conundrum
of Mr Cole Porter.

Holmes had gone to Poveglia himself on Monday morning, in a
boat he'd had to buy outright from its enterprising owner. He'd brought
away a parcel: the golden dress and bandeau Lady Vivian wore to the
Lido. That afternoon, it had sat on the littered *pietra dura* table while
Cole chatted and played, with Linda, the Murphys, several cats, and
various friends coming in and out. But when Linda went off to check
on lunch and the various friends went to see about a drink, Holmes had
laid the parcel, and his proposition, before the composer.

First he described the situation—or as much of it as he cared to
disclose: a desperate woman choosing freedom; her brother wishing to
control her money, her sexual preferences, and her person; the brother's
vulnerabilities, both here and at home.

What they required was a short man willing to wear women's clothing to a dress-up party. A golden costume, extreme and feminine. It had to convince—

"Sure," Porter said, reaching out to pick up the feathered bandeau. "Unless we can't get the dress to fit me."

"I'm told it is relatively voluminous."

"Fine, then." He dropped the bandeau and traded it for his cigarettes. "That's assuming I won't be the only guy in a dress. Linda won't like it if I am."

"As I understand it, the night is to be something of a free-for-all. Men in dresses, women in suits, women who prefer trousers donning frills, men who, well . . ."

"Lavender boys dressing butch?"

"As it were. The basic idea being, anything goes."

"Fine with me." Porter returned to the keyboard, his clever hands bouncing through the chords he'd been improvising earlier. It was a jaunty tune, the sort of thing a man would hum walking down the street. "Looking for some words for this one," he said. "Maybe your mixed-up costume party will give me an idea."

"One never knows," Holmes agreed. In this new world, wasn't anything possible? A curmudgeonly old detective could marry a girl half his age; a man could speak his painful truths from beneath a mask of lighthearted jokes; an island of madwomen could hide in plain sight.

Anything goes.

Author's Notes

....

1925 proved too early for the rise of Fascism in Britain. It was not ushered in until Oswald Mosley rose in the thirties. However, the impulse was already building, as witnessed by the founding of a proto-Fascist organization by Rotha Beryl Lintorn-Orman (described by Mycroft Holmes herein).

Women in 1925 Italy were regarded as being primarily a means of building the population of the state. Women were forbidden various kinds of jobs, including teaching history, Italian literature, and Greek or Latin in the high schools.

Ida Dalser, who claimed to have been married to Benito Mussolini in 1914, bore him a son in 1915. She persisted in demanding her rights, although any paperwork disappeared after the Fascist government took hold, and she was put into the San Clemente asylum in 1925. Their young son was told she was dead, although she lived until 1937. When the boy later asserted that his father was Benito Mussolini, he, too, was committed to an asylum, near Milan. He was murdered there at the age of twenty-six, in 1942.

"Moral management" of the insane came to the fore in Bethlem Royal Hospital and other facilities during the nineteenth century, following a long history when the mad were simply locked out of the way. In 1925, the predominant approach combined talk therapy, physical treatments, and comforting routine, but as the century went on, anti-psychotic drugs and shock therapy came to the fore. Ironically, society's way of dealing with the unbalanced has come full circle, with all but the most violent turned out of any asylum and put back onto the streets.

The Porters hired Ca' Rezzonico, now a magnificently restored eighteenth-century museum, for several summers (though Duff Cooper's 1925 diary mentions them in the Palazzo Papadopoli, further up the Grand Canal). Two years after this, the Milizia raided a too-riotous party involving drugs and cross-dressing, and Porter was invited to leave the city.

1925 found Cole Porter frustrated by his musical failures. Not until *Paris* in 1928 did he begin to make a name for himself. Porter's songs that find a place in his conversations with Holmes include "Babes in the Wood" (which may in fact have been written in 1924—a shocking instance in which Mary Russell's Memoirs may be mistaken); "Let's Misbehave"; "The Land of Going to Be"; "Don't Look at Me That Way"; "Let's Do It (Let's Fall in Love)"; "Wake Up and Dream"; and a number of others—including "Anything Goes." His songs are eternal because they are not, as Holmes notes, merely fluff entertainments. As one story has it, Porter was once badly beaten by a truck driver—and his response? The song "I Get a Kick Out of You."

The island of Poveglia stands in the Venice lagoon, and its pre–World War I history is much as given in this book—plague, mass burials, and all. In 1922, a mental institution did open there, under a doctor reputed to perform crude lobotomies, who is said to have hurled himself from the tower after being driven mad by ghosts. The asylum, which became a home for elderly indigents, closed in 1968. Sensational television shows and websites adore Poveglia, and it remains to be seen whether the island's recent sale will see development into yet another Venetian luxury resort—complete with skulls.

Acknowledgments

....

A city like Venice has many professional guides, but few who so instantly grasp what a visitor needs as the two who helped guide this book. The Hôtel Londres (formerly Beau Rivage, and as welcoming today as when Russell and Holmes stayed there) put me in touch with Daniela Zamperetti, who took time out from her "Tribal Fusion" dancing to show me around the excellent San Servolo museum and explain much about the workings of the city and its people, then later coax my flawed Italian into something recognizable. And guide Christina Gregorin (found at www.slow-venice.com) swept me from one end of the city to the other, talking politics and history. Not that this book is about politics: no, not at all.

The fabulous ladies of CineLit, Mary Alice Kier and Anna Cottle, have been a constant source of support, ideas, and enthusiasm for years now, and no time more than in 2017. A writer could ask for no better travel partners, whether the path leads to Venice or the wilds of Hollywood. Mary Alice and Anna, I raise a glass of Campari to our many future projects.

Bethlem Royal Hospital is still an active and vibrant mental health community, now in the southern reaches of London. Archivist Colin Gale was very helpful and patient with my questions and research, and I highly recommend a visit to their museum or their archives, for a look at the transformation of mental health care from priory hospital to "moral treatment." Their excellent website is at www.museumofthemind.org.uk.

San Servolo in the Venice lagoon, in addition to being Venice International University, houses an excellent museum (Museo del Manicomio), which one may visit in both actual and virtual senses. I dream of holding a writing conference in the San Servolo facilities . . .

And to my friend and walking Sherlock Holmes Reference Library, Leslie S. Klinger, I promise: next time I'll look it up in your *New Annotated* first.

Naturally, all of these generous individuals and organizations gave more than any writer could use, and all of them now suffer from seeing the inevitable corruption of their expertise by a mere storyteller. If I got things wrong here, it's really not their fault. They tried their best.

As always, my friends at Bantam Books (Penguin Random House) make my books possible. If this is in front of your eyes, it's thanks to them.

Or if this is in your ears, you can thank the great folk at Recorded Books.

As for me, I thank you all, collaborators and readers alike.

ABOUT THE AUTHOR

....

Laurie R. King is the *New York Times* bestselling author of fifteen Mary Russell mysteries, five contemporary novels featuring Kate Martinelli, the Stuyvesant & Grey novels: *Touchstone* and *The Bones of Paris*, and the acclaimed standalones *Lockdown*, *A Darker Place*, *Folly*, *Califia's Daughters* (written under the pen name Leigh Richards), and *Keeping Watch*. She lives on California's Central Coast.

LaurieRKing.com
Facebook.com/LaurieRKing
Twitter: @LaurieRKing
Twitter: @Mary_Russell